My whole body

The scent of coconuts. I had seen that perfect ass before. My heart raced as my mind frantically replayed that night.

No, no way, it couldn't be. I tried to calm my nerves as the woman sauntered and swayed to the pole standing in the middle of the room. She jumped up and spun slowly, before twisting around into some upside-down position and lowering her legs into a split as she spun. She was incredible and the way she moved her body was mesmerizing. All that black hair whipped around as she moved. When she descended from the pole in some sort of wide-legged pike, I got a clear view of her face for the first time.

My perfect Raven, that sexy woman who had stolen my sanity, stood before me almost completely bare. Grabbing the pole, she slowly thrust her hips toward it and then away, before grabbing a stiletto clad foot and pulling her leg to a standing split position and throwing her head back, sending all that black hair flying and whipping around.

I was too in shock to say anything, too hypnotized to move. She walked seductively back toward me, an audible gasp, a stutter step, a whirlwind of emotions held captive in her eyes. My face burned as I fixed my eyes on her.

Hide Us Away

by

Sonnet Harlynn

Hide Us Away

Cover Art by *Diana Carlile*

The Wild Rose Press, Inc.
PO Box 708
Adams Basin, NY 14410-0708
Visit us at www.thewildrosepress.com

Publishing History
First Edition, 2022
Trade Paperback ISBN 978-1-5092-4579-6
Digital ISBN 978-1-5092-4580-2

Published in the United States of America

Dedication

To Eric, whose belief gave wings to my dreams.

Acknowledgements

First of all, I want to thank my wonderful husband, Eric. He put in the work! From reading chapters to encouraging me when I had doubts, to making sure I met editing deadlines, he was active in making sure I crossed the finishing line. Thank you, love!

To my kiddos. You have been so encouraging throughout this journey. I appreciate you so much. Even if you never want to read this book (and I don't blame you), just know that you were a part of this process. Thank you, I am so lucky to have such lovely, funny, inspiring children!

Thank you to my incredible agent, Gwyn. I remember being so excited when we connected, but throughout the course of this book, I learn more and more just how lucky I am. From your input to your encouragement to your patience, I know for sure this wouldn't be a finished work without you. I cannot thank you enough!

And to my editor, Morena, whose edits and feedback have made me into a better writer. It's hard to express how grateful I am for the time you took to work with me and make sure these characters really came to life. To have the time of someone so talented is truly humbling, so thank you so much!

To my family. Mom, Dad, and Jenny, who have constantly entertained my wild ideas with genuine belief and curiosity. Your support has always given me the confidence to tackle my dreams. Mom and Dad, maybe skip the spicy chapters. Jenny, you know who I am. Thank you all so much. I love you like crazy!

To my dear friend Roxas, whose friendship, kindness, and humor, has kept me laughing and moving forward when I needed a break. Thank you for helping me when I was stuck on a chapter or struggling with the words. I'm so thankful to have a talented writer like you in my orbit. I adore you always. Thank you!

Chapter 1

Raven

The red and blue lights blared behind me, and the sound of sirens whirred in my ears.

"Seriously?" I whisper-screamed. Zara stirred and fussed in the back of the car.

Despite it being new to me, this car was nowhere close to new. It was well worn. Okay, it was beat up, and even though it came with all the necessary parts working, it also came with a smell that could only be described as warm cheese. Not good, but good enough for me. I was changing my life. Drastically. And those changes came with sacrifices. The first thing to go was style, and I couldn't help but wish that my olfactory nerves had gone right along with it.

Zara's fussy whimpers quickly turned into painfully loud screams, the kind of screams that make your nipples stand at attention and start spitting out milk.

We were almost there, after leaving Redlands at two in the morning under the cover of darkness. I had been driving for twelve hours on what felt like an endless trip with very few breaks between and we were just arriving at Brooks Falls, our new home, that, from the looks of it, was perfectly tucked away in the mountains of California. It was situated fairly northwest of Sacramento in the beautiful Coastal Mountain Range, close enough for a day trip to a few different cities, or west to the ocean. Most importantly, it was far enough away from Redlands. And my Zara had been a trooper the entire time. It helped that our sweet Australian Shepherd, Maus, was back there keeping her entertained, resting his head on her car seat or licking her face every so often, drawing out those cute little baby giggles that warmed my heart and reminded why I had left in the first place.

"Hey, Zara, shh, I know, honey. Believe me, Mama can relate. We're almost there, though." I could hardly blame the kid. At any point over the last twelve hours, I could've easily lost the very tenuous grip I had on my sanity too. I was tired and hungry, and most of all, I just wanted this nightmare to end.

I put on my turn signal and tossed on a pair of sunglasses as I found a spot to pull over. I took a deep breath and exhaled slowly through my nose. The stress of the last twenty-four hours was finally starting to catch up to me as the adrenaline wore off.

Once I had calmed my mind, I turned to the back of the car and reached for Zara, gently rubbing her chubby little hand and cooing softly to her, hoping the sounds would quiet her. She was still whimpering, her wails an appropriate and accurate soundtrack for the day.

After a few spirited sobs, Zara's breathing evened out as she hiccupped through waning cries and soon enough, they became short little puffs of baby breath. Her big brown eyes began to fully rouse from sleepy fussing. She shot me a big toothless smile, her fat red cheeks reaching all the way up to her eyes as she kicked her tiny legs and arms. Oh, how I wished I could recover from emotional distress that quickly.

"Mama nananana."

"You know, that's exactly what I was thinking."

"Bah, bah mama."

"Really? You also think one of the biggest problems facing our country today is healthcare accessibility for everyone?" I asked, like I was expecting an answer. Clearly, I was losing my mind. Twelve hours on the road with an infant and a life like mine could do that to a girl.

While I waited, I pulled out my license, registration, and insurance card and scanned over the names on each, suddenly worried that they didn't all match up. I sighed out a breath of relief when I saw that my name was the same on each and then immediately inhaled a breath of anxiety as the man neared.

Over the years, on the rare occasion that I drove, I had only been pulled over once and managed to talk my way out of that one. I was petite, full breasted, small waisted, and I had a nice ass: all of which I could use to my advantage. I wasn't proud of it, but I wasn't above using my looks to get out of a ticket. Especially this one. Not only did I have to stay under the radar, but I was also broke and couldn't afford a speeding ticket. I had barely had enough money to pay for gas to get to Brooks Falls.

I pulled down on my white tank top, making sure my boobs were prominently displayed. I should have been ashamed of myself. And I was. I was so full of shame; I wasn't sure there was much else to me at this point.

As the tall figure approached me, I felt a twinge of guilt and subtly yanked up my top. Just a bit—I was still desperate, after all.

I rolled down my window, the crisp spring air and the smell of trees filling my nostrils. I watched in my side mirror as the cop got out of his truck and made his approach. My eyes widened when he came into full view. He was gorgeous. And tall. When he stopped in front of my window, I looked up at the man towering over my car and staring down at me with dark gray-blue eyes that sparkled in the fading sunlight. His face was smooth shaven, his jaw chiseled, and his thick chestnut hair was tousled perfectly on top of his head in that "I woke up like this, except it really took me fifteen minutes to style my hair" kind of way. And the man was a wall of muscles. Muscles that I could actually *see* through his uniform. He was truly a sight to behold. I had zero interest in men at the moment, but I still had eyes, and my eyes were telling me that this man was sinfully sexy.

"Afternoon, miss. Do you know why I pulled you over?"

My traitor eyes roamed over his rock-hard body like they had a mind of their own.

"Excuse me, Miss?"

"Yes?" Jesus, was I drooling?

He furrowed his brow and studied my face. "You were going twenty miles over the speed limit. Did you realize that?" His tone was condescending.

"I'm sorry. I didn't realize I was going so fast." I smiled at him, friendly, but not *too* friendly. "I'm just moving into town and—"

"Did you realize you were going fifty-five in a thirty-five zone?" He pointed to the speed limit sign, which I saw now that I was sitting here in my car staring at it, but did not notice when I was blazing into town. I pressed my lips together, hoping he would just issue me a warning. This was a small town, after all. They did things differently, didn't they?

"Well, no." *Oh, good response, That'll definitely do it.* I internally eye-rolled at myself. "I was just caught off guard because I was on the highway, and the speed limit was fifty-five, then all of a sudden the speed changed, and I didn't have time to slow down." I looked at his nameplate and my eyes widened slightly at the sight of his broad chest. My mouth went dry as I tried to avert my gaze. *Focus.* "Officer Jameson, I don't normally speed. I've never even gotten a ticket."

"Da da da da baaaaaah!" Zara interrupted. I peered back to see her bouncing gleefully in the backseat without a care in the world. Maus was laying down next to her. Thankfully, I had invested in a seatbelt for him or else he would already be on my lap, assaulting the cute officer with wet kisses. *Cute officer and wet kisses, yes please.*

Officer Jameson peeked through the driver's side window into the back with a smile. Except no sooner had he looked than his smile turned to a scowl. "How old is your child?"

I would normally be very excited about this question. I loved talking about Zara. But something in his tone, and his menacing glower, told me that we were not about to have a nice little chat about parenting.

"She's six months old."

"And how much does she weigh?"

"She—" Wait, what? I stuttered, confused by the question. "She, uh, weighs about twenty pounds, give or take a big snack." I laughed nervously and swallowed hard. My joke was clearly not appreciated, because there were no smiles coming from this guy.

"Twenty pounds? Hmmm."

My heart started to pound in my chest as I realized

where this was going.

"Where are you from?" he asked with a hopeful curiosity.

"I'm from Redlands, but I'm just moving here today, actually."

His blue eyes glinted with something. "Ah, so you *are* from the state of California, then?" He asked, his tone insinuating that, as a native, I should know all the rules. What was I, a lawyer? No. But I was a mother and as desperate as I had been, I should've known how to keep my child safe. Shame washed over me and that place, somewhere deep down, where I kept all of my secrets, twinged, reminding me what a failure I was in all things.

I knew what to do here. It was a suck-it-up-and-eat-shit kind of moment. Admit my shortcomings and take the hit. My pride didn't allow it.

"Yes, well, I do have that California license you are holding *and* California plates, sooo…" I let my *sooo* hang like a catty schoolgirl, and even I cringed at it. My mouth was going to get me into trouble, just like it always did. His jaw flexed. Other than that, the man was unreadable. I supposed that was a great quality for a cop, but bad for a…what was I? A perp? I laughed to myself. I really needed to stop watching so many cop shows.

"Right. I'll be right back. You three sit tight." The man gave a two finger tap on my door before he walked away, and the child in me reappeared as I mocked him in my most infantile way, using my hands like puppets to act as his face.

"I'll be right back, because I'm an officer of the law, so I'm better than you. Are you from California, with your California license and your California plates? I'm a big, dumb, sexy cop." I had gotten so carried away with my rage play-acting that I was startled when I heard the clearing of a throat. Oops. I bit the inside of my cheeks nervously, not really knowing what to say and thinking it was better if I said nothing at all.

"Did you know that your license was suspended?"

Um, what? I opened my mouth, but nothing came out. I opened it again and still nothing. Suspended? No, that was impossible. Wasn't it? Thoughts of that sleazy, greasy little man entered my mind. It had to be a mistake. He promised me I was clean. I didn't manage to ask why it was suspended, because I was just opening and closing my mouth like a beached fish struggling to breathe. But I was cuing in on the fact that these were rhetorical questions, because without skipping a beat, he continued with the good news.

"And did you know that in California, all children under forty pounds need to be securely fastened in a *rear*-facing car seat?"

Well, that I did know. "Officer, no. I mean, yes, but she, well, okay, we…really?" Oh yeah, some of my finest work. At this point, my nerves were hanging on loosely by a single frayed thread. And with each new question, this man was whittling away at them. I blinked my eyes at him in disbelief. Maybe I could just blink away all the bullshit. It felt like the dam that held back all of my emotions was threatening to break, fractures in my already cracked foundation splaying and splintering, branching off into thousands of disconnected pieces.

That's when a tow truck pulled up behind us. My heart pounded in my chest and my eyes started to sting, because I knew exactly what that tow truck meant. I stared, dumbfounded, at the officer. His hardened demeanor softened slightly as we locked eyes.

"I'm sorry, Ms. DeLuca, but I can't let you drive with a suspended license *and* the incorrect child restraint system. Unfortunately, we are going to have to tow your vehicle. These are your citations." He handed them over. "Driving with a suspended license, improper child restraint system, and driving fifty-five in a thirty-five zone."

I laughed, the ridiculousness of the situation hitting me full force. "So, what, do I just walk the rest of the way into town with my baby and my dog?" I snort-laughed when what I really wanted to do was scream at someone. Specifically, him.

"Of course not. I'll drive you to the station, and you can call whoever you need to come and get you."

"Great." I threw my hands up in surrender. "It's a good thing that there are cops like you to take down the real criminals of this world." I mean, at that point, what was he going to do? Throw me in the back of his truck and haul me off? Oh wait, that was already happening.

Officer Jameson ignored me and took a rear-facing car seat from the driver of the tow truck and brought it around to the backseat of his police truck. He glanced back at me briefly, his face smug as he hooked the seat in. "You can take this car seat with you, all right?"

I was thankful he had gotten back to the car seat installation, because his words hit like a hammer on my heart. My voice came out soft and cracked. "Thank you."

His back was still facing me when he gave a curt nod and then backed out of the truck. Officer Jameson eyed my dog, tipped his head toward the truck, and said, "Get in, boy."

My traitorous dog, who rarely listened to anyone

except for me, hopped in effortlessly while I looked around for a step and found nothing. Just as I was calculating the velocity I'd need to achieve to successfully launch Zara and I into the truck, a large pair of hands lifted my baby gently out of my arms and loaded her into the car seat. My heart squeezed at the simple action, but before I had time to think on it, I was next. Officer Jameson wrapped one hand around my bicep and lowered the other to the small of my back. I prepared, shifting my large purse behind me. In seconds, I was hoisted into the truck and sidling up next to Zara, crushed between her and Maus.

As we drove into town, I shamelessly listened in on his phone calls. A boring call to the station first and then a call to his...wife?

"Hey, baby, are you all packed up and ready to go?"

My heart melted with every gentle word he said. In his voice was love—the kind of love that held a lifetime of letters and stolen kisses. I was pathetic, basking in this love that belonged to someone else.

"Aw, don't worry, honey. She'll come around."

I looked into the rear-view mirror at the man, studying his face as he spoke. Whatever she said back to him made his eyes smile, forming little crinkled edges at the corners.

She was clever and witty and beautiful, I was sure of it, and it was guaranteed that they were totally in love. She was probably a schoolteacher or a librarian. They had two perfect little babies that they took to church on Sunday and then out to brunch right after. One boy and one girl, with pristine little coordinated outfits and hair that always stayed in place. They took family pictures together by bridges and farm fences, the sun glistening on all their beauty and flawlessness.

Rhapsodizing about their fake life had originally felt like a sugar high, but now felt more like an overdose, so I closed my eyes, drowning out their chatter.

Don't come looking for us. I have everything I need to take you down. Flashes of memories filled my mind. Splatters of blood, a bag of money, and a cold, callous smirk that I'd seen more times than I could count. All that bravery in a single pinpoint moment, and now here I was, terrified about what I had done. Regret and worry inundated me, but I couldn't turn back now. I had cut the cord once and for all. What was done was done.

Eventually, I felt the truck slow as we turned into a parking lot in front of a well-kept but small, light gray building with four police trucks parked in front of it. Officer Jameson parked and got out of the truck.

As for me, I wasn't exactly sure what to do. I grabbed a purple hoodie that I'd shoved in my purse, deciding to cover myself up before I went in. When I turned my head back to the window, Officer Jameson stood there, staring in the car door window, with his brows raised as if to say, "Are you gonna get your ass out of my car?" Startled, I jumped and smacked my face on the window, which was curious. Even in my stupefied state, I had to wonder how I jumped forward, *toward* the perceived danger. Leave it to me to dive in headfirst. I placed a hand over my face, groaning in pain. Okay, it wasn't so much painful as it was embarrassing.

"Jesus Christ superstar." I groaned, feeling defeated.

"Whoa, Ma'am, are you okay?"

I glanced sheepishly through my fingers at him, wishing I could disappear. "Yeah, I'm fine."

"Let's get you out of my truck with everyone in one

piece, huh?"

I got out, unbuckled Zara, and grabbed Maus's leash. We had finally arrived. *Welcome to Brooks Falls. First stop, the police station.*

Chapter 2

Raven

"Hello?" a cheery voice said on the other end of the line. I heard the chattering of voices and the clinking of silverware in the background.

"Tessa?" I said hesitantly. "It's, uh, me." I heard nothing except background noises and then, complete silence. "Tessa, hello?" I was about to hang up, but I heard a scream and a squeal.

"Dan—"

"No! Well, yes, what you were going to say, but no. It's Raven DeLuca, officially," I whispered.

"I see." Sounding like she was trying to connect the dots with a long "Hmmmmm", Tessa whispered back to me. "Cool, Raven, but why are we whispering?"

I let out a small laugh, the tension I had been carrying starting to dissolve at the sound of her voice.

"Well, I know we haven't talked in a while, since, well, you know."

The last time I spoke with her had been a bad night, and it was the last we'd talked in at least a year. She was my best friend and losing her like that, my only support, had just about crushed me. "The thing is that I finally listened to your advice, and I left. Me and Zara and Maus, we all left."

I felt her shocked gasp more than I heard it, because

12

yeah, it had been a long time coming, and I was betting she hadn't thought I'd ever leave.

"Oh, honey, I am so proud of you. I know that took a lot. I know it must've taken everything," her voice was low and serious.

"So, where are you? Where did you end up going?" She was talking a mile a minute, back to her chipper, chatty self. "Please tell me you didn't stay in Redlands."

I dropped my shoulders and sighed, knowing this next part would come as a bit of a surprise since we hadn't spoken in a year, and seeing as I had no way to tell her that I was coming. I didn't know if this would be a good or bad surprise.

"No, I'm not in Redlands."

Tessa blew out a relieved breath. "Well, that's good news. That place is nothing but trouble. Where are you, then?"

I squared my shoulders in determination, getting ready to drop the bomb on her, hoping it would feel more like a glittery bath bomb and less like a nuke.

"We're actually in Brooks Falls," I said hesitantly. After about five seconds of a tortuous silence, she squealed.

"Are you messing with me right now? Girl, if you are seriously here, please get your tiny ass down to the Blue Rose. It's easy to find, right smack in the center of town on Main Street. Whoa, hold on, am I finally going to see my goddaughter? And Maus? Oh, I haven't seen him in so long, since he was just a little fleabag. And you, you get over here and come hug me already!"

I closed my eyes and considered not telling her the truth of the situation and just walking the rest of the way into town. But this was Tessa.

13

"That was the plan. I was going to come see you today. Actually, I was going to surprise you; I had a whole thing, maybe do a little song and a dance, like 'we're here, we're here, we're here.'" I sang like I was in a barbershop quartet, not giving a single thought to who was listening in. "But then, when I was driving into town, everything went so horribly wrong. I got pulled over, and it turns out my license was suspended, and I don't even know why." There were those pesky tears again, the cracks finally giving way to pressure and bursting wide open to release the floodgates. This always happened when I talked to Tessa. She was too good-natured, too genuine, and I knew she loved me. Her concern always whittled away at my exterior and drew out the tears.

She urged me gently in that sweet voice of hers. "Oh no! Go on, tell me."

I inhaled a calming breath that sounded more like sputters of breath.

"I'm at the police station with Zara and Maus. My car is impounded, we rolled into town in a police truck and I'm now the proud owner of no less than *three* traffic violations."

In all my despondency, I had gotten louder as the tears poured down my cheeks. I looked up from my no-longer-private phone call to see everyone, and I mean *everyone*, in the department staring at me. Zara bounced happily in my lap, with her chubby little hand wound around pieces of my messy hair. I felt the slightest draft of air on my chest and I glanced down, seeing what everyone was *actually* staring at. Zara had unzipped my hoodie and yanked the right side of my tank down. All the way down, bra and all. Ah, thank you breastfeeding.

I nodded like it made sense, because the way my day was going, it did. Tits out, broke, and in a police station—was there a better way to arrive at your new hometown?

"And to top it all off, Tessa, my titty is out. Like right now, it's just out."

So, I was losing it. The voices on the other end of the phone got louder, and I heard Tessa shout, "Maisy! I need to take off. I have a family emergency!"

A woman's voice yelled back, "All right, darlin', we got it covered. Go take care of your family."

"Raven, I'm headed to you. Put your tits away, dry your tears, and take care of those babies. I'll be there in ten minutes, babe."

"It's just one tit," I told her, as if that mattered at all.

Tessa giggled into the phone. "Put it away, babe."

I yanked my tank top back over my breast and kissed my sweet baby on the head. "Okay, see you soon."

Ten minutes later, I saw the familiar face of my best friend enter the station.

"Well, hello boys!" She looked around the room, and her gaze landed on the only woman in the place who sat at a large square desk in the center of the room with a silver desk plate that said *Mika Dawson—Dispatch*. Tessa's eyes widened, and she added with a flirtatious wink, "And *girls*."

The woman blushed, and I saw something flash between the two before Tessa spotted me. Her smile lit up the room, and my heart. I smiled stupidly back at her, so relieved to see her face. And in true Tessa form, she sashayed through the office, her confident strides highlighting her tanned, toned legs and curvy body. Her blue eyes sparkled and softened as she made her way toward me. I felt the stress melt away the nearer she got, reminding me how easy she was to be around.

We had met six years ago, back when we both lived in Redlands. After five years of working together, crying together, and sometimes dancing together, we were closer than ever. When her elderly grandma became ill, Tessa packed up her life and headed back to Brooks Falls, trading in five-inch stilettos for a black aesthetician smock. And she never came back after her grandma died. I knew she was working at the Blue Rose, but I didn't know if she was still dancing.

"Raven!" Tessa screeched, standing tall in front of me, a huge grin spread across her pretty face. Even in the drab lighting of the police station, she was a knock-out, with her perfectly symmetrical smile that revealed straight, white teeth behind full lips. I stood up, outstretched my arms, and before I knew it, she'd scooped me up into a tight embrace. Pulling back a few inches, she studied my face.

"I can't believe you're actually here, that you actually did it."

I gave her a weak smile. I really didn't want to talk about it. It was too soon. Sensing my discomfort, she lightly put my cheeks in her hands, squeezed them so my lips puckered up, and in true Tessa fashion, she planted one on me. My face heated, even though I knew exactly what she was doing. She was doing what Tessa always did, no matter where she was—she was going to give a show and leave the crowd with something to remember. My eyes drifted over to Mika, who looked particularly uncomfortable. I tried to be annoyed, but instead of rolling my eyes like I wanted to, I laughed. I truly was happy to see her.

"You always gotta make a whole scene, don't you?"

She laughed and nudged me playfully with her hip. "Me? Look at you barreling into town the way you did. Seems like I have competition in the growing field of 'making a scene'." She bent down to pick up Zara from her car seat. "Baby girl, hi, little monkey." She peppered Zara's face with kisses as Zara squealed in delight. "I'm your Aunty Tessa."

Zara blew a raspberry at her.

Officer Phillips, according to the name tag I spied on his chest, hustled over happily and said hi to Tessa as if they already knew each other.

She drew her brows together, looked him up and down, pursed her lips and then looked him back in the eyes and simply said, "No."

His face fell.

"Tessa!" I chided.

"What?" she asked as she bounced Zara on her hip. "Don't give me that look. I told him it wasn't going to be a thing." As she said it, she gave him another disapproving glance.

"Oh." I was a little taken aback, as men were usually her last choice. She considered herself pansexual with a bent toward masculine women. A strong bent. "You two?"

Tessa shot me a warning look.

"Do you want me to leave you here, or do you want to come home?"

I followed Tessa and noticed that her voice got louder as we walked past Mika's desk.

"Listen, I told him that it was a fun date, but I'm just way more into the ladies."

I side-eyed Tessa just in time to catch *her* side-eying Mika.

17

"You know me, men are too…hard and sweaty." She sighed dreamily. "Women are soft and pretty, and they usually smell better. Besides, men don't know what to do with their mouth half the time, and I swear, it's too much effort for a sex I don't even find that attractive. And while I could go on about the fundamental differences between the sexes that makes one far superior to the other, I think we need to get you all home." Tessa winked at me, a gentle smile playing on her face. Once she'd grabbed Maus' leash and Zara's new *rear-facing* car seat, I followed, carrying Zara and more than happy to get out of there.

As we walked out of the door, Tessa glanced behind her, before turning to me with a half-whisper on her tongue. "Did you see that chick back there? Oooh." She bit her knuckle. "Raven, I've never seen her before. How have I never seen her? The dating pool for me in this place is *shallow*. I'm going to meet her. Did she look interested? Tell me she looked interested. Please don't break my heart. If you think she's just one of those tomboy women who will break your perfectly honed gaydar, I'm going to scream."

"Okay, okay, calm down. I saw the way she looked at you. She looked *very* interested."

"Really? Wait, what am I doing rambling on about my love life? You're here!"

I couldn't believe it either. "Tessa, don't apologize. You talking to me about your love life is the kind of normal that I need right now." It was the truth. It was a kind of normal that I'd never really had, and I planned to cherish it.

I installed Zara's seat in her car before I placed her in and expertly wiggled those chubby little arms through the seatbelts and clicked her in. Maus followed and curled up on the seat next to Zara.

We got into Tessa's car. I let my body melt into the seat as I tried to let go of some of the day's stress. Despite the final events of the day, we had made it and our escape had been successful. I rolled my head over on the seat and smiled at my dear friend.

Tessa turned toward me and with a sympathetic smile. She paused, and we looked at each other for a beat before she asked, "Do you want to talk about it?"

I gave her a resounding "No." I calmed my voice before trying again. "Not right now. It's all really fresh. I just need a little time."

Tessa nodded in understanding and squeezed my arm. "Take all the time you need. We'll be living together, so we'll have plenty of time to catch up on everything when the time is right."

"What?"

Tessa scoffed. "Did you think I was gonna dump you at the nearest motel?"

"I didn't come here expecting you to take me in. I still have a little money saved." That was a lie. I had nothing.

"Good. Save it. I have a three-bedroom house, and I swear that if you argue with me, I'll dump *you* at the motel and keep your babies with me."

I laughed, but my gut tightened as her kindness wrapped around me like a blanket, warming places in me that had been cold for so long. My voice came out as barely a whisper when I told Tessa, "Thanks."

She smiled and reached for my hand. "This is what family does, hun. We take care of one another." Tessa gave my hand a squeeze and started the car.

"Family," I repeated. I turned to look out the window as Tessa drove forward. I watched the police station shrink in the side mirror, just as I had watched Redlands fade away behind me only hours before. My eyes stung, but my heart filled with hope. We were going to be okay. I was hundreds of miles away from my past and grabbing onto a second chance, surrounded by those I loved most.

Chapter 3

Raven - One year later

I cooed softly to my baby, who was no longer a baby but a toddler. "Zaraaaaa. Wakey, wakey, little snakey!" Her heavy eyes barely opened, and she graced me with the cutest sleepy smile. Delicate strands of her ebony hair were scattered across her precious face, stuck in some places from nighttime drool.

"Time to get up, my little lovebug. It's Saturday, and you know what that means!"

Zara stretched her tiny arms over her head and yawned.

Today was our fun day together. After a long week of work and school, we always took a day for "Mommy and Me" time.

"Do you want to pick out some clothes?" I usually let Zara help me pick out what she wore. Even though she was only eighteen months old, I wanted her to learn right away that she had a choice and that even though I was in charge of taking care of her, she was still her own person. After all that I'd gone through, I didn't want her to have to climb her way out of a mental hole like I did. She needed to know from the get-go that she was in charge of her life, and she got to make decisions. But most of all, I wanted her to understand that she had the power to say no. Of course, for the first nine months of her life, all she heard was "no".

Zara rifled through the storage bin that was flung over the closet door.

Twenty minutes and two leggings changes later, we were dressed and ready to face the day. With Zara's tiny hand in mine, we stepped outside. It was the middle of May, the sun was out, and the only sound I heard was the faint whistle of the birds that made this place their home in spring. I took a deep breath, inhaling the clean mountain air and the smell of evergreens. Though we were still in California, it was a stark contrast to the smog of Redlands, a thick air that had been laced with the subtle smells of gasoline and garbage. Not a single part of me missed the city, even with all of its conveniences.

I buckled Zara into her now legal front-facing car seat, then tossed the diaper bag and my purse on the passenger's side. Life had never felt so simple. And even though it was far from perfect, we had built a nice little life here in Brooks Falls. And above all, Zara had a safe place to be and a house full of love and laughter.

I drove toward the town center, which was nestled between the mountains, tall pine trees flanking it from every direction. I loved it here. The people were friendly and the town itself was perfect. Unlike the mishmash in Redlands, where half of the buildings were abandoned or boarded up, Brook's Falls stuck to strict zoning ordinances that ensured the town maintained its charm. And it had worked. Main Street was filled with businesses that looked more like cottages, with well-maintained sidewalks leading from one store front to the next. Most of the buildings were surrounded by gardens in the spring and summer, and snow in the winter, guaranteeing a certain amount of charm no matter the season. And although I hadn't really been anywhere else other than Redlands, I couldn't imagine a place more lovely than here.

We pulled out onto Main Street and drove past the Blue Rose, and I told Zara to say hi to Ms. Maisy.

Zara shrieked, "Maisy!"

She loved my boss, and Maisy loved her.

"We're here, little bug!"

Zara answered with a squelch and a, "Sumshines!"

I unloaded us from the car and followed behind Zara as she toddled clumsily up the steps towards Sunshine's.

"Careful, Zara." I pleaded, trying to keep up with her erratic steps. I was definitely ready for coffee. Tired from my long week, it had taken everything I had this morning not to inject last night's stale study coffee directly into my jugular vein. Zara stumbled through the door, and I looked down to see that both of her shoes were untied.

"Come here, honey. Mommy needs to tie your shoes back up."

Zara scrunched her nose. Okay, I guessed we were having an attitude today.

"It'll only take a second. If we don't tie your shoes, then we can't get muffins."

Her big brown eyes darted around, not even attempting to hide her intentions and instead planning the world's most obvious escape right before she turned around and ran forward, screaming, "Mama, no, I do it!"

****

Cameron

The sun peeked out through the clouds, casting a morning haze on Sunshine's. It looked quiet inside, the tables mostly empty, and the line that extended past the front door most mornings was nearly non-existent. This morning was my first day on the early shift in over a year. The bells chimed on the door when I walked in, and Layla's head popped up from the display case, first searching and then beaming when she saw me.

"Hey, Layla."

"Officer Jameson." She looked at her watch as if she was checking the time. "You're here early today. How ya been, dear?" Layla said softly, her head cocked, one side of her mouth pulled up into a half-smile. I knew she meant well, but that reaction was exactly what kept me away from everyone. I didn't want their sympathy, and I certainly didn't deserve their pity. What I wanted was to be left alone. But Layla was a good woman. She was the owner of Sunshine's, the best and only place to get good coffee in Brooks Falls. Aside from Shea's, the bar owned by my best friend Jet, Sunshine's was one of my favorite places. With oversized sofas, local art on every wall, and coffee to die for, the vibe was one of a kind.

"Not too bad."

"Hey there, Cameron."

I heard the familiar voice of Laurel, one of the baristas, as I turned to see her blinking at me through her thick lashes that were only thick because they were plastered in black goop. She was a cute girl, with short blonde hair and a nice body. Not my type, but she was cute.

The problem was that she seemed to be *very* interested in me lately, and I wasn't interested at all. I had no clue what to do when women threw themselves at me, and that was exactly what was happening more and more since she'd died. Died.

A pit formed in my stomach the size of the lie. And it *was* a lie. It had been a year, but it still felt so raw. So raw that I considered burying my dick in something just to hide the pain for a little while. But no way would it be Laurel. I had tried to tell her gently, when she asked me out a few weeks ago, that I really wasn't ready to date. I didn't mention the part that even if I was ready, she wouldn't be the one. I wasn't that much of a dick, and I wasn't the kind of guy to openly reject a woman. Hell, I didn't know what kind of guy I was anymore. Eleven years of being with the same woman will do that to a man.

"Hi, Laurel."

"What can I get for you, Cam?" She leaned over the counter, pushing her boobs out like that would change my mind.

"I'll just have a medium breakfast blend and a banana nut muffin."

"Of course, I don't know why I ask. It's always the same thing for you," she said with a playful wink.

I nodded and was about to pull out my wallet when I felt something, or someone, knock into my leg and bounce away. I looked down to see what the hell had just happened.

"Mama, no, no, I do it!" The high-pitched little voice screeched as I looked down to see a toddler sitting on her butt on the floor. The girl was adorable, with a ton of wild dark hair flying out every which way and big chocolate-colored eyes. Cute.

"Well, hey there, little one, aren't you a pretty princess?" This kid had some sort of superpower, because the instant she glanced up at me and smiled, a big gap-toothed grin, my cold heart warmed in my chest.

25

Defrosted with one look.

"Zara, come here. I just need to tie your shoes, silly girl."

The voice coming from behind me pierced me, pinning my feet right in place. It was the sweetest, softest voice that sounded more like a purr. I found myself wondering how a few words could send jolts of awareness straight to my cock.

And then I saw the woman.

"I'm so sorry about that. I swear, she is all over the place and despite the great cardio I've been getting lately, I can hardly keep up with her." She giggled while shaking her head, then knelt right at my feet next to her kid. The woman hadn't even made eye contact with me before she was rustling around in her bag, looking for something.

"Mama, I do it!"

"Okay, honey, you can do it, but you have to learn first. How about I do it this time, and you take Tigery. See? I have him right in my bag!"

"Tigeewy!" The kid squealed happily when the woman gave the girl a small, ratty stuffed tiger.

Good lord, the woman was a knockout. My eyes were glued to her perfectly rounded ass that popped out as she leaned on the floor. The woman was at my feet and Jesus, I was only a man. I couldn't help where my mind wandered to when the woman with the sweetest ass I'd ever seen was on her knees in front of me. I wasn't trying to be a creep, but with those jeans and a pink, curve-hugging shirt that I could see straight down...*Fuuuck*. Who was this woman? I was sure I'd never seen her around town before—there was no way I wouldn't remember those tits and that ass. Sure, I had been married, happily even, but I was still a man.

When she finally lifted her face, I felt a twinge of recognition, some sort of familiarity that I couldn't place. I was stunned into silence when a pair of big brown doe eyes landed on me.

Christ. I had to brace myself when I noticed her jet-black hair that tumbled down to her waist and settled right above that perky ass. Her creamy skin probably tasted as good as it looked. The girl was inked with delicate tattoos across her shoulders and arms. My cock took note, and I was, for the first time ever, thankful for the immovable uniform fabric.

She furrowed her brow, taking me in before she…sneered at me? Wait, what?

"Hi there." Wow. What a tool. I was a man struck silent by a beautiful girl. So much that the words were jumbled in my head and trapped on my tongue. She blinked up at me, her big eyes staring directly at me. Into me. I was drawn to her. I hadn't felt this way since…had I ever felt this?

I shook my head like I could shake the stupid right out. And then, like a pro, I nailed her with a winning line. "I'm sorry, but do we know each other?" Yep, it was official. I was a tool.

"Ha!" She snorted.

I fought a grin. I liked the attitude. I also liked that she didn't react to me like some women had. She didn't bat her eyes. She didn't stick out her tits.

What she did do was sit on her heels below me and pop out her hip with one hand on it. "No, *Officer*, we most definitely do not know each other."

Right. I was cueing into the fact we did know each other somehow, and the way we knew each other had to do with my job.

So, two things stuck out—why didn't I know this woman, and what had I done that was so bad to her? There was something about her that made me want to poke at her. In more ways than one.

"Ah, I see. I wrote you a ticket, didn't I?" I smirked, and she glared at me. It didn't accomplish what she intended. If anything, it made me want her more. I wanted to yank her up off the floor and pin her to a wall with my body. Spear her with my dick. Yeah, I was hard up and needed to get laid, but it was more than that. Her energy was magnetic, pulsing between us, drawing me in.

"Not quite," she said, with a petulant huff.

Hmm, interesting. "Did I...arrest you?"

She rolled her eyes while rolling her head back to the ceiling, and despite the fact that I could tell I was pissing her off, I was enjoying the hell out of it. I was also enjoying having this conversation while she was looking up at me from the ground.

"No! Of course not. Geez, do I look like the kinda person that gets arrested?"

No, but you look like the kind of person I'd like to put into handcuffs. I tilted my head, teasing her with a look that said, *Maybe*.

She huffed at me again. "No, you did not write me *a* ticket, you wrote me all the tickets!" Ah, now that made sense.

My voice got low for some reason, and I was pretty sure I no longer had control of all of my faculties. "Wow, you must've done something really bad."

"You impounded my car, drove me into town in a police truck, and gave me three tickets. On my first day in town." Her death glare would've been adorable if I hadn't remembered exactly what she was talking about. That entire month was branded into me. Every word said, every event leading up to the worst day of my life. I'd relived each moment, analyzing the details, searching for an explanation. Pain hit like a punch to the throat, knocking the wind out of me and pulling me out of the moment with her.

"Cam?" Laurel's sickeningly sweet voice floated over and dropped onto us like a wet blanket. "Your coffee and muffin are ready." She sounded innocent enough, but when I turned to grab my order, she was glaring at me. I didn't care what she thought, but I was grateful to have an out. *Walk away, asshole, leave the girl alone.*

Instead of doing what I should've done, I knelt down to face the woman, who was still fussing with her kid on the floor. I knew it was a mistake as soon as I got into her space. I shouldn't have gotten so close, because she smelled like coconuts and the fresh mountain breeze, all that sass and unintentional sexiness sending me straight into a tailspin. Before I could stop myself, I leaned closer than I should've, intrigued by the little gasps of breath she was taking in as I closed the gap between us. Sucked straight into those eyes that were now wide with shock.

"What are you drinking, sweetheart?" *Sweetheart? Jameson, what are you doing?* Her head snapped back in disbelief as she took me in.

"Who? Me, sweetheart?" She placed a delicate hand over her heart and tilted her head.

She said it as if I could possibly be talking to someone else. I was practically on top of the woman, on my heels, eye to eye with her. Dangerously close. I

29

glanced around.

"Yeah, you, sweetheart." I grinned at her, like the fool that I was. I didn't know how to do this anymore. I didn't even want to be doing this. Jesus, this woman could be married or have a boyfriend. I stole a glance at her hands. Just as I hoped, no ring. I shouldn't have cared. I couldn't have her, but I couldn't help but think that I didn't want anyone else to have her, either.

"Oh no, that's not necessary." She looked down at the ground, her cheeks blossoming with a pink hue that made her look even more adorable.

"I'm getting your order, so just tell me what you want so we can get out of this line." I tilted my head, motioning to the line behind her. She looked frantic as she turned to see a few customers stacking up behind us. The girl had to be new to this town if she didn't know this was the most easygoing place to be.

"Oh crap, I didn't even notice that. Okay, I'll just have a black medium roast."

"And?"

"Aaaaand, thank you?" She lifted one shoulder to her ear, and I couldn't help but smile at her confusion.

"No, gorgeous, I mean, would you like anything else? You need to eat, and what about your little one?" *Gorgeous?* I was losing it, and I just couldn't stop myself.

"No, really, you don't have to do that. I probably deserved all of those tickets, so if you're doing this because you feel bad for me then—"

I cut her off with a stern look of warning that felt way more intimate than it should've. "Tell me what you want."

Her eyes went round in what looked like a little bit

of fear. "All right then. I'll take a blueberry glazed donut." She looked down at her kid. "And what do you want to eat, Zara? The nice officer is going to buy our breakfast today."

"Boo mummin!"

She smiled at her daughter and then looked back up at me. Holy mother of Jesus. Her smile shot a pang of warmth to my stomach. Her perfect white teeth showed through a smile that was like the sunset. A warmth and beauty that left only darkness when it disappeared.

"She'll have a blueberry muffin and a milk."

I swallowed hard and tightened my fists to stop from reaching for this beautiful stranger. Except, when I stood up, I reached for her anyway, my mind and body completely at odds with one another. I grabbed her hand to help her up, and when we touched, the contact stirred something in me, and we both jumped a little and quickly backed away from each other. I looked away and cleared my throat.

"Did you get that, Laurel?" I asked, my voice strained.

Laurel nodded slowly. Her eyes were narrowed and her lips pursed to form a line across her face.

I ushered the woman and her kid out of the line, placing my hand gently on the small of her back. Her body quaked with the contact, and she turned to look at me over her shoulder, her eyes searching mine. We stopped a few paces away, my coffee in hand, the kid at her foot, and stared at one another.

"I'm Cameron." I said abruptly, pulling her hand when I should've shaken. She stumbled toward me, her lips parting on a quiet puff of air.

"I'm Raven, Raven DeLuca, and this is my

daughter, Zara." She placed her hands on her knees, bending down to talk to her daughter.

Christ, don't look, be a gentleman. Yeah, I looked, and it was worth it because that ass was something. I was sick, depraved. Here she was introducing me to her kid, and I was trying to memorize the contours of her ass.

"Zara, can you say hi to Mr. Cameron?" The little girl looked up at me and scrunched her tiny fingers together in that "hi" motion that kids do. Adorable.

"She's a cutie. You and your husband must be very proud."

She side-eyed me while looking at her daughter. It appeared it was obvious to her what I was getting at, but it wasn't obvious to me *why* I was getting at it, because what business did I have with this woman? Hitting on a single mom out with her kid was shameless, and I wasn't *that* guy.

"I'm not married." Her tone gave off a hint of sadness. A boyfriend maybe?

"Of course, you and your significant other, then."

She turned her head to stare directly into my eyes, throwing me off my game with just a single look. Ha, my game. I had no game. I had been out of the game for so long, I didn't remember the rules.

"I'm a single mother, always have been. No strings, no *dead weight*." Her face was closed and stoic and everything in between that, with a dash of bitterness that told me she was protective of what she had.

"Well then, would you two like to have a seat with me?" I asked her. She seemed surprised, her head tilting to the side as she looked anywhere but at me. *Yeah, sweetheart, that shocked the shit out of me too.*

"Oh. I really can't. I promised this little one a

breakfast picnic at the park before we put on our suits and play at the splash pad." Her beautiful face beamed at her daughter. "Saturdays are kind of strictly mother-daughter days, and part of that is getting breakfast and playing at the park. The weather is so nice, but the pool isn't open yet, so splash pad it is!"

I gave her an interested look, and she must've taken it differently, because she blushed and then quickly added, "Sorry, I don't know why I'm rambling and telling you all about our plans, like you care." I smiled at her and wanted to tell her that it didn't matter, because I really didn't hear much after she mentioned being in a bathing suit.

"Feel free to tell me all about your bathing suit plans." *Jesus, Jameson, that was too much.* Not to mention that I was in uniform, and failing miserably at maintaining professionalism.

No sooner than the words came out of my mouth did I feel all of the things I should've been aware of before I started talking—guilt, shame, anger. What was I doing other than breaking every single promise I'd made to myself a year ago? Just a year, and there I was, in uniform, flirting with some woman I didn't even know. She just looked up at me, no blush, no smile, just beautiful, wide, brown eyes staring up at me, taking me in. We shared this awkwardness for an uncomfortable amount of time.

"Medium black roast, milk, blueberry donut, and blueberry muffin!" Laurel called from behind the counter.

"Oh, thank god," Raven said quietly under her breath and then rushed to the counter to grab her things. Instead of heading back to continue whatever had just happened, she walked up next to me. "Thank you for buying us breakfast today. Be safe out there and, um, thanks for your service to our country and…" Her voice trailed off as she saluted me, and I heard the faintest whisper of a "what was that?" as she swung the door open and left in a hurry.

I had to admit, I was a little curious as to what else she was going to thank me for, or if she was going to break out into the national anthem. As awkward and cringey as it all was, I had to laugh. I swiveled my body to face the counter.

"Hey, how often does she come here?"

Laurel pressed her eyes closed while she inhaled a long breath. "Every day."

"She ever come with anyone else?"

Laurel gave me a deadpan look because she knew what I was asking. "Sometimes," she said, with a tilt of her head and a bite to her voice.

"Who?" I demanded, like I had some claim to her. Christ, I was jealous over a woman I didn't even know.

"Jesus, Cameron, she isn't married, and she doesn't have a boyfriend. There, are you happy?"

That made me happy, and I tried not to overthink why. I nodded slowly, trying to tame the upward twitch of my lips, wondering why I was about to do what I was going to do. "I want you to charge me for everything she gets here, okay?"

Laurel's eyes crinkled. "What? Why?"

"It's not what you think. It's more of a pay it forward kind of a thing." Or pay it back more accurately.

"I don't understand."

"Not that it's your business, and not that I have to answer to you, but she's a single mom, and I kind of

34

saddled her with a ton of tickets a while ago. I cost her a lot of money. I don't want her to know it's from me, though. Can you just do that for me, please?" I left out the part where I wanted to bend the woman over one of those fluffy-ass couch cushions and impale her with my cock. Laurel didn't need to know that.

Laurel's face softened. "Sure, Cameron, I can do that. That's actually really sweet. I thought you were interested in her."

"All right, thanks. Now, you have a nice day and don't forget, I'll just pay every day for what she gets, okay? And if I don't come in that same day, you know I'll be in, and I'm good for it."

"Of course, I know you are. I'll let Layla know." I was about to walk away when she added, "Wait, if I do this for you, will you do something for me?"

I furrowed my brow curiously. "Sure, what can I do?"

"You can take me to lunch."

I opened my mouth to shoot the idea down, but she put her hand up.

"And before you say no, it's not a date. I know you're not ready to date. You already said that to me. But you know, people do things other than date, like make friends. I'm new to town, and it would be nice to have a friend." She peered up at me through those thick lashes.

I knew what she was insinuating. And I knew that I didn't want it, but Laurel was going to do me a big favor. Plus, I could do friends.

"Not a date, huh?"

She nodded.

"Okay, sure, we have a deal." With a wink, I tossed a five-dollar bill into the tip jar and walked out of

Sunshine's, reminding myself that paying for Raven was just me trying to help out a single mother, nothing else. I was just a good Samaritan.

Chapter 4

Raven

For the love of all that is unholy, did I just salute that gorgeous man? I had not been prepared for what had gone down back there, and I didn't even know what that last thing was. And anyway, last year, when he was welcoming me to Brooks Falls, I was pretty sure he was married. He still could be. Even the sincerest man couldn't be trusted. I was frazzled as I walked out of Sunshine's, to be sure. So, in order to deal with myself, I did what any mature adult would do—I whined to my toddler.

"Zara, what are you going to do with Mommy?"

"We spash! You got a babing zoot, I gotsa baby zoot. We has fun, Mama!"

That was exactly what I needed to do. Have fun and not overthink what had just occurred, but probably didn't really occur the way I thought it did.

My phone started to ring, and while I wanted to leave it and let it go to voicemail, I knew I shouldn't. It was either Tessa, whom I never ignored, or one of my jobs, which I couldn't afford to ignore. I picked it up and looked at the number. Tess.

"Hey."

"Hey girl, where are you? You and Zara snuck out this morning. Are you at the park already?"

"Yeah, we are just getting here. I got coffee and breakfast from Sunshine's. Wanna join us?"

"Do I want to get in my bathing suit in public and splash around at a kids' park?" Pause for dramatics. "Hell yes I do! I'll be there in fifteen."

I laughed. I loved how free-spirited Tessa was. She was a natural spark of light, and her vibrant energy made everything fun. When we used to work long shifts together at the club, while the other girls were fighting for prime time, she and I were laughing and joking about customers.

"Great. Come whenever you can. We're gonna eat first, and after I inject this coffee directly into my veins, we'll get wet."

"Oooooo, I might go get wet tonight."

"Not what I meant."

"I know, doll, but it should be. Anyway, we can talk about that later. I'll see you soon."

We hung up, and no more than twenty minutes later, Tessa arrived in style. The wonderful, and curious, thing about her was that she was always the same person with everyone. With her, what you saw was what you got, every single time. So needless to say, she arrived in true Tessa style with cutoff booty shorts that showed off her perfect tan across all those long limbs, a cute coral knit halter top, big sunglasses, and her blonde hair thrown up into a carefree ponytail. When she found us, she gave me a strange look.

"Why are you dressed like my grandma?" She grabbed the hem of my dress with a disgusted face. "Did you go through her stuff and find that abomination?"

I looked down at my smock with a frown. It was a cover-up, something that moms wore over bathing suits.

I'd seen it when I took Zara to the municipal pool for swim lessons months ago and I learned the hard way that moms did not walk around in two-pieces.

"No, but I am at a kids' park, so I threw this on over my bathing suit. I'm not trying to show off everything in my arsenal like some people who just showed up here, whose name I won't say, but if I were to give them a name, it would definitely be something that rhymes with Schmessa."

Tessa smiled at me and nudged my hip with hers.

"You're such a jackass. Now, please tell me you have something underneath that hideous smock so you can take that ugly ass thing off."

I rolled my eyes and took a deep breath, sucking in the fresh mountain air. "I do have something under this *cover-up.*" I emphasized, because it was not a smock. It was a perfectly normal for women to wear cover-ups, especially when they were at a children's parks. "My bathing suit isn't really kids' park appropriate."

Tessa fingered the hem of my smock and eyed me. "Good. And since when do you care about being appropriate?"

I shot her a look. "Since always. Since I started a new life and have a chance to start all the way over."

"So, you're starting over as a seventy-five-year-old woman?"

I laughed, even though I was irritated. "No, I'm starting over as a responsible mother with modesty."

"Oh Christ, Raven, forget modesty when you have a body like that. You're not going to have it forever. Save modesty for your sixties or seventies, depending on how you age. And even then, who cares? Now take that ugly potato sack off and show me what cute bathing suit you're wearing!"

At that moment, Zara came running over and yelled, running to Tessa, who scooped her up and tickled her tummy.

"Ah, if it isn't my little partner in crime."

"Cwime!" Great.

"Baby Z, please do Aunty a solid and tell your mama to get her bathing suit on and stop being a prude!"

I rolled my eyes at Tessa, wanting this argument to end. Realizing that the park was empty, I decided to give in and yanked off my white linen cover-up. Underneath, I wore the only bathing suit that I had. It wasn't quite as modest as my linen cover-up, which was now scrunched up in a tight wad in my bag. I was wearing black boy shorts that barely covered my ass, and my top was a bright blue bra style that was a bit too revealing for a kids' park.

Tessa whistled at me and slapped my ass. "Okay, now we're talking! Woo-hoo, you got that T and that A, you better flaunt it before your T's are sagging all the way down to you A!"

She was ridiculous. But also, she was right. That's not why I was doing it, hiding myself. I was doing it to protect Zara and I. But as soon as the three of us started playing, I forgot that I was in the middle of the town wearing nothing but a bathing suit.

I left Tessa and Zara at the splash pad, while I ducked out to a park bench for a quick break. I was sipping my water, watching them from a distance and enjoying the cool mountain breeze, when a shadow cast over me.

"Hey there, sexy, remember me?" A deep voice rumbled from behind me.

When I spun around, I saw a tall man with a cutoff T-shirt, basketball shorts, and a tribal tattoo that wrapped around his large bicep. I looked into his eyes, trying to register if I knew him from somewhere, but nothing came to mind. I was positive that I didn't know him. But his presence was imposing and unwanted. I had experience with arrogant men like him, so I knew exactly how to handle them—carefully. Because as tough as they acted, they were the worst kind of fragile.

I dug out my most submissive and polite voice. "I'm sorry, but I don't think I know who you are." A timid smile formed at my lips. I was so weak, slipping so easily into old habits, cowering beneath an unpredictable man.

He studied me for a moment, his eyes darkening and wandering over me in a way that was far too familiar for a stranger. His devilish grin grew and sent shivers down my spine.

"I'm hurt you don't remember me." His voice was almost theatrical as he threw a hand over his chest and widened his eyes. Despite the drama, the rejection I saw in his eyes was real. "Well, you might not remember me, but after I saw what that little body can do, I couldn't forget you if I tried." He chuckled, and his repulsive gaze swept over my body. I shuddered and took a step back. I turned away, contemplating my next move. *Fight or flight? Fight or flight?* Helpless and trapped. Broken and alone. My whole body tensed, and I froze at the sudden influx of memories suffocating me. I gasped for breath. My eyes landed on Zara, who was happily playing with Tessa. Tessa made eye contact with me, and she tilted her head as if to ask me if everything was okay. I shook my head, insinuating that everything was fine and to stay where she was, and keep Zara away from this situation.

Fear came in waves, and before I could fully give over, I pushed myself, ready for a fight.

"Listen." I turned slowly, my eyes downcast as I steadied myself as best I could. "I'm just here with my family, trying to relax and enjoy my weekend. I don't remember you and I'm sorry if that offends you, but I dance for a lot of people, and I don't remember most of them." The truth was, I didn't remember *any* of them. "You seem nice." Bald-faced lie. "But I'm really not interested, so I hope you have a good day." I waved one hand and took a few steps back, hoping to make a full exit. I felt it and saw it simultaneously—a tingle on the back of my neck just as his eyes darkened and the veins in his neck dilated. The man grabbed my wrist tightly, spinning me and pulling me into him so that my back was flush against his sweaty frame. My body slammed against his and I whimpered. Instantly everything caught up to me, the weight of it all threatening to crush me underfoot and before I could stop it, I was trapped in a nightmare.

My wrist throbbed, and I went limp under his grip. My back hit the wall with a loud thud as the plastic grocery bag I had been holding went flying across the room. On impact with the wall, my chest seized, and I was suddenly wheezing, unable to draw new breath.

"Why are you late?" He screamed into my face, stabbing a finger in my direction.

A high-pitched whistle escaped my throat. He shook my body, spit shooting out from his gritted teeth, his wide eyes bloodshot and trained on me, before he hollered the question again. My head spun, and I loosened my body, preparing for the inevitable.

A cool gust of wind struck my face, and I blinked

several times, reorienting myself to the present moment, pushing past the memories that I carried silently, shamefully, deep in the bones like a disease.

"Now listen, you little slut." The man growled in my ear. "I enjoyed you shaking that ass for me at my friend's bachelor party the other night. Now you wanna pretend that you're some classy little princess with a family?" He laughed in my ear. His breath was warm against my face as tears stung my eyes and my heart pounded in my chest. "You're nothing, just some small-town stripper. You think you're better than me, huh? You were a hoe last weekend, and you're still one right now. A costume change won't change that."

Wasn't that the truth. A name change, a costume change, a location change. I still was who I had always been, and that girl was weak and broken and shameful. My eyes fell out of focus as his fingers clamped harder onto me, digging into my skin. The pain was something so familiar that in a sick way, it felt right. It felt like home, and as much as I wanted to buck against his hold, I melted into it. *It's the only way to survive, it's the only way.*

Between tears and panic, Tessa and Zara were a blur in the distance. I couldn't see them, but I could sure hear Tessa when she shouted, "Hey!" I raised a hand, hoping she and Zara would stay put. I didn't want Zara to see this—she had already experienced enough trauma to last a lifetime.

"Now, how about you and I go step into that bathroom and you can show me what's under this bathing suit, huh?" He wrapped an arm around my front, his hand flat on my stomach, pulling me into him. I felt him hard behind me, and I was sure that I was going to pass out or throw up. Maybe both.

It was then that a terrifying voice, so deep and steady, boomed from behind us. "Sir, get your hands off of the woman. I'm only gonna tell you this just the one time."

The man holding me spun around with me still pressed against him, while sputtering, "And who the fuck do you…" But before he finished that sentence, his angry voice trailed off. He dropped my arm and pushed me off of him, softening his tone as he spoke to the furious beast of a man that stood before us with his jaw flexed and his eyebrows pinched together. Cameron.

"I'm sorry, Officer. I was just talking to the girl."

"With your hands on her? Against her will?" Cameron roared. The man was so terrifying he didn't need a weapon. He was a weapon. Cameron turned to me. "Are you okay?"

I nodded my head because even though I wasn't, I wanted this man to go away right now. I at least had the presence of mind to know that the very last thing I needed was to be in court with my name and face made available to the public.

"Sweetheart, you're not okay. Tell me what this man was doing." His voice was soft and gentle, like honey to my soul.

"No, I just want him to leave me alone," I said, my voice a whisper, my gaze fixed on the ground.

Cameron's voice rumbled. "Go. But if I ever see you talking to her again, the next place you'll go after that is a cell and then a courtroom. You got me?" The man nodded and ran off like he hadn't just tried to assault me in a public park. My body trembled, and I was fixated on the ground, when a large hand rubbed the red marks on my arm. I lifted my head up to meet Cameron's eyes. Oh, he was beautiful, but he was more than that. Those gray-blue eyes gently searched me.

"Raven? You're not okay. You're shaking. Did he hurt you?" His words sounded strained and his voice cracked on that final word. He didn't sound like any cop I had ever met.

I let the cool sound of his deep voice wash over me like a wave of calm. The spike of adrenaline drained from my system, and before I could get my bearings, my legs gave out. I collapsed, ready to hit the ground, but was surprised when, after I closed my eyes, I didn't feel the grass. Cameron held me up, with one arm wrapped loosely around my waist, his gorgeous face just inches from mine, all that dark hair tousled perfectly on top of his head, his worried eyes boring into mine. "Sweetheart, did you know that guy? Did he do something to you?"

Sweetheart. Oh lord, this man. I melted into him more, allowing myself to be comforted. I laid my head on his firm chest, soaking in the genuineness, breathing in his compassion. I clutched onto his biceps for more support.

"No, I haven't seen him before." I lied because what was I supposed to say? Oh yeah, he's some creep that I danced half-naked for at a bachelor party the other night. Since I currently have no skills except dancing and waitressing, that's what I do for extra money. Wanna go out some time? No. I was not about to tell him that or anything else. Besides, what I said was a half-truth. I didn't remember the guy.

"All right, well, I've got you." His voice was soothing, and when his thick finger brushed away a stray tear, my heart fluttered. I remembered his phone call to his wife over a year ago, and I wondered what had happened between them since then. They'd seemed so happy.

Steadying me on my feet, but still holding me up, he reached into his breast pocket and pulled something out. "Here, take my card. If he, or *anyone* else, ever bothers you like that again, you just let me know. Okay?"

I took the card. The break in our connection sent a flash of something I couldn't identify across his face. For me, it was loss, because my body wanted to be back in his arms. I'd known this man for all of two seconds, and somehow, he made me feel safe.

"Okay. Thank you, Officer Jameson." And I meant it. I was mesmerized by him, and even though I knew that I'd have trust issues for the rest of my life, I wanted to believe this was a good man.

"Please, call me Cameron," he said with one side of his lips upturned into a smile that made the corners of his eyes crinkle. He was so handsome.

I blushed. I could feel the heat all the way from my neck to my face. "All right. Thank you, Cameron." His eyes shifted downward before he forcefully drew them back up and swallowed hard. I was still in my bathing suit, and I'd fallen into the man wearing practically nothing. My blush covered my entire body. Sure, I was used to being scantily clad in front of strangers, but that was different. It was my job. I didn't ever throw myself at men outside of work and I'd definitely never done it half-naked.

"I'm sorry, how embarrassing." I bent over and reached for a towel. Yeah, even worse. As I felt the cool mountain breeze hit my ass cheeks, I shot up and faced him without a towel, eyes widened as my mouth formed an "O".

He chuckled, a deep, rumbling sound.

"That's not quite the word I was thinking."

My blush blushed.

"I'm sorry. That was rude." He seemed sincerely remorseful as he bent over to grab my towel. He held it like it physically pained him to hand it over.

"Raven, is everything okay?" Tessa's voice broke the awkward towel silence as she walked over carrying Zara, wearing a look of concern and smugness at the same time.

"Yeah, I'm fine. Officer Jame—uh, Cameron, was just helping me with that guy. Some handsy creep."

Cameron stood up straight and tipped his head toward us. "You have my card, Raven. Please use it if you need to. Or want to. Have a good day, ladies." He tipped his head one more time and walked away toward his truck.

Tessa didn't wait for the man to leave. Oh no, she jumped right in. "Hey, what was that all about?" Tessa asked, setting down Zara, who swiftly ran back to play on the splash pad. Tessa sat down and patted the towel for me to join her.

"That guy, the runner, he was from the bachelor party I did the other night, and he recognized me."

"Oh, sweet Jesus, one of those." Tessa breathed out. "That party was thirty miles out of town in a rental. They weren't even locals. I guess that doesn't mean they didn't stop here, but still, I'm so sorry. Are you okay?"

I nodded my head at her. "Yeah, I'm okay, just a little shaken up. It's not your fault." She sidled up next to me and pulled my head onto her shoulder, stroking my hair.

"I promised you that any of the parties you did would be so far out of town, you wouldn't run into anyone you knew."

I gave her a half-smile. "True, but I knew the risk, because you can't really predict that. Unless you're God. Are you God?" I teased, wanting to lighten the mood, hoping it would calm my frayed nerves.

"Well, I was going to wait to tell you, but yes, I am."

"Well then, as your first order of holy business, can you get rid of all men like that?"

Tessa shot me a sly grin. "Please! You damn well know that if I had that power, I'd just get rid of all men. I got no use for most of them, personally. But if I did that, you wouldn't have any hot cops to whisk you off your feet."

I rolled my eyes at her ridiculousness.

"Seriously though, are you okay?" I knew what she was asking. The answer was no, I wasn't okay. I would never be okay. But it had nothing to do with that man in the park.

"I'm fine. You don't have to worry."

"Well then, if you're really okay, can we please get on to the most important topic at hand?"

Lifting my head from her shoulder, I tilted my head in confusion.

"The hot cop coming to save the day and then giving you his number?"

I rolled my eyes. "Oh, that. You mean the one who gave me all those tickets and who I'm pretty sure used to be married? Might *still* be married."

Tessa gave me a serious look. "No, honey. His wife died a while ago, shortly after you got into town, actually." My stomach clenched with a pang of sadness for him.

"It's been a year. Maybe he's ready to start something. Lord knows all the single, straight women in this town have been impatiently waiting for that. Which, I must point out, is most of the women in this small town. Remind me again why I moved to the middle of nowhere in Straightsville, California?"

I shook my head. "To take care of your granny and get your aesthetician license without any distractions? And he was just doing his job. He's on duty and he saw that guy bothering me. It's in his job description to serve and protect."

"Is that why you called him Cameron instead of Officer Jameson?"

I shifted uncomfortably and avoided eye contact with her. "No, we met earlier at Sunshine's, and he bought us breakfast." I mumbled that last part.

Her eyes about popped out of her head. "Oh, okay. I knew I saw something there. He's gonna serve and protect all right—serve you up some of that supersize dick and protect your vag from atrophying!"

"Seriously, Tessa, I don't think you could be any more crude!"

She shoved me playfully, laughing. "Oh, come on, you know that's not true. I can be much worse." She wrapped her arm around me as I giggled, knowing it was true; she could be much worse. "Seriously though, honey, if some fine as hell man is interested in you, maybe you should—"

"No," I cut her off. "I am not going there. Not now. Especially not now, and you know why. But definitely not before I get my life together. I'm a twenty-eight-year-old single mom, waitress, and part-time stripper. I have nothing to offer him or anyone else."

Tessa's lips twisted to one side and she peered up through her lashes. "I'm also both of those things. Do you think I have nothing to offer?"

Ashamed, I sighed. "Of course not, but you also don't have a baby and enough emotional baggage to fill every overhead bin in an airplane. You're also much closer to your aesthetician certification than I am to my nursing degree. But even if you chose to just be a waitress and part-time stripper, you have *everything* to offer. You are incredible and have always kept your life together. It's not my job that I'm ashamed of, Tess. It's my entire life. I can't afford to be close to anyone."

She nodded. "I know it's been a tough go for you, but I'm so proud of all you've managed to do in such a short period of time. Nursing is not easy. Those classes and all that anatomy crap you talk about and memorize is complicated. But you've aced every class. And what happened with you and—"

"Don't!" I didn't mean to shout. It wasn't anger; it was fear. It was that flat-out panic that couldn't be contained if we spoke of it.

Tessa eyed me warily. "Sorry."

I breathed out, wanting to change the topic, wanting to get our conversation back on track. "You know I couldn't be doing this without your help, right? I mean, there is no way I could afford evening childcare or rent or food."

"Oh, I know," she smiled. "I'm the best husband you'll ever have." Wasn't that the truth. "Come on, babe, let's go get some junk food and wine. We're having a girls' night tonight. We need pizza and chocolate and wine and some classic movies."

Zara ran up excitedly, and having overheard that last part, yelled, "Moobies!"

Tessa and I looked at each other and cracked up, then she nudged me, whispering, "I gave a lap dance to a guy with moobies the other night. He had full C-cups, almost bigger than yours."

I snickered. "You're unbelievable."

"I know, but you still love me."

Chapter 5

Raven

Girls' night was exactly what I needed. We checked all the necessary boxes. We did mani-pedis and makeovers and watched *Tangled* on loop since that was Zara's favorite Disney movie. And because I drew the short straw, I had to let Zara do my makeup, instead of the trained aesthetician in the house.

"Mama, you a pwincess." She squeezed my cheeks and examined her handiwork.

"More like the clown from *It*." Tessa mumbled, and I tossed a pillow at her.

I carried Zara off to bed when her movie ended for the hundredth time and tucked her in, planting a light kiss on her forehead. "Mama loves you, angel girl. Sweet dreams." Maus curled up on the floor, next to Zara's toddler bed, where he always slept. I patted his furry little head. "You watch over our girl, okay, Mausy?" His little nub of a tail wagged at the sound of his name, and I took that as an affirmative.

Tessa and I began the rest of our big girls' night, which included a slew of Tom Cruise movie classics, our favorite pizza from Mariani's—and of course, too much wine. After two movies and a bottle and a half of wine, Tessa shot up from the couch with a face that told me she was up to no good and walked to the back of the house.

Except she was heading straight for my room.

"Hey, where are you going? Don't go in there. You're gonna wake the baby!"

Tessa pressed her finger to her lips. "Shhhhh." She tip-toed dramatically, pulling her limp wrists in front of her chest, like a cartoon character. Oh yeah, she was drunk. She giggled quietly at herself, and I couldn't help but laugh at how ridiculous she looked.

After a few minutes, she came out of the room with a small card in her hand. *What was she up to?*

"What were you doing in there, crazy?" I asked her. She smiled suggestively and held up the card.

"I was looking for this." She waved the card around as if revealing a big secret. "You are going to call that hot cop from the park!" If I were to be honest with myself, I'd thought about Cameron all day. The way he swooped in and saved me from that creepy guy. And his sexy blue eyes scouring me in my bathing-suit-clad body like the answers to all of earth's mysteries could be found in my booty shorts.

"No, he said to call if I ever needed anything, like if I'm in some sort of danger, not if I'm drunk and hanging out with my annoying best friend." I reached for the card, trying to snatch it from her. I must've been a little more drunk than I thought because my movements were slow and uncoordinated, not even close to getting the card. Tessa raised her eyebrows, pulling her head back and giving me a look that told me she was about to tell me what was what.

"Hello! You *need* to talk to the hot cop because your pussy is in *danger* of drying the fuck up."

"You're impossible! I'm getting more wine, and when I come back out here, there needs to be another movie on so we can continue girls' night. This is not 'girl calls boy night.' It's just girls' night."

"Ooo, clever!" Tessa mocked me and rolled her eyes. "Fine. Prude. Go get more wine and bring the dark chocolate. I need a snack."

I went into the kitchen and poured myself another glass of wine, a glass that I really shouldn't be drinking. But it felt good the way it made my limbs relax and my mind buzz, a welcome feeling after the stress of the park incident. I grabbed the dark chocolate, and before I could turn back to the living room, I heard Tessa giggling.

"Hello, is this the sexy cop that stole my best friend's heart today?" *Oh no, what was she doing?*

I hurried to the couch where she was sitting, talking on the phone, looking so smug I wanted to slap that smirk right off her pretty little face.

"Tessa!" I whisper-yelled at her and threw the chocolate in her lap. "What are you doing?"

"Ouch!" She laughed maniacally at me. "Hey, guess who it is?"

"Get off of the phone, now! Hang up your phone." But Tessa waved *my* phone in the air and laughed. "It's not *my* phone, Raven!" she said, clear as day. Tessa on a normal day was a bit of a loose cannon, but drunk Tessa? She had enough ammunition to start and end the next world war.

"Give me that, now!"

She giggled and tossed the phone at me, then stood up with her wine and chocolate and sauntered away proudly, shouting over her shoulder in a singsong voice. "Have fun!"

I was hoping that by the time I had put my ear to the phone, Cameron would've hung up. I glanced at the clock. It was one in the morning, and she had probably woken him up. With any luck—if he was still on the phone—he was half asleep and just simply annoyed by an early morning prank phone call.

I put the phone to my ear, not saying a thing.

"Um, hello?"

Ugh, dammit Tessa, I thought. I cleared my throat, trying to sound sober. I didn't recognize my own voice as it came out high and panicked. Humiliated. That was the correct word.

"Yep, I'm here. It's, uh, Raven, from the park today. And the tickets from a year ago. I am *so* sorry about my friend. We were having a girls' night and probably too much to drink. I guess she thought it would be funny to call you, which was not funny at all. It was childish and rude and out of line to use your business card like that. I am seriously so embarrassed and sorry."

The phone line went dead. Well, ouch. That kind of stung. I mean, I wanted him to not be there when I answered, but hanging up on me after I apologized? I groaned. I was going to kill Tessa in the morning.

A second later, my phone blipped with the sound of a text message, and I swiped to open it, figuring it was Tessa texting me something stupid from her room. I checked the messages:

Unknown—*It's Cameron, answer your phone.*—

What? My phone rang again, and I wanted to throw it, like the thing was going to burn me. But I was a glutton for punishment, so I answered it. "Hello?"

"Hey there." Oh. My. Holy. Wet. Panties. Just two words from the deep, sleepy voice that rumbled on the other end of the line, and I was done for. "Sorry I hung up on you. You called my work cell, and I can't take personal calls on it. And whatever you were saying sounded pretty personal."

Right, that made sense. "I was just apologizing about my friend. I'm really sorry," I said in a voice that came out much huskier than I intended. "We were having a girls' night and drinking more wine than we probably should've. I think she got carried away."

"A girls' night, huh? What does a girls' night involve? Pillow fights in your pajamas?"

I laughed. "You wish." I also died a little, because his deep, sleepy voice was so sexy. I pictured him lying in bed, wearing nothing but a tight pair of boxer briefs, his hair messed up from sleep and his eyes half-shut in that sexy bedroom-eye look. My head was telling me to shut this down, but my neglected girl parts, spurred on by alcohol, were begging me to keep going. So, I grabbed a blanket and snuggled up on the couch. If he wanted to hear about girls' night, what harm was there in telling him?

"No pillow fights, but we did watch some movies and eat pizza. And obviously drank too much."

I heard a deep snicker, before he asked, in a smooth as silk voice, "What movies do you watch on a girls' night?"

"Well, we watched *Top Gun* and *Risky Business*, and we were about to watch *Jerry McGuire*, but then I guess we called you instead." I shrugged like he could see me.

"A Tom Cruise marathon, huh?"

"Yup, if you're going to have a girls' night, there are two things you must have: Tom Cruise and red wine."

"Mmm." He hummed into my ear, and lord help me, could I orgasm from a voice alone? I was definitely in a bad way. I pressed my thighs together, enjoying every last drop of his masculine voice. "I'll remember that for my next girls' night."

"Oh yeah? Do you have a lot of girls' nights?" I felt a little irritated by the thought of him having other women at his house, as if I had any right to feel that way.

He chuckled quietly. "No, but I might schedule one soon." My body tensed in annoyance.

"Well, that sounds nice," I snipped, more harshly than I intended. *Jesus, Raven, calm your tits. He's not yours.* "I hope you have fun, and make sure to choose only the classic Cruise movies. And definitely avoid *Vanilla Sky.*"

He chuckled again. "Maybe I'll just let you choose the movies for our girls' night." Aaaand, I melted right back into the couch. Yes, I was pathetic.

"*Our* girls' night?"

"I guess it would be more of a boy-girl night." Oh. I liked where this was going. No, I hated it. Loved it. Hated it! Loved.

He interrupted my internal battle. "Sweetheart?"

Oh lord, kill me now. I succumbed, my voice dripping with all kinds of desperation for this man. "Yes?" Ugh, my own voice reverberated in my head, and oh yeah, I sounded thirsty. I was too desperate.

"How drunk are you?"

"Hmm." I pretended to ponder it. I really wasn't that drunk. Just a little tipsy, right? "Drunk enough to stay on this phone call, but not drunk enough to forget it in the morning."

He was quiet for a second before I heard movement in the background and the clanging of a glass bottle.

"That sounds like just the right amount of drunk. I

57

better catch up."

"Were you in bed when my roommate called?"

"No, I was asleep on my couch." I thought that was weird. I didn't take him as the type of guy to fall asleep on the couch in front of the TV, but then again, it's not like I really knew him. I wanted to ask why, but he cut me off with a question.

"What are you wearing?"

Okay, well, that escalated quicker than I expected. I guessed we were going there, and since I was already going to regret this in the morning, why not really go for it?

"Oh wow, no lube. We're just jumping right in, huh?" I asked.

He groaned a little and once again set my body ablaze.

"Do you want the truth, or do you want the new-relationship answer?" I squeezed my eyes shut, cringing at my own words. I hadn't really just said "new relationship," had I? I was an idiot. But in truth, why would I expect anything different? I didn't know how to do this. Instead of hanging up on my inexperienced ass, he laughed.

"I want the truth."

I let out a small sigh of relief. "I am wearing gray sweats and a white tank top."

"And?"

"Aaaand, my hair is up?"

"No, sweetheart. What are you wearing underneath all of that?"

I was well aware that I was going to regret this tomorrow; but tonight, I was feeling all in for it. "Underneath all of that, I'm wearing a red lace thong."

Cameron groaned. "No bra?"

"No bra," I cooed. I wasn't baiting him. It was true. As soon as I got home, I let the girls roam free after a long day of being locked up.

He breathed heavily into the phone. "All right," he said, his voice strained.

"What are we doing?" I asked him, trying to calm myself down. I was too turned on by him. By a singular phone call.

A deep breath pushed through the phone. "I don't know," he answered, sounding a little defeated. Or regretful. "I haven't done this in a long time. I'm sorry if I took that too far just now."

"You haven't asked a girl what she was wearing?" I asked, trying to lighten the mood.

He laughed. "No. And I haven't tried flirting with a girl in about twelve years. Guess I'm pretty out of practice."

"Oh, I don't know if I'd say that. It was kind of working for me. I just don't really know you, and it seemed like an awfully intimate way to start."

"Yeah, it was. Raven. I'm sorry." He sounded embarrassed, and I didn't like the way that made me feel, so I tried a new approach.

"I just mean that it's not really fair that you know what I'm wearing, but I don't get to hear about your current fashion choices?" I teased. There was silence. "Well, what are you wearing?"

His deep voice somehow got deeper and lower. "Boxer briefs under black sleep pants. No shirt."

"That sounds...pretty nice," I said stupidly. And I lied. It sounded like my next self-inflicted orgasm, but I wasn't going to tell him that.

"A picture for a picture?"

My heart thumped in my chest. This was getting a little more serious much faster than I expected. Screw it, what did I have to lose? Only everything.

"Okay, hold on." I pulled my phone from my ear and turned the camera to face me. "Oh my gosh." I burst out laughing when I saw the face staring back at me.

"What? What is it?"

I kept giggling, trying to steady my hands to take the picture? "Do you really, *really* want a picture?" I asked, sounding overtly sexy.

"Yes, I really do."

"Okay, but just remember that you asked for this." Before I could think better of it, I snapped the picture and sent it via text. I waited.

"What in the hell?" he asked.

I burst out into uncontrollable laughter. "That blown away, huh?"

"Raven, why do you look like a clown-school dropout?"

I kept laughing and then said through tears, "Listen up, Cameron, if you can't handle me at my clown-school reject, then you don't deserve me at my bathing suit in the park!"

He laughed and then asked, "Seriously, what really happens on girls' nights? I'm not even sure I want to know anymore."

My giggling died down as I tried to get it together. "Zara did my makeup earlier, and until I went to take the picture for you, I completely forgot I still had it on. Do you like what she's done to me? She put so much on that I think it might be permanent, so I hope you like it!"

"As Insane Clown Posse as you look, you're still

gorgeous." Well, that was sweet. "Besides, I can see your hard nipples through your shirt, so I think I can look past it."

At the word nipples, my laughter turned down, and I was turned *all* the way up. "Now it's your turn. Send me a picture."

I watched as the dots on my screen appeared and disappeared. Then, a picture came through. Holy ever-loving calendar model hell. Cameron looked almost exactly how I had pictured him. He was stupid sexy. His thick dark hair was tousled messily on his head, his piercing bedroom eyes were so translucently blue-gray they sparkled a little with the light. And that handsome smirk told me he knew exactly what he was working with. He wasn't wearing just boxer briefs, unfortunately, but he was wearing some very sexy black lounge pants and just as he said, no shirt. I may have drooled on my phone a little. I had only ever seen him in his uniform, and even then I could tell he had a nice body. But this. This was much more. He had large, hard muscles and not a single ounce of fat. His body was chiseled like a working man's body, like he constantly used every muscle to do whatever manly things he did to get it that way. What did they do in the mountains here in Brooks Falls? Chop wood? Hunt bears? I'd never seen such a perfect man.

"Oh."

"Oh?" he asked. "Is that an 'oh' of approval?"

I nodded my head. Silence.

"Raven?"

My voice came out in a whisper. "Yes. Yes it's an 'oh' of approval."

"Good."

We sat in silence for a few beats. I didn't really know what to do next now that we had exchanged pictures and the conversation had gone from hilarious to downright seductive.

"Are you still there?" he asked me.

"Yes, I'm here. I just don't know what to do now," I giggled nervously.

"Uh yeah, this is new territory for me too. But, if hard-pressed, I can think of a few things we could do."

****

Cameron

There was no denying it now—this girl was as fun and funny as she was beautiful. But that wasn't what drew me to her. There was something about her. Plenty of pretty women had thrown themselves at me in the past few months, but I hadn't been interested until this one. With Raven, I had this feeling like I was standing on a precipice, about to jump over a ledge and free fall straight to my demise. The worst part was that I didn't even care. Self-preservation be damned. I had the feeling that if I went down a path with her, I wouldn't easily turn back, and that scared the piss out of me.

"Oh, really?" Her sweet voice cut through my fears. "And what are the few things you think we could do?"

"Hmm." I had plenty of ideas for what we could do, or more accurately, what I could do to her. But I had to slow my roll a bit. I'd known this woman for a day, and I was jumping in dick-first like a horny teenager, not the thirty-year-old man that I was.

"How about we play a game? Truth or dare."

She giggled. "Wow, this really is a continuation of girls' night. Also, I'm no mathematician, but you said a few things. and Truth or Dare is one thing, Cameron." My name slid off of her tongue like we had known each other for years, and that was exactly how comfortable it felt between us.

"Yeah, well, I lied. Truth or dare it is. Besides, what better way for me to get to know you than a friendly game between two semi-strangers?"

"Ugh, fine. You're lucky I'm still drunk."

I didn't know if this was a good idea or if I was just thinking with my dick instead of my brain. I shoved the doubts aside because what else could I do with this woman? Hanging up wasn't an option.

"Okay," I announced. "I'm starting. Pick your poison, gorgeous. Truth or dare?"

"Hmm. Well, since I don't really trust you yet, I'm going to have to choose truth."

"All right, truth it is." I looked up at the ceiling, thinking of the perfect first question. "Let's start easy. Where are you from?"

She chuckled. "Wow Jameson, I don't know if I can handle this kind of interrogation."

"We're back to Jameson now, huh? I thought you settled on Cameron."

"It really depends on how I'm feeling about you at any given moment. If you give me another round of tickets, you'll definitely be Officer Jameson." She laughed.

"All right, all right. Do we need to rehash the past, or are you going to answer the question, ma'am?" I teased, using my cop voice on her.

She scoffed. "I'm from Redlands, born and raised. I've never been anywhere else except here."

"Oh yeah? What brought you here?"

"Oh no, no, no. You get one question per turn. That was a nice effort, though, trying to slip that one in."

I wanted to slip something else in. "Fine, go. I choose dare."

She gasped a little. "Really? You hardly know me, and you're going to entrust me with a dare? You are a brave man, Cameron Jameson."

"What can I say? I'm a man who knows what he wants." Wasn't that the truth. I knew what I wanted right now, and it was her. Those tits in my mouth, that ass in my hands. Jesus. I took a swig of beer and waited for her challenge.

"Okay. Oh! I've got a good one! I dare you to get off of the phone with me, take off your pants, and video yourself running outside while yelling, 'I love clown-school rejects.'"

"You know I'm an officer of the law, right? You want me to send you video evidence of my ass streaking outside and screaming about clowns?"

She laughed into the phone and whispered, like someone could hear us. "Oh right, I didn't think about that! I didn't say you had to streak. You can do it in your underwear."

"You're so generous," I deadpanned.

"I know. Okay, FaceTime me then, and you can do it that way."

I cursed technology and hung up on her without a word, went to my FaceTime and called her back.

"Hi," she answered, looking much different than her picture.

"No more clown face?" I asked.

"No, I took it off while we were talking. I learned in clown school that it's really bad for the skin to go to bed with makeup on, so I always make sure to clean the day's work off my face."

She was so beautiful that all I could do was stare at her. All of that silky, long, black hair framed her face, highlighting high cheekbones and large, sparkling brown eyes.

"Cameron?"

"Right, clowning is serious business. Okay, let's get this over with." I didn't want to put my phone down. I would've rather stared at her like a creep, imagining all the ways we could defile each other. But a dare was a dare, and I supposed I had asked for it. I stood up from my couch and walked out the front door.

"I'm going to set you on the railing of my porch so you can see this, ok?"

I set the phone down and heard, "Okay! You better be enthusiastic! A jump or two wouldn't hurt things. Think high school pep squad and then dial it up a notch!"

This girl. I proceeded to make a complete fool out of myself and completed the dare, thanking my lucky stars that I lived out in the middle of nowhere. When I got back to the phone, I could hear her laughter as I picked it up and headed back inside.

"I'm glad you enjoyed that. Now it's my turn, and don't think for a second that I'm gonna go easy on you now! Truth or—"

She interrupted me. "Dare! Now give it to me, Cameron. I'm ready. Do your worst." She was so playful and carefree and just about the cutest thing I'd ever seen. I licked my lips, trying to push down the rush of lust that came over me. I definitely wanted to give her something.

"Oh yeah, you're ready for me, huh?"

She pursed her lips and rolled her eyes. "You know

what I meant."

I shook my head from side to side. "No, actually I don't. I don't really know you that well, so I think for this dare, I want to get to know you much better."

Her eyes narrowed in concern. And yeah, she should be concerned. I was about to push this much further than it should go, but I also wasn't going to be presumptuous. Sure, we were flirting hardcore, but that didn't mean I could just say anything to her. I wasn't about to cross a line she had no interest in crossing.

"Sweetheart?" Her face softened with the pet name that I was apparently going with, like we had stepped into something way more serious than either of us intended.

"Yes?" Her voice was all innocent vulnerability and breathy words.

"I want to say and do things tonight with you, but I'm not going to take this there if you aren't interested. Am I free to speak my mind, or do you want me to stop?"

She blinked once and then stared. I figured that meant she wanted to stop, so I opened my mouth to apologize but was stopped when she said, shyly, "No, I don't want you to stop."

I played it cool, but internally I was freaking out. I hadn't been with another woman since Callie. Not in any way, ever, and I was about to jump over this invisible line that I had drawn in the sand. At that moment, I felt like a teenager again, about to touch a woman for the first time. Excited, unsure, and a little nervous. Okay, I was really nervous. I tried to hide the shaking and the nerves from my voice.

"Okay. For your dare, I want you to take off all of your clothes. Except for your panties."

"Okay." That sweet, sweet voice made me feel like I was violating her. I hesitated.

"Raven, you don't have to do it. You can stop this at any time if you feel uncomfortable."

"Stop, Cameron. Just tell me what you want me to do." Her eyes were defiant, unashamed, open to me; her determination was on full display.

"Put the phone to where I can see you. All of you. Then slide your panties to the side and listen to me while I tell you all the dirty things I want to do to you while you fuck yourself with your fingers, thinking about me, about us." Yep, I said that. I was horny and my cock was rock hard. I halfway expected her to tell me to suck it and hang up on me, but when Raven's eyes got heavy, and she stood up looking around for a place to set the phone down, I stilled. All right. This was happening.

She stood in front of the phone and bent down so I could see her face. "Hang on, okay? I'll be right back. I need to make sure my roommate is asleep, and I want to grab something."

When she came back, she messed around with her phone again and then put on subtle wireless headphones. Smart. "Can you hear me?" she asked, standing in front of the phone, her sexy body in full view.

"Yeah, I can hear you and see you."

"Okay, time to complete the dare. But first, can I give you an advanced dare, just in case you get bored watching me make myself come to the sound of your voice?"

She had gone from innocent woman to vixen in seconds, and I wasn't sure my dick would hold out for too long without exploding if she kept that up. My mind was racing, thinking of her touching herself, wishing I was there with her. This woman.

"I don't think there's a world in which I could get bored watching you come, but go ahead."

She shrugged her shoulders. "Maybe, maybe not, but I really like to prepare. I'm just that kinda girl."

I tried to laugh, but it came out as a deep moan. Just looking at her kept me hard, but knowing she was about to touch herself? I could blow just thinking about it. It had been so long since I'd really been with a woman. I had to take it slow, or I was going to come in five seconds like an amateur.

"I'll take that as a yes?"

My words came out on a crack. "Yes." Jesus, what was this girl doing to me and how did she have so much power over me when I didn't even know her?

"So, just in case you get bored and need something to do while you wait, I dare *you* to take your cock out and stroke it while you listen to me and watch me touch myself. And just know that I'll be thinking of you stroking yourself the entire time. I'll be picturing every. Single. Thing."

I had already taken my dick out the moment she said it. My breathing was unsteady, and yeah, she knew what she was doing to me.

"I'll take that as another yes." She bit down on her bottom lip and batted her lashes before the corners of her mouth upturned into a perfectly even smile that would've knocked me on my ass if I hadn't already been sitting.

Then, she dipped her thumbs into the waistband of her pants. I was ready to see it all, except instead of taking her pants off, she began to circle her hips slowly as if dancing to a silent song. She caressed her hips as she moved, lazily sliding her hands up around her waist to her tits in a rhythmic motion. She bent forward slightly and grabbed her full breasts through her shirt.

I watched in awe, realizing that this girl had moves. I didn't think I'd ever seen a woman move the way she did.

She ran her hands up her delicate neck, twisting and winding them through her beautiful, long black hair and then continued to circle her hips until her back was facing me. She was a full-on seductress as she pulled the top of her pants down just enough so that I could see a string of lacy thong on the top of her perky ass. She looked back over her shoulder, and I had to stop stroking my dick or I was going to end this ride before it began. She spread her legs slightly, hinged at the waist, and slid her pants down until they were at her ankles.

My breath hitched at the sight of her bare ass, and I stopped stroking myself.

She lifted one foot and pulled her pant leg off before lifting the next and doing the same. With her back still turned to me, she bent completely at the waist, touching the ground with her hands, her perfect ass on full display, before slowly coming back up, arching her back as she did. My head was going to explode, along with my dick, which was pulsing, begging for some sort of release.

"Raven, you're perfect. I'm gonna come too quickly. You gotta slow it down for me, baby. It's been a long time."

She turned to face me, grinning shyly, like she wasn't the same woman who just completely rocked my world and spun it off its axis. She sauntered to the couch and laid herself down.

"You looked like a pro dancing like that." And with a bit of jealousy that I had no business feeling, I asked through gritted teeth, "Have you done that for a lot of guys?" I couldn't see her face too clearly from the distance we were now at, but I swear she cringed.

"Um, no. I've never done *this* before. Ever."

Feeling a little relieved, I watched her get settled on the couch.

"Do you have any instructions for me?" She asked.

I moaned, wanting to stroke my cock and come right now just to relieve the feeling that I was sitting in a pressure cooker about to implode. Shakily, I managed to get out the words.

"Take your hand and put one finger in your mouth, and suck on it like you're sucking me."

She put her finger in her mouth and sucked it hard, making a little gasp that caused me to groan. I didn't let myself touch my pulsing cock yet. I was going to make sure she was taken care of first and that I didn't humiliate myself with the stamina of a virgin.

"Now move your panties to the side, take that wet finger and slide it inside yourself. But look at me while you do it."

She did it and never stopped staring into the phone while she did. "Are you touching yourself, Cameron?" she asked me with a whimper, and my needy cock jerked at the sound of her voice.

"Not yet, baby. I need to get you close first."

"Okay, yes. But I wish you were here doing this to me."

"I don't know if I could maintain control if I were near you right now. You're so perfect, Raven. So beautiful. So sexy. So sweet."

"Cameron." My name left her lips like a plea. Her breaths sped up. While she worked herself with one hand, she tore her shirt off with the other, exposing her perfectly round breasts. She was going to kill me. I wanted those nipples in my mouth, wanted to be sucking, licking, biting them.

I grabbed my hard length, not able to hold myself back anymore. "Put another finger inside of yourself and then use your thumb to circle your clit. Christ, Raven, if I was there right now, it would be my hands inside of you and my mouth would be kissing your lips and sucking your nipples while I pumped my fingers in and out of your tight little pussy."

"Yes, I want that," she told me, her voice breathy and quivering. I stroked myself slowly, just enough to ease the pulsing, but edging myself closer. I kept my eyes wide open, watching her pleasure herself.

"I'm going to come, Cameron. Can I come now?" she pleaded. She was asking me. I had never been asked that question before and I was caught off guard by how much it turned me on.

"Yes, sweetheart, let go for me. Come all over your hands." I sped up my rhythm, pumping my cock harder and faster. "Come with me, baby," I gritted out, my throat tight, feeling the build-up in my groin as it spread to my thighs. I was close. Raven arched her back and thrust her hips into her hands, moaning as she found her release, her little body writhing on the couch in utter abandonment. I pumped harder until my body tensed, my balls tightened, and I released into my hand.

"Oh yeah. Raven, you're perfect." My words came out in a grunt. I did not understand the range of emotions swarming my body, or how this woman had so quickly gotten underneath my skin. Our rapid breaths mirrored one another as we both came down from the high.

71

Until I broke the silence. "I'll be right back. Don't go anywhere."

"Mmm, I don't think I could move even if I wanted to," she said sleepily.

I pulled my pants on and walked to the sink to wash my hands. When I came back to my phone, she hadn't moved. Her breasts were still in full view and my cock sprung to life at the sight. "Are you asleep?"

"Hmmm?"

"Why don't you go to bed, and we can talk about this tomorrow."

"Really?"

"Yeah, really. Tell your roommate I said thanks for the drunk dial, okay? You can drunk dial me any time."

Her cute face produced a lazy smile as she sat up and walked to the phone. "I'll be sure to tell her that." There was a pause before she added, "Cameron?"

"Yeah, sweetheart?"

She bit her lip and paused, before admitting hesitantly, "That was the best I've felt with a man in a long time."

I wanted to give her the same, that I felt the same way with her, except that guilt crept in and I had a million questions for myself that I couldn't begin to contemplate right now. A million reasons why I couldn't, shouldn't, be doing this with Raven.

"Yeah, that was pretty amazing, wasn't it?"

"Mmhmm. Goodnight, Officer Jameson."

"Raven," I warned her. "It's definitely Cameron now."

She stood up from the couch and laughed. "Fine. Cameron." Then she stood in front of the camera, winked, snapped to attention and saluted me, her perfect tits still out, before she ended our video chat. I burst out into laughter. This woman could easily destroy me.

Chapter 6

Raven

I woke up way too early to an eager Zara who was ready to the start the day before the sun was barely up.

"Well, well, well, Raven, how was *your* night?" Tessa strolled into the kitchen where I was drinking coffee and feeding Zara while nursing the world's worst wine hangover. I peered up through my disheveled hair and in a voice that could only be described as belonging to a fifty-year-old smoker after a rough night at the bar, I said, "it was fine."

Tessa bowed over in laughter. "Yeah, sounds like it was just fine. How did the chat with the hot cop go?"

"Also fine." I wasn't in the mood to elaborate. I would need at least two more cups of coffee for this talk.

"Just fine, huh? Would you like to thank me now or later when you come back to life?"

"The talk was a talk. It wasn't anything." Okay, maybe I was grumpy and a little regretful about how forward I'd been last night. I mean, did I really think that stripping for a guy on video was the new beginning to a great relationship?

"Nothing?"

"I know you have something to say, so just say it. I'm too tired to do this back and forth." I whined at her like a spoiled kid.

Tessa waved her thick blonde hair, gripped it in her hands, and started throwing her head around dramatically, doing her best impression of a woman either in pleasure or pain. With Cameron, probably both.

"Mmm, Cameron! Oh yes, give it to me, big boy!"

I felt the red crawl up my body, heating my neck and then my face, stinging my cheeks like red ants. Mortified at her insinuation, or even worse, her knowledge. I slammed my face into my hands, doing it way too fast because a sharp pain shot through my wine addled brain.

"Ouch. First of all, I did not say 'big boy'. And secondly, I thought you were asleep! I checked on you."

She laughed. "Did you now? How very thorough and well thought out. Well, I *was* asleep, but I was woken up by my best friend orgasming in our living room. Jesus, Raven, I hope he was still on the phone for that, otherwise I feel kinda sad for you. You're more desperate than I thought." Her laughter was unbridled, bordering on maniacal.

I sneered at her, wanting to slap that smirk right off her gorgeous face. "Yes, of course he was still on the phone. It was video chat."

She sat up straighter, her eyes bugging out of her head in disbelief.

"You saucy little minx! I honestly thought it was just you. Oooo, Rave, I'm so proud of you." She placed her hands on her face in feigned sincerity. "My little prude is growing up!"

I rolled my eyes so far up into my head I thought they might never come back. I did not want to talk about this. "Can we please let this go? I was drunk and stupid. What I did with him was out of character, Tessa. I don't even know what to say for myself right now. I've never done anything like that."

She, of course, ignored my serious concerns. "So, what's the deal? Did you make plans? Are you going to go on a date? Is this more of a hookup thing? What did you two talk about? Tell me, tell me, tell me!"

Her questions were the same ones I had mulled over all morning. Would I see him again? Was it a one-time thing? Would we date? Panic resurfaced at the thought of dating. I had never dated, and when I'd made my swift escape to the mountains of California, it was definitely not on my list of things to do once I got here. But when I told her how our night ended, she was going to be disappointed in me.

"Well, we said good night. I was kind of tired after, you know. And he was really sweet about the whole thing." I could feel a dopey smile forming across my lips, showing my hand to her, but even more than that, I was feeling more than I wanted to. "Then I, uh, saluted him with my tits out, and that was that." I said that last part very quietly, hoping she would just let that one go.

She blinked her eyes open once, twice, three times.

"I'm sorry, what did you just say?"

I sighed, knowing I was not going to get out of this. "I said, we got off the phone afterward."

Tessa closed her eyes and shook her head back and forth, as if to shake off the fact that her best friend had zero skills when it came to men.

"No, no, I got that part. But right after that, I'm pretty sure I had a brief hallucination, because I know I didn't just hear you say that you saluted him. Again."

My head pointed to the floor and my guilty face told her everything she needed to know. Tessa pressed her lips together, holding in a smile.

"Oh, no you didn't! Girl, you are *way* worse off than I thought! I mean, seriously, how can you be so freaking sexy, and at the same time, soooooo clueless?"

My face was hot with shame as I threw my head back in frustration.

"Geez, Tess, I'm such an idiot. I don't even know why I did it, and I'm not even talking about the salute. That's the least of my worries! I mean, why did I have"—I lowered my voice so Zara couldn't understand me—"phone sex"—I brought my voice back to a normal volume—"with him? You know more than anyone why that was a stupid idea. I have no business getting tangled up with a man. Not right now, and maybe not ever. Oh god, I'm going to have to change my name again and get face plastic surgery so he won't recognize me in this tiny-ass town!"

Tessa wrapped her arm around me. "Okay, okay. Calm down, crazy. You don't have to alter your face. It's not that big of a deal. People hook up all the time, and if you really don't want anything, maybe just lie low for a while and ghost him until he moves on to the next one. Lord knows every single, straight woman in this town is lined up for a piece of him."

My brows furrowed in annoyance.

"Oh, great."

Tessa could read me like a book. "Ah, you don't like that idea either? Maybe that was more than just a quick phone eh-eh," she said as she made a tunnel with one hand and moved her pointer finger in and out of it.

"I swear, Tessa, if I didn't know better, I'd think you had a guy living inside of you."

She shrugged her shoulders and scrunched up her nose. "No thanks. You know I prefer a woman living inside of me." She winked suggestively.

"Not like that. Is your mind ever not on sex?"

She pretended to think about it, and then, as if the answer surprised her too, she said, "No, not really."

****

By ten o'clock, I had drank enough water to rehydrate myself from all the wine, and it was a good thing I had because my shift at the Blue Rose started and the lunch rush was completely insane. It was the place to be on a Sunday after church, and the seats were always filled. Thankfully, after about 1:30 p.m., the place slowed down to a steady pace. My feet were sore, and I had only two things on my mind—all the homework I had to do for class tomorrow, and Cameron. I was chatting with one of the cooks when I heard the bell chime above the door.

"I guess that means my break is over."

Charlie, an older gentleman who loved to talk to me about his grandkids while he worked the grill, nodded at me. "All right, you get out there, kiddo. Thanks for the chat." He was a sweet, dedicated family man who worked hard and worked nonstop to provide.

I tied my apron back on, sighing, letting the memories from last night float to the surface. Sexy cop Cameron and those gorgeous eyes. Cameron and that filthy mouth. Cameron and that ridiculous body. Cameron and…that chick from Sunshine's? My new customers, Cameron and Laurel.

What? No.

I looked around in a panic, hoping to find Maisy so I could bail, pretend to be sick, have a sudden family emergency. Anything. But she wasn't up front. I hustled to the back unnoticed, leaving Cameron and Laurel waiting at the hostess stand. Our hostess, Tiffany, was an adorable seventeen-year-old high school student who was the epitome of pep. I heard her greet them in her cute, high-pitched voice as she started walking them to a table. *Dammit. And, also for good measure, shit.*

"Maisy?" I questioned frantically, looking around the kitchen for her and having no luck. "Charlie, have you seen Maisy?"

He tipped his head to the back where her office was. "Back there, darlin'. She's been on the phone for a while."

I darted past the kitchen staff in a frenzy. Finally, I heard her and followed the sound of her voice. Before I could interrupt her, her angry voice carried into my ears.

"No! No, John, you can't do that without me! You need to let me be there for that decision." Silence. "Oh, Christ, I know you're the executor. But it's executor, not executioner!"

Ohhhh, no thank you. I backed away slowly, not wanting to be anywhere near that powder-keg of a conversation.

I was going to have to get my ass out there and face the man I had phone sex with last night while he was out to lunch with another woman. It would be fine, and surely that would be better than telling Maisy, who sounded like she was in the middle of making actual life-or-death decisions, that I couldn't work right now because some guy that I video-banged last night was on a date. Sitting at my table with another woman. A cute woman. The woman from the coffee shop who flirted with him and gave me nasty looks.

My heart sank. *This is how it is for you. You don't get the good ones. It's why you need to stay single.* I gave myself a solidly negative pep talk before I brushed off my apron and walked my proud self out to their table, like this was just another day and these were just regular customers.

Yeah.

Right.

I avoided all eye contact with them while issuing my standard greeting to the floor. So much for my proud self.

"Hello, welcome to the Blue Rose. I hope you're having a colorful day today." Ugh, I felt foolish, standing there with my face to the ground, wishing Cameron and Laurel a *colorful* day.

"Can I get you started with some drinks?" My heart was pounding in my chest, and even though my voice sounded pleasant, it sounded cloyingly so. It sounded like exactly what it was—fake. I felt equal parts fury, embarrassment, and shame, which, when mixed together, created a very nice cocktail for tingling, warm cheeks.

"Hey, Raven. Nice to see you this morning!" Her saccharine tone, which rivaled my own insincerity, caught me off guard. "I'll have iced tea, no sugar, just lemon." She tilted her head and pressed her lips into a thin smile.

I nodded once. When I lifted my head up, Cameron was staring at me, looking just as stupefied as I felt. *Yeah, jerk, it's me. Surprise!* Laurel put her hand on his arm, lightly touching him. I tried to hide my annoyance, but I was sure it flashed across my face like a neon sign.

"Cameron? Are you going to get something to drink?"

He shook his head slightly, still staring at me, before he subtly pulled his arm away from Laurel. "Oh, yeah, just water for me. Please."

I gave them a very unconvincing, tight-lipped smile. "Great, I'll be right back with those."

"Can we have some menus?" Laurel asked. Ugh, what a bitch for asking for menus. Okay, technically giving them menus was part of my job, but still, couldn't she see I was trying to get my humiliated ass out of there?

"Menus!" I yelled. From the corner of my eye, I saw Tiffany jump and the few other customers look up at me. I lowered my voice, wishing that for once I could be the girl that plays it cool. "Yes, of course. I'll get you those menus right away." I reached into my apron pocket, which was the size of a small notepad. Obviously, the menus would not be in there. I patted myself front and back as if I stored menus in my freaking pants. "I'll be right back." I walked over to Tiffany, who was by now staring at me like I had lost my mind, which, to be fair, was probably accurate.

"Tiff, can you please bring some menus to table five? I thought I had some, but I can't find them," I said through shaky breaths, as if the menus were to blame for my impending breakdown. My eyes started to sting, and I could feel the tears pooling.

She gave me a sympathetic look. She really was such a sweet kid. "Are you okay?"

I sniffled and nodded. "It's just been a long day, and I have a lot to do. I think I'm just feeling a little stressed. Since it's slowed down a bit, can you get them the menus and their drink order? I'm just going to get my face right, and I'll be back in five minutes."

Tiffany smiled at me sweetly. "Of course. Take all the time you need. I got you, girl." I rushed to the back, not stopping as I passed Maisy, who also had a red, tear-stained face. Weren't we a barrel of monkeys today?

"Just taking five, Maisy," I hollered as I passed her quickly. I didn't want to talk to anyone about this, especially her. Maisy was one of the best people I knew. She had a heart of gold but a mouth that ran like a well-oiled machine. Anything I told her was bound to get around, and the last thing I needed was to make myself known in town as the girl who kinda, sorta hooked up with the newly single hottie who was apparently hooking up with everyone.

I ran to the restroom and locked the door behind me, hoping to collect myself and resurface as a woman who was not heartbroken over a man she'd met, video sexed, and lost, all in the matter of two days. *I'm not going to cry. No, not crying.* "Dammit." And then the tears started to run. What was done was done, so I let them flow. No point in putting Band-Aids on a dam. I didn't understand why this hurt so much. I didn't even know Cameron. And Tessa had said it herself this morning: It was just a hook-up, and people did it all the time. If I was going to put myself out there, which I wouldn't be doing ever again, I'd have to get used to it.

A soft knock on the door took me from my thoughts.

"Someone's in here." Another knock. "Someone is in here," I said louder, in my shaky voice. More knocking. "Geez," I mumbled and flung open the door. "I said someone is in…" I stood face to chest with him. All sexy, six-foot-something, solid Cameron, standing with one hand above the door frame, leaning in.

"Raven." He said in that same deep voice that made me do stupid things last night. He said my name like we were about to hop back into bed together, as if he wasn't on a date with another girl right now.

This was not happening. "I can't do this. I have work to do. And you and your *date* need to eat." I had wanted to play it cool, but my words came out sharp and did nothing to hide my hurt. I wanted to push past him, but he stood in front of me, his solid body unmoving. He stared down at me, his gaze shifting between my mouth and my eyes. I bit my lip and pressed my thighs together, fighting the unwelcome urges this man elicited in me with just a single glance. Cameron looked down to where my hands were folded in front of my squirming legs. And then, he groaned. My head snapped up and my chest heaved, the pained sound igniting every inch of me. I immediately reached out and grabbed one of his muscular forearms before taking two steps back, pulling him in with me. He did nothing to resist. Instead, he moved easily, kicked the door shut behind him, and flicked the lock.

He released a long breath, his head dipping down, when he said in a whisper, "Sweetheart, I'm so sorry."

At his apology, I returned to my senses and let go of him. "Oh, no you don't. Don't 'sweetheart' me!"

"Raven, I know this looks bad."

I lifted my chin and pretended my face wasn't covered in tears. "I'm not sure what you're referring to, Officer Jameson. Whatever it is, you don't owe me any explanations for it."

He was staring deep into my eyes, searching for something. Something I refused to give him—my vulnerability. My truth. I shifted my eyes down, trying to conceal the sadness swimming in them, the disappointment that was evident with each tear.

"Baby."

No. I did not want him to see me like this.

"I can tell you've been crying. I know it's because of me. I'm not with Laurel—Christ Raven, we aren't even on a date. It's just lunch between friends."

Was he serious right now?

"First of all, I am *not* your baby. And you don't owe me anything. I get it. Whatever happened between us last night was a one-time thing, and it was foolish. I made a mistake. Believe me when I say it won't happen again." My words were strong, but my intentions were feeble, my resolve weakening before the words even came out.

Even so, he looked wounded. Good.

The softness in his eyes dissipated and his jaw ticked. "A mistake?" he asked.

"Just lunch?" I retorted. He had no right to be mad at me. If that's how he wanted to do this, I would lay it out for him. "I did things last night with you that I've never done with anyone. And we haven't even had lunch! Christ, Jameson, we haven't spent any time together." I laughed bitterly at my own stupidity. Now I was pissed. "So, you just have lunch with a girl that is clearly in love with you and think that she doesn't think it's a date? Why would you go to lunch with a woman if it's not a date? Is she your sister?"

He shook his head. "No, she's not my sister," he said through gritted teeth.

"Are you close friends? Old friends? Best friends?"

"No."

"Okay, then why would you go to lunch with a woman who wants you if it's not a date?"

His face fell, and he pushed out a long breath. "She did me a favor."

I rolled my eyes. "Oh, I bet she did. I bet she'd like to do all kinds of favors for you. I feel much better. But like I said, it doesn't matter because you and I are nothing!" I whisper-screamed, right in his gorgeous face, like I had any right to be mad, to be as jealous as I was. I tried to ignore the forward pull I felt toward his lips. Those kissable lush lips.

"And," I began, but before I could say another word, he took a step forward and placed his hands on my hips. His touch burned and, once again, I was melting. I latched onto his arms and sunk my nails into them. Our eyes were locked, my panties suddenly drenched with desire, my nipples showing up to play as well.

Cameron gritted his teeth and ground out, "Raven, it's not what you think it is. Last night meant something to me. It meant a lot. You are the first woman I have been with since—" He paused, and my heart broke a little. I could see the honesty and sadness in his eyes. I touched my hand to his jaw, not overthinking it, not wondering why I was trying to comfort him. And then, without a warning, he turned into my hand and bit my finger gently. *Bye-bye, favorite panties.* I stared at him as he slowly moved his head back, sliding my finger out of his mouth through his teeth.

I planned to push him off and continue yelling at him. Really, that's what I was going to do. Except the signals got crossed somewhere between thought and execution, and I just stood there, paralyzed by this man. His nostrils flared, and I couldn't tell if it was desire or anger or both.

"Sweetheart."

His deep voice pummeled me. Instead of pushing him away, I inched closer. He bent down, so close to my face that our warm breaths mingled together. Cameron nudged my nose up and slowly lowered his lips to mine, plucking tender kisses from them before running his tongue across the seam of my lips. I opened for him. I had a feeling that I would always open for him. He tasted delicious, like mint, and he smelled like cologne and working man. *Screw it*. I fisted his shirt and jumped up onto him, wrapping my legs around his waist. I had no shame.

Cameron sucked in my bottom lip, his eyes glinting. I didn't protest. I couldn't. I was riding a wave of desire, and I didn't ever want it to end.

Our tongues met, dancing in a violent kiss. Our hands roamed like we were trying to touch everything at once. I ran my fingers over his large shoulders, feeling every hard muscle as I trailed a path up his neck until my fingers were buried in his hair. Our movements weren't coordinated, but they were certain. We were in a space and time where everything was completely primal and raw. I arched my back and pressed into him, needing more, needing friction, wanting to be as connected to him as I could be.

"Jesus, Raven, you feel good." He ground his hips into me, and I felt his hardened cock rock against my center.

And oh my, I could feel all of it through his snug jeans. If the imprint in his jeans was any indication, he was not a small or even average man. Sure, I had imagined it last night when he was driving me to do crazy things with his voice, but I hadn't seen it.

My mouth watered. I was completely wet just from looking at the man, but grinding into him like this, it did me in. With one hand, he untucked my shirt while still using the other to grip my ass and hold me up. Sliding one of his large hands underneath my shirt, he reached to the top of my bra, pulling it down below my breasts. His fingers played with my nipples, gently pulling the hard peeks as he moaned into my mouth.

"Baby, after last night, I need to have you." He ground his erection into me. "This is for you, Raven. This is what you do to me."

"Cameron, I want you so bad." I sounded like someone I didn't recognize—a girl so taken by her emotions that she didn't hold anything back. I could easily lose myself in him, and that terrified me.

"Mmm. I barely know you and you do this to me? You feel so good, so right."

"I know, you too," I said breathily, between kisses.

A knock at the door interrupted us. We simultaneously froze in place, as if staying still would make everything disappear. Another knock. I gathered my voice together, and when I spoke, my voice cracked like a prepubescent boy.

"Who is it?"

Cameron's head snapped to look at me and with stifled laughter, he leaned in, his mouth brushing against my ear as he whispered, sending chills straight down my spine.

"Did you just answer the bathroom door like you would answer the door at home?"

The realization struck me, and I could feel the mortification heat my face.

"I mean, there's someone in here. I'm, uh, I had a bad sandwich." I said proudly, like I had recovered from the situation. Realizing I was slandering my place of business, I tried to backtrack. "Not here though. All the food here is good and won't make you sick. I had a bad one before I came here. I'm gonna get a better sandwich when I finally get out of here, but first, this. I'm probably going to be in here for a while, but the men's room is available." The pitch of my voice seemed to get higher and higher the longer I allowed words to leave my mouth.

Cameron stared at me, stupefied and blinking.

****

Cameron

I set Raven down, reluctantly pulling my hand from those perfectly rounded tits and her tight, perfect little ass. I was being reckless and stupid with this girl, but I couldn't seem to stop myself.

"Raven." I said her name like a prayer. She was a prayer. Or an answer to one. She was beautiful and sexy, but she was also spontaneous and goofy. I stared at her, completely overwhelmed. Kissing her felt like something new, something real.

"Cameron," she whispered.

I pressed my forehead to hers, needing the closeness. Wanting my mouth to be on hers again. Our chests were heaving, and as the fog cleared, I realized that this was the first time in twelve years that I'd kissed a woman who wasn't my wife.

Raven broke the silence. "I had better get back to work. You stay until I get out, and I'll give you a knock if the coast is clear." She smiled at me and fixed her clothes.

I wasn't ready. Not to let go of her and not to let go of this moment, because I knew that as soon as that door opened, I'd no longer be insulated. Guilt would spread like wildfire, consuming my soul and spitting it back out just to do it all over again.

I latched onto her small waist and pulled her into me. "But I'm not done with you yet," I teased, tugging a strand of her hair. I bent down and pressed a kiss to her pouty lips, fighting the urge to pick her back up and take her right then and there. It wouldn't be right. I definitely wasn't going to take her for the first time in a restaurant bathroom. She deserved better.

"I have to go back to work, and you should probably get back to your, whatever it is."

Reluctantly, I let her go, but not before kissing her one last time. She leaned in and sighed into our kiss before slowly pulling away, running her nails along my waist as she backed up. I groaned.

"Do that and you'll never get out of here." I reached for her and tugged her back into me, rocking my still hard cock into her.

Raven stifled a squeal, then broke away. "Cameron! If you do that, I won't leave, and then I'll lose my job, and it will be all your fault. Is that what you want?"

Giving in, I nodded my head toward the door, my eyes narrowed, my balls blue. "Get outta here before I ravage you."

She smiled at me before cracking open the door and walking out. A few seconds later, I heard one knock on the door. I opened it, peeked down the hallway, and walked out. Raven was already at my table talking to Laurel, who had a fake smile plastered to her face. Laurel looked uneasy as she craned her neck side to side, trying to look around Raven toward the bathrooms.

I walked up to the table and took my seat.

"There you are. Everything okay?" Laurel looked between Raven and me, searching for any sign of what she had probably guessed had just gone down back there.

"Yep, I actually just got a call from the station that I had to take. I hate to do this to you, Laurel, since I promised you lunch for that favor you did for me, but I'm still going to make good on it right now." I looked at Raven and handed her a $50 bill. "Here, sweetheart. Whatever Laurel wants is on me today. She's a good friend who helped me out recently." I put the emphasis on "friend," hoping to clarify the situation for everyone.

"The rest is a tip for the prettiest waitress I've ever laid eyes on," I said as I stood up. I should've left it at that. Raven and I weren't together. We weren't anything. I was acting foolish, like a kid in love and not a grown man who had nothing to offer. I ignored reason and snaked my arm around Raven's waist, pulled her close, and planted a soft kiss across her lips. Her lips that felt like silk and tasted like honey. I clenched my fists, holding back when all I wanted to do was wrap her back in my arms and carry her all the way back to my bed.

"Text me later?"

She expelled a long breath as her eyelids fluttered open. "Yeah, sure." Her eyes were heavy and glazed over. I had to get out of there, because if I held her any longer, I would have to sit back down and let my cock settle. I loosened my grip on her and stepped away.

****

I looked around my half-renovated house. It was a mess. We had been in the middle of renovations when Callie was diagnosed, and after that, well, our lives just fell apart.

I still hadn't moved any of her things. Her clothes hung in our closet like she was coming back for them, and her side table next to our bed was still stacked with books. My knees buckled, giving way to all that grief that waited just under the surface.

My phone buzzed in my pocket, pulling me out and then pitching me right back in when I saw who was calling. Susan, Callie's mother. My muscles tensed and I dropped the phone. No way was I going to talk to her. And not a chance in hell was I going to try to explain how I destroyed her daughter. Susan had been trying to call me every month for the better part of a year, leaving messages, imploring me to call her. Why? So she could tell me how I ruined her daughter's life, her life, and my own life all in the matter of a day? I already knew that, was well aware that Callie was gone because of me. Didn't need anyone to remind me of what I had done, how clueless I had been.

I grabbed a beer from the kitchen and gulped it down. Then another bottle and another and a few more, until my mind was nice and fuzzy. I went back to the bedroom and pulled some boxes out from the overhead storage in our closet. Memories. I rifled through the many pictures Callie had taken of us over the years. Callie's death was my own, and I knew that I had nothing left to give anyone, nothing of value. A few aimless nights, a few meaningless hookups.

Sleep took me down demolition style, hitting hard and fast, the stress of all that my life had been, sucking me into a hole that I could never climb out of. When I woke up in our bedroom for the first time since Callie died, it was dark and empty. And it felt wrong. Groggily, I grabbed my phone as the screen lit up with a new text. I barely had the will to move, but I pulled it out to check anyway. And of course, it was her.

Raven—*Hey, you told me to text you later. So, it's later, and this is me texting. These past two days were* *fun. <wink emoji>*—

Two days. It was only two days. It was nothing. She would easily forget about me, and I, her. Twenty minutes later, my phone pinged again.

I shut my phone down. I couldn't be with her. She was a single mother with everything to lose. I had nothing to offer her. What had I been thinking? Rage, disappointment, and that wild, uncontrolled fire lit up inside of me. I grabbed one of the many bottles surrounding me and threw it against the wall.

"Fuck!" Burn it all, I wanted to burn it all down, just like Callie had done to me. Destroy the life we had made, just like she had destroyed me and her.

I stumbled to the kitchen and drank until I forgot about Raven. I fell asleep surrounded by beer bottles and memories, knowing that I wouldn't reach out to Raven tomorrow. Or ever. I hated myself for leading her on only to drop her without an explanation, but what did it matter? I would just add it to the growing list of all I'd messed up.

Chapter 7

Raven - One Week Later

I stared at my phone as if I could will it to ring or vibrate with a text. I was being an idiot.

Cameron had ghosted me. He never answered my messages or gave me a single reason to believe he was interested beyond the time we had already spent together. I should've been pissed and deleted his number, but instead, I was glued to my phone for a week.

At this point, I would still accept a family emergency or a dropped phone in the toilet. Hell, I'd take an "oops, I lost your number, and I was too busy with work to come find you." I was pathetic because I knew that none of those things were true.

I knew this because I saw him leaving Sunshine's with his coffee yesterday, and it took everything in me not to chase him down like a deranged stalker.

Two days. Two days was all we'd had. I should've known that he was dangerous, that after two days this man I barely knew could wreck me like this. There was no denying the way that man looked and all the many ways he had made me feel. And I hated myself for loving it, but I had loved it. It all had felt so good.

"Yo, babe!" Tessa wandered in, pulling me from my thoughts. She took one look at me, then announced, "Dang Rave, you look like death warmed over."

"Thanks. That means a lot to me that you would go out of your way to tell me that." I deadpanned, in no mood for her prods or her jokes. Or maybe she was just being honest.

She rolled her eyes at me. "What are best friends for?"

"Ummmm, telling you that you look terrible?" I said, annoyed with her. Annoyed that she was right. I knew I looked like garbage as much as I felt like it.

"Yep, you know it. And I am tired of seeing my hot, but pathetic, bestie, sitting in front of her phone waiting for some lame guy, who can't get his head out of his ass, to call. It's sad, Rave. You need to get over this man. I know you haven't been a part of the dating scene for like, well, ever, so let me explain how these things work now."

I closed my eyes, hating that she was right. I'd never dated, not once. And I didn't know how these things went.

"You spend some time with the person you're interested in. You talk on the phone a lot. You might hook up. And then, after all of that, you wait to see if they're going to pick you or one of the many other people they are *talking* to."

I gasped, appalled, because that was not my style. Ha, as if I had a style. "You mean to tell me that Cameron was 'talking' to other women the way he was 'talking' to me?" I put air quotes around "talking" because yeah, we were not just talking, we were "talking."

"They always are, Rave. That's just the way it is now. With all kinds of apps to sift through, there are almost too many options."

I looked up at her like the lost little puppy that I was,

feeling stupid for being clueless, thinking that Cameron and I had been going somewhere.

Tessa gave me a look that said exactly what I knew to be true—*it was two days.*

Two glorious days that made me feel ways I'd never felt with a man.

"That's it. I'm done with your moping around. We are going out tonight. Okay, well, I am going out because I kind of have a thing, but you are coming with me, and you are going to dress hot and get drunk and have fun. No more staring at your phone. Watching you like this is starting to make *me* feel sad."

"Fine."

Tessa's eyes widened. "Fine?"

"Yes, fine."

"Oh, okay." Tessa assumed a look of disappointment. "That was way easier than I thought it would be. I actually had a whole convincing argument and now I feel a little cheated that I didn't get to give it. Do you mind pushing back a little so I can say my thing?"

I shook my head at her because she was truly ridiculous, but I gave in to her inane demands. "Oh no, Tessa, don't make me go out. I can't. I am too much of a sad girl. I have a baby, so I can't just go out." That last part actually was true and had some merit to it.

Tessa rolled her eyes at me. "Never mind. I don't feel like you deserve the argument. And Maisy will watch Zara. She's been asking to fulfill her honorary grandmother duties for months now. Besides, it's already arranged." She smiled, a wicked grin that traveled from her mouth to her eyes. "Now, for the clothes." She clapped her hands together. "I have the perfect outfit for you!"

Three hours, a messy closet, and a full face of makeup later, we were ready to head out the door.

The drive to Shea's, the pub, was quick. It was a little on the outskirts of town in an old brick building that looked more like it should have a Law Offices sign on it. It was definitely not the bar or club scene I was used to, and I liked that. It put me at ease.

"Hey, who are we meeting here, anyway?"

Tessa blushed. That was new. It was rare to see her nervous about anything.

I raised my eyebrows at her. "Ah, is this"—I made an animated gasp as I clutched my chest—"a *date*?"

She rolled her eyes to the high heavens. "It's not a date, it's just a…" She paused thoughtfully. "Hangout." She tried to say it casually as she shrugged her stiff shoulders.

Upon opening the door to Shea's, I was immediately slapped in the face by the noise. No doubt, Shea's was the place to be on a Friday night. It felt like the whole town was here. As we walked inside, I took the place in. Exposed metal piping lined the ceilings, and brick walls surrounded the inside space where people could either sit in booths or stand at tables. A glass panel separated the bar from a room where I could see a man standing in front of three very large, steel containers. He was tall, with sleeves of tattoos running down his muscular arms. His hair was swept up into a man-bun, and when he turned around, I noticed that his face wore a few days' worth of stubble. He wasn't my type, but it was undeniable that this man was attractive.

Tessa nudged me. "That's Jet Bensley, the owner. Cute, huh?"

I shrugged. "Not my type."

"Too many tattoos?" she asked, as she raked her eyes over me, acknowledging the tattoos hidden under my jacket.

Tessa looked around the room until her gaze landed on a woman sitting at a table with a bunch of guys.

I grabbed Tessa's arm. "Is that your date?"

Trying to appear casual, she shrugged her shoulders and pursed her lips. "Yeah, I guess it's a date. She's nice."

"And cute!"

The woman had flawless dark brown skin with a bronze glow and relaxed green eyes, and her umber hair was styled in a faded mohawk. She wore fitted jeans and a tight white tank top, showcasing a few tattoos of her own and toned arms. *Definitely* Tessa's type. As we approached the table, Tessa gave a short wave to the woman, who got up to walk toward us.

"Mika, this is my best friend and roommate, Raven. Raven, this is my…" She paused, her eyes darting to one side and then the other before she looked at me and sputtered, "My Mika." I pressed my lips together and looked between the two of them, my eyebrows high.

I reached out my hand toward Mika, smiling broadly at Tessa's uncharacteristic fumbling of words. "Nice to see you again, Tessa's Mika. Not sure if you remember, or if I should even remind you of how we met, but we did meet at the police station on my first day in town. That was about a year ago, though."

She laughed. "Oh yeah, I remember you. I mostly remember this one," she said, as she squeezed Tessa's side playfully. "You look"—she looked me up and down—"different than I remember."

Tessa side-eyed me. I kept a smile at bay, amused that she was jealous, but not about to make it a thing. Tessa interjected, her head tilted to the side and one hand on her hip. "Yeah, she doesn't normally look like this. I covered her in makeup, and these are *my* clothes."

I was pleased to see this side of Tessa. She wasn't a jealous person or a relationship person, so seeing her spun up about this woman gave me a little ammunition to torture her back. Mika turned her eyes back to Tessa, gave her a sexy half-smile, and slung an arm over Tessa's shoulder before whispering something into her ear, something that made Tessa's gorgeous smile reappear.

"Come on. I'll introduce you guys to everyone." Mika gestured to the table.

Tessa turned her face up to Mika, and I saw every ounce of insecurity melt from her expression. We walked over to the table full of guys, and every single one of their faces lit up as they saw us.

"Guys, this is my girl Tessa and her friend Raven. This is Bram, Ryan, and Gray. We work together."

The men were all attractive in their own right. Bram was tall and built, and I could tell he had that effortless charm about him. With his sandy blonde hair against his lightly tanned skin and a pair of piercing green eyes, he reminded me of the male version of Tessa. Ryan was not quite as tall as the rest, and he was much leaner, with the body of a runner rather than a weightlifter. I recognized him as the one that Tessa had gone on a date with, and by the look on his face, he was clearly still in love with her. Tessa rarely went out with men, and when she did, they were not the dominant male type, so it made sense that she had chosen him. Gray was very cute, and I couldn't help but notice that he was staring at my legs. Well, the part of my legs that weren't covered in tall boots. His upper body was cut, his hard muscles stretching the fabric of his shirt. He was hot. Not Cameron hot, but he looked good.

"Hey, you're all here tonight, with a few new additions I've never met." A voice boomed behind me, and I turned around to see the man who had been behind the glass walls. "I'm Jet, the owner of Shea's. And you are?" He was looking at me. The man was even more beautiful close-up.

"I'm Raven. It's nice to meet you," I said shyly. He put his hand out toward me and shook it gently before turning to Mika.

"And this must be Tessa," he said, as if he already knew who she was.

"The one and only." Tessa shot out her hand to him while mouthing to me in the most obvious way, "He's cute." Oh, Tessa. She had no clue that I was still hung up on one gorgeous, confusing cop. Jet snickered.

"How's Nash doing, man?" Bram asked in a sweet, genuine tone that I wouldn't have expected from a guy like him.

"Ah, he's good, growing like a weed. Little man starts kindergarten this year."

My ears perked up. "You have a son?" I asked.

"Yeah. You got kids?"

"Just the one. She's almost two."

"Right on. Two's a fun age, but just wait till she's three. They always talk about the terrible twos, but three is where it gets really dicey. They're capable *and* full of attitude."

I laughed, feeling more lighthearted than I had all

week. "Thanks for the tip. I'll remember that. Right now, my little one is all sass and sweetness, and I've just been telling myself it's always going to be this way."

"Ah, lying to yourself. I get it." It was all in good fun.

"Jet here is a single father," Bram announced to the table, looking at me. I was sure everyone else at the table already knew this, so I wasn't ignorant of Bram's insinuations. "Any prospects lately, Jet?"

He laughed. "Unless a woman shows up at my doorstep ready to take on a five-year-old, I'm all the way outta that game, man. Having kids changes everything." Wasn't that the truth.

"I get what you mean. When you're a single parent, the only thing that matters is your child and someone else will have to fit into that. It's just the way it has to be."

"Ah, it's nice to have another parent around here that gets it. I'd say come around more, but if you got a toddler running around, I'm sure this is a rare outing."

I nodded, because it was true. This was the first time I'd gone out since I had Zara.

"Hey, it was nice to meet you ladies. Seems like Rachel needs a little help behind the bar."

I looked over toward the bar, which had gotten busier in just the last few minutes.

Tessa nudged me as Jet walked away and whispered, "That'll make you forget about Cameron."

Jet was nice, and of course he was attractive, but that thing wasn't there, that spark that couldn't be replicated. My heart started to pound as all thoughts went to Cameron, and I couldn't help but feel a little disappointed that he wasn't here. Here I was looking my best and a table full of guys was staring at me, but the one man I wanted to look at me that way wasn't there. And even if he had been there, he wasn't interested, and he'd made that clear. Gray stood up and pulled out a seat for me right next to him. I sat, committed to being in the moment and ignoring any thoughts of Cameron.

****

Cameron

I stood at the bar with my entire jaw on the floor, my heart in my stomach, and my dick straining in my pants. She was here and more beautiful than I remembered. She had on a short, dark purple skirt that was tight at her slim waist and flared out, landing right below that sexy ass to leave a large space between her boots and skirt, showcasing the sexiest part of her slim legs. She was a tiny little thing, but Christ, those legs.

I had watched Raven and her friend walk in, my eyes never blinking as I noticed every dickhead in the room staring them down. And, of course, there was Jet with that easy grin he gave her. It was all bullshit. There was nothing easy about Jet. His past was sordid, and his attitude was bad most of the time. I wanted to punch him right in his teeth. So, what if we were all friends? He'd touched my girl.

Gray stood up from his seat and pulled out the chair next to him, motioning Raven to sit down. I glared at him, seething as I watched him hit on her. She wasn't my girl. She was no one's girl and fair game for Gray to make a move on.

"Hey, man, you okay?" Jet asked, unaware of how just not okay I was.

"Yeah, all good," I gritted out unconvincingly.

He waved an inked arm in front of my face, my gaze

still fastened on Raven. "You know that girl?"

"Yeah."

"She's something, huh?"

I turned to him slowly, with a stern look of warning. "Yeah, she is something. But she's nothing to you."

Jet's eyes widened in shock before he laughed. "Oh man, you got it bad, huh?"

"Fuck off." I tossed a ten-dollar tip on the bar top as I walked away to the sound of Jet's booming laughter. I slowly walked to the table, inhaling deep breaths and balling my fists. There wasn't a seat next to Raven, so I lazily dragged a chair over to sit next to her, the sound of the chair scratching against the floor announcing my arrival. The girl on Mika's lap widened her eyes when she saw me before she whispered something in Mika's ear. Yeah, she knew. She gave me a narrow-eyed look that I couldn't give two shits about. She was Raven's roommate, probably.

Raven visibly stiffened, as if she sensed me behind her. God knew I felt her the moment she walked in tonight. She hadn't even turned to look at me when I saw her body go tight. Could she feel me the way I felt her? She slowly circled around to me, her smile disappearing quickly from her face as she looked into my eyes. Gray stopped talking and looked at me, irritated. I ignored him. If anyone should be irritated, it was me.

"Yo, bro, there you are. Cameron, this is Raven, Raven, Cameron. That's Tessa, Mika's girl," he said, motioning between us hurriedly before pointing to the woman on Mika's lap.

I saw her roommate, who I now knew as Tessa, cringe out of the corner of my eye. I was about to say that we knew each other and stake my claim when Raven reached her hand out to me.

"Nice to meet you. Cameron, was it?"

I narrowed my eyes at her, but felt the tiniest smirk form on my lips. I grabbed her hand and both of us jumped slightly, reacting to the buzz of electricity that hummed between us. I didn't want to let her hand go. Her skin was soft and warm and it felt good being close to her again. What I wanted to do was throw her over my shoulder and haul her ass out of this place, push her up against a wall and finish what we started at the Blue Rose.

"Yeah, it's Cameron. Nice to meet you as well." I held onto her hand as we stared one another down. She didn't even bother to pull away.

Our strange staring hand-holding contest was disrupted by Mika clearing her throat. "You guys already know each other," she said in a slightly tipsy voice. Mika laughed at us. "Jameson, you pulled her over on her first day in town, dickhead." She swirled her beer in our direction. "Gave the poor girl three tickets and towed her car."

We both let out a breath like that was the best thing Mika could've said. Relief. Until I noticed the group of guys with their jaws dropped to the floor.

"No way! I remember you." Bram slapped the table, and I saw Raven jump out of our stare down. "Shoooooh! You know, the whole department talked about the new, beautiful girl in town for that entire week! Except for this dickhead." Bram heisted his thumb over his shoulder at me.

Mika snickered and turned to Tessa. "Not me, baby. I was talking about you."

Phillips rolled his eyes at the statement and

mumbled under his breath. "Yeah, she wouldn't stop asking me about you."

Tessa laughed. "Well thank you, Ryan. I never meant to break your heart after just *one* date, but come on, look at the two of us. Aren't we perfect?"

"I'll toast to that!" Gray laughed and tipped up a beer to them.

The conversation had veered off course in the best way possible, because the last thing I wanted was to rehash the first time I met Raven. Except, I could always count on Bram to home in on the one thing I wanted to avoid.

"Man, you really know how to welcome the new girl. Can't believe you don't remember this one." Bram said, pointing to Raven.

"Well, I pull over a lot of people," I said, quickly silencing myself with a drink of my beer. "Don't remember them all." If she wanted to play it like this, I would happily oblige. Raven looked to the side, hurt filling her eyes. I was a dick. Gray wasted no time in turning it all around for himself. I had to give him credit; when he saw an opening, he took it.

"Really, Jameson? If I had seen this face at any point in my life, I wouldn't forget it." He shot Raven a lighthearted smile, nudging her with his shoulder.

"Well, unlike you, I'm not picking up women when I pull them over." Yeah, I snapped at him. He looked shocked. There he was trying to lighten the mood, but I was brooding and apparently everyone was going to feel it tonight.

"Relax, man, I was only complimenting the girl." Gray had such an ease about him that I usually appreciated. He was like a member of the bomb squad, knowing exactly which cords to cut to stop an explosion. Right now, though, seeing him sitting this close to Raven was pissing me off, and the only thing he could do to defuse this situation was get out of her face.

When Gray went to the bar to get a few more beers for him and Raven, I leaned into her. Being close to her like this without touching her was killing me.

"Hey there. Raven, was it?" I whispered, my lips barely grazing her ear. Her breath hitched, and I watched her throat as she swallowed hard. She turned her head slowly toward me, her lips just inches from mine before she pulled back, her eyes flashing something devious.

"You know, it's gotten really hot in here." Next thing I knew, she was standing up in front of me, her gorgeous legs and ass right in my line of sight. "Not a lot of room here, is there?" She said slyly, moving closer to where my legs were, barely putting one of her legs between mine. I could see everyone staring at us from my periphery, and I didn't even care. She slowly peeled off her leather jacket, revealing her toned body in a tight-fitting black sleeveless shirt. A few tattoos spread across both of her thin arms and shoulder, but one in particular stood out among the rest. The only one in color. A flower drawn in watercolors graced the delicate underside of her forearm. My breathing became ragged. The barely there touch of her leg on mine caused my dick to stand up in awareness.

"Ah, that's much better." She cocked her head and smirked.

I adjusted my pants. She raised her eyebrows right before she turned around and bent down, her ass on display, and put her jacket across the back of her seat. I felt my jaw tense, and all I wanted to do was reach out

105

and grab her, bring her back to me where she belonged. Bram snorted across the table, and Mika catcalled the girl, while Tessa smacked Mika playfully on the arm.

Gray came back with their beers, and it took everything in me not to yell at him to go away so Raven could finish what she started. His greedy eyes flashed to my girl's arms, noticing all her ink, drinking her in.

"Wow, you have a lot of tattoos. I like them. What is that one?" He touched the flower on her arm.

I was seeing red.

"It's a lotus flower." Her soft voice cut through my rage.

"Wow, it's beautiful. Do they all have a meaning?"

Before she could answer, Tessa chimed in. "She did that tattoo herself." Raven shot Tessa a glance and rolled her eyes while we all stared at her. Beautiful and talented, no surprise there. I couldn't help it. I couldn't resist the urges. Something in me snapped, and I had to get back to her.

"I didn't do the tattoo myself. I just designed it and drew it out for my artist."

"Really?" I reached out to her arm and traced the lines of her tattoo. "It's beautiful. What does it mean?" If her shallow breaths were any indication, she was affected by me just as much as I was affected by her.

She swallowed, leaving my hand on her arm, and reached out with the other to take a drink of her beer. "Thank you," she said softly. "The lotus flower symbolizes survival."

"How so?" I was still outlining the tattoo with my finger, ignoring the daggers I could feel Gray sending my way. He might've thought he had some sort of dibs, but he had no claim. The girl was free to do whatever she wanted. I could see his jaw tightening and his face reddening next to her.

"Well, the lotus flower is tough and resilient. It can grow in any environment and climate. Everyone knows that it can grow in mud, but a lot of people don't realize it survived the Ice Age when most other plants died. It symbolizes the kind of person I would like to be." There was a sadness to her voice that resonated somewhere deep in my soul.

"No, honey, it symbolizes the kind of person you *are*," Tessa cut in, her tone genuine and soft.

Raven shot her a gentle smile before she turned back to watch my finger trace her tattoo over and over.

"It's amazing that you did this."

She raised her head to look at me, the tense ridges of her face melting as her cheeks went pink and she said softly, "Thank you."

Too Close by Sungrazer started to play as the center floor cleared for dancing as it always did after ten. Tessa shot up and grabbed Mika, dragging her to the dance floor. All eyes were on us, and I didn't care.

Phillips, who had been silent and brooding all night, nudged Gray. Yeah, that's right, welcome him to your club. "I think you might wanna sit this one out, man."

Gray didn't bother hiding his irritation as he stormed off to the bar.

"Sweetheart?"

"Yes?" Her words came out in a breathy whisper, a plea, a call to my spirit.

"Dance with me." It wasn't a question. It was a demand, a need.

"Yeah."

I slid my hand from her forearm down to her small

hand and clasped it. Yanking her up, I walked us to the dance floor and pulled her in to me. Exactly where she belonged. Her head rested against my chest, and I could feel my heart thudding. Could she feel it? Did she even know what she did to me? I rested my chin on her head, breathing in her hypnotic scent.

"I'm sorry." My words came out like a broken whisper.

She tilted up to look at me. "Let's just dance. I'm still hurt, but I can't seem to stay away." Her raw, honest admission pierced me from every angle. I didn't want to hurt her.

"Trust me, sweetheart. I was trying to do you a favor. My life is a mess. Doubt you want any part of that."

She scoffed. "Maybe. Maybe not. But I guess we'll never know."

"Hey," I tilted her chin up, forcing her to look at me, thinking that I was going to say something profound when all I could do was stare at her. She crushed me like an avalanche. Her beauty was immense, but it was what was hidden behind those dark eyes. She had depth, and I wanted to dive right in.

"Cameron?"

"Yeah?"

"Just shut up for a little while and let me enjoy this." She rested her head back on my chest, and I grinned, pulling her closer to me, wrapping my hands around her curvy waist. Her fingers dug into my back, sending my thoughts straight to that corrupt place. A place I wanted to go with her. We swayed gently to the music, and I swear to Christ, I didn't know what was coming out of my mouth when I sang quietly into her hair.

I was happily losing myself in her when a loud voice interrupted our moment. We both stopped and turned in the direction of the sound.

"Oh, come on, let me cut in. Don't you want to dance with your own kind?"

Raven's eyes bugged out of her head as she launched forward toward Tessa and Mika, but I grabbed her arm, holding her back. If anyone was going to deal with this, it certainly wouldn't be her. I held her close, my arms wrapped around from behind.

"Hey, don't you go running into trouble. If they can't handle this, there's plenty of us that will."

Tessa snorted at the man who was way too close for my liking, and if he got any closer, I'd be game to lay him out.

"My own kind? Are you stupid? Obviously, I'm *only* into my own kind. Go away, I'm not interested."

"Hey, man, I'm just trying to have a chill time with my girl. You can be on your way," Mika told the dude calmly, some drunk preppy-boy that had clearly been told all of his life that he could have anything he wanted whenever he wanted it.

"I wasn't talking to you, bitch. I'm not interested in talking to people like you. What I want is your girl, and what I want is for your kind to stay with your kind."

And that was enough. I released Raven and started to walk over there, noticing that the other guys were already on their way. We stood behind Mika, who looked like she was about to rip into him. The dude didn't seem to care because he went to get in Mika's face, except before he could get too close, Tessa pushed the guy away, cranked back her arm and threw her entire body into the single blow that laid him right out on the bar floor. He groaned, holding his nose in shock, while me and my friends gathered around the douche rolling around the floor like the weak-ass he was. Jet came storming over.

"Hey!" the man yelled from the floor. "That cunt just punched me. You gonna do anything about that?"

Jet leaned down while the rest of us gave him some space. Yeah, we were cops, but why call that out when everything was under control? "Yeah, I am. I'm gonna tell you that we don't allow *your* kind here. And when you try to put your hands on a woman and get decked for it, that's on you. So, what I'm gonna do about it is tell you not to come back to my bar ever again."

The guy stumbled onto his feet and ran out of Shea's. Raven ran to Tessa and Mika. "Tess! Are you okay?"

"I'm fine," Tessa said, sounding rattled.

"Babe, you're bleeding." Mika grabbed Tessa's hand and inspected it. Sure enough, her knuckles were bleeding.

"I'm fine. It just hurt a little bit. It's not the first time I've punched a guy in the face for being a waste of space." Tessa placed her hand on Mika's arm with a smile. "Are you okay, though? The things that guy was saying. And he was going to put his hands on you!"

Mika laughed humorlessly. "I'm a gay black woman, Tess. I got three strikes against me in this world, so yeah, I deal with this shit all the time."

Tessa's eyes filled with a softness that was a full 180 from the face she just wore. "Let's get out of here. Come home with me?" Tessa wrapped herself around Mika, tears forming in her eyes.

Mika spoke. "And please don't do that again.

You're going to get yourself hurt."

"I did it for us. People like that don't listen to reason. It's better to just shut them up quickly."

"We all had your back," I said. "I was about to break his face."

Tessa shot me a half-smile. "Yeah, but it felt good to do it myself. I wasn't about to let one of you take that away from me."

Raven's eyebrows knit and she frowned. "Tessa, you really gotta be more careful," Raven said before she wrapped her arms around both of Tessa and Mika, pulling them away from the dance floor.

"Let's go home," Raven said gently as they all walked away. She shot a sad glance my way before she left the bar.

Chapter 8

Raven

Maus's loud barking interrupted my studying, something I didn't mind at all, because I was elbows deep in pharmacology and my brain was breaking a little. A sleepy Zara walked out of our room, dragging her disheveled blanket on the floor. The same blanket I bought for her the day I found out I was having a baby. It was a little pale, yellow blanket with honeybees on it that was now closer to gray in color and torn in several places from being dragged everywhere.

"Hey, honeybun, did Mausy wake you?"

Zara crawled up into my lap and rested her head on my chest, closing her tired eyes and pressing the blanket to the side of her red face that was imprinted by her pillow.

She was still half asleep and in lazy snuggle-mode, so I went back to reading about carbenicillin. Nursing school was tough. Between classes, two jobs, clinicals, and Zara, I was stretched pretty thin. My personal life was no longer in shambles, and aside from the few Cameron hiccups that seemed to disappear just as quickly as they reappeared, I was happy for the first time ever.

As for Cameron, I hadn't heard from him since the bar incident. And still, I didn't know what to make of what we had shared. I couldn't help that I was drawn to him, and if I was reading him right, he was drawn to me as well. I should've taken Tessa's advice that night at the bar. I should've let him go and put myself out of my misery, but I couldn't resist him. I couldn't walk away. It was a magnetic pull that I was powerless to resist.

My phone buzzed with an incoming text. I picked it up to see the name "GFH Joany." With a sigh, I set the phone down. I was exhausted, but the money was good, and I had bills to pay. Time to lace up the stilettos.

****

Cameron

"Grab whatever seat you want. I'm gonna hit this spotlight on and shut down the lights. Your girl will be out in a minute. No touching unless she tells you to, no kissing, no groping, no abusive remarks."

The bouncer tossed a few strips of fabric on the table. He was a big burly guy, a combination of muscle and fat. One of those dudes that may not move fast, but it didn't matter; he would knock someone out with a single hit. He was there to provide security for the stripper the guys had hired for me.

"She likes to work with blindfolds. She says it enhances the senses during the dance or something. You can put it on or not. I don't really care."

"It's just gonna be him," Bram said, pointing to me. "The rest of us will be out back. That all right?"

The bouncer shrugged. "Sure man, I don't care how you do it as long as you follow the rules. I'll be right out there." Then he hit the lights, and everyone left the room.

I was pissed at Bram for this. I was also glad that I was buzzed at this point, but I still wanted to bash his head in. Some surprise this was. Had I known about this earlier, I would've stayed home.

Now, I sat in the chair, having placed the blindfold over my eyes like someone that needed to pay for a girl's attention. What if she was young? Christ, I would get up and run my ass outside if she was too young. I wasn't some depraved creep.

The music started and I heard a door open. I felt fingernails run through the back of my hair in a slow, steady motion, up to the front, right before a hand brushed up against my chest. It actually felt good. A hum of electricity sent jolts through my body, this awareness of a familiarity bringing me back to my senses. I brushed it off.

A muted seductive voice spoke into my ear, "Are you ready?"

All of a sudden I understood the blindfold, because it was hot. My head actually tingled with anticipation when her sweet, breathy voice swept over me. I swallowed hard and shifted, my dick responding to the sound of her. There was something there, and I mentally scolded myself for even thinking that.

"Good. Is it okay if I touch you?"

I was barely able to croak out a yes.

"Okay, that's very good."

As the music kicked up a little, I felt her ass lightly grinding against my now hardened cock. It took everything for me to keep my hands to myself. I wanted to grab her hips, to feel this woman, to slam her down on top of me and get some sense of relief. *Remember the rules. Be respectful, asshole, she's just doing her job.*

As her body undulated over me, I felt her turn around to face me. Holding my shoulders as leverage, she thrust her hips toward my chest in slow, sensual movements. I didn't expect it, but she lightly moved her hands down the length of my arms until she got to my hands. She grabbed my hands with hers and placed them on her hips. Holding me in place, she moved my hands to make her grind just above me, letting me feel her movements, allowing me to take part in the kinkiest thing I had ever done.

"I thought I couldn't touch you," I grumbled, trying not to sound as needy as I felt and failing miserably.

"I set the limits. This is all you can do."

Her hands snaked around my head, running through my hair until she found the tied ends of the blindfold and released it, and it fell from my eyes. I opened slowly, my eyes adjusting to the lighter darkness that we were bathed in. Her back was still facing me, and her long, black hair reached down her back, covering everything up to the curve of her ass. Her slim hips were still grinding just above my lap, a tiny black lace thong adorning her perfect ass and a lace bra on top. My eyes surveyed her every move. I took in every inch of her that I could see from behind. On her hip, peeking out from the side of her thong, was a small dragon tattoo, along with a few other tattoos on her arms that I couldn't quite make out.

She leaned her head back to rub lightly against my neck. Swiping her beautiful hair to the side, she reached back once again and unhooked her bra, still moving with the sounds of the music. She stood up from my lap, moving my large hands off of her, and then bent down in front of me, slowly getting up while still moving to the music.

My whole body tensed. Familiarity, electricity, fire.

The scent of coconuts. I had seen that perfect ass before. My heart raced as my mind frantically replayed that night.

No, no way, it couldn't be. I tried to calm my nerves as the woman sauntered and swayed to the pole standing in the middle of the room. She jumped up and spun slowly, before twisting around into some upside-down position and lowering her legs into a split as she spun. She was incredible and the way she moved her body was mesmerizing. All that black hair whipped around as she moved. When she descended from the pole in some sort of wide-legged pike, I got a clear view of her face for the first time.

My perfect Raven, that sexy woman who had stolen my sanity, stood before me almost completely bare. Grabbing the pole, she slowly thrust her hips toward it and then away, before grabbing a stiletto clad foot and pulling her leg to a standing split position and throwing her head back, sending all that black hair flying and whipping around.

I was too in shock to say anything, too hypnotized to move. She walked seductively back toward me, an audible gasp, a stutter step, a whirlwind of emotions held captive in her eyes. My face burned as I fixed my eyes on her.

Our breathing became heavy, almost in unison. I narrowed a heated gaze at her, my jaw tighter than it had ever been, and I gritted my teeth. She recovered quickly, like a professional, and I wasn't sure if that made me respect her more or pissed me off knowing she wasn't new to this. She set herself, thrusting her chin up as she continued to move toward me.

As she got closer, I whispered angrily, "What are

you doing here?"

"What does it look like? I'm doing what I was hired by *you* to do."

"Jesus, you're a stripper? Don't you think I should've known that?"

She didn't stop at my questioning, instead she scrunched her nose up and narrowed her eyes at me but kept on dancing. Except her movements became volatile—a hip thrown into my gut or a slap of her hair to my face, followed by a flash of her eyes and a smirk. Her sass was entertaining. And most of all, it did nothing to quell my desire for her.

"And when would I have told you that?" Grind, rub. "When we were having video sex?" Thrust, caress. "Or maybe when you had me shoved up against a bathroom wall with your hand up my shirt?" Scratch, rotate. "Or should I have told you in front of your friends when we pretended we didn't know each other?"

"Goddammit, Raven."

"No. You don't get to have a say in this or anything else regarding my life. This is my job, and I work hard, and do what I have to do to provide for my family."

"Do those guys touch you?"

She ran a finger from my lips, slowly down my chest, lazily watching her finger go down my body, almost like she was in a trance. Her voice was distant when she told me, "Sometimes, but it's a rule that they don't touch me. Doesn't always stop them."

"I don't like it," I gritted out, my teeth so firmly pressed together I thought I might grind them to nubs.

"I didn't ask if you liked it." The bite of her tone traveled straight from her mouth to my dick, and I was positive that any vitriol this girl had was fuel to my fire.

Or she was the fire, warming and lighting up my entire world.

"Dammit, Raven, why does everything have to be so hard with you?"

Her lips curved up on one side, forming a sexy half-smile while her eyes darkened. "Hard, huh?" She teased, dipping her chin to look at me through her lashes. I swallowed hard and tried to keep my cool, but it was no use.

"Let me touch you. Please." I begged her, my voice cracking with the plea. I didn't care, not even a little. I was in hell, with her in front of me like this, and not able to touch her.

"I don't break rules at work, Jameson. You might be turned on, but this is my work."

Did I respect that? Yes. Did I like knowing that she set boundaries for the men she danced for? Absolutely. Did I like that I was one of those men? Not at all. She was mine.

"Sweetheart, please. Put my hands on you again. Please." I agonized, eyes closed tight in pain, showing her just how much I needed her, how much she owned me already. And I hoped she saw it; the cracks in my spirit, the desperation in my eyes, the truth of who I was, the truth of who she was to me. She wasn't some quick lay or some hot stripper I wanted to get my hands on— she was mine. "Who touches you?" I asked her again, my tone harsh and demanding.

"No one," she whimpered and ground into me. I was about to burst when she grabbed my hands and placed them on her hips. "Better?" I exhaled sharply and squeezed her hips. It was a relief to touch her again, but now I was wound up in a whole different way. I pressed her down onto my aching cock and growled, "Who touches you, Raven?"

Her lips parted as she moved with me. "No one does, Cameron."

I slammed her down on me, and she let out a loud gasp, her eyes filled with lust and that same depraved darkness I'd recognize anywhere, as she rode me. Her lips were close to me and I could feel her short, warm breaths against my face. She lifted herself from my lap and turned around so I could see only her round ass. I moved her hair to one side and got closer to her ear, taking it in my lips and biting down gently.

"Baby, who? Tell me who can touch you."

"You. Only you." She gasped, throwing her head back as she leaned into me. Fuck the rules. I didn't care about Bruno or his agreements. I didn't even think about my friends who were waiting just outside.

"That's right. Only me. Only you." And I knew then that I was done for. I wasn't this guy. I wasn't forward. I wasn't possessive. I had never made anyone tell me that they belonged to me.

As if my words snapped her out of the trance, she sputtered, "I, I can't. I don't trust you. I barely know you. And you've managed to do nothing but hurt me." Her words struck as she backed away from me, shaking her head slowly. "Keep your money. I need to get out of here."

"Raven, please. Please don't go."

"I can't." The fear and hurt in her eyes pierced me, drove nails into my guilty heart as she scooped up her belongings, running out the door. She was right to run from me. Except she ran out the wrong door, the door that all the guys stood outside of, shooting the shit and waiting. Christ. I followed her.

"Oh dayum…is that?" Gray mumbled beneath his breath.

"Yes," I answered sternly, not wanting him to say her name or even look at her.

"What did you do? Is she okay?" Gray started to walk toward her. I grabbed his shoulder hard and yanked him back.

"I didn't do anything. Mind your own business and get inside. I got this." I barreled toward her in the dark, not sure where she was going. "Raven!"

"Wait!" Bram yelled desperately, Jet standing right next to him, looking just as interested. I looked back at them and was going to seriously punch him if he kept me from going after her for one second longer. "You and her?"

My face said it all.

He nodded in approval, looking her over. Disgusting. Maybe I would punch him for even looking at her. "Nice job, man."

I rolled my eyes at him. "Fuck off."

Chapter 9

Raven

How is my luck so awful that the one man I am trying to avoid is here, at a house, in the middle of nowhere? And how did I not recognize him? I was drawn to Cameron, but the truth was that I couldn't trust him. When he told me that I was his, I lost it. I wasn't going to be anyone's ever again. The rational side of me knew that Cameron wasn't trying to control me, that this man didn't have it in him to be cruel, that he would never intentionally hurt me. But that broken, terrified woman, whose only experience with a man was suffering at his hands? Well, she put up a fight. A strong one.

Except my fight only led me here, through the wrong door, standing behind a shed in someone's backyard with just my panties on. At least I'd had the foresight to grab my bra before I ran outside. Not that it mattered now. I saw the recognition on *all* of his friends' faces as I stormed by them. And now it was just me, my underwear, and my black stilettos sinking into the moist parts of the turf. Great.

I heard heavy footsteps approach from behind me, and I didn't have to turn around to know it was him. I could feel Cameron's presence with my back turned to him. I must've looked like a fool, standing outside, mostly naked, my thong-clad ass on full display, staring off into the distance like I was pondering life's mysteries. As he stepped up behind me, he gently grabbed the back of my arm as he steadily spun me around. I cast my eyes to the ground, refusing to look up at him. I was going to get sucked right back in if I wasn't careful. But he wasn't going to get my feelings tonight. He hadn't earned that.

"Raven? Will you look at me?"

"Why? So you can make up some lame excuse as to why you're hot and cold with me and then continue to drag my heart around whenever you please, like I'm just sitting here waiting for you to come around?" So much for holding back my feelings.

"That's not what I want. I just-it's hard for me to do this. I don't want to hurt you, but I also can't let you go. This isn't right, I'm sorry." He ran his calloused hands through his thick, dark hair.

It hypnotized me, looking at him. He was handsome and strong, but more than that, despite all the back and forth, his eyes were full of compassion and regret. All the thoughts and desires swirling around my head made me want to accept his apology. Except I had been the doormat before, and that way of life had done me no favors. Besides, I wasn't going to fall at his feet every time he up and ditched me and then decided he wanted me again.

"It's fine." I refused to make eye contact with him.

"Sweetheart, it's not fine." He stepped toward me, the heat of his body reaching me before he even got to me, and all of what he was, drew me in. Stupid moth, straight to the flame. I unintentionally took a step toward him. Cameron moved a strand of hair behind my ear, brushing his knuckles across my cheek.

"That's why I'm apologizing. I just saw you here,

half naked and beautiful. I couldn't—I can't—imagine you doing this for anyone else. I don't want another guy to touch you or even look at you." His voice was growing more irritable.

Was he for real? That yanked me right out of my lust-induced haze. "Excuse me?" I snapped, just inches from his face. "Who I touch and let touch me is *none* of your business!" I pointed my finger into his broad chest and pushed him backward toward a shed a few feet away from us. "You don't own me, *Officer* Jameson, so you don't get to tell me what I can and cannot do. Who I can and cannot touch. Who I can and cannot *fuck!*"

He was fully backed up against the shed, his eyes now blazing with anger.

"Who you can and cannot fuck? I'll tell you who. No one. No one in this goddamn whole town, okay? I'll tell you exactly what—"

But before he could finish, I raised my right hand to strike him across the face, the anger at my situation lifting like a pulley up, up, up until it fell on Cameron like an anvil.

He caught my wrist.

I raised my other hand, but he caught that, too.

I'd never hit a man before this. Well, I had still never hit a man, but the point was that I'd never tried before. Right now, I was brazen, and I liked it. He held both of my wrists gently before letting them go. Then he leaned down.

"Don't do that," he admonished. "Can't you see that you're driving me crazy?" He asked through clenched teeth, close enough to my face that if I wanted, I could just lean up on my toes and kiss him.

"Me?" I laughed, incredulous at his insinuation that

123

I held any power between the two of us. "I haven't done anything. You're the one who is driving us both into crazy town! You want me and then you don't. You kiss me and then you stop talking to me altogether. You dance with me, sing me a love song, and then poof, you're gone. I don't deserve this, Cameron, and I definitely don't need this."

He got closer, so we were face to face, his hard body pressing into mine, and oh holy mother of mercy. Zaps of lightning bolted down my spine, bringing every cell in my body to life, every nerve ending to awareness. I was panting, out of breath, and I couldn't tell if it was anger or lust or something in between. He leaned towards my ear, grazing it with his lips. Lust, it was lust.

"Just stop, please?" His voice broke. "I can't take another man looking at you like this. I can't take you being mad at me. I can't take being without you, and I can't be with you. It's messed up, I know it."

My heart melted with his confession, but it also stung. As much as it hurt, I did understand. I couldn't resist him either, but deep down, I knew I couldn't have him. I took a step back. My lip quivered as I shook my head. This would never work, and we both knew it. I turned around and began my defeated walk back to the house when his growly voice pummeled me.

"Raven.".

I jerked to a halt, my body instantly stiffening. I wanted to run from him. I knew it was the only way to free myself from this hold he had on me.

"Get. Back. Here." It was a command that drove me right into action. I whipped around and spasmed when I saw how he was looking at me. Like he was an animal about to devour his favorite meal: Me. I promptly forgot all of the reasons why this was a terrible idea and I ran to him, jumping and crashing into his solid frame. He caught me easily, and I wrapped my legs around his waist. I pressed my mouth to his and kissed him hard until we both couldn't breathe. Until I didn't know which breaths were his and which were mine. Until I forgot about how much he had hurt me, how much life had hurt me.

He moaned into my mouth, his soft, smooth lips humming against mine with each low sound he made. Firm hands squeezed my ass and as I gasped, he captured my bottom lip before slowly pulling away. He freed my lip from his mouth with a muted "pop." Cameron rested his forehead on mine, his deep, heavy breaths the only other sound I could hear besides the rapid beats of my own heart.

"Come here and give me that mouth again," he said, his voice low and coarse. I lifted my head and drew closer to his lips, compliant and willing. Cameron parted my lips with his tongue, and I let him take everything he wanted. One of his hands slid from my ass as he moved it slowly toward my center, skimming the outside of my panties before pushing the soaked strip of lace to the side. The tender caresses of his rough hands against my soft skin were tantalizing, and I couldn't help but want more.

"Jesus, Raven. You're so wet for me. Let me in?"

"Yes." I tried to play it cool, but I was in pure need, and he saw it.

He smiled against my lips as he played with the outside of my pussy, grazing his fingers around my swollen lips. He swirled around in all the wetness before sliding one thick, long finger inside of me. I moaned into his mouth, pulling away from our kiss, arching my back into his finger and forcing him to go deeper. His eyes were hooded and his breathing rapid as he moved his finger in and out of me. I rested my head against his clenched jaw, my stomach twinging with pleasure as I reveled in the feel of his breaths against my cheek.

He pulled his finger out of me, and I couldn't control the "No!" that escaped me. Cameron kissed my lips gently and grinned, then slid back inside of me with two thick fingers.

"That feels good!" I told him breathlessly, rolling my hips in sync with his movements.

He was no longer being gentle when he glided in, stretching my pussy and dragging his fingers in and out through the wetness.

"Cameron." I whimpered, shuddering beneath his touch. "That feels so good. Please, more? I need more."

He raised his eyebrows and pulled his fingers out of me.

"What-What are you doing?" I stammered. "No, you aren't done." My words came out petulantly as I shook my head back and forth a few times.

Cameron said nothing, but set me on my feet and knelt down in front of me. I stiffened and my eyes widened as I stared down at him.

He gazed up at me, eyelids heavy, the moonlight flickering in his blue eyes. "What's wrong, baby? You don't like this?"

I felt my cheeks heat. How did I tell him that I didn't know if I liked it because I had never done it? I was twenty-eight years old, but I had the sexual experience of exactly the kind of person I was—a damaged and traumatized woman.

"I don't know." I said it quietly, hoping to hide my embarrassment, but when I saw his gentle, knowing expression, I knew he understood. His gentleness morphed quickly into passion. His hands roamed greedily over my hips before squeezing my ass hard.

"Jesus. All mine then." He whispered into my thigh, and I wasn't entirely sure whether he was talking to me or himself. "Let me be your first." Cameron closed his eyes and inhaled a deep breath.

I nodded first and then whispered, "Yes."

His head snapped up, eyes opened, as he let out a long breath and dropped his shoulders away from his ears. My nerves transformed to lust when I watched a lazy smile form on his face, showcasing his full lips. The very same ones that would soon be between my thighs. I squirmed at the thought and stumbled in place a bit.

"Useless little panties," Cameron whispered as he ran a hand along the lace edges of my thong. "Let's get rid of these, huh, baby?"

He didn't wait for my reply, and he didn't have to, because I was already shimmying my thong down, trying to help him get the damn thing off me.

When I was completely bared to him, he took my right leg in his hand and stretched it out straight before placing sweet kisses from my ankle all the way up to my knee. He slung my right leg over his shoulder and began kissing and licking my inner thighs. His hand slid up my leg to my core until he was exactly where I needed him with his two fingers back inside of me, continuing to work me relentlessly. He moved closer to my pussy so that I could feel his warm breath against my slit.

"Jesus," he whispered, so quietly that I barely heard him. "You're stunning."

One lick was all it took. I was done. He started out slow, licking me gently with his tongue, until my need became so great that I couldn't stop myself when I raked my fingers through his hair, pulling him closer to me. My message was clear. More. He started using his tongue to devour my pussy. He licked along the wet seam of my body, sucking my swollen clit into his mouth. I was gone, lost to something so achingly delicious that I didn't know if I'd ever felt this good. I was nothing in his arms as he completely broke me down, giving me the kind of care and attention that I'd never experienced.

My own voice broke through the sounds of him licking me. "Cameron, yes! That's. Yes!"

I ran my hand through his thick hair and used it as leverage to pull him closer. His tongue flattened and flexed on me, while he used his fingers to add to the intense pleasure that was building inside of me. I was without words as he worked me over. One skilled hand pressed into me, while his other hand reached up to my breast and played with my hardened nipples.

"Yes!" I screamed, completely forgetting where I was.

His left hand grabbed my hand, and he placed it on my swollen clit. I massaged and rubbed it in slow circles. "Cameron, please."

He didn't stop, he didn't speed up or slow down, he just kept at me, drawing me closer to the edge, to that intensity that coiled like a spring. And then, bliss. Absolute bliss. My core tightened and spasmed around his fingers, in his mouth. The burning feelings of pleasure pulsed through my entire body in one long, earth-shattering orgasm.

"Please don't stop! So good, it feels so good," I cried

out.

He licked up every last drop I gave him, thirsty for me, lapping me up until nothing was left. When my body relaxed, he pulled his mouth away from my pussy but kept his fingers gently and slowly moving inside of me, taking from me every last bit of pleasure.

Cameron set my leg down from off of his shoulder and slowly pulled his fingers out of me. My mind was jumbled, in awe of what this man had just done to me. I held onto him, my knees threatening to buckle beneath me. As I came down from the greatest orgasm of my life, reality bit like that coldhearted bitch that she was.

Shame, regret, fear—it all crept in like a bandit, stealing my peace. What was I doing with this man? I couldn't do this, not with him—not with anyone—but especially him. I was certain that, given time, Cameron could destroy me over and over again. And hadn't I been ruined enough? Did I even have anything left to break?

I snatched my panties and hurriedly put them on. "I have to go." My voice trembled with the realization of what I had just done. I was a mother, for chrissake. I had a kid at home, and I was acting like an irresponsible kid myself.

"Can we at least talk?" Cameron asked.

I gave him a bewildered look and scanned my own body. Did I really need to remind him that I was barely clothed?

"Right."

"I can't do this with you." My voice wavered, every last bit of me dissolving into a panic. The fear sprouted from the depths of my soul and hammered into me like a freight train. I knew what came next, and I had to get out. My breaths became heavy and rapid, and I knew that any minute, I would be curled up in a ball, reliving those nightmares I'd worked hard to forget. I would be inconsolable.

So, I ran.

Chapter 10

Raven - 8 years earlier

I woke up on the floor of Candy's trailer at six in the morning, my legs tucked up between my arms in the only position I could fit in stuffed away in this tiny, cramped space. I had planned to be out in fifteen minutes, long before her three kids woke up. A small trailer wasn't room enough for the four of them, let alone an extra person. I was small, but when space is limited, any extra body is in the way.

I inhaled deeply, trying to motivate myself to get up and get moving. It was the only way. I dropped my blanket and gathered my things. If anything, I had a routine when I stayed here, and it was nice. It didn't quite feel like home, but it was something familiar, something normal. I stuffed my few belongings into my ratty Salvation Army backpack that had seen better days and headed off to the showers so I could wash up before taking the bus into the city. I would spend my day the way I spent most days—looking for a job.

The trailer park was on the outskirts of Redlands, and transportation to and from was inconvenient. But my only other option was to stay in a shelter downtown, and, well, that wasn't going to happen. Not because I was too good for it, but plenty of women had told me stories of what happened to them at shelters, and I wasn't about to put myself in that type of environment. I was getting tired and every day I felt the cards stacking up higher and higher against me, but still, I knew something had to break.

By the time I finished getting cleaned up, I had just missed the bus, which meant I had about twenty minutes until the next one. It wasn't a big deal. It was still early, and most places wouldn't even be open yet. I walked over to the makeshift pond and picked up a few rocks that were sitting on the edge. I stood on that fake plastic grass stuff and tossed a rock, throwing it in sideways, trying my best to skip it. *Plunk.* I tried again. *Plunk.* I was just about to try another when I heard a smooth as silk voice behind me.

"Didn't your dad ever teach you how to skip a rock?"

I startled a little and turned toward the deep, intoxicating voice that belonged to a tall, handsome man. He looked to be in his late twenties or early thirties. I may have stared at him a little too long, but he was very good-looking, with a freshly shaven face and styled brown hair. He wore a sleek gray suit, a crisp white dress shirt, and a black tie. I looked him up and down. He definitely didn't belong in a trailer park. He looked like a politician or a business owner. Did politicians come to trailer parks? I didn't know.

"I don't have a dad," I said with a shrug, the weight of the statement feather-light. A fact, nothing more.

"Ah, well, lucky for me, I guess. I can teach you how to skip a rock."

I laughed, a little shocked at the idea that I was lucky to be an orphan. "Wow, no one ever says I'm lucky to not have a dad."

He stared at me, squinting his eyes together as if he was trying to study me, read me, find something hidden behind my eyes. What did he see? "What's your name?"

Caught off guard by the shift in conversation, I stuttered. "Oh, I'm Danica, but most people just call me Dani. And you are?"

"I'm not most people." Okay, someone was impressed with themselves. "Nice to meet you, Danica. I'm Trent. Trent Petrov."

"Nice to meet you, Mr. Petrov. Are you the owner of this park?"

He scoffed and looked around, disgusted, like I just spat in his face and told him to go directly to hell. "Most definitely not. I'm here looking in on an employee who lives here. She left her shift early last night, said she wasn't feeling well, so I came to check on her. Do you live here?"

How to answer that one? Seemed like a simple enough question. No, I sleep here sometimes, when I'm not sleeping on someone else's couch. Not that.

"Um, no, I was just visiting a friend," I lied. "I'm on my way to the city."

"Ah, me too. What business do you do in the city?"

I looked down at my clothes, confused. I definitely didn't look like someone who *did business* in the city. No, I looked more like I was the person who cleaned the toilets for the person who brought coffee to someone who did business in the city.

"I, uh, I was actually on my way to a few interviews."

He slowly looked me up and then down and then back up. "Hmm."

I blushed. I didn't know this guy, but I was sure that

I knew what he was thinking. He was thinking the same thing that every employer I met with was thinking—*why would anyone hire you?* My shoulders fell a little, and I looked away.

"What kind of work are you looking for?"

I glanced at him and shrugged. "I'm mostly looking for waitressing jobs, but I'm pretty much open to anything at this point," I told him in a moment of unexpected honesty.

"I see. I guess we are both in luck today. I'm actually hiring waitresses at my club, and you are *exactly* the type of girl we are looking for." His dark eyes raked over me again, sending a chill down my spine.

"Me? I am?" I was kind of miffed. How did he know that I was what he was looking for? I'd never even waited tables before. Maybe he was looking for cheap labor, and I certainly looked like the bargain bin at the thrift store.

"You are beautiful."

I opened my eyes a little wider, taken aback by the forward compliment.

"How old are you?"

I stuttered, unsure of myself, not used to being called beautiful. Sure, I got catcalled by most men, but I knew that didn't mean anything. Guys would shoot their shots, as many as they could, hoping one would go in. "I'm twenty."

His lips twisted a bit, and he looked disappointed, nodding his head and looking up at the sky. I really was dense sometimes. This man said he owned a club; he was probably looking for someone who could serve alcohol.

I added quickly, "But I'll be twenty-one in a few weeks."

A slow smile spread across his face. "Well, that's

good news for us both." He said, looking down at the watch on his wrist and back up at me. "Come with me to the club, Danica. I'll show you the ropes and introduce you to some girls who can help you learn the job."

Something didn't feel right about this man, this stranger, offering me a job without knowing anything about me. Thinking that it would be totally naive to go with some guy I'd never met, I inched my way out.

"Um, I actually already have plans to head into the city. I have an interview scheduled." That last part was a lie; I didn't have anything lined up. I may have been desperate, but I wasn't a complete idiot who was just going to get into some stranger's car, no matter how nice his suit was. His lips formed a strange half-smile.

"Smart girl. How's this? I'll give you my business card, and if your interview doesn't go as planned today, come to my club and let the bouncer know you're there to see Trent for an interview." Then he reached into his breast pocket and held a card out to me. I hesitated before grabbing it. "The address is on there. But come today. I won't be hiring for long, and the job pays well. And here, use this for cab fare." He pulled his wallet out from his pants pocket, unfolded it, and took out a crisp $100 bill and thrust it at me. *One hundred dollars.*

I stepped back from him, confused as to why he was giving me money. Was I foolish to take it, or was I just so accustomed to the struggle that I couldn't see good when it came at me head on? But to take money from a guy I didn't even know felt, well, it felt *wrong*. I hadn't done anything to earn it, and if I had one thing, it was a strong work ethic and pride. I was frozen in place with my thoughts when the man took my hand and shoved the money in with his business card. His hand lingered on mine.

"Beautiful girls like you shouldn't ride the bus. It's not safe." A glint of something passed through his eyes, making me shiver. "Now call yourself a cab, Danica, and I'll see you later today."

Applying for jobs downtown was a bust. It didn't matter how many applications I filled out; no one wanted to hire a homeless wannabe waitress with zero experience whose clothes and hair looked like they were styled for the orphan scenes in *Annie*.

I pulled the card out of my backpack and looked at the address again. I could only hope that Mr. Petrov would still be there and hadn't yet filled the position.

****

Raven - Present Day

"Good morning sunshine!" Tessa strolled out to the living room, where Zara and I were watching cartoons. "How did your gig go last night?"

I breathed out a sigh. I'd been hoping to avoid this conversation, but I also knew that if I could talk to anyone about it, it was Tessa.

"It was…eventful."

Tessa yawned and pulled a sweatshirt over her body. "This sounds like a story I'll need coffee for. Hold your horses. I'll be right back."

"No, I'll come with you. Zara does not need to hear this."

Tessa raised her brows at me as I followed her into the kitchen. She poured herself an oversized mug of coffee and grabbed a croissant that she crammed halfway into her mouth. "I'm waiting."

"Fine, I'm just gonna say it."

I explained everything that happened up until the point where Cameron gave me the best orgasm of my life. Tessa's jaw hung slack, her face mimicking exactly how I felt about the night.

"You what? Tell me, tell me, tell me! I need all the dirty, slutty little details."

I was about to open my mouth and tell her all the dirty details when someone walked out of the hallway.

"Mika," I said in surprise. A huge grin spread across my face, and I turned to Tessa. "Did someone have a slumber party last night?"

She rolled her eyes at me. "Geez, we aren't schoolgirls, Raven." She paused. "Well, I might have been one last night. That and a French Maid and maybe also a sexy delivery girl."

"Tessa!" I smacked her, laughing. "I don't need to know all that." I glanced over at Mika, who shrugged and laughed, clearly used to my best friend's antics.

"I mean, she's not lying, Raven."

"Raven stripped for your coworkers yesterday," Tessa blurted out like it was the next logical thing to say.

"Geez, thanks for that." I wasn't sure how much of this I should talk about around Mika. She was Cameron's coworker and friend, and I was just her girlfriend's roommate. She had no reason to keep my secrets.

Tessa lifted one shoulder and let it fall. "Yeah, no problem. I thought we could catch her up quickly so we can move to the filthy bits of the story."

I glanced between Mika and Tessa, with a hesitancy in my voice and my face. "I don't know if that's a good idea."

"Oh, come on, she's not going to go back to the office and talk to him about it. Right, babe? You wouldn't do that." Tessa interlaced her fingers with Mika's and gave her hand a light tug.

Mika glanced down at their hands and grinned before looking back up at Tessa. "Nah, I wouldn't do that, I promise. They're my friends, but hoes before bros and all that good stuff." Mika winked at me and added. "But I can go if you want. I got stuff to do at home."

Tessa squeezed Mika closer to her and shot me the saddest pair of puppy eyes. "Don't make my girlfriend go home. I'm not ready to say goodbye." Both Mika and I smiled. I wasn't sure if Tessa even realized what she said.

"No, don't go. It's fine." I fumbled around for the words. What did it matter? If I didn't tell her now, Tessa would just tell her later, anyway. I inhaled what was meant to be a calming, cleansing breath, but felt more like heaving. "He. Well, we—"

"Babe, you already told this part of the story!" Tessa hounded me.

"Actually, not I." I paused. Last night was absurd, and it seemed pointless to even try to explain it.

"Wow, that sounds like a great story. Glad I stuck around for this," Mika deadpanned.

"All right, fine! I gave him a private dance, and then he ate me out behind a shed," I blurted out quickly.

Tessa rested her chin on her hand and grinned. "Sounds like a pretty good night to me. Actually, it kind of resembles my night." She winked at Mika and continued nibbling her croissant. Mika watched me with wide eyes while I contemplated how to explain my bizarre night.

The silence was becoming unbearable when Tessa looked up from her food and spoke. "Well, was it good?"

"Really, babe?" Mika gestured at me with a single eyebrow raised and one side of her mouth hitched. "Look at the girl. That's the face of someone who has been thoroughly taken care of."

I sighed and pressed my eyes shut briefly while I squeezed my thighs together. I could still feel the sensation of his slick tongue sliding along my pussy, licking and sucking me in like it was his final act on earth.

"See?" Mika said and shot Tessa a smirk.

I felt a burning prickle move from the back of my neck, up to my cheeks. "It was my first time doing *that,* so I have nothing to compare it to, but it was…" I searched for the right words, because calling it "good" felt like a disservice. "Everything. Like it was so everything that I'm pretty sure I left my body, watched him lick me, and then re-entered my body for a double orgasm. So yeah, you could say that it was good."

They both gaped, blinking in silence. Mika opened her mouth and then closed it. More blinking. More silence.

Then Tessa finally spoke. "Did you just say that was your *first* time?"

Seriously? That was their takeaway from my entire story?

My phone pinged on the table, and immediately I knew who it was.

Cameron: Hey you. Can we talk?

I could answer him and tell him no thanks. That would be the polite and courteous thing to do. But no. If I talked to him, if I gave myself just enough rope, I'd metaphorically hang myself when it came to this man. I had to have some freaking self-discipline, so I hit the trash button and deleted his text, then went into my contacts and blocked his number. It was the only way to keep myself away from him. And that was exactly what I had to do.

****

Cameron

The week dragged on. Raven wasn't taking my calls, and Chief continued to make me sit in my spot outside town, and all of nothing continued to happen there. It was a good way to spend hours thinking of all that had gone wrong in my life. All that I'd messed up. When Saturday finally came around, I was ready to drink until there were no more thoughts in my head. Except I had a ton of work to do on my property.

I spent the better part of Saturday afternoon clearing the fence line, taking only two breaks before getting back at it and going full force until about six at night. I turned off the tractor and heard a dog barking in the distance. It was high-pitched and filled with distress. I grabbed my rifle from the tractor. I could never be too careful out here. There were mountain lions and bears in this area, so I never went wandering without some sort of protection.

I hopped over the fence and followed the sounds of the dog until I got to a small clearing. I paused, trying to get my directional bearings. Except the animal stopped barking, and in its place, I heard the cries of a child.

My heart began racing and adrenaline shot straight through my veins. I ran through the woods toward the crying child, jumping over downed trees and running straight through spider webs. I crept up to the noise and saw the one person that I was truly not prepared for.

"Please, no!" she screamed as she wrapped herself around the child. Lying on top of the baby, she shook like a leaf and pleaded through tears. "Please no, please no, please just let us go. Please don't hurt her. I'll do whatever you want."

I was stunned speechless, standing slack-jawed, the rifle hanging at my side, trying to figure out what I was looking at. When I finally snapped out of my stupor, I slung the rifle to my back. Slowly ambling toward the woman who had been haunting my every thought, I knelt down and softly placed my hand on her back. Electricity. Lightning. All that fire compressed between the two of us. How could one simple touch elicit such a response?

"Sweetheart, it's me. It's Cameron."

Raven was shaking uncontrollably, and I couldn't understand what I had done that would cause such a response. I ran my fingers through her hair gently and soothed her in the calmest voice I could muster. But who I was kidding? I was a wreck, and my adrenaline was so high I could've lifted a large tree right then and there.

"Raven, baby, calm down. Look at me please and try to breathe. What are you doing out here in the middle of nowhere?"

She lifted her body off of her daughter and peered up into my eyes. Jesus, she looked right through my eyes and into my soul. It broke my heart to see her afraid like this.

Her daughter let out a soft whimper.

"Cameron?" Raven asked through heavy breaths. She leaned in close to me and ran the tips of her delicate fingers along my jaw.

After several seconds, she reached out and grabbed each side of my neck. "It's you...It's just you...Oh

141

Cameron, I was so scared. I thought that it was someone else, and I saw a gun, and I—" She choked on a gasp before she broke down into loud sobs as she held onto me for dear life, her small frame vibrating as her cries became erratic.

"Mommy sad." Her baby made a pouty face as she pushed a tiny finger into Raven's cheek. "It's okay, Mama. Zawa make it all better. I kiss your boo-boos and put bam-aids on it." The little girl leaned down and placed a kiss on Raven's ankle.

Raven sniffed back her tears and smiled at the child. Letting go of my neck, she placed a hand on the girl's cheek. "Thank you, sweet girl. You always make Mommy feel better."

I looked down at Raven's ankle, in the spot where Zara had just planted a kiss. The boot on her right ankle was untied, loosened to make room for a good deal of swelling.

"What are you guys doing out here? You realize this isn't a hiking trail, right? All the hiking trails are just north of here and marked pretty clearly."

"I'm out here being the world's worst mother." She laughed and immediately began to cry again. "It was nice weather today, so I decided to take Zara and Maus for a hike. We followed the maps, I swear. I even have this stupid, useless app on my phone, but we must've gotten off the path, and I tripped on a hole in the ground. I have no cell service out here and we've been sitting here for four hours. Four hours! I have some snacks for Zara, but not enough, and Maus is probably starving and thirsty." She cried harder. "I can't do anything right. I was just trying to give us a fun family day, and it sucked. I suck. You know, I tripped while I was carrying Zara, and thankfully I had enough sense to twist myself around or else I would've landed on her." She wiped her eyes, trying to explain through hiccupped breaths and tears.

I wanted to wrap the two girls up in my arms and carry them home. "Okay, sweetheart, I think that's enough berating yourself. We need to do less of that and more of getting you out of here, okay?"

She sniffled and took in a shaky breath. "Yeah, that's probably a good idea."

"All right. Good. Now let's figure this out." I scanned the area, trying to think of how I was going to get them all out of here. "Will your dog follow you without a lead?"

"Yeah. We were only using one because of the park rules, but he goes wherever I go."

"Good, then we won't worry about him. Zara can't walk all the way to my house, so—"

Her head shot up as she stared at me. "*Your* house?"

"Yeah, I live just about a half mile west." I could see the concern in her eyes, but this was a foregone conclusion. They were coming to my house. It would be foolish to try and hike our way out of here when she was in this state. And right now, I knew how to get back to where I lived from here. "Trust me, that's a much better option than trying to figure out what path you were on and then hiking back to your vehicle and driving home with an injured ankle."

She inhaled a long breath and nodded in reluctant agreement.

"Good choice," I told her, even though it was the only choice.

Raven grabbed the backpack at her side and held it up to me. "I have this carrier for Zara. I can put that back on if you can help me walk."

I furrowed my brows at her. The girl was crazy if she thought I was going to let her do anything, let alone everything.

"No, babe, I'll put the carrier on and manage Zara. You just sit there for now." I picked up the backpack, and after a swift lesson from Raven, I had Zara—who'd promised not to pull my hair (something her mother informed me she loved to do), strapped onto my back.

I set my rifle on the ground and helped Raven stand up.

"I'm gonna need you to carry the gun. Can you do that?" I pointed to the rifle, and she looked a little frightened. "The safety is on and I can even take all of the ammo out if you feel safer, but I do carry when I'm out hiking because we have mountain lions in this area."

Her eyes popped out as her head snapped to me. "Wow, if I would've known that, I wouldn't have taken my family out on this treacherous death march. You can leave the bullets in."

"All right. Now, just strap this to your front."

As soon as she slung it over her shoulder and settled the gun on her chest, I made quick work of scooping her up into my arms.

"Cameron! What are you doing? You can't carry both of us!"

"I can, and I am," I said before doing exactly that.

The hike back took some time, but Raven and Zara weren't all that heavy. Raven's dog, who seemed to be well-trained, stayed by my side the entire time, looking up at Zara and Raven every so often. As we got closer to the house, I felt little pinpricks on my neck.

"Ouch."

Raven looked up at me before looking over my shoulder. She pressed her lips together, holding back that gorgeous smile.

"Sowwy, Mama. Sowwy, Caca."

Raven's eyes were filled with mischief, nostrils flared as she looked into my eyes. I shook my head at Raven as she burst out into a fit of giggles.

Ignoring the lingering sting on the back of my neck, I told Zara gently, "How about you call me Cam, baby girl?"

But Zara, reacting to her mom's laughter and understanding that what she said was funny, began to chant, "Caca, caca, caca!" Raven and I shared a look before we both burst out laughing. Quickly, Zara joined in. The sound of their giggles reverberating in the woods hit me hard. My guts twisted and pangs of sadness shot through me. I had been alone for so long until I'd met Raven and her little girl. I hadn't realized how lonely I was. Yet, I couldn't keep these two girls in my life. I was no good for them.

Zara's gleeful shrieks pulled me from my thoughts, and my eyes refocused only to find Raven staring at me with those big, round eyes.

And suddenly, I knew. I was completely fucked.

Chapter 11

Raven

To say that I felt like I was in a fever dream would have been an understatement. I was wrapped up in Cameron's arms, my baby strapped on his back, and he was carrying us both without even stopping to rest, like some sort of rugged supercharged mountain man. And Maus followed behind, heeding Cameron's commands like he was his master. It didn't take long to reach his house.

After getting me situated on his couch, he unloaded Zara, and she jumped up on to the couch with me and snuggled in with heavy eyelids. His place was, well, a place. It wasn't messy, like a stereotypical bachelor pad, but it was fairly plain and undecorated and looked like it hadn't been updated since it was built, which was probably in the 1970s. It was a strange layout, with two hallways on each side of the living space. I had never seen a house with wings like this. The entrance on the right of me was draped over with a drop cloth, blocking the hallway from my sight. The other hallway had three doors.

"Are you redoing your house?" I asked him, curious about the drop cloth and closed-off spaces.

"Eh, eventually," he said over his shoulder as he walked through an open doorway to the adjacent room.

When he came back, he handed me two bottles of water and set down a bowl of water for Maus. "Here, drink up. You're probably pretty thirsty." Yeah, we were. "I'm going to order some pizza. I don't really have a lot of food here. Can babies eat pizza?"

"Yes, she loves pizza. Just cheese for her, and I'll eat anything."

He tilted his head and walked over to where I was sitting on the couch. Kneeling down in front of me, his gorgeous gray-blue eyes pierced me. I was done for.

"What do you like, Rave?" Rave. It was the first time he had called me that. I shook my head, freeing myself from these foolish thoughts, and stumbled over my words, not understanding the question.

"I, uh, like lots of things?" I asked, more than stated.

"No, baby, what kind of *pizza* do you like? I know you said you'll eat anything, but that's not good enough for me. I want to get you what you like."

Oh. What I like. That was new. I answered shyly, feeling stupid for not understanding the question. "I like veggie pizza. With extra cheese and extra olives." Cameron gave me a curt nod and stood up, heading back into what I assumed was the kitchen.

"Mama, milky," Zara cried as she opened and closed her fist, signing the word for milk as she said it. My poor little girl was probably starving and thirsty. We had been stuck out there for a while without much to eat or drink.

"Ok my little love, come here." I gestured toward Zara, and she hopped into my arms. I got up carefully and limped to the kitchen very unsteadily, with Zara hanging on my hip, to see if Cameron had any milk for her. He was already on the phone with the pizza place when I approached him, asking him if he had any milk before realizing he was already talking to someone. I mouthed the word sorry and started to walk out, but as I turned around, I felt his large arms grab my hips and come up behind me, my behind pressed against his body.

"I'm on hold, baby. What can I get you before you sit your fine ass down?" I felt his body jerk behind me as he tightened his grip on my hip. "Sorry. I meant, sit your lovely self on a chair."

I chuckled. He was sweet, and I appreciated the effort. But if he only knew the words Tessa had already unintentionally taught my kid, he wouldn't feel as bad. I turned to face him, carefully maneuvering my foot so I didn't fall. "Milk for Zara," I whispered.

Cameron nodded at me, pointed to a table with four chairs around it, and then put his arms out to Zara, who happily fell into him as he lifted her out of my arms and told me, "Sit."

"Yes, sir." I smirked.

Cameron's lips upturned into a wolfish grin. "Sir, huh? I could get used to that." I rolled my eyes but couldn't help my smile. Cameron laughed and shook his head at me. "Go on, sit down, I'll get you whatever you need." He was brushing a kiss on my temple when I heard a voice through the speaker on his phone. He stepped back and resumed his order with the pizza place, releasing me to limp to the chair, the lingering feel of his lips still on my skin.

When he was done with the call, he grabbed a cup and was about to pour some milk for Zara.

"Do you have a cup with a lid? She'll probably spill that everywhere," I warned.

"Nah, but it's okay if she does. I'll help the little cutie pie drink her milk."

My head snapped up. What was that voice? He wasn't even looking at me when he spoke in the sweetest baby voice to Zara. Nope, he was staring lovingly at my daughter. Cameron sat down with Zara in the chair next to me, set her on his knee, and gently helped her grip the sides of the cup.

Cameron spoke gently when he told Zara, "You gotta drink it slowly, little Z, okay? If you pour it too fast, you'll pour it all over, and then the milk will be gone."

"I do it, Camy!" Zara urged.

At Zara's attitude, my spine straightened. "I'm sorry. She can be a bit bossy. I'll take her." Frantically I reached out, ready to shield my daughter from anything or anyone that would hurt her or crush her spirit. Except Cameron laughed. He freaking *laughed.*

"She's fine. I can handle this monster. Besides..." He was looking at Zara again, bouncing her on his knee, and speaking in that gentle baby voice. "We want our little Z monster here to grow up strong and give *all* the boys a tough time. Boss away, babycakes."

My mouth closed. I slumped down. I opened my mouth. I closed it again. *Our* little Z monster? Babycakes? What was this man trying to do to me?

"Now you try it," he coaxed.

Zara tipped the cup up very slowly and then back down.

"Hey, you did it!" He clapped and looked at me with wide eyes that said, "Did you see that?" He was genuinely excited for her. My shattered heart slowly started to piece back together, and I wasn't sure how much more of this sweet, domestic version of Cameron I could take. I could avoid the lust-induced craze between us in the name of motherhood, but when this was all about my kid? Nope, just nope. I couldn't be expected to resist, could I?

"I get no milk, Cam-am. My cup empty, you go put milk!"

Cameron laughed at her and looked into the cup. "Ah, I see. You didn't tip it far enough. Can I help you do it this time?"

Zara looked at me for approval, and when I nodded, she responded. "Mama say yes." Cameron's large hands clasped around her tiny ones as he slowly tipped the cup up.

"I do it, I do it, Mama, see I dwink milky all bidy myself!" Zara bounced proudly, a milk mustache on display. "Cam-Cam not hep me dat much, Mama, I do it!"

I laughed and clapped for her. "You did it. Good job!"

Thirty minutes later, the pizza arrived, and if Zara wasn't tired before, that sleep-induced food coma, combined with the stressful events of the day, hit all at once. It was time to get home. I didn't want this evening to end, but my little one needed her rest.

"Hey Cameron, Zara is about to crash. She's had a long day, and I probably need to get her home in bed. I'm just gonna call Tessa to come and pick us up. She has a car seat in her car, so you won't have to write me another ticket." I nudged him playfully.

He nodded his head in understanding. "Sure, I understand that. Does she sleep in a crib?"

"No, she sleeps in a regular bed. Well, it's like a regular bed, but closer to the ground, so she doesn't fall far if she rolls off."

"I have a guest room, and before you say anything, hear me out. It has a regular bed in it, but I can put the mattress on the floor. I want you to stay with me tonight." He put his hands up as if calming me down, "And not for anything other than I want to get to know you, and, right now, we have this chance."

Sure, he wanted to get to know me, in the biblical sense. As if he sensed my apprehension, he went on. "I really do, Raven. You and I have been unconventional." Ha, that was the understatement of the century. "The way I've been with you, I haven't been the man I am, or want to be. I've been douchey, bordering on full-on asshole." These were all true facts. He had been all of that, despite the earth-shattering orgasms. Those were great. "Please, I'll only ask you once, and if you don't want to stay, I'll understand. But," He continued. "Tessa and Mika are hanging out tonight at your place, and chances are you'll get better care rest here."

My brows furrowed. "How do you know they are hanging out tonight?"

"Mika and I are friends. We talk."

I swallowed, wondering what he knew, hoping she hadn't told him anything about me. No, she was my friend too. She wouldn't.

"And since I don't have a car seat for her, the whole process of getting your car will take a long time, and poor little Z will never get to bed on time." He frowned, going for broke. It worked, because I hadn't even thought of the logistics. He was right. By the time we got it all sorted out, it would be really late, and Zara would probably wake up and never fall back asleep.

"Okay, yeah. I don't want to disturb their night. Anyway, one of them is probably all tied up by now." I

151

giggled.

His eyebrows shot up to his forehead.

"I'm joking!" I waved him off and then mumbled, "Sort of."

Honestly, they probably needed a night without me as their annoying third wheel. "Okay, we'll stay."

Cameron raised his brows and dipped his chin down. "Yeah?" He asked, his voice pitched higher than normal.

"Yeah." I lifted one shoulder, like this was nothing, like I wasn't freaking out inside. "Let me send a text to Tessa so she knows not to worry."

"Okay," He said decisively, with a curt nod. "While you do that, I'm going to go get the guest room ready for little Z."

"Thanks," I replied with a smile, patting my baby's back as she rested on me, squiggling and squirming the way she always did when she was ready for bed. I sent Tessa a text letting her know that the three of us wouldn't be home tonight.

I looked up from my phone to notice that Zara had wiggled her way out of my hold and wasn't in the room. The kid was stealthy and had somehow wandered off in a matter of two minutes, and I was really hoping she didn't wander off into the closed-off wing of the house. As I was about to get up, I heard Cameron's voice.

"Shhh, shhh, little Z."

I walked to the guest room and peeked in. My heart stopped. He paced the floor, rocking and swaying Zara side to side with her wrapped in his arms, her head laying on his broad chest. She was completely out. And I could hardly blame her for leaving me to snuggle with him. The man was a wall. Cameron's gaze drifted to mine, and his gray-blue eyes looked like pools of forever, and I wanted to slap myself for even thinking like that. I could get lost in this man, and I didn't really even know much about him.

He kept his voice low. "She asked me to pick her up and then kinda just crashed. I think she's asleep. That was pretty easy."

The words sat like concrete in my throat. How could I tell him that he was the first man to ever hold her? The first man that had lovingly rocked her to sleep? It was sweet sadness and melancholy bliss. Instead of jumping on him and telling him why this meant so much to me, to Zara, I nodded in agreement and decided on lightheartedness.

"Yeah, toddlers are super easy." I let him have this little victory, because if he put her to bed on any other day, he would be leaving her room like he was walking away from the final battle in *Braveheart*.

"You want me to put her down on the bed?"

I nodded, blinking back tears, mesmerized by the sight.

"All right. She's a little chunk, isn't she?"

I smiled and nodded my head yes.

****

Cameron showed me to the shower by the guest room and gave me some clean clothes to wear. I looked at them. Size medium with the tags still on, but they were women's clothes. I lifted my head to meet his gaze, wondering where these clothes came from and why they were new. He cleared his throat.

"They were my wife's, Callie's, but they were a gift that she never wore. Too small for her. She was very curvy, and you are, well, pretty tiny." He put his hands out and drew them in closer together. I guessed that was the universal signal for narrow?

My stare fell to the fireplace, where a picture of them sat. It looked like a wedding picture, and Callie was, well, intimidatingly beautiful. She looked like a freaking pinup model, and in a way, reminded me of Tessa. A twinge of sadness for him, for her, pulled at my heart. Nothing in life was ever fair.

"If this is weird for you at all, I'm fine just wearing one of your shirts to bed or something. It-it's not a big deal. I don't want to impose on your space, and I'm not that kind of person, you know. I'm not going to be weird about anything."

He shook his head. "Nah, it's fine. She never wore this. And by the way, you're cute when you're nervous." He grinned that panty-melting grin, and I squeezed my thighs, thankful to have some space for a little while. I needed to gather my thoughts and myself.

After a quick shower, I went out to the living room to see that Cameron had changed too. His hair was wet, and he was wearing gray sweatpants and a white shirt. He must've had another bathroom, with a shower, down the closed-off hallway. I wanted to ask, but thought better of it. If he wanted me to know, he would've told me. I sat on the couch with him, giving us some distance. Cameron sweetly put my foot up on the coffee table and placed a bag of frozen peas on it.

"You should probably elevate and ice this. I'm no doctor, but I think that's what they'd tell you to do."

"Well, it's good advice. As a nursing student, I give you an 'A' in patient care."

"What? I didn't know you were in school."

I scoffed, and the sound came out sour, more sour than I'd intended it to. "You and I never really talked, now did we?" I said with a sly grin, trying to hide the hurt that was behind the joke.

He gave me a regretful look before scooting closer, grabbing me and pulling me into him. I squeaked. "No, I guess not. We'll have to remedy that."

I settled into him, fully giving in to the tension between us. At this point, what *was* the point of resisting? He and I were a foregone conclusion. For tonight, anyway.

"So…" He started, letting the word hang.

I buried my head in his chest and giggled nervously. "So?" I asked, still hiding my face, but feeling my body relax into him.

Cameron shifted underneath me before running his fingers through my hair. "Want to watch a movie?" He asked. But I pressed my eyes closed and moaned, too focused on the delightful tingling sensation on my scalp. He stopped abruptly and cleared his throat. "How about *A Few Good Men*?"

I couldn't help but perk up. I lifted my head and shot him a toothy smile. It was cute that he remembered our conversation from that first night.

"Are we having a girls' night?" I asked him.

"Only if it's like the last girls' night we had." He paused for a second, then raised his eyebrows. "But better. You know, less phone sex, more actual touching."

My cheeks heated at his response, and a jolt of pleasure shot through my core. "Oh? Should I go put on my clown makeup?"

"Ha. Oh yeah, you know how I like it, baby."

We spent the next hour and a half eating pizza and debating the performances of Tom Cruise and Jack Nicholson. When it got down to the last slice, we agreed the first one to give in to a tickle fight was the loser and forfeited the last slice. With Cameron's hands on me, I didn't put up much of a fight and he came out as the clear winner. I did tally one point for myself when I managed to get his shirt off, but that was the extent of my success in the tickle battle arena. I didn't care; I'd take an eyeful of Cameron's abs over pizza any day.

My gaze swept the length of his ripped torso, and I was sure I looked thirsty for him. I stared at him, not knowing what to do, not wanting to move from the position we'd landed in with me on top, straddling him. Cameron set his hands on my hips gently while raising his hips just a bit so I could feel him a little more. Bursts of excitement roused my entire body, hairs standing on end, nerve endings at the ready.

Cameron's eyes darkened when he said, "This is what you do to me. Every single time."

I blushed and cast my eyes downward.

He lifted my chin with one finger, forcing me to look at him. "I haven't had this much fun in a long time. It's been a rough few years for me, and honestly, I wasn't sure I'd be laughing again, feeling again, and—" He let the words hang in the air, suspended in honesty.

The insinuation settled over us like a dense fog, capturing us alone in this moment together, the silence saying much more than words could tell. His eyes said "love," but also said it was too soon.

"Well," he continued. "Let's just say that I didn't think I'd be here, with you or anyone else."

"I'm glad I could be a part of that." My truth sat at the tip of my tongue. I didn't think I'd ever laugh again, either. I didn't think I'd ever feel safe. I didn't think I'd ever fall in love or know what it was like to feel loved.

No, not now, I told myself. He looked at me adoringly as his gaze traveled the length of my body, the air between us thinning. He licked his lips. He was going to kiss me, and I wanted it.

I was completely still. I inhaled deep breaths, trying to calm the violent beating of my heart as I waited for him to make his move.

Seconds later, his tender lips found mine. He plucked small kisses from me, giving me just a tempting taste of his lips before gently taking my lower lip between his teeth, clamping down softly and releasing.

His kisses were everything. They breathed new life into me, gave me hope, restored a bit of my soul. He swiped his tongue between my lips, parting my mouth, leisurely exploring, searching, and finding. I kissed him back, needing more.

Tilting my head to the side, I deepened our kiss, and it went from slow and gentle to a heated frenzy. He groaned into my mouth as he kissed me hard, both of his large hands stilled on either side of my hips. He was still holding himself back. I didn't know if it was fear or too much desire, too much built-up tension between us. We were both about to snap like a stretched rubber band. But we had gone too far now to hold back. This was happening, and if something didn't give, I'd be riding the magic wand into next year.

I reached around him and grabbed his back, taking control and pulling him closer to me, letting him know I wanted it too. He smiled into my mouth. I had never been one to take control like this, but with him, it was different. I felt safe.

"I want you, Raven," he whispered darkly into my neck as he trailed kisses along the path from my ear to my collarbone.

"Really? I hadn't noticed," I whispered back with an exhale.

Chapter 12

Cameron

A short bark of laughter escaped me, and I swallowed hard, gulping back the nerves as I traveled farther down her body, my lips getting closer to her breasts. It had been a long time since I'd been with a woman and even longer since I'd been with a woman other than my wife.

Nerves or not, my dick was hard anytime I was around this woman. No way I could resist. And I didn't have to because she wanted more. She was begging for it, needing it as much as I did. I looked up and down her body, Callie's clothes hanging on her delicate curves. I shook off the feeling that my wife was somehow here in this moment, standing between us. And I powered through the relentless ache in my chest to focus on Raven.

My gaze rose to her beautiful, heart-shaped face that was framed by long, shiny black hair. And her eyes. I could, and did, get lost in her golden-flecked doe eyes. They carried something more than what she presented. I could sense something there, stories she had yet to tell me. I wanted to know everything about her, and at that moment, I felt hopeful that one day I might.

"Cameron."

Raven's moans broke me out of my trance, and

without another thought, I gently kissed her swollen lips when she opened her mouth for me. I lightly pressed my body into hers, stopping myself from moving too fast when her moans became needy whimpers and she peered up at me through large eyes. She was irresistible, and I wanted all of her at once. But I wasn't about to speed through this moment with her.

I needed more than one night from her. She could be the safety and the deliverance from my dark thoughts. I wanted to feel her, to own her, and to claim every part of her.

I played at the hem of her shirt and instead of waiting, she thrust into me, pushing my hand under her shirt, my fingertips pressing into her warm skin. I ran my hand slowly up her shirt, starting low, pressing in as I crossed her navel, up to the center between her breasts.

Raven's chest expanded, and she locked eyes with me while I teased the area with the tips of my fingers. I enjoyed taunting her, but I also wanted to take my time before I lost my mind and fucked her senseless.

I reached behind her with both of my hands and unclipped her bra. She worked her arms out, and I pulled the bra carefully off of her full breasts, dragging it down. I bunched her bra in my fist as I wrapped one arm around her waist and leaned into her. She arched and let her head fall backward, exposing her long neck. She was graceful and the way she moved her body was damn near art. Instantly, I dropped the bra and trailed kisses along her exposed throat as I slid my hand back up her shirt, palming her round breasts that fit perfectly in my large hand. Her nipples were already hard as I gently swept my thumb over their stiff peaks, taunting her with my touch as I kissed her.

I continued to play with her, alternating between gently grabbing handfuls of her breasts and pulling her nipples. Raven grabbed my arms and pulled herself back up. She was panting, her chest heaving as she ran her nails across my spine, slowly making her way around to my stomach. She played with the waistband of my pants, teasing with her finger as she dipped just below and then out again. By the third time she did it, I'd had enough. I grabbed her hand a little harder than I meant to and put it over her head. She winced.

"Sorry, didn't mean to hurt you." In one motion, I flipped her to her back and hovered over her. "When I give you my cock, I want you begging me for it."

Her lips parted, and she exhaled as her body melted beneath me. Just how I wanted her. There was no inhibition between us, only this feeling, this raw, animalistic ache that made me want to bury myself inside of her until neither of us could see straight.

We grew primal, hands everywhere, the urgency of the moment pulling us deeper in. Raven pulled her shirt up higher, revealing more of her creamy, flawless skin and those large, round breasts that I wanted to get my mouth on. She was like art laying there beneath me. Arching her back, she thrust her breasts up toward me. I bent my head down and took one stiff nipple into my mouth, flicking it with my tongue. And Christ, I had to slow down or I was going to shoot off like it was my first time with a woman. I worked her breasts slower, licking and sucking as I gently held both of her wrists pinned over her head. Raven wrapped her legs around me, her warm center pressed against my stomach, the feel of her body driving me insane. My dick was grinding into the couch, my senses heightened as I came unglued, my body begging for its own relief.

I released her breasts from my mouth and moved back up to her. "I need your mouth, baby."

"Take it. Take whatever you want. I need you too Cam."

Cam. I paused, thinking the nickname might destroy me, bring me back to a simpler time in my life and wreck me all over again. But coming from her lips, the words were a healing salve, spread across all my wounded parts. Raven's words were more of a plea than permission. I clenched one fist when she leaned into me and the feel of her skin nearly undid me.

I had tried so hard to hold back, to go slow, but every cell in my body was awake and desperate for her. I crashed down onto her swollen, wet lips and kissed her hard, drawing out soft whimpers that did nothing but spur me on. I took everything that she was willing to give. Raven matched my passion, her hands running haphazardly through my hair, grabbing and pulling, while she kissed me relentlessly.

"Mmm." Her moans buzzed against my lips and my cock jumped. "Yes, more. Give me more." Raven wrapped her arms around my waist and dug her nails into my skin as she yanked me closer.

"Fuck." My voice cracked. "I wanna hear you say my name."

"Cameron!" Raven replied breathlessly, the golden flecks in her dark eyes glinting as she stared back at me.

I touched my forehead to hers and, with a primal growl, I let myself go. "That's right, baby. By the time I'm done with you, you're gonna scream that with this cock buried deep inside of you."

"Tell me more, Cam," Raven begged with a

whisper, our eyes still locked, bodies pressed close.

"I'll tell you exactly what I want, baby." I ground my body deeper into hers and gritted out the words, my voice strained with desire. "I want you to wrap those legs around me and ride my cock. I'm gonna watch those perfect tits bounce while you make that tight little body work for me. I want you to take all of me until you come screaming my name."

Raven's body trembled beneath me and she breathed out shaky, shallow breaths. I paused, thinking I'd gone too far. But then she pushed me off of her just enough for her to pull the shirt over her head and toss it on to the living room floor.

Grabbing the back of my neck, Raven pulled me back into her and parted her lips. Before I was close enough to take her mouth, I stopped, taking her in. I wanted to lick her every delicate curve with my tongue, taste her soft, creamy skin while I travelled her body.

Her long, black hair was strewn messily around her, covering the tattoos inked on her arms. I gathered her hair and moved it to one side, just taking her in.

We were laying the length of the couch, skin to skin, heat radiating and electricity thrumming between us. Raven reached down and pushed her pants off as I lifted just enough to accommodate. My dick twitched inside my pants at the sight of her lace thong. Her panties formed just a small triangle over her. My mouth had already been on her pussy, so I knew she was smooth under the thin strip of fabric, but seeing her again, it felt like the first time. Raven didn't wait for me to act. She pushed down on the waistband of my sweats and briefs at once.

"Greedy girl," I growled, ignoring this new man I

was becoming. This needy man who couldn't think about anything but being inside of this woman. I didn't care, because right now, I was going to enjoy every minute that she gave me. Raven looked up at me with hooded eyes. We were completely lost in each other. Kicking my pants and briefs off the rest of the way, they fell to the floor. I looked at Raven, ready to dive back in, but she was looking down, staring at where my cock bobbed between us.

"It's…" Her gaze shifted between my dick and my face, before settling on my dick again. "It's…" She looked up and gasped, eyes widening slowly, as she bit her bottom lip and murmured, "Cam."

With one elbow pressed into the couch at the side of her head and my knee bent, I hovered over her. I lowered my lips to her ear as I took my cock in my hand and gave it slow, languid pulls, sliding up and down my length as she watched. Reveling in the relief, I stroked myself over her and whispered into her ear. "I want you to take all of it, baby. We will start slow, but I need you to take every last inch of my cock. Do you think you can handle it?"

I wasn't an arrogant man, but I knew what I was packing. And Raven was small. As much as I wanted to be inside of her, I didn't want to hurt her. Raven nodded, her eyes glazed over as she looked through me.

"I promise, sweetheart, I'll be as gentle as you need. I won't hurt you. I'll *never* hurt you. If you need me to stop, I'll stop. I'll go easy until you get used to me." It would be a massive effort to hold myself back, but I wasn't an animal, even if I felt like one around her.

Raven looked up and shook her head back and forth. "I don't want you to go easy on me. I need it. I need *you*. I need you more than anything else right now." She looked up at me briefly before her eyes sparkled and her lips tugged up on one side. Her voice was playful when she demanded, "So give it to me."

Christ, I was going to blow my load right then and there.

"Good." I grunted out. "But first, I need to taste you." Without giving her a chance to speak, I was already at her slit, smirking at the little piece of fabric that acted like a weak barrier. I ripped the scrap of material off of her, and before she could react, I licked a path from the back to the front of her wet pussy. She tasted like pure heaven.

She whimpered pushing up into me, as I worked my tongue deeper into her. I placed one hand against her stomach, holding her in place. "Cam, baby, I, oh. It feels so—" I flexed my tongue on her pussy as I placed one finger over the opening of her ass and moved it around in slow circles.

"Ah!" She bucked and screamed.

"Is that too much?"

"No, don't you dare stop!"

I laughed into her. Licking her pussy up and down, I worked her walls with my tongue, tasting her, devouring her, making her mine. She bore down on my finger, threw her head back, and released a long moan. I tamped down my own reaction to pleasuring her, knowing I'd never forgive myself if this went too fast. I pressed my finger lightly into her ass and continued my motion, fingering her ass while sucking gently on her clit. Her thighs pressed against my head, her body becoming tight and tense.

"Cam, I'm gonna—I'm gonna come."

"Give it to me, baby. Let go for me."

I kept at her as her pussy clenched around my tongue and that tight little hole contracted around my finger. I didn't bother to stop. I was going to draw out every last ounce of her pleasure until she was so consumed by it that she had no choice but to beg for me. Her body pulsed and shook, her moans becoming louder and uncontrolled.

"Cameron—right there—that's—yes!" She thrust and circled her hips gently into my face and finger as she rode out her orgasm on my mouth, lost in the bliss of it, her eyes hooded right before they gently fluttered shut.

There was nothing sexier than a beautiful woman coming apart on my tongue. I slowly slid my finger out of her ass. Her breath hitched, and she opened her eyes slightly. Raven looked at me, her eyes glazed and one side of her mouth lifted into a half smile, right before she dropped her head back and let out a long sigh.

"I'll just get myself out of this headlock," I told her with a chuckle, as I carefully pressed against the inside of her thighs until her legs relaxed and fell into the couch with the rest of her.

"Mmmm," Raven hummed, her voice distant. I doubted she'd heard a word I'd said. I moved up next to her, rolling her to her side to make room for me. Raven's back was to my chest, and I wrapped an arm loosely around her. I felt the rise and fall of her body beneath my hold, as her rapid breaths evened out. Just when I thought she might be falling asleep, she reached up and grabbed onto my arm, a move that erased all the space between my throbbing cock and her bare ass.

****

I lay on the couch with her, letting her rest and enjoy the comedown from her orgasm. I wanted to get inside of her, I needed to, and with my hard as a rock dick pressed against her, I wasn't sure how long I could resist. But she needed a break, and I had to pull it together before I slipped inside of her and came in two seconds.

She shifted in front of me, pushing her ass into my cock. I was going to let her rest, but Christ, I was only a man, and if she wanted it, I wasn't going to say no.

"Are you ready for me now, sweetheart?" I whispered into her ear, pulling all that black hair to one side.

She nodded silently and thrust her ass back into me until my cock was pressing into the crevice of her ass. I groaned and reached around to grab her tits, palming them and playing with her nipples, while I ground into her. I flipped her around to face me and in one quick movement, I turned to sit and placed her on top of me, her legs straddling me, my cock bobbing against her, slapping her belly. Her eyes went wide with desire as she ground into me.

"Stand up and turn around, Raven," I ordered her with a growl.

She flashed me innocent eyes full of desire. And when her tight little ass was right in front of me, I grabbed it with both of my hands and kissed down her spine until I landed on the curve of her hips. I wanted to be gentle. I wanted to go slow and savor the moment. But staring at her like this, her round ass in full view, I couldn't hold myself back. Grabbing her waist with a tight grip, I pulled her down to me, her back still facing me. She let out a loud whimper. I bit her neck gently, trying to stop the urge I had to completely ruin her. I lifted her slightly, inhaling calming breaths of my own. I was going to give it to her slow. For her, but also for me.

I knew if I moved too fast, I'd go off immediately.

"Take me, baby, just a little at a time."

She lowered herself onto me so slowly it was near torture to my aching cock. Tossing her head back, she panted.

"That's it, baby, ease yourself onto me." I coaxed her to take more. I needed her to take it all.

"Cam," she said shakily.

"Are you okay, sweetheart?"

"Yes, just, it feels so good."

I smiled at her admission, glad she didn't want to stop here or else I was pretty sure my dick would detach itself from my body and dickslap me into the next millennium. I helped work my length into her, rubbing the head around her opening and circling the tip of my dick in all of her wetness. It was torture, because all I wanted to do was pound into her. When I was a little further inside, she stayed still for a moment, breathing in and out.

"You okay, baby?"

Shakily, she answered. "Yes." And then, Raven cautiously rode me up and down, taking more of me every time she went down.

"I want to take all of you," she moaned.

"Take your time, baby, just take your time. I'm going to give you every last inch, but I want it to feel good for you."

Raven nodded, and she slowly lowered herself, easing her way around me, almost fully on my cock. And then without warning, she dropped herself fast and hard onto me, burying me completely in her tight little pussy, her ass cheeks slapping against me. She screamed out, and I lost control.

"Ah, fuck!" I ground out, my fingers digging into her, the feeling so unexpected and intense that I nearly lost everything I had. But I held on. "Oh, Jesus, baby, you're really tight." I grunted out and gripped her hips so hard that when I realized it, I loosened my hold a little, hoping I hadn't left a mark. For a few seconds, she didn't move. She breathed in, getting used to the length and girth of me. And I was glad for it, because I needed to get used to her tight warmth or it was going to be over before it started.

"I feel full. You make me feel so full, Cameron."

I gritted my teeth, hanging on by a near-frayed thread. After a moment, she began to slowly move back and forth, up and down, alternating between rocking her hips and swiveling them around on my cock. She slid herself up and down my length, slamming down onto me so hard I wasn't sure how I held on. But I did, because she was going to come again before this was over. She ramped up her speed, and my jaw clenched as I hung on. I grabbed one hip and with my other hand, I reached around to her clit, massaging it steadily.

"Is that good, baby? Do you like that?"

She nodded. "Don't stop, please. I'm going to come," she said through heavy breaths.

I worked her clit as she rode me nonstop, using my hand on her waist to help push her up and down on my cock, making sure that she received every last inch of me. Her movements became erratic, and her breathing was heavy. I grabbed her hips and slammed her down onto my cock as I thrust up into her over and over until her pussy tightened and pulsed around me, squeezing my dick so hard my body jolted.

"Cameron, yes that's it, yes. Just like that, honey,

169

don't stop!" She screamed out, begging for me like we were the only two people in the world.

Her pussy continued to pulse around me as I lessened my thrusts, slowing down and letting her ride out her orgasm on me until she fully found her release. I wasn't done with her. I lifted her off of me and nudged her up to stand. She was drenched and I could see the juices dripping from her. I spun her around, taking in the sight of her disheveled hair and swollen lips. I couldn't get enough of the woman and sure as hell hoped she wasn't done with me when I asked, "Now, do you want more?"

"Yes," she replied, her voice quiet and her whole body relaxed.

"Wrap your legs around me," I demanded as I stood up and lifted her up onto me, her ass sitting just above my dick that was aching to be back inside of her. I walked her back to the wall as I kissed her, falling into the woman, losing myself entirely. She was taken care of, and I was going to lose my mind if I didn't come soon. I breathed her in, trying to slow myself down. She smelled like coconuts and the mountain breeze, and she tasted like a second chance. And I knew, for a brief moment, that if I let myself, I could fall fully into her, into us.

Pushing her against the wall as I supported all of her weight, I lined myself up with her and stared into her gorgeous eyes. Without any warning and without easing her in at all, I thrust my cock into her, burying the full length of myself inside of her in one motion.

"Ah, oh god!" She whisper-screamed into my neck and arched her back.

"You like that? I told you I wouldn't go easy on

you," I growled at her as I continued thrusting. She grabbed my face with both hands, and through the haze of it all, I thought I saw her: just as emotional as I was, just as desperate to feel something. Something real.

"Yes, Cameron, hard! Harder!"

I mercilessly pounded into her over and over, slamming her against the wall while we stared into each other's eyes. I was unrelenting, and she didn't know it, but she had me. I knew that I wouldn't last long like this. But I couldn't take it slow with her anymore. I had to have her. I had to be inside of her. I needed her to make me come. I would take her slow later if she let me, but now, I couldn't ignore the urgency of the moment. When I felt the tension begin to build at my shaft, I knew I was close.

"I'm gonna come, baby," I warned her through deep, guttural grunts.

"Come, Cameron. Please come in me."

My jaw tensed, my balls tightened, and my body went rigid as I pumped into her, thrusting erratically. My whole body shook and shuddered as I spilled everything I had inside of her, pumping in as deep as I could get. Her walls closed around me as she found her own release once again. The tightening of her pussy only increased my pleasure.

"Oh, that's good, baby," I ground out, still lightly pushing in and out of her as she milked the last remaining cum from my cock.

I held her up against the wall as we came down from the fog of our sex. Her small body collapsed against me, her head resting on my shoulder as we both tried to catch our breath. I nudged her face up with my chin and pressed a lazy kiss to her swollen, pink lips before I walked us to the couch, my dick still inside of her.

"Don't. No. Please? Want you to stay," Raven whined, her head falling forward onto my shoulder.

I smiled at her unintelligible pleas as I gently eased myself out of her with a gasp. My dick was sensitive after coming, but more than that, every sensation was amplified around this woman.

"I gotta clean you up, sweetheart."

Laying her down, I went to the bathroom to get a washcloth to clean her with. When I came back, her eyes were still closed as she lay naked on my couch, cum dripping out of her wet pussy. I wasn't sure I'd ever seen anyone more beautiful, and that thought fell on me like a new kind of burden. A burden that I couldn't consider right then. Right then, I was sure of one thing, and that was Raven's beauty. As I cleaned her off, she barely opened her eyes and grinned widely. I smiled back, proud that I was the one who had put that smile on her face. I looked between our naked bodies, my head still buzzing with euphoria, when I saw it.

I closed my eyes briefly. "Shit."

Raven's voice pitched and she sat up on the couch, her eyes now open and alert. "What?"

Embarrassed, I looked to the side. "I didn't wear a condom, Raven." I'd been so caught up in the moment, so reckless around this woman, it hadn't even occurred to me. Not to mention, I'd hardly had sex in the last three years. I also wouldn't even know where to find a condom in my house.

She let out a small groan as she sunk back down into the couch and sighed. "It's okay. I'm on the pill."

I let out my own sigh of relief.

"And even though I haven't been with anyone in

over a year, I had my annual exam a few months ago, and there's nothing you need to know," she added.

"Okay, good. I haven't been to the doctor recently, but before you, I was with my wife for eleven years and never stepped out. I can go again though, if it'd make you feel better," I told her as I snatched my sweats up off the floor and tugged them on.

"No, it's okay. That's good enough if you haven't been with anyone since your wife."

I stared at her naked body spread across my big couch. I wasn't sure I could tear my eyes away from her, until her shoulders lifted, and she shivered, hugging her arms to her body.

I went to the hallway closet and pulled out a few fleece blankets and some pillows. When I got back to the front room, Raven was sitting up, her arms wrapped tightly around her chest.

"Um, thanks." She reached out and grabbed one of the blankets. Immediately, she unfolded it and wrapped it around herself. She looked down, red spreading across her cheeks.

"Babe, what's wrong?"

Raven kept her gaze on the couch as she fiddled with the blanket. "Nothing."

"Sweetheart, I was just inside of you. You sat on my face. I had my finger in your—"

"Stop!" She shook her head and laughed uncomfortably. "Thank you. I know what we did. I was there. I don't need a replay."

"Hmmm, maybe you don't, but just so you know, I'll be replaying that on loop for a long time to come," I teased, waggling my eyebrows. "My point is, we're *well* acquainted now. You can tell me if something's wrong."

She worked her lip between her teeth, before she said in a hushed tone. "It's just that maybe I should go sleep in the room with Zara."

I jerked my head back, shocked at her suggestion. "What? Why would you do that?"

She scanned the room, looking at everything except for me. "I don't want to be out here alone on your couch. It feels weird." She shrugged, her voice wavering when she said, "It's okay. I understand that it's like this with us. It was nice, but I'm going to head off to bed now." Her voice pitched and her lip trembled.

"What do you mean, 'It's like this with us'?" I asked, a bite to my tone.

Raven stood up and grabbed her clothes from the floor. "It's fine, Cameron, really. I'm tired and I don't feel like having this conversation right now." She took a few steps away, but before she got too far, I clutched her wrist and hauled her back to me. I wrapped her stiff body in my arms and moved her hair to the side.

"Raven, baby, stop. I don't want you to sleep out here alone, and I definitely don't want you to go sleep somewhere else."

She looked up at me, her eyes watering before a few tears fell down her cheeks. "You don't? Are you sleeping out here too?"

I laughed. Did she really think I would leave her out here alone? What kind of man did she think I was? Then it landed on me, heavy and shameful. Of course, she would expect that from me. After the way I had treated her up to now, why wouldn't she?

"Yes, I'm sleeping out here with you." My shoulders fell as I made my admission. "I know that I jerked you around and haven't given you much of a reason to trust me, but I promise I'm not really that guy. I was struggling when we first met." I shook my head. "If I'm being honest, I still am. I've never intentionally hurt you, but I know it still hurt. I'll do better, I swear. But right now, more than anything, after what we just shared, I need to be close to you."

Her eyelashes fluttered as she looked up at me. "Can I ask why we aren't sleeping in your bed?" She bit her bottom lip, her large brown eyes fixed on me. Expectant, waiting, coaxing my truth out of me.

My body stiffened. I felt it, the pain of those last years, the darkness of that final night. Poison coursing through her veins, the veins I filled for her, the ones I may as well have split open and bled dry. This perfect girl, this pure innocent woman, had no clue who I was or what I had done. I'd never slept in that goddamned bed again. I avoided that side of the house like a plague, sure that Callie's ghost lived there, haunting me, reminding me of my every failure.

"I haven't slept in my room since..." My voice cracked, the words hovering in my throat. Her face softened in understanding, and her body relaxed into me, telling me that she knew what I was about to say. Except she didn't know. I took a deep breath.

"I don't really spend much time on that side of the house at all. Sorry." I hung my head as all the reasons why I had pushed this woman away came flooding back. The memory of that fateful night was crystal clear in my mind; it was pure torment.

"It's okay, Cam. You shouldn't have to explain or apologize. I'm sorry I got upset. I didn't even think of that. I can be so thoughtless sometimes. I mean, I knew you had a wife."

I cupped her face with my hands, all of her beautiful wrapped in all my dark.

"You aren't thoughtless. I may not know you that well yet, but I know you're good." I kissed her lips. "And beautiful." I kissed her nose. "And kind." I kissed her neck, and she giggled, raising one shoulder up, creating a barrier between my mouth and her neck. "And ticklish." I smirked.

I let her go and unfolded some of the blankets onto the floor. I sat down and reached my arms out. "Come here."

Raven dropped the blanket she had been wearing and lowered herself to the floor next to me. I nudged her to lie down and then hovered over her, before I moved down to kiss her stomach. She giggled and pulled me up to her before kissing me softly.

"I would love to sleep with you out here. But, *no* tickling," she demanded.

I chuckled. I was sleeping out here with her, but I wasn't making any promises. Seeing her squirm was my new favorite pastime, and I was planning to make her squirm more than she knew.

Chapter 13

Raven

Cameron and I lay face to face on the blankets spread across the floor.

"I really don't know anything about you. Other than you are a single mom, you wait tables, and dance—and I believe you mentioned something about nursing school?",

I smiled. There were two things that I liked about his statement. One, he didn't hesitate when he mentioned that I danced. And two, he remembered that I was going to school. School seemed like such a small thing to a lot of people, but for me it was like scaling a wall to find safety on the other side. Dependence on a man had given me eight long years of trouble and pain. Education was my freedom, along with a few minor felonies along the way. It was the life raft that would take me from the deep, dark waters of my past to the shallow ground of my future.

"Those are all true, except I don't actually dance anymore. That time you saw me was my last gig."

He flinched, his face twisting up into a look I knew all too well. Regret.

"It's not what you're thinking, Cam. I didn't quit because of that night with you. I quit because my school clinicals kicked up, and I really have to focus on school and Zara. Tessa has been amazing to let me stay with her, considering I barely have time to pick up shifts at the Blue Rose anymore between school and being a single mom. But it's short-term sacrifices for the long-term payoff. That's what I keep telling myself, anyway. Money is tight, but it won't always be that way. Dancing was a great way to make decent money for a job that's easy for me."

"When did you start dancing?" Cam asked.

I shrugged. "Dancing is all I've ever done for work, really. I was twenty, a waitress at a club, and I quickly learned to dance from some of the other girls."

"Why dancing?"

I stiffened. I didn't want to talk about this with him or anyone. How did I tell him that I aged out of the foster system with no skills or opportunities, and not a penny to my name? I was homeless and without family, struggling to find steady work before meeting Trent.

"I was good at it, and it made good money. I didn't really do that well in high school, so college wasn't an option. I needed to do something, and I guess you could say I was scouted for a job."

It was a blatant lie. Scouted, ha. More like preyed on. But when it came to my past, the lies rolled right off my tongue as if deception was my second nature. "The owner gave me a job as a waitress first and then when he saw I could dance, I became a dancer. But I mostly worked the stage. Until I moved here, I'd never done much one-on-one or private parties."

"What's a stage dancer?"

I laughed at him. "You mean to tell me that you've never been to a strip club?" I didn't buy it.

His shoulders rose and then fell. "No, never. I was

with my wife since senior year of high school. I didn't exactly have wild nights out with the guys. That kind of place wasn't really my scene, anyway."

I knew his words were innocent, but they still stung. I could feel the redness crawling up my neck. I lifted my chin and scoffed, unable to hide my hurt. "*That* kind of place?" I asked.

"Hey," Cameron said, catching my gaze, "I didn't mean it in any kind of bad way."

I bit my lip and looked away, suddenly very aware of just how different our lives had been. I had never been embarrassed about my job and I wasn't now. Dancing wasn't dirty, not to me. But I knew how other people saw it and what they thought of the women who did it. Sure, men loved us for making their fantasies come to life, but they also hated us for it. We weren't people to them. We were pretty faces with nice bodies that we were willing to flaunt, and most of all, we were their weakness. An indulgence they were ashamed of giving in to.

I inhaled a breath and looked back up at him. "You sure about that?"

Cameron jerked his head back and his eyes went wide. "Of course I am. Raven, I don't care that you danced. Fuck, I've seen you do it and enjoyed the hell out of it. You're strong, but somehow still graceful." He grabbed a lock of my hair and gave it a light tug. "And I'm a muscular guy, but if I tried to swing my ass around that pole, I'd probably break my neck."

At his words, my body loosened, and I giggled. "I don't know, I think I'd like to see you try."

Cameron narrowed his eyes and shook his head at me. "That's never gonna happen, Babe." He said, before running a hand along my arm and coaxing. "Now, will you tell me what a stage dancer is?"

I lifted a shoulder. "It's exactly what it sounds like. It's a girl who dances on stage. Except at my club, that is all I did. I never really worked the floor, didn't do lap dances, and never did private room dances. Like, uh, what I did for you, I didn't do that before. I was, well, am, kinda shy, so the owner decided stage dancing was a good fit. I could go out, do my thing, make some good tips and disappear into the back without having to flirt with anyone for tips."

It was a partial truth. I only did stage dancing because Trent would kill me if anyone touched me. And no, Trent would not kill a paying customer. It was always my ass on the line.

"Don't a lot of men try to grope you?" His question was asked through gritted teeth, and it almost seemed like he was jealous.

"No. It's an elite club with very strict rules, not some small-town seedy place." The lies just kept coming. Sure, the club was elite, and the rules were strict for certain people, but I knew what really went on behind the scenes.

"So why did you choose nursing now?"

Ready to be done with this game of twenty questions I inadvertently stepped into, I ran my hand over my face feeling flustered. Was this how relationships were? Men never asked me questions—aside from a few nice and uncomfortable men whose friends dragged them to the club. I wanted to tell Cameron that I didn't choose nursing *now*. I wanted to explain why it had taken me five long years to complete two years' worth of classes, but I couldn't bring myself to utter the words. I didn't want to hide myself from him—I owed him the truth—

but it was too painful. Saying them felt like bringing the danger closer than I could handle. My life with Trent was a montage of painful memories that I kept buried deep in my bones, and it felt like if I said the words, they would come to life again, replaying like a movie reel, haunting and tormenting me all over again. And I wasn't sure if I would survive it this time. So, I lied.

"When Zara came into my world, I had to slow down and really focus on her for a while. I knew dancing had a shelf-life and being a forty-year-old dancer was never my dream. I don't regret dancing, and I don't begrudge anyone who chooses to do it. But it wasn't my dream. I don't like the constant loud music and bustling activity. I wanted a slower life. And now that I'm finishing up my last few semesters, I'm even more excited." Cameron looked at me like he wanted to ask a question, but wasn't sure if he should.

"What is it?"

"Zara's father. Were you married, or is he in the picture?" he asked hesitantly.

The lies spilled out once again, and I hated how naturally they came. "No, we never married, and he's never been in the picture." It was a half-truth. Trent was not in Zara's life, not even when we were around him. He didn't want a baby, and she was nothing but an annoyance to him. The older Zara got, the bolder and more irritated he was going to get with her, and I could only protect her from him for so long. The thought sent shivers down my spine.

"But it's fine. I'm glad he's not part of her life. Trust me, it's better for everyone." At least that much was true.

"Well, I'm glad you ended up here. What kind of nurse do you want to be?"

"I don't know. My clinicals right now are in a nursing home and I really enjoy that. You don't realize how many elderly folks are left in places like that, feeling abandoned and lonely. It's hard to see, especially with patients whose families never come to visit them. We forget about people as they age, and I think it's just wrong. No one should be made to feel invisible, like they've somehow aged out of mattering. I'm not sure if it's for me long term, but I really like it right now. I have some time to think about it, though."

Cameron smiled wickedly, his eyes glinting with mischief.

"What?" I asked, narrowing my eyes at him.

"I was just thinking, maybe you could combine nursing with one of your other jobs to give the folks at the nursing home something to look forward to every day."

I furrowed my brow in confusion. As the meaning behind his tease dawned on me, I slapped my hand over my mouth and smacked his chest with my other hand, before falling into a fit of giggles.

"I wouldn't want to give them all heart attacks. Besides, I'm not sure how sexy dancing in scrubs would be."

He laughed again. "I think you could make anything sexy, but when I picture you as a nurse, I am seeing something more along the lines of a Halloween costume nurse."

Smiling at him, I shook my head in disapproval. Typical guy. "Ah, of course. I think that sex-pot nurse is generally frowned upon, not to mention highly unsanitary in a hospital setting. You know, crotchless panties are fun for the house, not so much for the nursing home."

"I'm sure the old men would disagree." He waggled his brows.

"Okay, I think you're working yourself into an unrealistic frenzy. Let's move on."

He wore a look of feigned disappointment as he pushed out his bottom lip.

"Please don't dash my dreams. Does it really hurt you to let me have this one thing?"

I rolled my eyes at him. "I think we're done with me for now."

"Oh, baby." He pulled me into him tightly and rolled his hips into me. Oh, this man. "I'm definitely not done with you yet. I'm not sure if I'll ever be done with you. I might just keep you forever." His tone was playful, but his words caught me off guard. Forever. The thought of forever with him was too much to bear, too perfect, too hopeful, too soon.

"We're done with talking about me. Now you tell me something."

Cameron's body stiffened, and he released me, turning to his back and staring up at the ceiling.

"I'm originally from here, but I spent a lot of time in LA for school. I had a football scholarship. Then, after school, I joined law enforcement. Then I moved back here."

I stared at him and then gave him that nod that said *and*? He let out a very small, sad laugh.

"There isn't much else to my story that you'd probably want to hear about."

I stared at him, confused. Was he really not going to mention his wife? Everyone knew he'd had a wife. He knew that I knew he had a wife, so why was he hiding it?

I gave his arm a light squeeze and looked him in the eyes. "If you want, I'd love for you to tell me about her." I shot him a half smile and ran my fingers along his bicep. I wanted him to feel comfortable talking about his wife. I wasn't the kind of person to make a guy pretend he didn't have relationships before me. And Cameron hadn't just had a relationship; He'd been *married*. To his high school sweetheart.

"Not tonight," Cameron clipped out immediately and with a finality that told me to let it go. And could I really blame him? He'd lost the woman he loved. If I knew anything, it was that some things were just too painful.

"Oh, okay," I stammered, dropping my hand from his arm and shrinking back.

Cameron inhaled deep and pulled me to him. "I'm sorry. I just can't talk about it yet. It's too soon."

And that was that. We lay there staring at each other in silence until the night swept us away into a peaceful sleep.

****

Months passed and Cameron Jameson remained a god in the bedroom; that was almost a given. It would have been absolute lawlessness for a man that sexy to be anything but skilled in bed. And while he was the epitome of sex, he was so much more. He was a sweet, attentive, and protective boyfriend.

That's right. *Boyfriend.*

And Zara loved him too. They were wild together. Cameron could match her crazy energy the same way that Tessa could, which gave me a welcome break from entertaining my spirited toddler. Most of their play involved Cameron chasing her around the living room and usually ended with Zara in a fit of giggles over a tickle fight. They were cute together, and I couldn't deny that he was quickly cementing a place in our lives.

I'd also enrolled in Summer classes and on the evenings I had clinicals, Cameron would watch Zara while I went to work at the hospital. I had been shocked when he gave me a key to his place so I could let myself in after my shifts. And I'd been completely smitten on the nights I had come back to him and Zara conked out on the couch, surrounded by stuffed animals and toys, with Maus's head laying over Cameron's lap.

We were good. And when we weren't working or studying, we'd spent the summer months hunkered away at his place or hiking around one of the many lakes around Brook's Falls. But each day that passed without me telling him brought me more and more terror, and the further from the truth I traveled. And the harder it was going to be when the time came. I felt trapped and held back by my own lies, but at the same time, completely unwilling to tell him the truth or let him go. I was in limbo. I was in too deep with him, yet somehow, not deep at all. I managed to skirt around all of his questions about my past for now, but I would have to tell him eventually. I wanted to tell him when everything was done. Except, I didn't have the first clue how to get the ball rolling. It was easier to ignore my past and all the shady things I'd been involved in. What I had done to get us out of Redlands and what I would have to do to be rid of Trent for good, *that* was what kept me up at night. *That* was the stuff my nightmares were made of.

I rushed Zara and myself into Sunshine's, trying to escape the chill in the air. Fall had come fast and my wardrobe hadn't quite caught up yet. Cameron was already there when we walked in. His back was facing us, so I took a moment to appreciate this gorgeous man that I somehow managed to snag. His hair was gelled perfectly today, and it looked like he had just gotten a haircut. There was a war going on between his muscular body and the fabric of his fitted sky-blue sweater, and I would have been completely fine if the sweater lost this battle. The world was a better place when Cameron Jameson wasn't wearing clothes, and that was a fact. I could smell him from where I was standing: the musky scent of his cologne, working man, and cedar. I sniffed the room like a weirdo. Zara finally noticed him and instead of admiring him from a distance, she jumped up and ran.

"Camyun!" She cried, scampering toward him, arms outstretched, ready to pounce.

I watched as he turned around and straightened, his toothy grin widening at the sight of Zara. When she reached him, he scooped her up, tossed her lightly in the air as she squealed, and gave her a little snuggle before placing a kiss on her forehead. She snuggled him back and my heart melted into a puddle on the floor.

"Hey, little Z. How's my favorite princess today?" Cameron carried Zara over to where I was standing, watching their interaction.

"I is so good. I go poo-poo, pee-pee on the potty, and Mama give me a special treat because I a big girl and that's what big girls do, Camyun." I winced a bit, not sure he was ready for poop talk.

"Wow! You *are* a big girl! I knew you could do it. I'm so proud of you. You keep doing big girl things and keep growing bigger and bigger. One day you're going to be bigger than this building."

"Yay!" Zara bounced and wiggled in his arms, but he held tight. Zara pointed a finger at Cameron's face and tilted her head, her sass on full display. "You silly, I not gonna be bigger than dis bilbing. I's be big yike Mommy."

"Big like Mommy, huh? That's quite a challenge." He smirked at me, and I smacked him. "What?" He laughed, stepping back. "You're like five feet tall, babe."

"I am not!" I thrust my chin up to the air in pride. "I'm five foot two."

"Oh, my apologies. You can't forget those two inches."

I snorted in the most unladylike fashion. "Ha, that's what he said." God, I was turning into Tessa.

Cameron lifted his eyebrows at me and shook his head, before leaning down to whisper in my ear. "I would say that I didn't expect that from you, but I know all your dirty little secrets and depraved sex needs now."

I rolled my eyes at him. Although, it was true. He and I did some *interesting* things, things I'd never done with anyone. Ever. He bent down to kiss me, and as it happened, my body tensed as I felt all eyes on us.

Even though we'd been a steady thing for months now, this was the first time we had been affectionate with each other in public since we'd gotten serious. I hadn't considered until that moment how weird this might be for everyone else who had known his wife. How strange it might be for him. How uncomfortable it might be for me because all of a sudden, I felt very out of place and like the other woman. It was stupid, but I couldn't help how my body reacted as he got closer to my lips. A feeling of unworthiness sprung up out of my depths like a monster that had been lying in wait for the perfect moment. Cameron wrapped his free arm around my waist and kissed me gently on the lips, making me forget all about those ghosts.

"My girls," he said sweetly. "Good morning. I missed you last night."

"Good morning, *Officer* Jameson." I raised my brows, alluding to the wake-up he'd given me yesterday morning, one that involved his handcuffs and my blindfold. It was probably against some sort of police code of ethics, but I couldn't let my man get out of practice. We chalked it up to training.

"Mmmm. Baby, what are you trying to do to me in public? You know I can't think about you without waking something else up." He used his eyes to point to his crotch and groaned against the top of my head.

I blushed at his admission and wiggled out of his hold. If I couldn't have him right there and then, I needed to put a little distance between us.

"Right. Let's just get breakfast before this gets out of hand." I fixed my hair and wiped away the brow sweat that had formed from being in proximity with him for just two seconds.

We turned together toward the counter to find Layla and Laurel staring at us. Well, Layla was staring. But Laurel, she was glaring. Layla was also beaming, her broad smile reaching ear to ear.

"Cameron and Raven and Zara! Three of my favorite people. Here. All together. Well, well, well, imagine that!"

Layla was a cheerful, outgoing woman, who I'd come to know as a result of the many hours I'd spent at Sunshine's. If I wasn't there having breakfast with Zara, I was there studying. She and I chatted regularly about a lot of different things, but the one thing I'd never mentioned was Cameron.

I shifted nervously from side to side and smiled back at her. "Morning, Layla. How are you today?"

"Oh, I'm just fine. Not as good as you two seem to be, though." She raised her brows and looked between us. "What is happening here? Or should I say, what has *already* happened here?" she asked with a wink.

Cameron laughed and leaned in. "Oh, I think you know what is happening here, and I'm not sure if you want the details of what has already happened here."

"Cameron!" I slapped his arm, my face heating, as he and Layla laughed.

"Oh my. You're right, I don't need the details. That's what romance novels are for." She wiggled her eyebrows at us. "Now, what can I get for you guys?"

Now was probably as good a time as any to tell Cameron that I had been freeloading off of some secret admirer for months. I wasn't sure how he would take it, and I wasn't sure how I felt about it anymore, now that Cameron and I were a thing. I tapped his arm, getting his attention.

"Uh, Cam?"

"Yeah, baby?" He said in a low, distant voice as he and Zara looked at the food in the display case.

"What do you want to eat, pumpkin?" He asked Zara, as she studied the food in earnest. I pulled on his arm, and he turned to me.

"So, there's this weird thing that I should probably tell you."

He tilted his head, now focused solely on me. I cleared my throat, suddenly feeling like I had been cheating on him somehow or doing something wrong.

"Well, a while ago, someone started paying for my food and drinks here. I don't know who they are, and I kind of gladly accepted it since I have been pretty strapped for cash for, well, always. And I just wanted to tell you, because now that I think about it, I guess it's kind of weird because it could be another guy. I'm sorry. I didn't really think about it." I bit my lip, scared he was going to be mad. And I was slightly ashamed of myself. Layla looked between us with a grin, and Cameron smiled at me.

"Yeah, I know about that, babe."

Wait, what? He knew? Unable to speak, I gawked and waited for him to explain how and *what* he knew.

"Remember when I bumped into you and Zara here the first time?"

"Yes, of course," I answered. I would never forget that day—more specifically, that first night.

"Do you remember yelling at me for slapping all those tickets on you on your first day in town?"

I scoffed, rolling my eyes. "I would hardly call that yelling."

Cameron's lip hitched up at one side and he shook his head at me. "I felt bad and wanted to make it up to you, so I had Layla charge all your orders to me."

My jaw fell to the floor.

"And, sure, I thought you were beautiful and hilarious. That definitely didn't hurt, but I wanted to do something to pay you back for the hardship."

I felt my eyes begin to well with tears. Instead of speaking, because I was certain if I did that the tears would shoot out like freaking water cannons, I nodded. I rolled my tongue around my cheek to stop my stupid lips from quivering. Trying to swallow back the emotion that bubbled up to the surface, I plastered myself against him and cupped his face in my hands. Zara put her tiny little hands over mine as I closed my eyes, because looking at him might just rip me apart at the seams.

"You are too good to us. I don't even know what to say. It may not seem like a big deal to you, but this has been the place where I study. This is where I've been plugging away at my dreams of a better life. And in a huge way, you're a part of that now, because I couldn't afford to do this as much as I do, and I wouldn't have a quiet place to study. So, there it is. Thank you for being an investor in my dreams." I tried to hold back the tears, and for the most part I did good, considering what kind of ammunition I had in there. A few small ones slid down my cheeks, and Cameron wiped them away with his thumb.

We looked at each other, and it was a dangerous look, one that said things neither of us was ready to say out loud.

Chapter 14

Raven

I was on my hand's knees, clutching the cushions of his couch, trying to keep myself steady as Cameron worked my clit from behind. He had two fingers in my pussy, and I was achingly close. I bucked back into him, ready to explode when he pulled out of me and flipped me around so I was straddling him. I loved the way he man-handled me during sex. I got off on it. Heck, sometimes I even begged for it. But at that moment, climbing toward my orgasm, I needed him back inside of me.

I gasped, and an unintentional "No!" escaped me.

Cameron smirked and the moonlight peaking in from the window cast a shadow on his face, making him look just as evil as he was. "Ride my face, baby," he commanded as he pulled me closer to his mouth, my pussy just millimeters from him, his breath warm against me. "Jesus, you're wet. I need to taste that pussy right now. Do you trust me?" His large hands slid up the curvature of my spine, holding me in place while he drew me closer to his mouth.

"Yes. Do anything. Just get back inside of me," I whined, impatient to feel him again.

His lips quirked up and he squeezed my ass. "Okay, filthy girl," Cameron teased, and I rolled my eyes, in no mood for his jokes when he'd just ripped me away from a pending orgasm.

I had never been a prude necessarily, but I also had never done half of the things I'd done with him. With Trent, our sex life, if you could call it "ours," had always been about him. Trent was hateful and greedy, taking and taking, hollowing me out, until I was too empty to protest. But with Cameron, I wanted to do *all* the things, and I knew if he asked me, I'd let him command my body however he wanted. I trusted him. I longed for his touch, and I relished every single thing he did to me and let me do to him.

He finished bringing me all the way to his mouth as he started to lick up and down my pussy. The sounds of his tongue lapping against my skin worked me up. I tensed, holding back my orgasm, wanting to feel so much more before I let go. His tongue worked against me, pushing me closer and closer to the edge. He started to move so hard and fast that I had a difficult time focusing on any one sensation. From behind me, he slid two fingers inside of me, pumping them in and out slowly, and I knew that when he was ready for me to come, he would hit the spot that always did it for me. With his other hand, he slowly moved down my back and down my ass, pushing farther and farther down until he pressed and circled his finger gently around my ass. That was it. I was going to lose it.

"Cameron, that feels so good, honey, so good!" I whimpered loudly, uncharacteristically letting myself go. With Tessa babysitting Zara, it was one of the rare nights we had alone, and we were capitalizing on it.

Every nerve fiber was stimulated, every cell in my body alert and attentive to the sensations being doled out by this generous man. Before him, I didn't know I could feel good in this many ways. My entire body was melting over him as he licked and sucked and fingered me everywhere he could get his hands or mouth on. I was done.

"Let me come, please!" I pleaded with him, now thrusting my hips forward into his face, desperate to get my way. "You're torturing me. Let me come in your mouth. Please. Cam!" Sure, I was playing dirty. I knew that saying the words 'come in your mouth' was not playing fair. He couldn't ignore that request and pretend like it didn't do things to him. But he wasn't playing fair either. He was pleasuring me every way he could without his cock, and I was dying a slow death.

My strategy worked like a charm. Cameron began to devour my pussy. He pushed his fingers deeper inside and began to work me fast and hard. He hit that spot with his fingers, and the floor fell out from underneath me. I fell over a ledge and collided with the moon and the stars, moaning so loud it echoed through his house. My body quaked, chills racing down my spine to the tips of my fingers and toes. I felt it all. I didn't want him to leave any part of my body. I wanted him to keep going because I was certain that if he kept moving, I could come ten more times just like this.

He slowed down, easing himself out of me. The loss of him left an emptiness I didn't want to consider the ramifications of. I fell to the couch on my side, reveling in my post-orgasm ecstasy. Cameron rolled over, half on top of me, his hard cock resting on my thigh, and stared down at me.

"Baby," he groaned. "What was that?"

"Hmmm?" I hummed, fully relaxed as my muscles

liquefied under him.

"Mmm, that was hot. Sometimes I can barely handle the way you make me feel. And just when I think you can't turn me on anymore, you go and do something like that." He brushed a strand of hair from my face and pressed a lingering kiss to my temple.

At his words, my heart fluttered, and I pressed into him.

"I need to be inside of you. Now, Rave," He whispered, his deep, rough voice commanding my body.

My pussy throbbed, and I looked up into his gorgeous eyes. "You know I want that."

He didn't wait for me to say more. He pushed himself up, hovering over me, and shoved my knees apart with his legs. I was waiting for his large cock to spread me open and slam inside of me. He liked it like that sometimes, hard and rough and fast. And so did I.

Except he didn't move.

"Are you okay, Cam?" I asked.

Cameron's blue eyes flickered as he leaned down and pressed his forehead to mine. "Yeah, babe, I'm good. With you, I'm better than ever, actually."

My heart squeezed and his simple, affirming words filled me with hope. He peered deep into my eyes as he lowered his thick length down to my entrance. I was already soaked, and he could easily slide in fast and hard. Instead, he lined himself up at my opening and, ever so slowly, he thrust inside. I turned my head to the side, unsure I could even process all of the emotions swirling around inside of me. Cameron grabbed the sides of my face, his elbows rested on either side of me as he held me. He held my gaze.

"Look at me," he demanded.

And I did. I looked at him. I was terrified of what I saw in his face, scared of what I felt. We watched each other as he slid in, so slowly that I felt every single inch. My eyes widened at the feel of him, my breath hitched at the sight of him. Intense blue eyes gleamed and his jaw was tight. Desperation and longing filled the space between us until it was suddenly snuffed out by the closeness of our connection.

He left nothing of himself out, fully seating himself inside of me from tip to root. And then he froze, buried so deep, I could feel only him. And then, we fell. We both saw it, our bodies fused together in something much more profound than simply sex. Awareness began to rise up from inside of me, and a small tear fell from the corner of my eye.

I hoped he missed it. I didn't want to explain why I was crying during sex. I didn't fully understand it myself. But I knew he saw it, because he leaned down and kissed the tear from my face as he pushed deeper into me.

I gasped into his ear, and he whispered into the side of my face. "I want you to feel everything, Raven. You and I are more. I think we always have been. I'm feeling it all too, baby." He captured my mouth with his and brought me into a passionate, slow kiss that matched the speed of our bodies. "Do you feel that like I do?"

"Yes," I whimpered, because I did. I felt it all, and it was killing me and reviving me at once.

"Just like that, babe." He moaned into my mouth. I wasn't sure either of us knew what we were feeling or how to articulate it. "Raven." He growled my name as he grabbed my hips and started pushing harder into me. Each thrust was harder than the next until he was slamming into me, our sweaty flesh smacking together, his body pounding against mine.

"Christ, baby. I—"

"Cameron, don't stop, don't you dare stop."

"Never," he ground out as he pulled out of me and turned me onto my belly.

Before I could even consider the loss of him inside of me, he slid back into me until all I heard was the sound of him cursing as he buried himself inside.

"Need you to come," He grunted. "Now."

I happily gave in to his demand. I lifted my hips from the couch and pushed up into him, taking every last inch inside of me. Cameron grabbed my thighs and thrusted into me. His body was tense, and I knew he was barely hanging on. And he wouldn't have to hold on for long. Between the way he felt inside of me and the emotions he stirred up in me, I lost it. My pussy clenched and convulsed around him. And seconds later, I felt the pulsing of his cock as his warm cum shot deep inside of me.

Cameron groaned, holding me to him, still lightly thrusting, milking his pleasure and mine, until the bittersweet end.

I was shaking and exhausted, ready to collapse when he rolled to his side and brought me with him, his semi-hard dick still inside of me.

"Cameron," I whimpered, unable to move.

"Raven. That was everything. I, I," he stammered. Was this it? Was he going to say it? I wanted to say it. I had said it in my head to him a thousand times. I wanted to hear him say it, but if we went there, I would have to tell him everything, and I just wasn't ready. So I interrupted, spewing out the only thing I could think of.

"I'm starving!" I blurted out, mustering any remaining energy to speak even though the last thing I wanted to do was move.

Cameron chuckled. "Yeah? Okay, babe, you lay down. I'll clean up and make us some food." He pulled my hair back and kissed me on the cheek before carefully sliding out of me. I whined my displeasure.

"I hate when you're not inside of me." He leaned over me, his hard body hovering over my back.

"I don't ever want to be without you, Raven. You're mine, baby."

"I am. And you're mine."

"Yes, I am."

And I knew right then that I had to tell him. It couldn't wait any longer. I just didn't know where to begin.

****

Cameron

"Hey, baby, I'm here. You girls ready?" I hollered through the screen door.

"Hey, *honey.*" Tessa's mocking voice came from the kitchen.

"Oh hey, Tessa. I'm here to pick up the girls."

Tessa popped her head out from the kitchen. "Geez, come inside, Cameron. Don't stand out there like a weirdo."

I opened the door and went into the kitchen where Tessa was standing, wearing an apron and high heels. Underneath it was some sort of very revealing lingerie. I didn't spend too much time looking before I realized what she was wearing.

"Jesus, Tess. What are you doing?" She laughed as

198

I shielded my eyes like I was looking straight into the sun. The last thing I wanted was for Raven to think I was creeping on her best friend, or any woman, for that matter.

"Calm down, tiger. This is not for *you*. I've been known to dip my toes in different waters if someone really, really special comes along, but I've always had a stronger preference for women. No offense, but ew. Not enough *this*." She made the universal sign for boobs by cupping her hands and placing them in front of her chest. "And too much of this," she said as she stroked an invisible penis.

I rolled my eyes at her and folded my arms over my chest, my body wooden and uncomfortable. I didn't know how to take this woman sometimes. I kept my face turned away as I spoke to her. "I didn't think you were hitting on me, but a little warning about your clothes, or lack thereof, would've been nice."

"Oh, right. Sorry. Let's try it again." She was mocking me. "Come in weirdo, I'm in the kitchen making half-naked sex stir-fry for my girlfriend. Is that better?"

"No." I deadpanned. "But what in god's name is sex stir-fry?"

She tilted her head to one side and pointed at me with a spatula. "Ugh, you have so much to learn. Well, as you know, I am a terrible cook."

I nodded, because it was true. Tessa had trouble boiling water.

She continued. "And as you also know, my girl works hard and deserves to be taken care of. I can't cook to save my life, but I still want her to know I care, so I figure if I make this disgusting rendition of a stir-fry but look so hot that she forgets about dinner and moves straight to the sexy part, I'm golden. By the time the sex is over, and Cameron, it *will* be a while—because oh, lawdy, Mika, the girl has stamina. I don't know what you and Raven have going on, but just know that if you *ever* need tips, you know where to go."

I blinked, wondering how those two polar opposites had ended up together. I knew that if I dared asked Mika anything about her sex life, she'd tell me to piss off. Mika was a private person, unlike her spitfire girlfriend, who freely discussed her personal life. "Anyway, I'm hoping it works. I don't know if you can cook, but if you want, I'll let you know if sex stir-fry is a go."

"Okay, well, thanks." I pulled at the collar of my shirt, wishing I had waited in the truck.

"Sure." She shrugged. "When we have it as good as you and I do, we gotta pull out all the stops."

"Hey, honey. Hey, oh geez, Tessa, what are you doing?" Raven slapped a hand over her face. Then a smile formed as she peeled apart the fingers over her eyes and looked at Tessa through them. Raven pressed her lips together and then giggled.

"I'm cooking," she said with narrowed eyes.

"I see that, hun, but why aren't you wearing clothes?"

Tessa dropped her head back and rolled her eyes. "Mika is coming over."

Raven paused before her eyebrows shot up to her forehead. "Aw, babe, that's cute! Are you trying to be, dare I say it, *romantic?*" She threw a hand over her heart, and Tessa scoffed.

I chimed in. "No, babe, she's trying to—"

Tessa cut me off, her nose scrunched as she shot me

daggers. "I'm trying to be romantic and cook, yes."

"That's so sweet. Isn't that sweet, baby?" Raven peered at me, her eyes full of hearts. She had no clue.

"Camyun!" Zara hugged my leg, burrowing her face into it. My heart squeezed. This kid was everything. She was a spark of energy and light. A tornado of giggles that zoomed out of rooms as fast as she zoomed in.

"Hey, little Z!" I grabbed her up into my arms. I would normally give her a little toss in the air, but she buried her face in my chest for a snuggle. Zara was bundled up today. Her chubby cheeks were popping out of a big, puffy jacket that was zipped up to her face and had puppy ears coming out of the top. Zara put her head up and squeezed my face, her eyes wide with excitement as she spoke a mile a minute.

"We going to a festival, Camyun! I a puppy, yook at me." She pulled the ears of her coat up. "Puppies go woof-woof just like Mausy. It cold outside, you have a jacket? Mommy say I need a jacket, and so do you!" She pointed her chubby finger at me and booped my nose as she said it. "Mommy say I be a good girl, and I get a special, special treat!" Zara bounced in my arms and squealed in delight.

This little girl had completely won my heart. Hell, even if she wasn't good today, I'd get her whatever she wanted. I was creeping into dangerous territory with the new girls in my life, and as much as it terrified me, I couldn't stop.

Zara released my face and surveyed the room. When her eyes landed on Tessa, she pointed and kicked her legs excitedly.

"Babing suit! Aunty Tessy, you go swimming? Where Aunty Mika? She gon swim too?"

"Oh yeah, you know Aunty Mika loves to swim!" Raven covered her mouth and snickered into her hand, then pulled on my arm. "Come on you two, let's get out of here. Aunty Tessa has to prepare for the big…swimming race." Raven shot Tessa a mischievous look and laughed. "Good luck, I hope you get the gold!"

Tessa pursed her lips and tossed her hair. "Raven, please, you know I *always* get the gold."

Raven laughed and then proceeded to push us out the door. We buckled Zara up in the car seat that I'd purchased recently. We had been spending so much time together lately that it only made sense for me to get something for my truck, rather than uninstall and install Zara's seat over and over. When Zara was situated, I snagged Raven and carried her around to the back and set her down on the bed of my truck. I grabbed her thighs and pulled them apart to nestle myself between them. She wrapped her legs around me and tipped her head back to look up at me.

"I'm really glad I have you girls. You know that right?" I asked and then kissed her before she had a chance to reply.

When I pulled back, Raven's face was soft. She closed her eyes for a moment and breathed in. Opening them, she said, "Yes, I think I am starting to get that."

"Good." I kissed her soft lips again. This time, Raven parted her lips, and I explored her mouth with my tongue for a few glorious seconds. Raven squeezed her legs and lifted her hips to press into my growing erection.

"No, baby, you can't have this right now," I admonished her, after giving her one of my own thrusts.

Raven scoffed at me and smacked my chest. "Tease!"

I unpeeled her legs from me, lifted her up by the waist, and set her back down on the ground. "Get in the truck." I ordered. As she narrowed her eyes at me and turned around to walk away, I couldn't help but land a hard smack on her cute ass. "That's for turning me on."

She whipped around and stalked toward me, her eyes wide, before something flashed across her face, and her lips pulled up to form a smug grin. When she got to me, she reached out with one hand and ran the tips of her fingers along my waist and swayed her hips side to side, her other hand playing with her hair as she lowered herself. When she was eye level with my crotch, she peered up through her lashes and bit her lip. "And that's." She purred. "For." Raven let her head fall back and her mouth fell open. My pulse quickened with the thought of those plush lips wrapped around my cock. I lurched forward just as she backed away and shot up to standing. "Turning *me* on!" She tossed her hair back, lips pursed.

"Raven," I warned, my jaw tight and nostrils flared. "Get in the truck before I do something I'll regret." I lumbered toward her and with a shriek followed by giggles, she ran away and jumped into the truck, slamming the door before I could get to her. She smiled at me from inside as I narrowed my eyes on her, trying to hold back a laugh of my own. This woman was already under my skin and knew how to drive me crazy in all the right ways.

****

The annual Oktoberfest was busy, with plenty of people coming in from out of town. The town council had decided years ago that investing in an Oktoberfest would be profitable in more ways than one. Not only would it bring visitors to town when tourism was down, but it would introduce more people to Brooks Falls in the hope that they would come back in the fall for the foliage or the winter for the snow. It was just one of the many attractions that kept our little town from becoming another forgotten, run-down place in the middle of nowhere. The streets were filled with vendors, many of them local craftspeople and artists. Several of the dance studios showcased their kids' skills, and we even had a stage with a group of older folks performing traditional German dances.

"You girls hungry?"

"Starving!" Raven held Zara's hand as we meandered through downtown, stopping at every booth.

"Let's find some food for you, babe. I can't have you wasting away and losing that ass of yours," I teased. Raven's half-smile was anything but happy. Her lips pulled tightly together as she turned her head away and stared off into the distance. I opened my mouth to ask what was wrong, when she perked up, gaze focused on the booth in front of us that had little knit hats and crap.

"Oh, can we look?" Raven squealed and Zara chimed in with a few small jumps and a, "Yes, yook!"

They hurried over and Raven immediately fawned over the items. "These are adorable." She looked between a bunch of hats and the woman at the table.

"Thank you, dear. I started making them when my grandbaby was born and never stopped. I had so many hats and I thought, why not?" The woman laughed.

"How old is your grandbaby now?" Raven tilted her head, her eyes glowing.

"Oh, he's five now. Much too cool for wearing these now." I walked up behind Raven and placed a hand around her waist.

"Hey Ms. Bensley," I said, making my presence known.

A smile spread across her face, and she pointed a finger at me. "You know to call me Lillian." She scolded. "How are you, dear?" She asked as she hustled around the table toward me. She hadn't changed a bit since I was a kid or since the last time I'd seen her. Lillian had always been a free spirit and even though she'd aged, her green eyes still sparkled with youth. She wore a floor-length, long-sleeve dress and furry boots with fake rabbit tails pinned to them.

"Get over here and give me a hug!"

I released Raven and met Lillian where she stood waiting. "Wow, look at you. I think it's been about a year since I've seen you." She winced and quickly changed the subject. "You see my Jet lately?"

"Yes, ma'am, every Friday and sometimes Saturday."

Lillian's face became contorted when she asked, "Did he tell you that he was considering looking back into *that* woman?" I knew who she was referring to. Jet's ex and the mother of his child. "He thinks he should make everything official, but I think he should just let her stay gone. I never trusted her. I wouldn't put it past her to be up to no good! Oh, but who knows, and poor Nash, never having a mother in his life. He deserves so much better, and so does my Jet."

Lillian had openly loathed his ex for their entire short relationship, and I could hardly blame her once I found out all that the woman had been into, and what she nearly dragged Jet into.

"Did he ask you to help him find her?" Lillian asked

with narrowed eyes.

"Yeah, he's mentioned it, but you know I can't use resources like that without opening an investigation." It was true, and if we did that, Jet wouldn't have the anonymity he wanted.

Lillian grabbed my shoulders. "And thankfully you can't. Why in mother nature's green earth he would want to find that woman is beyond me. She was always trouble." Lillian shook her head and breathed. "Well, enough of that. It's good to see you and…?" She raised her eyebrows, motioning at Raven and Zara with a tilt of her head.

"This is my girlfriend, Raven, and her daughter, Zara." I lifted up Zara and pulled a beaming Raven in close.

"It's nice to meet you." Raven shot her hand out and her sweater slipped up, revealing a few of the tattoos on her arm.

Lillian, who was never one to shy away, pushed up Raven's sleeve and held her arm, studying the ink. "Ah, my kind of girl!" Lillian stated proudly. Raven laughed. "I like someone with a story, and I always find that people with tattoos have a good story." Raven smiled weakly. "Well, please, take a look and see if there's anything you like." Lillian released Raven and gestured to the knitwear spread across her booth.

"I love all of them." Raven picked up a small, pink knitted band with a huge yellow sunflower attached to the front of it and held it up to Zara. "But I think I need to have this one. How much are they?"

"That one is $10 flat."

Raven nodded and reached into her purse. Not a chance. I grabbed her wrist and pulled her hand out of her purse.

"I don't think so, babe." I yanked my wallet from my back pocket and pulled out a twenty. "Do you want anything else?"

Raven's head jerked back. "Cam, you don't have to do that. I have money. I can pay for it."

"I know you have money, and I know you *can* pay for it, but you're not going to pay for anything when I'm around. Get used to it, babe. Look around and see if you want something else for Zara."

Raven's cheeks flushed, and her features softened. "No, honey, I think this is good. Thank you."

"I have matching gloves for an additional $10," Lillian said, pointing to a pair of pink gloves with a smaller sunflower attached to where the back of the hand would go.

"Oh!" Raven cried, pressing her hands to her cheeks.

"We'll take those too." I chuckled as Raven looked up at me with something. Something akin to love, and damn if I didn't feel it too. I had almost said the something the other night in a moment of weakness, and after the best sex of my life. But it was too soon, and I think we both knew it.

Raven took the hat and gloves and showed them to Zara.

"What do you think, baby girl? Cameron bought these for you."

Zara jumped and reached out for her presents, struggling to put them on. I lifted Zara, and Raven pulled Zara's dark hair back out of her face and placed the band around her head. The huge sunflower rivaled only the size of her cheeks, and I had to admit, it was pretty cute.

The gloves were harder to put on. Zara squirmed in my arms while Raven giggled the entire time, struggling to get the little fingers in each compartment.

We said goodbye to Lillian, and as we turned around to head to another booth, I saw *her*. She was standing there, for who knows how long, staring at us. Susan. My heart pounded right before it fell to the floor. We both stared back at one another, silent and speechless.

I jumped when Raven touched my arm. "Honey, are you okay?"

I yanked my forearm from her and took a step away. Raven's brow furrowed as she stumbled slightly back. If I hadn't seen the hurt in her eyes, I would've felt it. "Here," I murmured, handing Zara off to her.

"Cameron," Susan said quietly as she took a step in my direction.

I shook my head at her as she took small, slow steps toward me like I was a wild animal. And she was right, I was.

Susan stopped her advance when I took a step back. "Cameron, please?" Her voice broke.

I backed away, the horror of that last night crashing into me like a battering ram, gutting me in an instant.

"No. I gotta get out of here," I managed to push out between mumbled words.

"Please, I need to know!" Susan begged, and I ran from her, from the truth, from the reality of it all, just like I had been doing since the day I killed my wife.

Running from that weak *thrum, thrum, thrum* of a heartbeat, of fingers twitching. Blue lips and black souls. And that final puff of air before she dragged me straight to hell with her.

Chapter 15

Cameron

A knock on the door crackled through the dense fog that only four glasses of bourbon could deliver. I stumbled to the door, eyes out of focus, limbs so relaxed I could fall over and sleep for a whole week right on my ugly-ass fifty-year-old shag carpet. I swung open the door and scoffed. "What?"

Raven. She stared at me with those wide eyes, so vulnerable and foolishly lost in me. She had no clue what she was getting with me, and as much as I had tried to be what she needed, I knew was going to mess it up eventually.

"What? Is that all you have to say?" Tears poured down her cheeks. She made no effort to hide her distress.

It clawed at my heart, thrashing that useless organ to pieces.

"You left us there," she said, astonishment in her voice.

"Believe me, sweetheart, is for the best." I slurred. "You're just so fuckin' beaufil. I don't deserve you, Raven. Not a guy like me."

"Cameron, what are you talking about? What happened back there?" She pointed a thumb behind her.

"I did the bes' thing for you, baby. Come in, come in. We can't figh' out here." I pulled her in to the house, tripping over an empty bottle of beer on the floor.

"I didn't come here to fight with you, Cam. I came here so you could tell me what is going on. One minute we were fine, and the next, you bailed on me. What's worse though, you bailed on Zara." She grabbed my face and turned it to her. I swayed, trying to still, trying to focus on her red eyes. "I've watched you walk in and out of my life since the moment I met you. I'm a big girl, Cameron. I can handle that. But Zara? I let you into my life because I trusted you with her. If you're going to jerk both of us around, you can't be in my life. I won't let you hurt her. She was bawling when you ran from us. Jesus, Cam, she was confused, and I felt like such an idiot, standing there alone. We had to walk home. You can't keep doing this. I've let you do it and allowed you back in, but I won't let you do this to her."

"I know." I rocked back, about to lose balance, when Raven grabbed my arms and pushed me to the couch. "But I killed her."

That brutal silence filled the air, the room thick with the truth of what I had done. Raven stared at me in disbelief: chest heaving, eyes wide open. Did she really want this? Did she want to know who I really was? Because it was now or never for her to leave. Once the levee burst with all that I was holding in, it wasn't going to stop.

I laughed. "Pancreatic cancer. You would've thought that was what took her down. Two years of fighting it. Two of the longes' years of our lives. And in the end, she beat it but lost anyway."

Raven swallowed heavily but stayed completely still.

I shook my own head in disbelief, trying to make

sense of what happened. "She beat it. She beat cancer. Hurray, righ'? Yep, we were all naively celebrating, so happy for her, for us. We were so happy that she could live again, and we could finally move on. Have some kids, travel the world. Goddammit!" I picked up a bottle on the table and threw it across the room. It smashed against the wall, shattering into tiny pieces. Just like that. So quickly things could be destroyed.

Raven jumped and gasped out a breath. "Cam, don't do that. Please. Please calm down." She placed her hand on my arm gently, but I yanked it away. Her touch was like a deep, visceral burn that I felt in my bones.

"Don't touch me."

Raven's chin quivered, but still, she didn't move. She would leave soon, and it would be for the best. I looked away, my thoughts turning inwards as the room darkened around me. My voice cracked, and the breath was torn from me when all I could see was Callie's ghost.

I had been glad to be getting out of there for a while. Planning that trip was my last-ditch effort to hold our marriage together. Cancer had plowed through us like a tornado, but the debris left in its wake, that toxic sludge that I never expected, is what really did us in.

After six months of additional treatment after the cancer, I had just wanted an end to it. I wanted to see my wife again, to be around the woman I married. Not the lying, cheating, stealing woman that was so desperate for a fix that she'd do anything to get it. I didn't know this woman.

Our trip to Europe, to everyone else, had been a celebration of our anniversary. But Callie and I had really been celebrating her release from the addiction center. I hadn't seen her in twelve long weeks. Weeks that I wished I had missed her, but all I had felt was relief. It had been a break: from searching the entire house every day, from finding pills that weren't hers, from constantly wondering if she was lying to me, and if every time she stepped out of the house wondering if she was looking for that same high. That feeling she had been chasing for years.

I inhaled a shaky breath, my gaze still locked on Callie's ghost, as the truths I'd buried with my wife came spilling out. "We went to Amsterdam on our first stop," I told Raven, my vision blurring as tears filled my eyes. "Callie was a teacher. She taught history at the high school. World War II was her favorite period to teach, so she insisted the Netherlands be our first stop. She wanted to visit the Anne Frank House. I was so jet-lagged from the flight that when we got there, all I wanted to do was sleep. Callie was too excited to sleep, so she told me to rest and that she'd go explore the city alone for a while."

****

"Cameron, Cameron, wake up." Callie shook me from my slumber. I woke up feeling like I didn't know what or where I was; my body's clock was clearly off by at least by a full day.

"Hey, baby. What time is it?"

Callie's eyes were blood-shot and wild with excitement. "It's one in the morning. The city is amazing, Cam-Cam. It's freaking amazing! I loved it out there! I went to this club and it was crazy, so many lights and people and music that pulsed all the way to my toes!"

Oh yeah, she was wild with something all right. I knew I shouldn't have let her go out alone. I knew it and I'd done it anyway because I was tired, something I couldn't afford to be anymore.

"Cal, babe, are you all right?" Six months we had been dealing with this, and I still didn't know how to ask what I really meant. Are you strung out? Are you high as a kite?

"I am so good, Cam-Cam! I'm great!"

Yeah, she was strung out. I reached for her hand, not knowing what to say, not having the first clue how to deal with her anymore. Her hand was shaking, tremors rocked up and down her arms. "Babe, did you take your insulin today?"

"What?"

"Your medicine. Did you take it today?"

"You know, I don't think so. I completely forgot! With everything I had to see today, it must've slipped my mind."

We stared at each other, unspoken words between us, countless lies and constant pretending. She was okay, and I was ignorant. That's what we were playing.

"Why don't you let me give you your medicine, baby? You're shaking pretty bad."

"Yeah, okay, sure, yeah, yeah, sure. I'm going to go unpack it from the bathroom and get it ready."

Callie scurried off to the bathroom with that look in her eye. That look I'd come to know like a part of my new wife, where her sole focus had become the fix. Anxiously awaiting the next before the current one had even dissipated.

She returned with her insulin needle all filled up and ready to go. She was shaking way too much for me to let her do it herself. I injected it into her side. Immediately, her eyes shut and her head fell back as a sigh escaped her lips.

"That better, baby?"

Callie fell onto the bed, her limbs splayed out like a starfish. Completely relaxed. I lay down next to her.

"Much better, Cam-Cam."

I ran my fingers through her hair. The distance between us had grown wider with each passing day that this felt like the most intimacy we had shared in months.

"You want to change into your pjs?"

"Neh…" Callie's words came out garbled and nonsensical. I pushed up onto my elbows. Her eyes rolled around in her head, her skin pale.

"Callie…Callie! Wake up, baby, wake up!"

Foam bubbled from her lips that were now tinged with blue as her whole body jolted and tremored as if it was trying to extricate her soul from her body. It was violence and pure evil, before silence and stillness.

"Callie, Callie, no. No, no, no. Baby no!" I screamed. I begged her to stay, to come back to me. But she was dead, and I was pretty sure she took my heart right along with her.

****

Raven's doe eyes were unapologetically spilling tears as she shook her head. Her hands were wiping away all those tears. A futile effort.

My voice came out robotic, as the haze of alcohol settled as a heavy rock in my stomach. My eyes kept blinking, but Callie's ghost had disappeared. "The toxicology report said it was heroin, cocaine, and ecstasy in her system. The needle I had given her, her so-called medication, was heroin. Enough drugs to power an army." I turned to face Raven. "I delivered her the final dose, Raven. I told her to take the medication, and then I delivered it to her and watched her die. I just watched her. Completely helpless to do anything."

My own reality caught up with me, crushing any remaining pieces of my spirit, sending my mind straight into chaos. I lost it, drunk and crying, feeling too close to the memories I had kept locked away for so long.

Raven's soft voice cut through my loud sobs. "Cameron, no, no, honey, no! It wasn't your fault. You have to see that. Look at me, baby, please." She gently rested her hands on my face, pulling me to look at her. "She was sick, Cameron. She had an addiction. It wasn't your fault. You gotta know that!"

My voice cracked with sorrow. "I gave her the dose, Raven. I held the needle in my hands. And I gave it to her."

"No, you didn't know! How could you have? You were trying to take care of her, make sure she had her medicine. Cameron, that's what's true. That's the reality, honey."

"Don't ever lie to me, baby. I can't take it. Callie destroyed me with her lies. I can't take it." I fell into Raven's lap, my head resting on her thighs as she ran her nails through my hair and down my back. Over and over she did that, all the while telling me that it was going to be okay. I was going to be okay. I let her sweet murmurings calm my racing thoughts and let the stress of the day and the alcohol push me into sleep.

****

Raven

The weight of Cameron's confession was sitting on me like an elephant. My heart broke for him and for all he had been through. I wondered if I could ever tell him what I'd done in the past, and what had been done to me. His words echoed through my head. *Don't ever lie to me,*

I can't take it. I shuddered, because that's all I had done to him. Lie after lie, omission after omission.

He slept all night on my lap, rustling around in a restless sleep. I had a hard time sleeping myself. We had so much to overcome, and he didn't know the half of it. Cameron rolled to one side, his face pressed into my stomach before he groaned and turned to look up at me. His brow creased, and his eyelids shuttered between open and closed.

"Hey." I ran my fingers through his hair, hoping it would calm him the way it did last night. "Good morning."

"You're still here."

"Of course, I'm still here, Cameron." I ran a hand along his jaw.

"Where's Zara? Is she okay?"

"Yes, she's okay. She's with Mika and Tessa. They know I stayed over last night. It was fine."

"Nothing is fine," he rasped out, that same anger from last night in his tone, but instead of pulling away, he leaned further into me.

"It can be. It will be, honey."

"How can you say that after what you know?"

I looked down at him in earnest. I couldn't believe he thought any of what had happened in the past was his fault. "After what I know? You mean the fact that you stood by your wife through cancer and then tried to support her through an addiction? That you were trying to take care of her when she died? And no, don't say that you killed her, because you didn't. I *know* you didn't."

"How can I even live with myself, knowing I was the one who injected the drugs that killed her? How?"

I didn't know what to tell him. I was a hypocrite.

How could I tell him how to stop blaming himself? To stop running from his past, when all I had been doing was running from mine since the day I'd fled Redlands and made a new life in Brook's Falls?

"One day at a time, honey. And I'll be here with you, for you. As long as you want me to be."

Cameron's strong arms wrapped around my waist as he buried his head into my lap. "I'll always want you, baby. Always."

Always. I let the word and what it meant sink in. And it sunk. The word tied around my foot and pulled me so deep that I wasn't sure I would come back from it if I lost him. I had to tell him.

****

Later that day, I pushed my cart through the grocery store. An excited Zara was kicking her little legs in the front while we loaded our cart down with food. Money had gotten tight since I quit dancing, so more often than not, we had to get creative. Tonight's dinner was elevated ramen. In other words, we were eating cheap ramen with some fresh veggies and herbs for extra flavor and a little bit of soy sauce.

I was loading up with ramen and macaroni and cheese when I saw her. Laurel had never accepted that Cameron and I were together, shooting me catty looks any time I looked her direction. I ignored her. I wasn't in high school anymore and wasn't about to fight over a boy. I had plenty of experience disregarding jealous women sizing me up for my looks, and I just didn't have the energy to care. Besides, it wasn't in my nature. I was non-confrontational, and I'd rather shrug off a few harmless slights than create a scene.

"Hey, Laurel." I mustered as much kindness as I

could.

"Oh, hey." She looked me up and down quickly and when her eyes settled on Zara, I swear she gave my baby a scowl. I inhaled a sharp breath, wishing I could have run into anyone else.

"You making a fancy dinner tonight?" she asked, eyeing the contents of my cart.

Okay then. I guess we weren't being nice. I laughed, trying to keep it light, refusing to give in to my annoyance. "Yeah, you know I'm on that student budget."

"Oh. That must be tough living like a poor college student when you're...how old are you? Thirty?"

She was the absolute worst. I swallowed, kicking back the spiteful words I knew would accomplish nothing but making me feel guilty, no matter how good they felt in the moment.

"Around there, yes. But you'll learn as you get older that dreams don't really die at a certain age." I was not going to give her the pleasure of getting to me. I was twenty-nine, so I really was almost thirty, even though I still looked closer to my early twenties. "And it's not so bad. It will be worth having a marketable skill when I'm done, something I can support my daughter with." I smiled gently. I didn't want to hate the woman, even if she made every effort to irritate me.

"Right. Well, I guess Cameron doesn't care if you're eating like a bachelor," she said as she walked away.

I muttered under my breath, "Have a shitty day. I hope your bread turns out to be moldy in the middle."

"Mama, you says a bad word! Aunty Miky tell me you no say dat word, Mama, is bad. Aunty Tessy go timeout she use bad, bad words. Me and Aunt Miky put her to timeout. Say no cake for you!"

Whoops. There I was, being that great mother again.

"Sorry, honey, Mommy shouldn't have said those bad words. You can put me in timeout when we get home." I squeezed her chubby cheek.

I finished loading my cart up with some of the cheapest, but still relatively nutritious, foods I could find. Creativity was my friend in tight times like these and I was no stranger to living on a budget.

I wheeled us to the self-checkout. It was usually faster, and Zara liked to help me scan the items. As I tossed a box of dry spaghetti in a bag, Laurel walked to the kiosk next to us. I kept my gaze forward, focused on scanning and pretending I didn't notice her there. As if the self-checkout screen was the most interesting thing I'd ever seen. She also ignored me. Perfect.

I looked at the total. $73.65. Crap. I didn't think I'd spent that much, and I was positive I only had about $60 to spend on groceries. I wasn't about to pull items out in front of Laurel and ask the cashier to void them. Sure, I was being childish, but I had a little pride. I could pay $60 on my debit and the rest on my credit card. It wasn't ideal. I only used my credit card to pay for school stuff, but it was only $13.65—not that big of a price to pay for a little self-respect. After paying for $60 on my debit, I reached for my credit card, which was buried in the back of my wallet from lack of use. Stuck between two other cards, I yanked it out hard, sending all my cards flying straight toward Laurel.

She turned and glowered before she knelt down and gathered the cards, staring longer than she needed to, narrowing her eyes at them. Nosey.

"Sorry about that. I was trying to get my card and

they just went flying. I can be so clumsy sometimes."

She stared up at me and handed me the cards. "No worries." She lifted a shoulder and turned casually back to her screen.

Well, that was the least bitchy she's ever been. I grabbed my things and shoved them back into my purse before I ran my card, charging the rest of the groceries to credit. Who knew the grocery store could be so overwhelming? Broke people, that's who. But still, I didn't even miss the days where I didn't have to worry as much about my grocery store total or how much I charged to a credit card. Those days of financial freedom were anything but free, and I never wanted to go back to that.

I never would, no matter what the cost.

Chapter 16

Cameron

"Well, she's finally asleep," Raven informed us as she walked down the hall, before making her way to the loveseat and collapsing next to me. After a moment, she sat up, fixing her gaze on Tessa and pointing a finger at her. "This is the last time I let you give her sugar after six p.m." Raven narrowed her eyes. "Unless you want to start putting her to bed all riled up?"

Tessa bit her lip and glanced to the side where Mika was sitting, sipping a glass of wine.

"Don't look at me, Tess." Mika said, averting her eyes from Tessa to look at Raven. "I was on your side, remember? One bite of cake seemed fine, but a whole slice? Mmm, I've spent enough time with Zara to know that with just a little sugar she's like a wet gremlin after midnight."

Raven laughed and relaxed back into me. "And tonight was no exception," she said, lifting her arms and studying her shirt. "I'm still wet from giving her a bath. In fact, I think we ended up with more water out of the tub than in."

I wrapped an arm around Raven and pulled her into me. "I can confirm," I told the women. "It took three towels to clean that floor up."

After Raven had carried an energetic Zara from the

bathroom to the bedroom, I'd gone in to clean up, knowing what a sugared-up Zara was capable of.

"Sorry, hun," Tessa interjected, folding her hands together under her chin and making her eyes wide. "I promise I'll work on it, but she's just so cute when she asks me for things, and I haven't quite learned to tell her no yet."

That, I understood. Zara was smart, and she knew just how to wield her big, brown eyes to get what she wanted. It had worked on me on more than one occasion.

Raven scoffed, but I knew she was being playful when she rolled her eyes with a smile. "I'll believe it when I see it." Her face lit up when she reached out and grabbed the glass of white wine sitting next to my beer on the coffee table. "This mine?" She asked me and then didn't wait for my answer before she took a sip.

"Yeah," I chuckled. "It's for you."

"Thank you," Raven sat back and rested her head on my shoulder. "It's exactly what I needed. Well, aside from a long, hot shower."

My dick took notice and jerked at the thought of Raven, hot and wet. I leaned down and muttered into the top of her head. "Hmm, I think I could help with that. You've been working so hard tonight; you'll probably need some help getting clean."

Raven tilted her head to look up at me. Her eyes had been heavy but widened and sparkled when she quirked her lips, giving me her silent endorsement of the idea. And that's how things had been going for us. We were becoming more and more connected in a way that felt meaningful, and after sharing about Callie, it also no longer scared me. I'd fallen deeper, trusting her and giving in to the idea of building something with her and

Zara.

"All right, lovebirds," Mika interjected. "Ya'll two did the cooking. We'll do the cleaning." She tapped Tessa's knee before she pushed up off the couch and offered Tessa a hand. "Come on, before I lose steam."

Tessa groaned but didn't argue. Instead, she grabbed Mika's hand and stood up, letting Mika pull her to the kitchen.

Just as soon as the two women were busy loading dishes and talking, I ran my fingers through Raven's long hair. My cock snapped to attention when her head fell forward and she moaned her approval. Winding my hand in those soft strands, I pulled her head back, exposing her throat. She whimpered and her lips parted. My cock strained in my pants. She released a small puff of air when I bent down to kiss her neck, gliding my lips over all that sweet, soft skin. She smelled so good that I wanted to bathe in her scent, the smell of whatever coconutty stuff she used in hair with the mild floral aroma of her perfume. I worked my way up to her ear, breathing her in as I went.

"Raven, Raven, Raven." Her name was a prayer, a plea on my lips, a placeholder for the one thing I needed to say.

She released a breath. "Cameron," she begged, just as anguished, just as telling as the way her name fell from my lips. I knew we were both falling. The truth I had unloaded on her a few nights ago had only drawn us closer, pulling us deeper into what we were becoming.

"Come on." I grabbed the glass from her hand and set it back on the table, before grabbing both her hands and pulling her up to standing. Without another word, I scooped her up and walked us to the bathroom, closing and locking the door behind us.

I set her down and started the shower, letting it warm up while we got undressed. Raven peeled off her shirt slowly, staring at me the entire time, her perky tits bouncing slightly as she pulled her shirt up. I needed those in my mouth, and soon. Raven unbuttoned her jeans and slid them down, kicking them to the side, leaving her wearing nothing but that little useless strip of fabric she called panties. I stared intently, mesmerized by every subtle curve of her body.

"Now you," Raven said, her low, husky voice grabbing my attention and inspiring a quick reaction.

I yanked the back of my shirt over my head in one swift, hurried motion, and she giggled.

"I don't understand how guys do that. I would strangle myself with my own clothes." Her voice trailed off as my shirt hit the floor. Her gaze swept over my body, darting up to my eyes every once in a while, and then, almost silently, she said, "Seriously? It's just not fair. A girl has no chance when you look like that."

I smirked, feeling confident and loving that she reacted just as helplessly to my body as I did to hers. I wrapped my arms around her waist and pulled her in until she was flush against my chest. Her full breasts were pressed into me, and her warm, silken skin felt so good against my roughness. I drew a long, calming breath and then growled. "These need to come off now." I dipped my hand under the waistline of her panties and worked my fingers down to her slit. She was already wet. I mumbled unintelligibly. "Useless little panties. Take them off before I tear them off."

Raven squeezed her thighs together and whimpered, before stepping back from me. My hand lost its place between her legs, and I groaned, already missing the feel of her. I forgot my annoyance when she slid the thong down her legs and kicked it to the side. At the sight of her glistening pussy, my already hard cock, jolted. "Fuck, you're gorgeous." I took a step toward her and lowered my head until our lips were barely touching. I ran a hand down her back, along the curve of her ass, continuing down and around until my finger was back between her thighs, sliding along her cunt. She was dripping. "And fuck, you're wet," I rasped.

"Mm," Raven moaned and bucked her hips into me. "That's because of you."

"Only me?" I asked, gliding one finger inside of her.

She gasped and dropped her head forward. "Yes, Cam, only ever you."

It felt good to hear her say it, but more than that, I felt it. We belonged to one another. When I closed my eyes at night, she was always the last person I thought of. And when I woke up, she was the first to come to mind. "You're the only woman for me, you know that, right?" I wasn't this guy. This guy that needed to constantly discuss his feelings about a woman. But it was all I could do to stay above water, stay sane, knowing we were on the same page. I knew with the way I was feeling, the woman could wreck me if she wanted, and after all I'd been through with Callie, I couldn't take it. Not again. Not from Raven.

"Yes," Raven whispered and lifted her head so we were face to face again. "And it's only ever been you. It will always be you."

She placed her hand on mine and pressed my finger deeper into her. She was unraveling me with her words, with the way she felt under my touch, and the look in her eye when she said it would always be me.

"Always," I repeated back to her before dropping a kiss on her lips.

I pulled back. Raven focused on my crotch and a pout formed on her face as she pushed down on the waist of my jeans. "Now take these off. It isn't fair that I'm standing here naked while you still have clothes on."

I grinned, suddenly enjoying the idea of torturing her and turned way on just hearing how much she wanted me. "It's not fair, huh?" I asked, working my finger slowly inside of her, grazing her clit with my thumb just enough to tease her. "Maybe you should ask me nicely." I suggested.

Raven narrowed her eyes at me, her annoyance only spurring me on. I was about to open my mouth and taunt her more when Raven's eyes widened, and she smirked. My hand fell away from her pussy when she lowered herself slowly, running a finger down my torso as she went. Raven settled on her knees in front of me. She was face to my crotch when she leaned in and bit the waistline of my jeans.

"Fuck," I whispered, my dick jerking in my pants.

Raven released my pants from her teeth and looked up at me. "That's better," she said, her big, chocolate-brown eyes glinting with mischief. She locked eyes with me and undid the single button before she leaned back in and grabbed the zipper with her teeth. My chest heaved, and it took every ounce of willpower I had not to grind into her face. Then, she threw down the gauntlet, and I was done. I was putty in the woman's hands. Raven's eyes flashed as she pulled the zipper down with her teeth, still staring up at me, while she undid my pants and any control I had left.

"Jesus, fuck." I ground into her face, unable to stop myself.

Raven put her hands on either side of hips and yanked down on both my jeans and my briefs, pulling them down until they were at my feet. I lifted my feet, and with one foot, flung them to the side. They hit the bathroom wall with a thud before falling to the floor.

Raven snorted and her, "Wow, now you're motivated," ended in a stammer when she turned back to face me. She shifted on her knees, her lips parting with a small gasp. My cock stood long and harder than ever. She was lips to tip and practically salivating. And so the fuck was I.

"Should we get in the shower now?" Raven asked my dick. If I wasn't so damn turned on, I would've laughed. Instead, I croaked out a, "Yes."

I was about to offer her a hand when she slanted forward and used her tongue to lick a slow path from the base of my cock to the tip, where she finished with a long suck.

I groaned when she released me, my balls tightening, my cock now dripping with pre-cum. Raven stood up and bit her lip, before smiling and saying, "Now I'm ready," in a voice that sounded way too sweet and innocent for someone who had just licked a cock. But it worked for her. I didn't know how she did it, but the woman made pure evil look cute.

I followed her to the shower, staring at her round ass the entire time. Steam billowed out when Raven pulled the shower curtain to one side and stepped in. I got in behind her, entranced by the pearly rivulets falling down her skin. Raven turned toward me and it was all I could do to hold myself together at the sight of her wet tits.

When she grabbed my bicep and stepped around me, I followed. Unable to tear my eyes from her, I turned with her, until I felt the warm water roll down my back. "I need more of that." Her half-open eyes were fixed in a heated gaze on my cock.

Christ, she was trying to kill me right here in this shower. I tried to play it cool when I grabbed my dick and gave it a stroke. "More of this?" I asked, my voice deep and low as I grunted out the words. "*All* of it," Raven replied.

Too turned on for any other words, I managed to rasp out a, "Yes," the image of her taking all of me in her mouth the only thought in my head.

Raven got closer, and I wrapped my arms around her back and pulled her in. My aching cock was pressing into her stomach, and I didn't know why I was prolonging this. I wanted those lips wrapped around me and now. Instead, I bent down to kiss her, taking her lips in a deep, wet kiss that I felt in my soul. Our kiss reminded why I wasn't in a hurry to get to the main event. Raven and I were connected. It was more than sex with her, it always had been.

She kissed back, matching my intensity. When we broke the kiss, we were both panting, lost to one another. She didn't wait long before she began kissing every part of me, running her lips and tongue down my chest, paying special attention to my abs, as she lowered herself to her knees, water splashing at my back with the woman in front of me like an offering.

She ran her tongue over my tip, swirling the bit of pre-cum that had formed on my cock.

I exhaled a sharp breath and dropped my head back with a moan. "God, that feels so good." She licked from root to tip right before she wrapped her swollen lips around me and slid me into her mouth, sucking and drawing me in.

"Hmm," she hummed, sending vibrations down my dick that made my knees weak. My jaw was tight, and I could feel the heat traveling up the back of my neck when I looked down at her. I must've looked as crazed as I felt, because her eyes flashed when I caught her gaze. Placing a hand on the back of her head, I thrust gently into her mouth, needing more.

Raven whimpered; her sound muffled. I tensed and was pulling back, afraid I'd gone too far, when her fingers dug into my thighs and held me in place.

She lurched forward, and I lost my mind when my cock slid in and hit the back of her throat. "Oh, shit." I managed to growl as she stole a glance up at me. Her movements sped up as she increased the suction, tightening around me like a vice grip. She wasn't being gentle at all, and I loved it.

"Yes, baby, just like that," I groaned, losing myself with every suck. Raven pulled back and released my cock. Her lips were wet and swollen and she was panting for breath.

"Fuck my mouth," she demanded breathlessly, before planting her lips back on my aching cock.

I stilled because, Jesus Christ, she *was* going to kill me. I'd never done that. I'd never been rough with a woman. I hadn't wanted to, that is, until she suggested it and fucking her mouth was suddenly the only thing I wanted.

I started slowly, thrusting my hips gently into her face. After a few tentative thrusts, Raven took control. She wound her little hands around me and grabbed my ass, digging her nails in and pulling me into her mouth harder and faster and deeper.

I groaned, unable to comprehend the sensations: the slick of her tongue, the hollow of her cheeks, and the tightness of her throat.

The intensity was overwhelming, and I turned wild as I bucked into her mouth. Feral, I fucked her mouth as she moaned around me. The vibrations from her sounds sent jolts of pleasure straight down to my balls. Fisting her gorgeous black hair in my hands, I used it as leverage to shove her mouth onto my dick, enjoying how my cock felt sliding down her throat.

"Raven," I gritted out, thrusting erratically without any rhythm, her mouth consuming every inch of me. I watched as I pulled out of her, then slammed back in, disappearing into her mouth. She ran a hand up my thigh and grabbed my balls, tugging them and sending my body over the edge.

"If you keep doing that, baby, I'm gonna come in your mouth," I warned, sounding as savage as I felt. She looked up at me without pulling away, my dick all wrapped up in those lush lips. Jesus Christ, she wanted me to. She sucked and swirled and tugged and worked the base of my cock. I leaned my head back, with my hands still in her hair, and shot my hot cum down her throat as I pulled her as close as I could get her.

"Yeah, that's it. Easy, baby, finish me slow." I groaned while I continued to thrust into her mouth. She released her hands from my balls and the base of my cock. My hands in her hair kept her mouth wrapped around me, slowly and gently sucking me, swallowing every last drop. It felt so good that I couldn't let go. And she didn't stop sucking until I released her. Unhurriedly, she pulled her mouth away, freeing my cock with a pop.

I reached down for her. "No one, baby, no one but you, Raven. You're incredible. That mouth is incredible. I've never done that, baby, and I just—I lost myself a little. I hope I didn't hurt you."

She shrugged. "I've never done that either and I must say, that was really sexy. Everything that you have going on up there and down here, well, it's really not fair to womankind."

I pulled her up to me and kissed that mouth that was just on my cock. I tasted myself on her tongue, becoming increasingly hard with each kiss, the image of Raven on her knees taking me, still playing in my mind.

"No one is as beautiful as you. Sometimes I think you're too good to be true." I told her, when we finally stop to catch our breath.

She looked away momentarily before turning back and looking down between us. "You're, um, again?" she asked, tipping her head to the side. Yeah, after just a few minutes of kissing her, my dick had risen and was ready for round two.

"For you, always." I chuckled and pushed her dripping hair to one side. "Come on, let's get out. The waters getting cold." I ran the back of my hand along the goosebumps that had formed on her arm.

"I didn't even get clean," Raven pouted. But she was trembling, and the water heater in Tessa's old house only had so much to give. And it had given it. Besides, I had other plans.

I grinned, reaching around her to turn off the shower. "You got dirty as hell, though," I teased. "And I'm not done with you."

She bit her lip and her eyes widened. I ushered us

out of the shower and quickly dried us both off, before taking her to the double vanity. I set her in front of the large mirror, enjoying the way her body looked, all naked and wet.

"Turn around and grab onto the counter and don't you let go," I told her

I leaned in and wrapped my arms around her from behind, taking the full weight of her breasts in my hands. "I need to see your perfect ass when I'm inside of you tonight, and I also need to see your beautiful face. You keep your eyes on me, baby, understand?"

I had never been this demanding with sex before, but with Raven, I didn't just want certain things. I needed them, and she gave them freely. Raven nodded her agreement. I lightly clutched her hips while working my cock inside of her, using the wetness around her pussy to slowly slide myself in. She was dripping. I pushed into her, and she leaned her head forward, a puff of air leaving her lips.

"No, I said look at me. Do not stop looking at me. I need to see your face when you come for me."

That earned me the buck of her hips as she stared into my eyes from the mirror. I held onto her tighter, dipping my hand down between her thighs to coat my finger in her juices, then used that finger to work her clit, circling as I sped up my thrusts.

"Cam, that feels so good. Oh, it's feels so, ah!" I drove in as deep as I could, giving her every inch of me. "Baby! I'm going to come."

"No, not yet. You're going to come with me."

"Okay, but then you can't—" She cut herself off with a moan of pleasure. "Can't play with my clit like that. It's too, it's…" She trailed off.

"Oh, I can't?" I asked. "You don't like this?" I teased and continued to work her with the pad of my finger.

"Cameron! I…" She moaned and bucked her hips back into me, driving my dick deeper. I rode her harder, not giving her any reprieve..

"You can let go now. Come with me, Raven." I commanded. I rode her until I felt her pussy tighten around me. "Let go, baby. Give me everything. Come all over my cock." She thrust back into me, and with a whimper, she let her orgasm roll over her.

"Yes!" she whimpered as my whole body spasmed, and I spilled inside of her with a few final hard bucks of my hips. I clasped a handful of her hair to keep her head in place.

"Do you see us? Do you see this?" I growled, as we stared at each other in the mirror. "So perfect."

"I see it, baby, I see it all, I feel it all."

As we came down from the bliss of the moment, I kept languidly pumping my dick into her, reveling in the heat of the moment. That is, until we heard a small knock on the door. We both looked up.

"Um, Raven, we heard a noise. Are you okay in there?"

Raven shut her eyes and pressed her lips together. Before she could start to ramble the way she always did when she got nervous, I answered for her. "Yeah, Tessa, we are *really* good here."

Silence for a moment, and then a snicker. "Oh, I see. I thought you might've snuck out and gone home. I guess this makes more sense. Well, don't mind me, I'll get back to what I was doing, and you guys, uh, seem like you're done, but—"

"Oh my god, Tessa, go away!" Raven hissed, the apples of her cheeks turning such a deep shade of red, that I couldn't help but laugh at her. Tessa snorted and mumbled something, her voice getting further away until we no longer heard her.

Raven's head snapped up, and she locked eyes with me through the mirror. "I cannot have a conversation with my friend while you are still inside of me!" She whispered harshly.

"Did you want me to get out?"

"No." She whined. "I wanted *her* to get out."

I bucked into her, and she pressed her eyes closed with a sigh. "I'm going to stay with you tonight. Is that okay?" I asked.

"Definitely, but you know we can't have sex in my room. I share a room with Zara."

"I know, why do you think I brought you in here?" I smacked her ass, gave her one final thrust, and then gently pulled myself out of her.

Raven gasped and then frowned. "I still hate when you're not inside me."

"Mmm, don't say that, or we'll never get out of this bathroom," I warned.

She smiled lazily with her eyes at half-mast, and I could tell she was exhausted. I knew she probably had a ton of homework to do and still had to work the next day. I put my underwear on and wrapped her in a towel, then lifted her in my arms. She didn't even protest. She just nestled her head into my chest.

I'd never seen her room before and I was surprised by how small it was. Maus was curled up on the floor next to Zara's small bed, where Raven told me he slept every night. I lay Raven down on her bed. "Where's your clothes, babe?" She pointed to a three-tiered plastic dresser in the closet. I pulled the top one open and found some panties and a large shirt. She was already half asleep, so I carefully unwrapped the towel from her, exposing her naked body. She shivered a bit.

"Shhh, it's okay, baby. I'm gonna get you dressed." I worked her legs in the underwear and put the shirt over her small body. She was completely out as I lay down next to her and pulled her into my chest.

"I love you, sweetheart." I kissed her forehead and fell into a deep, peaceful slumber.

****

"Morning, Laurel!" My voice surprised me. I sounded chipper. And I couldn't remember the last time I felt this happy.

"Hey, Cameron." Laurel glanced at me with an expression I couldn't really read. "I was hoping you would come in soon. Do you have a minute?"

I did have a minute, but I really didn't want to give it to her. I just wanted to get my coffee, pick up my girls and get on the road. "I really don't. I surprised the girls with a weekend at a cabin in Deerfield Bluffs. It'll be Zara's first time playing in the snow, so they're pretty excited to get going. I do need to grab some things, though. I'll get a—" But before I could finish, she cut me off.

"Well, it's kind of about them."

Them? A flash of heat shot up the back of my neck and my eyes went wide. I don't know why it made me mad, but I also didn't know why Laurel had anything to say about Raven. And more so, she definitely shouldn't have *anything* to say about Zara. That really pissed me off. I furrowed my brow. I knew Laurel was sour about me seeing Raven, but I figured she would have let it go by now.

"I'm not sure what you would have to say about them," I told her through gritted teeth. She was getting on my last nerve and I knew that whatever was about to come out of her mouth was rooted in jealousy.

"It will just take a second. As a friend, I promise." She held up her hands, the look on her face uncharacteristically unreadable.

Still, I wasn't buying it. "As a friend? You mean a friend who's hated my girlfriend since the day she and I met?" I didn't have time for this, and she was ruining my good mood. I searched the room for Layla, hoping she would run interference so I could get my coffee and treats and go. But she wasn't anywhere to be seen.

"Cameron, listen to me, please. I learned some things about Raven that you really want to know."

I pressed two fingers to my temple and inhaled a deep breath, ready to walk out without buying anything if she didn't stop. "I'm not sure there's anything you could say that I don't already know. I'd really just like to get my order and go."

"Oh. So, you know that she's a stripper?" she blurted out loudly, her head cocked to the side in a way that said, "got ya!".

Okay, if I wasn't pissed before, I was now. I motioned for her to step around the counter and away from listening ears.

"Jesus, Laurel, of course I know that she *was* a stripper. Not that it matters, nor is it any of your business, but she doesn't dance anymore. She's a nursing student. I would appreciate it if you didn't spread Raven's personal life around, though."

Laurel nodded her head in that way that someone nods when they know something you don't. I rolled my eyes and threw up my hands, realizing it would be better to skip breakfast today. She'd already put a damper on my happy-go-lucky mood. I was about to walk away when Laurel opened her mouth again.

"Sorry, Cameron, I didn't realize you knew everything already and that you'd be so chill dating a married stripper. I mean, *ex-stripper.*" My heart stalled in my chest, and I froze. Time stopped as I tried to make sense of what I'd heard.

"What did you just say?" I whispered, the weight of her words sitting on my chest like an elephant.

"Ex-stripper?" she asked.

My face was red-hot. "Why would you say that Raven is married?"

She raised her brows at me. "Because *she is*. But don't search her fake name if you'd like to find out for yourself. You might want to use her real name," she said with a bitter, mocking tone that was nearly lost on me. *Real name?* What was she even talking about?

"Why are you making up lies about my girlfriend?"

She placed her hand on my forearm and softened her voice. "I'm just trying to be a friend."

I yanked my arm away from her. "By spreading rumors about my girlfriend?"

"They're not rumors, Cameron. Ask your girlfriend, Danica Petrov, about her husband."

No. No way. It wasn't true. There was no way any of this made sense. I searched Laurel's eyes, desperately looking for some sign that she was making this all up. I didn't find it.

"I saw it for myself at the grocery store, Cameron.

She dropped an ID card on the ground, and it was her picture, but not her name. I thought it was odd, so I looked her up. And Danica Petrov, from Redlands, has been married for eight years."

"No. You're making this shit up. You're lying. You're lying." I repeated, thinking if I said it enough, it would be true. Like the words could somehow get rid of the sudden sinking feeling I had in my stomach.

"You know I'm not. Why would I lie about this? I'm telling you, it's true. And if you don't believe me, all you have to do is a quick Google search like I did. Geez Cameron, you're a cop. You could find that information out easier than I could."

I was done with this conversation and I was done with her. She had crossed a line. I shook my head at her and stormed out. Laurel was the liar. *Raven wouldn't lie to me. There's no way she is married.* And a different name? That was nuts. She told me specifically that Zara's father wasn't in the picture and that they never married.

I sat in my truck, Laurel's words swirling around over and over in my mind, settling in, taunting me. *Danica Petrov.* No.

"Fuck!" I slammed my hand on the steering wheel, confused and frustrated, knowing that the only way to get these doubts out of my mind was to prove Laurel wrong. So, I did the one thing that I knew would ease my mind. I drove to the station.

I quickly exchanged hellos with the guys on duty and hustled to my desk. A feeling of unease washed over me as I pulled up a court records database.. It was easy enough to find out if someone was married or divorced. It was public record. I could get this one question answered real fast, assuage my worries, and move on with my life. I knew that Raven had grown up and moved here from Redlands, so I at least had the county name, which would make the rest easy to find.

I felt guilty, like I was betraying her trust. But I also knew that if I didn't ease my mind, the thought that Raven was married, that she was someone else entirely, would be hanging over me until I got an answer. The fact was that if I didn't get some answers now, it would ruin our weekend away, and I wanted to give Raven and Zara the best of me. That was what I told myself to justify looking into Raven without talking to her first.

I navigated to the San Bernardino County website and typed in the name Laurel had given me. I only had to press the search button and it would tell me that Laurel was full of it. Except, I had this gnawing feeling in my stomach that made me want to get my ass out of here and talk to Raven. I held my breath, hit search, and closed my eyes for a minute. There was just one record available for a Danica Petrov. My breath hitched in my chest. I needed to cool it. For all I knew, it wasn't even her. I decided to check the DMV database for her. Maybe there would be a picture. I searched for Raven DeLuca, finding her picture quickly there. I felt my whole body relax. She didn't have a fake ID; she was in the database as Raven. Raven was real.

Don't do it. Just leave now and forget you were ever here. But I knew I had to do it. I hit the keys, spelling out Danica Petrov. One record in California. I selected the name and waited for the picture to load. When I saw the picture staring back at me, the entire floor dropped out from underneath me. It was her, it was Raven, or Danica, whatever her name was. Shaking, I navigated back to the county database and clicked on the one record for Danica Petrov.

Chapter 17

Raven

"Hey girl! You look happy today." Tessa spun into the kitchen, a bright smile on her face. She was looking more carefree than ever since Mika had come into her life, but today she was glowing.

"So do you." I tipped my head down, studying her.

"Yeah, well Mika and I have the entire house alone for the whole weekend this time, so we're probably going to do it everywhere."

"That's sweet, hun."

Tessa furrowed her brow at me. "Sweet? I just said I was going to have sex with my girlfriend all over the house. I didn't say we were going to braid each other's hair and talk until the sun rose." Tessa blushed, and I couldn't help but laugh at her.

"I know, but I can tell that you and Mika are really something. She makes you happy, and that makes me happy to see. It's cute, and you two are definitely relationship goals." I drew a heart in the air for her. "Can't I just be happy for my best friend?"

Tessa rolled her eyes and swung open the refrigerator door. She grabbed the milk, untwisted the cap, and opened her mouth to say something sassy no doubt, but then she closed it. Pouring some milk into a mug for her coffee, she faced away from me. I could feel her hesitation sifting through the thick air.

"I am happy. I haven't been this happy with someone since, well…I've never been this happy with someone. She makes me feel good about myself, and I think she actually might like me for me. Mika and I get each other."

I was stunned by her admission. Tessa had a big heart, and she would do anything for the people she loved, but one thing she was not was sappy. She rarely let people into her little world, and when it came to love and romantic relationships, she kept it pretty superficial. In fact, love had always been something she reserved for friends, not lovers.

"Wow, Tess." I choked up a little, feeling the weight of her statement, knowing that if she said all of that, she meant it. "That's pretty big." She turned around and wiped a stray tear from her face. "Oh no, babe, why are you crying?" I asked her, frowning and wiping a few of my own tears away.

"They're stupid happy tears, happy tears! What a load of crap." She hiccupped a few breaths before shaking her head and throwing her arms up dramatically. I smiled at her. Tessa deserved the world. She was the best person I knew.

"You deserve everything good, hun. And Mika likes you because she's smart and knows a good thing when she sees it."

"And she has really, really good taste," she added, narrowing her eyes and sneering at me, like I had just insulted her. "She's hot as sin, Rave, but so am I. Don't tell me that's not part of it."

A teary laugh caught in my throat, because it sounded like a joke, but I knew she was dead serious.

"Obviously. I didn't think I had to say it." I hugged her to me, beaming with pride. "Thanks for sharing that with me. I know talking about your feelings isn't really your thing."

Tessa waved me off and took a sip of her coffee. "Don't get used to it. I'm close to my period and you just caught me at a vulnerable time, you sneaky little bitch."

I giggled, glad to see that her sarcasm was still fully intact.

"So, you're going for a weekend away with Cameron? That's a big deal." Tessa spoke into her coffee.

"Mmhm," I hummed the words and sighed dreamily, thinking of how much fun this weekend was going to be.

"Babe, I know it's not my place to say anything, but being the wise sage in relationships that I am all of a sudden, do you think maybe it's time to tell him?"

I stiffened, becoming anxious at the mere mention of it. The thought of telling Cameron sent a whirlwind of emotion through me. Fear that pummeled me like a crashing wave: suffocating and devastating, scattering me across the expanse. Just the thought of Trent sent me into a panic, but speaking of my life with him, my life before Brooks Falls? Impossible. Tessa was right; I was going to have to tell him. I owed Cameron the truth. I just didn't know how to tell him.

I was a ticking time bomb and eventually I would explode, destroying everything around me. Knowing this made not one shred of a difference. I was paralyzed when it came to this part of my life. Not even Tessa knew the full extent of it. Sure, she knew enough to know that Trent was bad news, but she was smart enough not to press for information. And even if she had, what would I say? How could I take that kind of pain and transform it into words? Trent had done permanent damage and if Cameron knew, he wouldn't want me. I was damaged goods and no one, not even Cameron, could love me.

I inhaled deep, shaking the heaviness away. "Tessa, I just want to be happy right now." It was full of guilt and hesitation and remorse, because admitting she was right and having the strength to do anything about it were two very separate things.

"Oh sweetie, I want you to be happy. You know that, right?"

I nodded at her, my throat tightening as I held back a sob.

"I just don't want the shit to hit the fan with Cameron. You two are getting serious." She threw a hand up and sighed. "I know you'll figure it out, hun. I'm sorry I brought it up. I'm a hormonal disaster right now. Just go enjoy your weekend and forget about me!" She forced a laugh, and I faked a smile.

Still, she was right. I had a looming feeling that this entire bubble I'd built around myself could pop at any second, and then I would be back to square one. Or worse. Shaking off those feelings and reminding myself that I was about to go have a wonderful weekend away with my man and my little girl, I stood up.

"I'm going to wake up Zara and get her ready."

"Are you mad at me?" Tessa asked, her voice pitched.

"Of course not. I know you mean well and I know without a doubt that you love me more than you love anyone else, except for Mika." I raised a brow and grinned over my shoulder as I walked out of the kitchen toward my room.

Tessa hollered at me from the kitchen. "I *never* said I loved her!"

I scoffed. She was lying to herself if she believed that. She did love Mika, and I could see it plain as day. I would let her live her little lie for now, because in all fairness, she was letting me live mine, even if my lie was far more dangerous.

****

A loud banging on the front door startled me. I popped up from the floor, where I was playing blocks with Zara.

"I'll be right back, honeybun." I kissed Zara on the head, but she was too engrossed to care.

I swung open the door, surprised to see Cameron. "Hey, I thought you weren't coming for another hour," I said, my words tapering off when I focused on him. "Honey, are you all right?"

I reached out to touch his arm, but quickly retreated when he spoke. "You're fucking married."

I swayed, his words knocking me back. It wasn't a question, but a statement. My lips went dry as the desert and my thoughts shifted into overdrive. My chest tightened, and I clutched it, heaving, trying to catch my breath while Trent's wolfish grin played on repeat in my head. When I looked up, Cameron was nodding, as if I had given him all the confirmation he needed.

"Wh-what?" I managed to get out.

"You're married, *Danica Petrov*."

That name, that godforsaken name, felt like a curse, like a brick tied to my ankle as I was thrown into the sea. Drowning. I wanted that name wiped from my memory. I pressed my chest as if I could hold my heart in place and stop it from breaking all over again.

I braced myself against the door jamb and leaned over, my stomach turning and my head spinning. I tried to say something, anything, but all I could think was *Zara*. My nerves activated and I pushed out of the door, letting it slam behind me.

"How do you know?" I asked, enraged, terrified, but brazen, because all I could think was *Zara, Zara, Zara*.

Cameron's already clenched jaw, ticked, and anger turned to rage. He scoffed, looking down at me like he finally saw me for what I really was—trash that wasn't worth his time.

"How do I know? I just told you that I found out you've been lying to me, about being married, about who you are, and all you have to say is 'how do you know?' Christ, Raven, or Danica, whatever the hell your name is, you can't be serious?" he yelled at me. But I heard none of what he really said.

"Don't ever call me that name!" I screamed at him like he was the one who had done me wrong. I was spiraling, searching for some sort of anchor in the chaos that was my life. "How did you find out?" I straightened, thrusting my chin in the air, committed to getting answers. I didn't care if I sounded unreasonable. Cameron was the least of my concerns in that moment.

"You're unbelievable, Raven," he spat, tossing an arm out.

I grabbed both of his arms and with all of the courage I could muster, I stared into his eyes and repeated slowly.

"How did you find out?"

He pushed my hands off of him and then stepped toward me. I backed up, not cowering, but not completely unafraid. Memories engulfed me, tempting my body to crumble beneath the fiery gaze of a man, but I fought them. I fought them for her. He backed me up until my back hit the door. We stared each other down, intensity burning between us. But not that beautiful kind that made me forget who I was. No, this was rage, this was darkness. I stood my ground, unwilling to back down. I *would* get answers.

"Tell me, Cameron!" I yelled, just inches from his face.

"Not that you deserve to know anything, but I found out your real name and searched it in a database. Found your picture, your real identity. Jesus, Raven, I saw your marriage license, Trenton and Danica Petrov, married for eight goddamn years!" My stomach knotted at the sound of those two names together, coming from his lips.

"*How* did you find out my real name?"

"I don't owe you answers! You're in the wrong here, not me!"

"Tell me!" I screeched, the sound so shrill that I didn't even recognize my own voice.

He inched toward me, his hand on my hip, his voice low. "No, you don't get to be mad about getting caught in a lie. Several lies."

His touch threw me, and I shrunk back a little. "It's not what you think."

He was so close that it hurt. I wanted to throw myself into his arms, feel his strong body wrap me up, hear him tell me everything was going to be okay. But that wasn't mine to have anymore, not after today.

"It's not what I think? Are you married? Is your real name Danica Petrov? Or am I the crazy one here? Don't you dare stand here and lie to my face anymore! Christ, that was the one thing I asked you not to do." The air was thinning as I felt my world, the one that had become my safe haven, close in on me.

"Yes, I am but—"

He cut me off. "Have you filed for divorce?"

"No, but—"

He cut me off again. "Then it's exactly what I think. You've been married this entire time and have lied to my face about it. Repeatedly. You're someone else entirely! I don't know anything true about you. In fact, I know so little that I didn't even know your real name!" He bent down into my face. "You're a liar."

The words sent prickles of pain throughout my body. He pushed away from me and ran his hand through his hair, pacing back and forth, his eyes red and bloodshot, his face pale.

"What is this? Are you some kind of criminal?" Yes. But I wasn't about to tell him that. "Do you latch on to vulnerable widows and pretend to be whatever you are, then extort them for money or favors?"

My mouth fell to the floor. Was he serious? I had never asked him for a single thing.

"What money? What favors?" I asked, angry at the accusation. "I would never do that. You know me, Cameron. What have I ever asked you for?" I cried.

"I know you? Don't you think that if I knew you, I would have known your name? And don't you think that if I knew you at all, I would've known that you were *married*? I don't know you. I've been replaying these past few months over and over in my head, and I realized you've never told me much about your life before you moved here. Every time I brought it up, you changed the subject. Ha, I'm the idiot here, aren't I?"

He slammed his hand against the wall. My eyes were spilling over, blurry with tears, as I reached out for him. He stepped back, his face screwed up when he looked at me.

"If I knew you at all, I wouldn't be standing here dealing with the realization that I've been loving some other man's wife and kid, playing house like all *this*," He swept his hand in a wide circle, "Belonged to me!" he shouted, but all I heard was love.

I was sobbing, my heart torn in two, my soul laid out bare. "You love us?" I asked through tears. He stopped moving and looked at me, all that betrayal and hurt staring back at me.

"No. No, Raven. I don't love you. I loved the person that I thought you were. I don't love you because I don't even know you. And I don't love you, because I don't deliberately step in the middle of a fucking marriage."

I couldn't breathe. He was slipping away from me and I was powerless to do anything to stop it. "Cameron, please," I begged. But he had no interest in what I had to say. And the truth was that I had nothing to say. I wasn't going to tell him, or anyone, my story.

He wasted no time in issuing one final blow. "You're not the person I thought you were, Raven. You're just another disappointment, and I don't ever want to see you again."

And then, he got into his truck and drove away.

He'd loved me. Loved. I had lost the one man who had ever truly loved me. The only man that I ever loved. Once again, I was shattered, wrecked, strewn across the horizon and my pieces would never be recovered again. And I had no one to blame but myself.

****

"Thanks, Maisy," Tessa hollered as she backed out of our driveway. I waved my hand, mustering as much pep as I could.

"Bye-bye, sweety, have fun. Be good!" I called out to Zara, who waved back at me and squealed through her partially rolled down window.

"Bye Mama, bye Aunty."

I smiled big at Zara, who had been excited all day about her sleepover at Maisy's. One more fake smile before I could take the night off from pretending. I'd been faking it all week, refusing to let my breakup with Cameron bleed over into Zara's life. She didn't deserve to pay for all my mistakes. When Maisy's car was no longer in sight, I let my face fall and I turned to Tessa.

"Do you really want me there with you?" I asked glumly. "I mean, look at me, I'm a depressed mess. I'm just going to ruin your night."

"Yes, Rave, you said you'd go, and of course I want you there. Mika and I both want you there. You need to get out of this funk, babe. It's not good for you, and it's not good for Z." She stroked my hair tenderly, passing over the knots that had formed from a week's worth of neglect.

"Come on, time to get ready," Tessa said as she ushered me toward the house.

"Fine. But I'm not dressing up. Can you just get me some comfortable clothes to wear?" Moisture pooled in my eyes. I was on uneven ground and still hadn't been able to get through one day without crying. My throat was raw, and my heart was heavy. "If I must go, I don't want to wear anything sexy."

Tessa chuckled as we stepped through the door. "Okay, babe. I'll get you my most comfortable potato sack. How's that?"

"Perfect," I told her, falling onto the couch and sinking in.

I eyed her as she ventured down the hallway. I didn't trust her not to try to put me in something cute, but when she went to *my* room, I was relieved. I didn't have anything in there that she liked. She pulled out my softest and most cozy ankle-length skinny jeans, a short baby-pink Henley tee, and my Toms. When Tessa threw my army green baseball hat on the pile, I shot up to sitting with my eyes wide and my mouth ajar.

"You really do love me, don't you?"

She snickered and rolled her eyes at me. "Obviously. I just gave you a baseball hat to go out in. Besides," she frowned as she studied my hair, "I'm not sure that even I can work miracles on that bird's nest you are currently calling hair. So, a hat will have to do."

"I think you're my soulmate."

"I know," she said and then blew me a kiss. "Now get dressed."

Later that night, I sat at a table in the bar and watched my friends. Mika and Tessa were annoyingly adorable. I wasn't a jealous person, but I couldn't help the twinge of envy that niggled at me when I saw them together. They were uncomplicated, their dynamic easy and carefree, filled with affection. I wanted that. I'd had that. And even if Cameron and I had been a rollercoaster of ups and downs from the very beginning straight to the bitter end, I'd enjoyed every second of the ride.

Shea's was busy like usual. Jet managed the bar like a pro, doling out drinks and chatting with patrons who accosted him. Mostly women. He was very handsome in that brooding, tattooed kind of way that women liked, so

I understood the appeal. Jet glanced over and winked at me, waggling his eyebrows. I rolled my eyes and looked away, ready to make faces at him from across the bar. It was pointless. He was already surrounded by a new group of women by the time I looked back.

A few men looked at us, but thankfully, next to Tessa, I was pretty invisible. She was wearing a short, black dress that hugged her ample curves and showed off her breasts, which she had plenty of. Mika was quick to sense the room and wrapped an arm around Tessa, claiming her and letting everyone know to back off. I sighed. If I was going to have to watch them all night, I would need a few drinks to take off the edge.

"Hey, ladies, I'm gonna get us some drinks." I announced. "What do you two want?"

"Corona with a lime for Tessa, and I'll have a double vodka cranberry."

"Oh, I love when you order for me. So domineering." Tessa ran her finger along Mika's lips before planting a soft kiss on them. Cue internal eye roll. Cute couples in love were so not my jam right now.

"That's what you always get," Mika retorted. "But noted on the dominating." She twisted her lips into a smirk and Tessa leaned in closer.

I forced out a tight-lipped smile and nodded. "Got it. I'll be right back."

When I got to the bar, Jet was surprisingly not covered in women. "Yo, Raven, how goes it?"

"It goes," I said, unable to hide my sadness.

"Yeah," He drew out. "Sorry to hear about you and my dickhead friend."

I figured everyone knew by now, especially those in Cameron's inner circle. But it still hurt. I lifted one shoulder, hoping to downplay the hurt and failing miserably when I stammered. "It happens. People break up all the time."

Jet leaned in, his voice somber. "You were good for him, Raven. The shit he was going through the past few years with his wife, I don't know if he told you, but it messed him up. He hadn't been happy in a long time. Until he met you." He slapped a hand on the bar top. "I don't know what happened between you two, but I bet he'll come around."

If he thought Cameron would come back around for me, then he definitely didn't know what had happened between us. At least I could be grateful for that.

"Thanks." My voice broke and thankfully Jet took my order and made the drinks without any more mention of Cameron.

I carried our drinks back and quickly downed my own vodka cranberry, and in a matter of thirty minutes, I had downed one more. I didn't usually drink hard liquor. I was a wine girl. So, after two doubles, I was drunk. It was exactly how I wanted to feel. My head was fuzzy, my limbs were buzzing, and for the first time since everything had gone down, I wasn't whining about Cameron. I was feeling loose and more easy-going than I'd felt since we'd broken up a week ago.

I was laughing at a story that Tessa was telling about a student in her aesthetician class when my eyes caught a couple walking into Shea's. Tall and muscular, with thick, dark hair styled flawlessly on his head. The most beautiful man with gray-blue eyes that made me stupid. My laughter died in an instant and my heart fell straight to my stomach when I saw who he was with.

"Oh lord. What is he doing here?" Mika asked no

one in particular.

"Wow, he has a lot of nerve." Tessa mumbled, before turning to me. "Ignore him, babe. He's not good enough for you, especially if he's here with another woman already." Tessa studied them. "Hold up. Hold the hell up! Is that…?"

"Yup," I clipped.

Tessa stared at me open-mouthed for a few seconds before Mika asked. "Who? Who is it?"

"That's bitch-brows from the coffee shop, babe!"

Mika squinted in their direction. "*She's* the one who's been chasing after him?" Mika asked, raising an eyebrow. "And what are bitch-brows?"

Tessa tilted her head to the side and her eyes went wide. "Mika, baby, really? I have so much to teach you. But I can explain this one easily—over tweezed and over shaped. You know, the brows that make women look like cartoon villains."

Mika shrugged. "Gonna be honest, Tess, and I hope I don't offend your profession, but I don't notice that shit." Mika pulled Tessa onto her lap. "Except yours, of course."

"Guys, focus!" I scolded.

Mika snapped up, her attention on me. "Right, so bitch-brows is in love with Cameron, and he brought her here?"

"Yup. She's the one that he brought to the Blue Rose, pretending they were on a date." My soul ached thinking about Cameron. My thighs clenched too, and I loathed that I had absolutely no control over my body when it came to him.

"She's the worst!" Tessa exclaimed.

"Pretty much." I breathed out, wishing I was

anywhere but here. I hadn't seen him for a week, but thoughts of him still consumed my every free second. And now, here he was with not just any woman, but Laurel.

I looked between Tessa and Mika. "Let's forget they are even here." I begged, wanting them to understand that I needed all talk of Cameron to be over for the night. "I'm gonna get some water."

Tessa stood up. "I got you, babe. You hang here and relax."

I spent the next twenty minutes pretending that I wasn't staring at Cameron and Laurel. It still stung seeing them together. What did they even have in common? He was Cameron, funny and good-natured, and she was Laurel, the living worst. I watched in disgust as she inched in closer and closer to him as time wore on. He didn't seem to notice, but she had scooted her chair so close that she was almost between his legs.

I knew Jet saw it too when I looked over and he was glaring at them before he glanced at me. I was feeling every painful emotion known to humankind. I wanted to punch Laurel right in her smug little face. I was also lamenting my clothes, because if Cameron did happen to notice me, I didn't even look my best. I snorted when Laurel stood up and reached over Cameron to grab something and shoved her boobs right in his face. And that was it. I snapped.

"I'm done with this. I'm not gonna sit here and just watch them," I announced to the empty table.

Tessa and Mika had been dancing for the past five minutes, and I was alone. Alone with my drunken plans. I drained my glass of water and slammed it on the table like it was a shot of vodka. I stormed toward the door, on a mission to get as far away from Cameron and Laurel as possible. I wasn't going to walk by them. I wasn't going to say anything. I would walk out and forget any of it ever happened.

Except my feet had a mind of their own and guided me right to the bar where they were sitting. Laurel and her stupid face were laughing—that was all I could see. It was all I needed to see. I breezed by, slapping Laurel's beer with my left hand, and flipping a middle finger with my right.

"Fuck you both," I said confidently as Laurel gasped and jumped.

It felt better than I thought it would. For five whole seconds, I felt like a champion. Then, the reality of what I had just done came boomeranging back and hit me.

I shoved my way out of Shea's and headed in no particular direction. "Shit, Shit." I pressed my eyes closed momentarily and sped up.

I didn't have my car, and even if I had, I couldn't drive. I didn't drive even after one drink, but this time I was actually drunk. I had no plan, just me and my loud-mouth and my reckless middle finger. I hurried down the sidewalk, heading absolutely nowhere. I'd walk far away from Shea's and call an Uber.

I heard heavy footsteps approaching behind me. I walked faster. The footsteps neared, and I could feel my assailant closing in on me. And as luck would have it, I was passing a dark alleyway. *Oh good*, I thought, *a nice quiet place to be murdered.* I felt a large hand wrap around my arm and yank me into the darkness. I squeaked, the presence overwhelmed me, and right away I knew it was him.

"What was that back there?" Cameron growled at

me.

I made a weak effort to pull my arm from his grasp, but he held tight. I opened my mouth to apologize or spit more venom. I wasn't sure which. But before I could, he grabbed my face and crashed his mouth to mine.

I wished I could say that I tried to resist, but my body had a will of its own and wanted what it wanted when faced with this man. I was powerless to stop it. Cameron gripped my hips and backed me up to a wall, taking my mouth like it was the last time. Maybe it was. But I couldn't think of that. All I could think of was just how much I had missed this. How much I missed him.

After I wrapped my head around what was happening, I threw my arms around him, pulling him tighter to me. I was thinking that maybe if this kiss never ended, he would never leave me again. When he broke our kiss, I stumbled, clambering for a breath.

"Cameron!" I was panting.

"Do you want me to stop?" He was frantic, unhinged in a way I'd never seen him. Not dangerous, but tortured.

"No," I breathed out against my own good sense.

"Unbutton your pants."

"Wh—?" I started to speak, but he silenced me with a kiss.

"Please." He bit down on my bottom lip, his voice cracking with the plea.

I started to unbutton, but I fumbled, shaking with the anticipation of feeling him again. Cameron didn't wait for me. "Now!" He growled as he tugged my pants down with my panties in one quick motion, before yanking my shirt off and knocking my hat to the ground.

"Jesus. Jesus, Raven, I missed this body." Cameron gritted out the words as his eyes roamed over me. He unbuttoned his own pants and pulled them down just enough to free his cock. My mouth watered at the sight of his thick length bobbing between us. He bent down to kiss me and slid two fingers inside me, moving them in and out for a few glorious seconds.

"You're wet," he said into my lips.

I whimpered. "Always for you."

Cameron groaned and stroked his thick cock. I watched him, loving every second of it, until my body begged for him and I was consumed with need.

"Enough," I said, reaching out and palming his length. He released a long breath and his head fell back, before he snapped back and clasped my waist in his hands.

"Yeah, enough," he said between heavy breaths. Then, he lifted me up and, on instinct, I wrapped my legs around him. Dropping his forehead to mine, we locked eyes. I felt the tip of his cock push through the opening of my pussy, and that was all it took for me to lose it entirely. I dug my nails into his upper back as he pushed himself inside of me.

"Ah!" I whimpered into his mouth, the suddenness of being completely filled with him bringing me both pain and intense pleasure. Cameron pulled almost all the way out of me. Torture.

"Do you want this?" he growled at me.

"Yes! Yes, I want it." My voice broke, and I pled with my eyes.

"How badly do you want it, baby?"

"Cameron you're all I want. I miss you, please just come back to me." I begged, unsure if I was asking for him right now or forever.

One side of his mouth quirked up into something

between a grimace and self-satisfied smirk, right before he thrust into me, his powerful hips rocking into me with abandon, just like he used to do. I let out a loud moan as he pulsed in and out of me, going fast and then slow, hard and then soft.

"Cam!" I gasped for air, so full it took my breath away. "I might. I think I'm gonna—"

"Come for me, baby," he said, his blue eyes warm, looking at me the way he used to. "Give me everything, I need this from you. I need everything from you."

I was too far gone to think about the regrets that might follow. Those were problems for future Raven— she could deal with the poor choices of my present self.

"Cam, honey!" I cried as my pussy convulsed around him. I sunk my teeth into his shoulder, quieting my moans as I rode the high of my orgasm. He rocked harder and harder, his bucks becoming more erratic, until he released a deep groan, his hips jerking and twitching as his cock throbbed and I felt that warm liquid spilling inside of me.

"Yes, baby." He ground out with one last harsh thrash of his hips before his movements slowed and I felt one final quake of his body against mine. "Why do you do this to me?" he asked, his voice cracking.

I rested my head on his shoulder, savoring the closeness. Just a little longer. Don't let me go.

He shook his head and set me down. I didn't know what to say as we put our clothes back on in silence. I moved toward him, wanting to touch him, but he put his hand on my arm, keeping me in place.

"I'm taking you home." His face was granite and his tone was sharp. I stared back at him, studying his hardened features that minutes ago bore a resemblance to the Cameron that was once mine. My shoulders sank. The moment was over and once again, my bad decisions would bite me in the ass.

Chapter 18

Cameron

What had I just done? I was a dirtbag of the worst kind. When Laurel invited me to Shea's to talk, I had been feeling desperate. She was the only one who knew who Raven really was and I needed someone to talk to about it all.

As soon as we had arrived at Shea's, it was clear that she only wanted one thing from me, and it wasn't to support me. Laurel let me know that she thought Raven didn't deserve someone like me while she not so subtly tried to worm her way into my space. I had been getting irritated with her and was about to end the night when a pissed off Raven blew by: her brown eyes filled with fire, her full breasts bouncing as she sauntered by with all that sass. Of course, my dick took notice.

It had me all kinds of hard, imagining that filthy mouth all over me, sucking me, kissing me, loving me again. And more than that, I missed her. I missed the warmth of her smile at the end of a long day together. I missed the sound of Raven and Zara giggling in the morning over tickle fights. And I missed that attitude of Raven's—the very same one that mouthed off to me and Laurel just moments ago.

I'd had no choice but to go after her. I was drawn to her as if on a string, tied to the woman that had me all messed up. Laurel had called out as I left to chase Raven. It had been useless to try and explain. There was no logic when it came to Raven and I. It just was. Nothing had changed. From the day we met at Sunshine's to now, I couldn't stay away from her even if I tried.

Now this lying, perfect, confusing woman was in my truck, her messy hair covered in a hat, still looking all kinds of gorgeous. Neither of us had said a single word since we left the alley. My head was still spinning from what I had just done. I was a cop. I had arrested people for indecent exposure in situations much tamer than what just transpired between us. I was losing my grip, and it was all because of her.

I looked over at her and her lip was quivering. Tears freely fell down her puffy red cheeks as she stared out the window. Even crying, she was the prettiest woman I'd ever seen. How was I supposed to stay away when all I wanted was to take her face into my hands and kiss away every last tear? I wanted to hold her and tell her that I still loved her. I wanted to reclaim her entire body as mine and forget about everything else. But dammit, she was still married, and I still didn't know the first real thing about her.

"Stop crying, please," I said as we pulled up in her driveway.

Running the back of her hand over her cheeks, she sucked in a sharp breath. "I can't." Her voice faltered. "I haven't stopped crying since we broke up."

I dove right in, asking the question I still needed the answer to. "Why didn't you tell me you were married?"

She glanced at me from the side of her eyes and then shook her head no.

"Are you in the process of getting a divorce?"

Please say yes. Just say yes. I wanted the answer to be yes—why wouldn't it be? No other answer made sense. She looked at the ground.

"No. I can't. Not right now."

"You can't what? You can't tell me anything? You can't talk to me? You can't get divorced? Say something, Raven."

I was giving her a lifeline, tossing it out to her freely, and I desperately wanted her to take it. I needed her to take it.

"Yes. All of that. I just can't, not now. I still love you, and I still want to be with you. I just need time to get my life together." Her voice was sullen and low.

I placed my face in my hands, trying to understand and hoping she would take this olive branch. I was giving her a chance to come clean so we could be together.

"You can't or you won't?"

"Both?" She said it like a question. "I will, but not now. It's about more than you and me." She wasn't even looking at me, her words sewn together in one long string of monotony spoken from so much distance. She was staring off, playing with a strand of her hair, like none of this mattered. Like the truth didn't matter.

"Get out of my truck."

Her gaze snapped to me, and I hoped that the only thing she saw in it was coldness. I had to do it. I had to shut myself off from her for my own sanity. I couldn't go down this path again, trusting someone who refused to be honest with me, waiting for them to undo me again and again. Callie pulverized my heart until it was nothing, only for Raven to bring new life to me and crush it all over again. I was done with it all. And if I couldn't be with her, I couldn't be around her.

"Cameron," she said, reaching for me and resting her hand on my hand.

Her touch was electric, sending sparks of life through my entire body. I wondered if it would always be this way. How was I going to survive knowing this woman was out there without me? With someone else? I took her hand and gently placed it back on her lap. It was time to end this for good. Stamp out her flames before she stamped out mine.

"I don't want to see you anymore. I mean it this time. Tonight was my fault, so that one's on me. I guarantee you that it won't happen again. If you see me out, just avoid me and I'll do the same for you. It's not a huge town, so chances are we'll run into each other. But Raven, stay away from me and lose my number. I don't want to see your face if I can help it. Now get out of my truck."

I held my resolve as I hammered her heart right in front of me. Tears were streaming down her face before she said sadly. "You're not who I thought you were, Cameron."

I scoffed at the irony of her words. "Yeah, neither are you."

Raven nodded once and without another word, she was out of my truck and out of my life. This time for good.

****

Friday night came quicker than I wanted it to. I usually looked forward to this night with the guys, shooting the shit and putting back beers, but after seeing Raven at Shea's last weekend and solidifying our breakup, I wasn't in the mood to be here.

"Dude, I heard you broke up with Raven." Bram

slapped me on the back, shaking his head, brow lifted, and for once, he looked serious. "She was a good one. What happened, man?"

"Wait, hold up," Gray chimed in. "You mean to tell me that you cherry-picked that woman right out from under me and now you broke up with her?" He snorted and then shrugged. "Guess she's fair game then."

I stared him dead in the eye, wanting to make my next words clear. "First of all, I didn't 'cherry-pick' her. We already had something going when you met her, dumbass. She made her choice—*me*. And second of all, she is not fair game. She's not a game at all, so you can continue to back off."

"Ah, I see. So you don't want her, but no one else can have her?" Jet asked, playing devil's advocate the way he loved to, always stirring shit up.

"Yeah, bro, you know she and I had some actual chemistry," Gray added.

"Shut up man. You and I both know those two aren't for us. If they were, one would be with me instead of Mika, and the other would be here with you instead of crying over this asshat," Philips said, strolling up with a few beers and inserting himself right into the conversation.

Gray admitted easily. "I know, I know, I just like to give this dickwad a hard time. Especially because what kind of idiot breaks up with a woman like that?"

"A guy who finds out that the woman he thought he knew is married, that's who."

I threw a shot back, hyperaware that the table had suddenly fallen silent. I was pretty sure it felt like the entire bar went quiet, with all eyes on me, watching me, waiting for me to elaborate. What was there to say? I said it all. Plain and simple. Married.

"Whoa," Jet's eyes went wide. "Does her husband live nearby?"

"Nope. He lives in Redlands, where she came from. They've been married for eight fuckin' years." I tossed back a shot of tequila. My second shot. Liquid courage.

"Jesus, Jameson, that for real?" Bram's casual charm was nowhere to be seen, because yeah, it wasn't funny or easy or light, just like everything else in my life.

I hit that third shot, ignoring the dirty look from Gray as I shamelessly swiped his tequila. It went down smooth as water.

"Yea. I gave her everything. Everything." I tossed my hand up and let it fall hard on the table. "After what Callie did to me, I didn't think I had anything left to lose." My voice was strained, the pain of it all coursing through me.

"What does that mean?" Jet asked, his blurry face bouncing back and forth as three consecutive shots hit my blood stream suddenly.

"It means that everyone is going to screw you over eventually, tha's what it means. They're gonna take your broken heart and rip it right out of your chest. But here's the kicker." I swayed side to side and leaned in close, like I had something important to say, and these weren't the drunken ramblings of a broken man. "You won' know it's happening until it's too late, and by that time you're head-over-ass." I slammed my hands on the table, not sure if I was pissed or devastated.

"Hey, man, hey, chill out and slow way down on the tequila." Jet handed me a beer. "Did she tell you why she hid that from you?" Jet probed, his eyes squinted, getting to the heart of the matter as only he could. For such a burly guy, he could sure deal with feelings.

"No. Just said she couldn't talk about it right now."

I took a swig of beer.

Bram cleared his throat, and glanced around at everyone, before looking back at me.

"You ever consider that maybe he's not a good dude? It doesn't make a whole lot of sense that she would leave with her daughter and the guy would never come around, especially if they're married or separated. Don't you think?"

"She lied to me." That was all I said, because he was making sense and I had been so wrapped up in the lie that I didn't bother to understand her.

Jet nodded his agreement and added, "Yeah, people do that when they're trying to protect themselves. I mean, maybe not, but Raven seems like a solid person and it just doesn't add up unless she had a good reason. She's got a kid, man. I know I'd do anything to keep my kid safe—cheat, lie, steal, whatever it took."

"You'd probably do that shit anyway," Gray teased, but I was stuck on my own stupidity.

The room tilted as understanding dawned on me. The hiding away in a small town, the name change, the secrecy. I stumbled to a stand, knocking over a few empty shot glasses on my way up.

"Hey, hold up man, where are you going?" Jet grabbed me by the shoulders.

"I gotta find her. I gotta get to her. Gotta talk to her. I need to do it now." The words tumbled out in one drunken string of nonsense.

"Why don't you come to my office? Drink some water. Calm down a little bit. Then you can give her a call. You definitely aren't driving anywhere right now, but you know that."

"Goddammit!" I clenched and unclenched my fist, needing somewhere to put this rage. I wanted to turn it on myself. I had been so caught up in my own hurt that I didn't even notice the truth that was right in front of me. I was going to fix this. I had to fix this.

Jet steered me to his office, but I couldn't wait. Stumbling along, I reached into my pocket for my phone. I hadn't deleted her number, despite my insistence that she forget mine. Hell, she was still on the list of favorites in my phone. I selected her contact and waited.

Her phone rang and rang, going to voicemail over and over.

I slumped onto the chair at Jet's desk and left message after message. "Raven, it's Cam, baby. Call me back. I need to talk to you."

"Sweetheart, please, I messed up. Call me."

"I love you Raven. I'm sorry, baby. Please answer your phone or call me back. I need to hear your voice."

Chapter 19

Raven

My feet throbbed in my shoes. It was finally Friday, and the weekend couldn't come quick enough. If I thought waitressing was tiring, nursing was exhausting. I spent all week on my feet, retrieving juice boxes and blankets and refilling refrigerators with juice boxes and heated bins with blankets. If I didn't know any better, I'd have thought I was back in the hospitality industry with all the waiting on people I did. Still, I loved it, and I was good at it. I was twenty-nine and finally figuring my life out. Sure, my personal life was in shambles, a special kind of disaster akin to a soap opera, but tonight, I wasn't going to focus on that.

I had just six months left until graduation and it was beginning to sink in that this was going to happen for me. I was just six months away from giving my baby girl the life she deserved, the kind of life that I'd never had. And the best part was that the trauma center in the hospital I was doing clinicals in had an opening. The hospital was twenty miles away in a larger town that I could easily drive to. Though at this point, moving seemed like the better option. I wasn't going to tell Tessa that now because I wasn't sure. I also didn't know if I could stay in Brooks Falls.

Seeing Cameron all the time, especially if he moved

on, would destroy me. I had never known such gut-rending pain. Sure, Trent broke my spirit, but Cameron broke my heart.

I'd spent the past year and a half trying to rebuild myself from the ground up. And the day I left Trent, I had been bold for the first time in my life. When I wrote him that letter, threatening to expose his crimes if he ever came looking for us, I thought the anxiety of what I'd done and the fear of what he would do if he ever found me, would kill me, but I'd survived. Leaving Trent was still the hardest thing I'd ever done, but losing Cameron had destroyed the last bit of me that believed someone out there could love me. I didn't think my heart would ever fully mend from Cameron. I needed to stop torturing myself with thoughts of him, and I definitely wasn't going to spend my thirty-minute commute fantasizing about a man who wanted nothing to do with me.

With my sore foot to the pedal, I pulled out of the hospital parking lot. It was dark out and late. If I'd learned anything about myself during school, it was that I was *done* with night shifts. I had already turned in my stilettos for ugly as hell, but also comfortable as hell, black clogs. Now, I was ready to turn in my night-owl ways for some single-mother daytime hours.

I spent my drive thinking about my future, imagining how I would decorate Zara's room once we finally had our own place and the money to spend. Maybe I'd buy a small house with a fenced yard for Maus and Zara. I day-dreamed all the way home and not only did the drive go quickly, but I felt happy and hopeful.

I pulled into our drive, noticing it was darker than normal. Tessa usually kept the porch light on. She liked to remind me that I was way too clumsy to be walking in the dark, even if I had sturdy, old-woman shoes now. She was such a brat.

There was a slight chill in the air as I got out of my car. An odd, but familiar, feeling swept over me, and a shiver raced down my spine. I looked around as I hurried to the door. Everything seemed okay.

I fumbled with my keys, anxiety rippling through me, when I heard and felt the crunch of glass underfoot. I trembled and my heart raced as I tried to calm down, reminding myself that plenty of teenagers in this neighborhood would think it was funny to take out a porch light or two. I was getting back my bearings and sorting out the keys again when I felt it. A dark presence emerged from the shadows and loomed over me. A hostile energy that I'd know anywhere. Hot breath hit the back of my neck, and before I could scream, a large hand wrapped around my mouth.

"If it isn't my devoted wife." His voice was playful in the way that a lion was playful with his prey before he ripped it to pieces.

Fear tore through my body at once. My heart plummeted to my stomach, and I was suddenly shaking uncontrollably. The hope I'd felt just moments ago was scattered in the wind, floating into the atmosphere like so many of my former dreams. His presence captured me, and just like he always could, in an instant, he tamed me like a caged animal.

"Shhhh, hush, hush. You wouldn't want to wake anyone up and make this uglier than it needs to be, would you, *dear*?"

I had thought that this day might come. I'd always hoped it wouldn't, but I knew that if it did, it was not going to go well for me. I had known the risks, but it had always been the better option, the only option after I saw what he'd done, knowing already who he was. And what had my choices been? Die out here alone by his hand instead of in a house that was more like a prison, with my daughter watching.

My eyes bulged out of my sockets while I gasped for breath under the force of his hand at my mouth. I shook my head back and forth. I was compliant, just like I always was.

"Good girl," he whispered into the shell of my ear. I gagged—his breath stank of bourbon and cigarettes. "Now open the door, Danica. We need to quietly get a few things before we get on the road." His voice was terrifyingly calm, like that stable air right before a storm hits. "You know, you might like to get some clothes, some snacks, our daughter, some *pictures.*" He clipped sharply as he squeezed my mouth in his hand.

I whimpered from the pain of it. My body remembered exactly what he was capable of. I held the memories deep inside, shoved so far down that they had become easy to ignore. Not now though. They rose to the surface, flooding my mind with visions of my former life.

Trent leaned down, nipping my ear with his mouth, his harsh voice a whisper, "You know how to sneak around quietly, don't you, darling? You know how to do a lot of things I didn't know you could do. I underestimated you, Danica. I won't make that mistake again." He pulled my head to the side violently, yanking on my hair and exposing my neck, before he ran his nose up the side.

"Mmmm," I cried, tears trailing down my cheeks, my voice muted under his hands. He kissed my neck, and

I cowered, tremors rocking my body under his violent hold, his unwanted false affections.

"What?" Trent crooned. "You don't like your husband touching you? Maybe you're just tired from all that work you've been doing. But don't you worry, I'll give you a nice long break. Workers' compensation for all the injuries." My eyes widened, knowing he had the power to make that statement come to life.

All hope of a better life drained out of me, and I knew it was over. I tried to speak under his hold, my sounds muffled under his grip. He released his hand from my mouth, allowing me to breathe and speak.

I sucked in air, trying to catch my breath through the panic. "Please, Trent, please. I'll go with you. I'll never leave again, I swear. But please, just leave her here. Then it will be just you and me. No crying babies, no extra messes, nothing to bother you. You'll have everything you want, and I promise, I promise I'll stay." His hand clasped around my mouth again.

"Promise, huh? Like the promise you made when we got married? You're the same trash you've always been since the day I found you, and I never should've given you so much freedom. You're going to pay for what you've done, but first, I need those pictures, you stupid bitch." I flinched. The pictures. If only he knew where the pictures had come from, surely I'd be toast.

"They're in my room." The words came out like a whisper, so quiet I barely heard them myself. It was almost everything I had on him, and it didn't even matter now.

"Well, let's go get them. You can be really quiet when you're sneaking around. I know that now."

"Please. Just leave Zara here. She'll be taken care of

and out of your way. You never wanted her anyway. I'll get the pictures. Just please leave her here."

"And how would that look if my estranged wife came back to me and we abandoned our child? Do you think I became this successful by being an idiot?"

"She'll cry. She'll wake up my roommate."

"Well then, you better make sure she doesn't."

I was becoming hysterical. I would beg, I would plead, I would scream, I would tell a million more lies to protect my baby.

"I'll write a note. I'll tell my roommate that I couldn't handle it, that I-I don't want to be a mother. She'll believe it. She knows what kind of person I am."

"The kind of bitch that leaves her husband!" He gritted out.

"Yes, and her child too," I said, my breath leaving me as I realized that I'd never see my baby again. It didn't matter. *I* didn't matter. Zara would be safe, and that was all I needed. "I'll do anything, please. Just let her stay. I won't contact anyone, and Zara will be taken care of. She's too young to remember me. Please, I swear Trent, I swear, I'll never come back."

I was falling apart. Losing Zara would be the end of me, but the beginning of her, and that was something I could live with. Or die for. Trent pushed my head up and turned me around to face him. Seeing his face again brought every memory to the surface, and I nearly fell over. But for her, I held on. I was staring down the devil, and I had just made a deal with him. One I would not regret.

His shriveled lips formed a wicked smile, that same one he always wore when he was making plans for me. I was filled with dread, but I couldn't think of that now.

"Let's go," he said in that commanding voice of his. I opened the door, praying to the universe that everyone would be asleep. Trent was like a wild animal, unpredictable, and I didn't know what he would do if he was confronted. The house was quiet, and as we made our way to my room, Trent tightened his hand around my throat. A warning.

"Maus, stay," I choked out.

Maus looked at Trent and let out a low growl. But my good boy, who I had trained so well, listened. He stayed put at the side of Zara's bed, his eyes trained on us. I dug out the box where I kept the prints, ready to go if I ever had to use them. I opened the box, my heart sinking as soon as he saw them. I was going to pay heftily for this once he saw all that I had on him. His eyes lit and his lip snarled when he saw the stack of photos. He snagged the box from me and as I turned to look at Zara one last time, the tears streaming down my face, he pulled me away from her. My baby. My world.

"Hurry the fuck up," Trent demanded, his jaw tight as he pulled out a pen from the breast pocket of his perfectly tailored suit. I nodded, gesturing with my head to the kitchen, where we kept a pad of paper in the junk drawer. He pushed me forward, his large hands wound tightly around my arms.

I penned a quick note to Tessa and taped it to the inside of the front door, before Trent dragged me outside. Away from my home, away from my family, away. But I was already far away, detaching myself, so I felt nothing instead of the unbearable pain and loss that would surely crush me. I closed the door behind us, closing my heart right along with it.

"You feel soft, and you look fat," Trent told me as

he dragged me down the long drive. "Did you spend the last year sitting on your ass and eating whatever you wanted?"

I had gained maybe five pounds since he last saw me, and those five pounds were a healthy and necessary five pounds that had settled quite nicely on me. His black Mercedes was parked on the road and just as I was about to get in and close myself off forever, hope beckoned to me as I remembered what I had done just a few months ago on a sleepless, anxious night.

Trent pushed me into the passenger's seat and buckled me up. My eyes searched for anything that I could grab. I just needed any little thing. I had maybe two seconds to find it, so I reached into the side compartment of the passenger door and gathered what felt like a handful of trash. I couldn't see it, and I didn't have time to look at any of it because Trent was opening his car door. I had little time to make my play.

"I need air," I told Trent as he got in.

"Shut your whore mouth."

"I'm going to vomit if I don't have air."

That worked. Trent loved his precious cars more than anything. He could control me, but I knew how to manipulate him, too. He glared at me as he hit the button to roll down my window. As Trent started the ignition, I grabbed my phone, opened it to the video, locked it, and bundled it with the trash before forcing my body out the window and throwing the contents of my hands as far back into my driveway as I could. He pulled me back in.

"Try to get away from me one more time, bitch!" He yelled right before my body jolted to the side and a sharp pain spread across my head. And then, darkness.

****

The left side of my head ached like I had been split in two. I reached up to touch the painful area and was met with hair matted in semi-dried blood. I didn't have to look to know what it was—no, this was all too familiar. My left eye refused to open, pounding painfully, reminding me that I had once again lost.

I looked around, noticing my old room hadn't changed since I last saw it. It felt eerie, like the preserved space of someone who had died. And hadn't she? Danica Petrov was nothing more than a memory, a woman I barely knew anymore. My stomach curled, and a ray of sunlight beaming in through a broken shade that Maus had once bent, was too much for my throbbing head.

The door creaked and I turned my head slowly to see Trent walking toward me. His jaw was set, his cold, steely gaze fixed on me.

"Well, you can't dance like that. And I don't even mean your face, I mean your body. You're going to stay here in this room until you lose that weight. You got that, darling?"

The dull ache of my head thrummed. Dizziness and confusion washed over me in waves, nausea swelling in my stomach the longer I kept my eyes open.

"I'm going to give you just one more chance, so don't throw it away this time. I know that I told you before if you ever tried to leave me, it would be the last thing you did. Do you remember that, or are you too stupid?"

"I remember." My voice was scratchy, and I was sure my throat was bruised.

"Good. And now that you know *exactly* what I'm capable of, I think maybe you'll listen. I'm going to break my promise this time and cut you some slack." He bent down until he was just inches away from my face. "But if you try to pull anything like that again, and I find out about it, if I even catch wind that the thought crossed your little mind, you'll be done. And *no one* will miss you. No one will know because right now, you're a ghost, Danica. You belong to me. No one else cares about where you are, except for me. You have no family but me, and that's something you'd better remember."

Trent found a sadistic kind of joy in reminding me of how unloved I was, how alone and dependent I was. And it had been the truth then, but it wasn't true anymore. Sure, I had friends in Redlands, but they all answered to Trent. They all needed him for something. Marissa had stuck her neck out for me when she helped me get out, but she wouldn't do it again, especially now that I was back. But people would miss me now. People would come looking for me. Tessa would never stop looking for me. And the friends I'd made in Brooks Falls? They wouldn't just forget about me.

"Do you understand me?" He grabbed my chin and forced me to face him.

"Ah!" I let out a cry of pain.

"Do. You. Understand. Danica?" he said, speaking to me like a child.

I kept my eyes locked on his hateful face. What did I have to lose? I'd already lost everything that mattered to me. My dreams of starting a career were over. I had no family. I had nothing, and even if my friends came looking for me, they might not find me alive by the time they found me. There was a sad, twisted kind of power in that, a power that I was feeling just irrational enough to use.

"No," I said, my voice a barely audible whisper.

Trent's head jerked back and his shock pleased me before his face turned colder than ever. He spoke through his teeth at me, "What did you say to me?"

I was unwavering in my eye contact. "I said 'no.'" I tried to sound indignant, but my muted defiance made me sound more like a scared child.

"No what?" he asked, baiting me and reeling me in.

"I don't understand what you want with me. Why do you want me here if you hate me so much? Did you ever even love me?" My words may as well have been whimpers for how feeble they were. But I wanted to understand. I finally wanted to understand, because I didn't. In all those years of torment, I didn't understand why he wanted me.

Trent drew closer, if that was even possible, erasing any space between us.

"Oh Danica." He ran his finger along the soft ridge of my jawline. "My feeble-minded Danica. You belong to me, dear. You've always belonged to me from the moment I plucked you out of that trailer park to now, and you'll belong to me until the day you die."

"But did you love me?"

Trent scoffed. "Love is for the weak. Don't you see? Don't you think I know all about how you were chasing love in that little hick town? And look how it turned out for you? Don't worry, your little cop is safe. Too messy for me right now."

My eyes widened and I couldn't hide the terror.

Trent lifted my blood-matted hair in disgust as he said softly in that calm, tense voice he always used right before he leveled me. "I told you before, I can see everything you do. Did you let him touch you?" He growled in my face and took my wrists, pinning them above my head. "Did you cheat on me, Danica, and let some other man fuck what's mine?"

I released a gasp. He was becoming irate. As for me, I was becoming stupid.

"No, Trent. I hate you! I hate you for all of it. I didn't *fuck* anyone. I made love to someone who loved me and treated me like I was a person, not a wild animal!" I yelled at him through tears, the bitter words sliding off my tongue like a death wish. Surely that's what this was.

His pupils dilated as he took me in. I braced myself.

"Loved you, huh, baby? You mean fucked? Do you need me to remind you who owns you?"

I tried to be strong. I tried not to show weakness, but it was impossible, because the mere thought of him touching me again sent me into a tailspin.

"No! No, please, please don't. I don't want to. I don't want you to touch me, please!" I cried out. I begged. I appealed to any shred of humanity that he might have. But I had given him everything his twisted mind wanted.

Trent grabbed my arms, dragging me out of the bed. The suddenness of it jolted me and I screamed. But before the noise fully exited my mouth, he slammed me against the wall, the full force of the blow pushing the air from my lungs. I wheezed and searched for oxygen, struggling to catch my breath.

Trent stood in front of me, my back against the wall, his fists on either side of my head. I cowered. He pulled one fist back and punched the wall so close to my head I thought I felt the pain of a blow, and I screamed again.

"You think you're tough now, huh? Let's test that. It's been a while, and you seem to have forgotten respect. Let me remind you that no one knows you're back yet."

Trent pulled out a cigar from his coat pocket.

"No. No, Trent, no. I'm sorry, I'm sorry, please don't."

Trent laughed at me, and I hated myself. *So weak, Raven, always so weak.*

"Ah, you're sorry? You seem to be sorry about a lot of things that you just can't stop yourself from doing."

He lifted his left hand and backhanded the right side of my face, and I fell to the floor and cried out. I tried to ball up into the fetal position and protect myself from what was coming.

"Please." I was shamelessly begging now, through what were either tears or blood. Maybe both. Trent unfolded my body from its protective posture and straddled me on the floor as he lit his cigar. He was not a small man, at least six foot two and solidly built. There was no way I was getting out of this. I was at his mercy, just like I always was.

"Danica?"

His tone was removed from the pain he so easily doled out. It was as if he was completely disconnected from the things he did to me. I was terrified, knowing he would kill me without remorse. Right now, though, I was his entertainment, his little plaything. "You know the funny thing about you? I gave you everything you ever wanted. I gave you a job, a house, a kid. You had money, food, a real nice life, baby. I just don't understand why you would leave me." He was goading me. He knew why I left him—his unbearable cruelty, his twisted ways, too many reasons to list off. He wanted to push me so I would tell him why I left. If I wanted to survive, and I thought I actually did, I had to play it safe.

"I don't know. It was a mistake. I never should've

left." I spoke to him in my most loving, apologetic voice. He snickered and lifted up my shirt to expose my torso.

"Huh," he scoffed, "You're a much more convincing liar than I ever gave you credit for. You know, I always thought you were my idiotic wife, but now I know that you're my idiotic, *lying* wife." With the word lying, he pushed the butt-end of his lit cigar onto my rib cage. I screamed out with unbridled pain. I was crying and screaming and begging. Garbled noises born from excruciating pain left my lips. The smell of burned skin wafted to my nose, the searing pain, Trent on top of me, all of it reminded me of my place in this life that I was a prisoner to.

"You're such a good liar that I think I may be able to use you for my other business ventures. Once you're involved, you might think twice about blackmailing your husband and landing us both in prison, huh?"

I could feel the blisters forming, my flesh continuing to burn even after it was snuffed out. I moaned, I heaved, sucking in air desperately, my erratic heartbeats pounding out of me, still dizzy with pain in my head and my face swollen so much more than before. When my breathing finally evened out, and I was silent, except for the few breaths of shock now exiting my mouth, he leaned down to my face and smiled.

"Now, let's try this again. Do. You. Understand. Danica?"

I nodded my head, my eyes glazed over in pain. I wasn't even looking at him. I wasn't looking at anything. My head was swimming with thoughts and fears. What if this was it? What if I never saw Zara again?

"Yes," I croaked out quietly. "I understand." *Please leave. Just please, get up and go.*

Trent sat back up and studied me. "Good." I breathed out a sigh of relief, but was injected with a new dose of fear when he started to undo his belt.

No. I couldn't survive it. Not again.

"Later, when you're not so disgusting, I'll remind you who you belong to." Trent warned, tossing his belt over his shoulder as he strolled leisurely away.

I had to shut everything out. The dank smell of smoke, the cold air blowing from the vents, the prison that was this house. I closed my eyes and escaped to that quiet place inside myself that I had lived in for so long.

Chapter 20

Cameron

I didn't remember getting home, but I woke up in my house with a splitting headache, feeling thankful it was Saturday, and I had the day off.

My cell vibrated on my coffee table and I considered throwing it across the room. But that small glimmer of hope that it could be her caused me to pick it up and check.

Bram—*You're going to want to get your ass to the station.*—

Me—*I really don't, man. I've got the hangover to beat all hangovers.*—

I tossed my phone to the table and closed my eyes, listening to the phone vibrate, and ignoring it. I wasn't going in on my day off, and I definitely wasn't going in like this. Minutes later, my phone rang.

"Bro, I'm not coming in."

He was quiet on the other end of the line. He cleared his throat. I heard a door close.

"Man, Raven was reported missing this morning."

"What?" Sobriety and awareness struck, overtaking the dull pounding of my hangover.

"She's been reported as missing as of last night."

I sprung up from my couch and ran to the medicine cabinet, downing a few tablets of ibuprofen as I hurried to the back of the house.

"On my way. Be there in ten."

I hung up and tossed on my uniform. Fear prickled down the back of my neck. My girl was missing. And what about Zara? Why didn't I ask about Zara?

Arriving at the station, I was relieved when I found Tessa with Zara. I jogged toward them.

"Camyun!" Zara ran up to me and threw her little arms around my leg as I bent down to pick her up. It was like no time had passed. Love. Love for this little girl filled the hollow places in my heart. The places that I had hollowed out all on my own when I ripped myself from their lives.

"Hey, little Z." I tapped her nose that looked so much like her mother's, it physically pained me. Tessa stood by us, her face pale and splotchy, twisting her hands together.

Tessa placed a hand on Zara's cheek. "Wanna hang with Aunty Mika for a bit?"

Zara nodded vehemently, and I squeezed her tight before setting her down. She ran toward Mika, who grabbed her hand. "If it isn't my favorite little button nose! How about we color something pretty on the whiteboard?"

Bram ushered Tessa into the conference room. Instead of sitting, she paced back and forth, running her fingers through her long hair.

"Her car is there. Her car is at the house, and she just left without it? She wouldn't do that! And the porch light was shattered…and…Oh my god." She was becoming hysterical. Bram reached out for her and wrapped his hand around her arm, gently urging her to sit.

"Why don't you try to calm down so we can get all

the information we need to look into this as soon as possible, okay?"

Tessa nodded and sat down in one of the chairs. Calm down? I was trying to hold it together while I was falling apart on the inside.

Tessa sucked in a deep breath. "She's been working the night shift for a few weeks now, for her school clinicals. She doesn't get off until really late, so I've been taking care of Zara at night. She wakes up with Zara every morning, and I mean *every* morning." Tessa turned to me. "Cameron, you know Raven is a devoted mom. She would never just leave her."

I nodded in agreement, because it was true. Zara had always been Raven's first priority, before school, before me, before herself. Bram caught Tessa's eyes.

"Was she spending time with anyone new or anyone at all that you know of? Maybe some school friends or," he looked at me and paused, before he said, "Maybe a new boyfriend?"

Tessa shook her head immediately. "No." It was a minor relief that didn't matter now.

"Was she still dancing?" He asked.

"No, she hadn't danced since, well, I think you were all there the last time she danced." Her lips quivered as she spoke. "She left this note. It-it doesn't make any sense. I swear she wouldn't do this. I know her. Something isn't right. It has to be him."

Him. My heart stopped and my body tensed. Who was "him?"

"Give us the note," I demanded, sounding harsher than I intended, but we didn't have time to waste. She handed over the note. And she was right; it didn't make any sense. "I thought she didn't go by Danica anymore."

"It can't be," Tessa cried out. "She doesn't. She *never* did. There was only one person that called her Danica. Even before she was Raven, we all called her Dani. Only Trent called her that, and I'm just so scared that he has her. I don't know how he would've found her, but if he did, Cameron, it's bad, it's so bad. He'll— he'll…" She broke out into uncontained sobs.

Trent. My stomach tightened and my jaw set. I was angry at Trent. At myself for letting this happen, and afraid to hear why Tessa was so scared of him.

"Her husband?" Bram asked. Tessa's eyes flashed to me and then back to Bram.

"He didn't know where she was. He didn't even know she changed her name. It was all…" she trailed off into hysterics. "Please, I don't want Raven to be in trouble."

"If you want us to find her, you have to tell us everything you know. The first twenty-four hours are the most important," I reminded her quickly.

"Okay, all right. Um…So, she bribed someone, a government official she met at the club, I think? Paid them off to get her and Zara's names changed. Off of the record."

Christ, this was deeper than I ever imagined.

"And why would she do that?" Bram asked, and I listened, waiting for Tessa's answer, thinking that I was glad Bram was here and he had his full head about him.

"I didn't know all of it until now. Only that something really, really bad happened before she ran. She wouldn't tell me because she didn't want me to be involved, but she said her life was in danger. That's all she would tell me." Tessa blinked before grabbing my arm. "I'm telling you, if she thought her life was in danger, it had to be bad, so I didn't press. And it was, it *is*. Her life was always in danger with Trent. He was…no he *is* the devil."

I clamped my teeth together, needing somewhere to put my anger. "Tell me what he did to her," I demanded.

Tessa shook her head and dropped her forehead into her hands.

"He beat her. And I don't mean a slap or a push here or there. He *beat* her. When we worked together, she would sometimes be out for weeks, healing. He…" Tessa swallowed a sob. "He forced himself on her. He starved her because he thought she was too fat."

My nostrils flared, and I was pretty sure my teeth had been pulverized straight into oblivion. I was going to kill someone. I was going to find this son of a bitch and murder him with my own two hands. Bram was nodding and taking notes like Tessa hadn't just turned my world upside down. And I was grateful for him.

"Were there domestic disputes or any cases that we could look into?"

She shook her head. "Not that I know of, but I do know that Raven said he was very careful. And Raven never tried to report him. She'd seen what happened to women who reported their abusive husbands. You both should know. The system rarely works in favor of the woman."

She wasn't wrong. It was true. Early in my career, when I worked beat in the city, I saw it all the time. Women who were in and out of abusive situations with no power to get out permanently. And just to add insult to injury, they knew they'd face worse consequences when they returned.

"Is there any chance that he could have found her?"

Bram asked. My stomach turned, my world was falling apart right in front of my eyes, by my own hand, by my own foolish choices.

"She stayed off the grid as best she could. I don't know how he would've found her." My mind flashed to Laurel and what she knew. And the timing of it all. No, even she wasn't capable of something so terrible, was she? "But I do know he would've done anything to get her back."

Bram jotted down a few notes.

"What about her family? Did they know where she was?"

"Raven doesn't have a family."

My head shot up, and I furrowed my brow. Raven had told me about her family, her parents, her siblings. She had shared little stories and anecdotes about them.

"Raven was raised by her grandma until she was nine, and then when her grandma died, she went into the system. She bounced around until she was eighteen and never really stayed with one foster family for too long."

I was gut-punched. My heart ached for my girl. And who was I? Just one more person in her life who had cast her aside without a second thought. There was so much she hadn't told me, and so much that I had missed.

Tessa glanced in my direction. "It wasn't personal, Cameron. She's not a liar. She was ashamed of her past. She thought it made her less of a person. She didn't talk about it with anyone except for me."

I wasn't sure if that was supposed to make me feel better, but it made me feel worse. I had berated her for lying to me, had yelled at her and shamed her. I had proven her right and treated her the exact way she expected me to and then left her to deal with the broken pieces.

"I found her phone in the driveway wrapped up in receipts from Redlands. Recent ones. I didn't know, I didn't know until now what had happened. When I found her phone, it was unlocked with a video up." Tessa threw her hand over her mouth, covering a wail. "I can't unsee it. Cameron, I can't, I can't. Please!"

"All right, calm down. Breathe in," Bram told Tessa, placing a hand on her arm as I reached out to grab the phone and immediately hit play on the video. Bram came to my side. The video was shaky from those delicate hands that trembled while she held the phone. My brave girl. Drugs, money, betrayal, standard drug trafficking. Except, my eyes widened when I saw what was about to happen. A gun with a silencer twisted on. An unknowing kid counting money. Her husband was deep in that world, and my baby, my life, my perfect girl, was stuck in the center of it. In danger.

"Jesus. Dammit!" I couldn't hold my anger in any longer. I couldn't be the professional that I was supposed to be. "I failed her. Fuck!" I shot to my feet, yelling, my hands running through my hair, pulling in frustration before landing a punch on the wall. A punch that was no doubt heard throughout the office. Tessa's hand landed on me, bunching my shirt in her hands.

"There's no time to search for blame." Her tear-filled eyes locked on me. "Just find her and bring her home." She was right. And that's exactly what I intended to do.

****

I'd driven to Redlands the same day Raven was reported as missing. I stayed in a shitty motel near the Redlands precinct for two of the longest days of my life,

290

while I waited for updates on Raven's case.

And I took what felt like my first breath in days when the Redlands Chief of Police called to tell me that they had finally obtained a search warrant, and due to the nature of the crimes, the circumstances were being treated as exigent. It was good news. It meant we could go in at any time. It was a not a "knock and announce" warrant. It meant that the scumbag wouldn't have time to do anything stupid before we got to him. The DEA, in conjunction with the raid on the Petrov house, was set to raid his business at the exact same time.

"Officer Jameson, pleased to meet you. I'm Chief Sanchez, this is Lieutenant Velasquez and Sergeant Donaldson. They'll be serving the warrant with you today."

"Good to meet you all." I lifted my chin, impatient to get moving.

Velasquez tipped her chin at me. "SWAT is gearing up. We looked into your guy. He has several guns registered to his name and potentially several unregistered. We don't know what we're walking into. This guy has managed to stay off of the radar entirely. Aside from that video, we don't know anything else, and because this case is in cooperation with the DEA, we have to keep a tight lid on it. Which, unfortunately as you probably know, means no informants, no questioning in the days leading up."

"So, no one has seen the girl?" I tried to cover my emotion. The words caught tightly in my throat as the worry crept up my spine in slow prickles.

Velasquez caught on, or she was already briefed, that this was personal for me. Her voice lowered. "No. But everyone, and I mean *everyone*, involved in this case, knows that there is a BOLO out for the girl. She's a key witness, and Law Enforcement knows what she will mean for prosecution. They'll be careful. We'll be careful."

"They scoped the place yesterday while the warrant was in progress. They currently have someone with eyes on, verifying the suspect is home. Last night, he left the residence at roughly 1900 hours and went straight to his place of business and returned to his residence at 0500. Our guys scoped for security devices and found three. Two in front appeared to be motion-detected. One in back, same. SWAT's gonna go in fast and hard. And then we follow." Velasquez glanced at the clock on the wall. "It's 1310 now, and SWAT goes in at 1400."

She didn't have to tell me twice.

"Let's go," I swallowed and followed the other officers out of the precinct.

I was amped and crushed all at once. Prepared for the worst, prepared to lose the woman I loved. Again. But this time, I knew there would be no coming back from it. We turned down a road that I did not expect to turn down. I knew her husband was a successful club owner, but for some reason, I never pictured that she had lived in a place like this. The sidewalks were lined with palm trees, the lawns were manicured, and the street was clean, reminding me just how deceiving appearances could be.

"Squad 220 approaching the residence."

"Ten-four. Standby. SWAT en route. ETA T minus two minutes."

Velasquez parked the vehicle farther down the road. Two minutes dragged on like two hours.

"SWAT passing on your nine."

As soon as they passed, we got out and followed. Keeping our distance, we watched as they surrounded the house, every officer moving skillfully as if they'd practiced this exact formation a thousand times.

And then I heard it, the loud busting of a door, shouts of, "Redlands police! Drop your weapons!" and gunshots. Once gunshots rang out, my body was no longer operating in unison with my mind. It was operating on pure adrenaline. I ran toward the house and through the broken door. When I was in, I searched the room frantically with my eyes. There was one SWAT member tenderly holding his chest where a gunshot had hit his vest. Below him, a man lay on the floor with a gunshot to what appeared to be his arm. He was being held down by an officer. I didn't have time to figure out if it was her husband. I was single-minded. Find my girl. The SWAT team continued to move through the house, carefully sweeping each room while I followed closely behind. I was careful to stay out of their way. Until I heard someone yell from upstairs.

"We got a room locked from the outside. I need the spreaders!"

Another member ran up the stairs with equipment to unlock the door. Before busting the lock, he knocked on the door.

"Is anyone in here? If you're in there, move away from the door. Can you hear me?" He listened to the door, but not too closely. They didn't know what was behind the door, and part of me was terrified of finding out. I braced myself for the worst.

"I got nothing. Let's bust it down, but carefully. Our hostage might be in there. I'll run the tool. You two hold the door so it doesn't swing into any occupants." In two minutes, the door was methodically opened, and SWAT swept the room.

I followed, frantically searching for her. What I saw eviscerated me, cut me from skin to bone. There she was. My girl. I didn't have time to blame myself for letting this happen to her. I ran to her, getting to her first while the team continued to sweep the room. Pulling out my CB, I called headquarters for an ambulance.

"This is Officer Jameson. Send an ambulance and put a rush on it."

"Ambulance already en route."

I knelt down by her side, not touching her. I wanted to. Every part of me wanted to scoop her up and carry her away.

"Raven. Raven, baby. It's me. It's Cameron."

Nothing could have ever prepared me to see the woman I loved like this—battered, bleeding, and restrained on the floor. Her frail frame laying there with rope restraints around her wrists like an animal. She had been beaten, her left eye so swollen it wasn't open. Bile rose from my gut, and I did everything in my power to hold it back. That asshole had put his hands on her, and I was going to kill him. Tears filled my eyes. Regret, shame, and anger. I let this happen to her. I failed her. I was murderous and sick and feeling deranged. Then my gaze traveled back to Raven, and all the anger turned to pain.

EMTs rushed up the stairs as I moved quickly out of the way. Raven breathed shallow breaths as her restraints were loosened. Her wrists were red and raw from the rope rubbing her delicate skin. I knelt down next to her as she received medical attention. Her eyes were closed, and I didn't know if she was unconscious or just too weak.

"Raven. It's Cameron. I'm here." I spoke quietly. "We are getting you out of here, okay? I want you to know that Zara is safe. She's with Tessa and Mika. And you're going to be okay, baby."

My tears started to fall. How could he have done this to her? The EMTs cut off her shirt, checking for anything that would prevent her from being moved. When I saw it, my eyes bugged out of my head. I knew what it was the minute I saw it. I had seen welts like this before, not usually this large, but just like this. I was going to kill him if he wasn't already dead. Raven groaned, but her eyes remained closed. Several other EMTs entered the room and set down a stretcher.

"Twenty-nine-year-old female. Likely three to four broken ribs, no neck or back damage, appears to have sensation in her legs. She has large burns on her upper left quadrant, so be cautious when lifting her. Ready?"

They gathered around her and gently loaded her onto the stretcher. I wanted to follow them down the stairs, but they needed to get her to the hospital. One EMT was packing up his equipment. I bent down to him.

"What hospital are they taking her to? I'm her family. I need to know the hospital and room number."

"You can take the ambulance with her, sir."

I ran down the stairs to catch up, the EMTs still there, taking their time moving her. She was in too bad of shape to move quickly. As they moved her down slowly, I saw him. He was standing with his arm wrapped, his hands cuffed, right next to Velasquez. I didn't wait, I didn't think. I moved in close and pressed my elbow to the gauze over his wound, and enjoyed his cries of pain.

"You'll never see her again. You'll never touch her again, and I'll do everything in my power to make sure you rot in prison for the rest of your pathetic life."

I wanted to kill him; but instead, I followed her.

Chapter 21

Raven

Two weeks stuck in a hospital room. Two weeks of seeing him every day. Two weeks without Zara. I missed Zara. When I was stuck in that room in my old house, I thought I would never look at her face again. I knew that I couldn't even begin to heal without holding my baby again. The few days I spent at Trent's were the worst days of my life. Worse than all the years I'd spent there before. I had lost all hope of ever leaving again, and the pain he inflicted on me didn't come close to rivaling the emotional distress.

During my hospital stay, I talked to caseworkers and cops and investigators from different agencies, spilling the facts of my life, the things I knew about Trent, as if it was someone else's story. I was detached. I could feel it. I didn't need to be psychoanalyzed to know what it was. I had been actively detaching from pain for my entire life. It was survival; it was self-preservation. But I told them everything. Every painful detail slid from my tongue like it was finally the right time and place for the story I had to tell. It was the first time I ever shared my whole story with anyone.

The only thing I recounted with pride was the day I left, the day I packed up Zara and Maus, hauled my babies on foot at three in the morning to the car I'd bought. I had driven out of town that day with nothing but fear, my babies, and that video they found on my phone. The very same video that I'd used to make the pictures I had blackmailed Trent with. That's what really saved my life, and I knew it.

I knew that the police would never have busted down his door to go look for a missing stripper. It wasn't fair, and it wasn't right. Reality was a bitch, but the truth of the matter was that there were forgotten women out there. Forgotten because of their occupations. Forgotten because they were deemed not important enough. The cold, hard reality was that I had something they wanted; I had information and a testimony. And that same information that nearly cost me my life is what also gave it back to me.

Cameron never left my side at the hospital, except to get food or coffee or anything I wanted. The first few days he just sat next to me, talking to me, sometimes holding my fingers. My wrists and hands were badly bruised, but he was careful and gentle in every way. Tessa offered to drive down with Zara, but we both agreed that she shouldn't see me like this. But I talked to them every day. Cameron had assured me that they were safe. My biggest fear was Trent's criminal network coming after my family. From the initial interrogation of Trent, it was made clear that he hadn't told anyone about me or the video. He was too afraid it would expose him as negligent and untrustworthy. As it stood now, I was invisible in this case and my testimony would be sealed.

"How are you feeling, baby?"

I sighed, hating that he was calling me baby and loving it all at the same. It still did things to me, had my heart in knots and my stomach fluttering like a girl in love. It was no wonder, though—Cameron had been here for me. He came back when I needed him the most, and I couldn't just ignore that. But also, I couldn't go back to what we had, and after everything, I didn't want to. My heart and body had been broken over the span of a few weeks, and I was just done with it all. So instead of communicating the feelings swirling around inside of me, I let it come out in irritation.

"I'm ready to go home."

I was getting grumpier each day I spent at the hospital. Could anyone blame me? It was boring, and I was tired of sitting around all day. Although I could go on walks around the hospital floors and then, eventually, on the hospital grounds, it was still stifling. Cameron stayed close by, like I would try to break away and drive home like this. Truth be told, the thought had crossed my mind. Besides, what was slipping away in a hospital gown like a crazy person compared to any of my previous harrowing escapes?

"I know you are, sweetheart. Only one more day, and then I'm gonna take you home. You had three broken ribs and a punctured lung. They're just trying to make sure you're fully recovered first."

"Mmmm." I rolled my eyes at him and grumbled at the thought of even one more day here. One more day of hospital food. One more day without Zara. I turned my head away from him, not wanting him to see my desperation, the brokenness so intrinsic to who I was that I wasn't sure if I was more me or just pieces of me.

Cameron rubbed the back of my hand with his thumb. "You'll be with her soon."

I loved that he knew exactly why I was so grouchy. And now he knew everything. He was there when I told the caseworker how I met Trent, and he heard me tell the cops about every awful thing that Trent ever did to me. He knew that I had committed felonies to get out. He even helped me strike a deal with law enforcement—my testimony for complete immunity for my own crimes, which, in all fairness, were nothing compared to Trent's. Cameron now knew that I had no family. He knew all the worst things about me, yet he never asked or pressed me for information.

"I know it's just one more day." I was full-on whining. But the events of the past few weeks were ones that I had yet to fully process. It was weighing on me, and all I wanted was to go home and get my life in order. Again.

"I just hate it here. I want my bed, I want to see Zara, and I want to talk to Tessa. I just want to go back to normal. I need to figure out my school, now that I've missed so much. I still have to work and pay bills. I have so much to do." I was starting to talk faster, becoming frantic when I realized how much I really did have to do to get my plan back on track.

"Baby, baby." Cameron pushed the hair back from my face and stroked my head. "You've been through a lot. You've been through trauma, and you need to heal, in more ways than one."

I blinked up at him, not knowing what to say. It was true, but that didn't make it any easier to comprehend. When I recounted stories and events, it always felt like I was telling a story about someone else. Over the years, I'd learned to separate my psyche from the facts, and quite honestly, I wasn't sure if I wanted to be attached to it emotionally. Ever.

"And you've spent a lot of time talking with

administration at the university. It seems like they are going to work with you, so you can still graduate on time. Right?" I nodded, because it was true. They had been so helpful and committed to getting me back in the swing of things as soon as possible. "You filled your admissions counselor in on everything that happened, and from what I heard, she might be more dedicated than you to getting your cute butt to graduation."

"Yeah, that's true. My advisor said to call as soon as I get back, and she'll go over the plan for getting me caught up."

"See? All good. As for your bills, you aren't behind. Tessa's been paying them."

"Oh, don't tell me that, Cameron. She can't afford that!"

"Don't worry, baby. She doesn't have to. I've been sending her money. It's all taken care of."

My lips slammed together, pressed closed by the actions of this man. The man who had come into my life like a storm, the man who was now the life raft keeping me afloat.

"And I spoke with your lawyer. It's guaranteed that you'll get a *large* settlement. And that piece of shit is going to be in prison for the rest of his life. The assets that aren't tied up in drug money those go to you."

I had given Cameron permission to deal with the lawyer for now. It was all too much. Cameron consulted me about anything major, but the long list of motions and injunctions to be filed were filtered through him.

"I don't want anything from him." I was defiant, disgusted by the idea of having anything that reminded me of that man.

"It's not about getting something from him, Raven.

It's getting your portion of the assets you deserve. It's getting compensated for what he put you through, and quite honestly, there isn't enough money he could give you to make up for it, so I hope for yours and Zara's sake that you get a lot."

I nodded, and our eyes met. Unsaid words floated between us, and it was all too much. I couldn't deal with my feelings for him, and I definitely couldn't deal with his feelings for me. But I was grateful for him.

"I really want to hug you right now," I announced.

Cameron's lips tipped up into a sweet smile as he stood up, his large, solid body hovering over me; all those mountains of muscles and hard ridges that I still wanted to sink my teeth into. I was still so attracted to him, my body reacting in ways that I couldn't prevent. But my heart was guarded. He leaned down, and I lightly wrapped my arms around him, burying my face in his chest, his cologne luring me into a deep trance. "Yum, he smells like heaven."

I felt his body quaking and heard a chuckle, a deep rumble in his chest.

"Are you narrating our lives now?" he whispered into the side of my head, his lips so close to me that it set my body on fire. I felt my cheeks heat, realizing what I had done. Instead of letting me make up some lame excuse, he bent his face down and kissed me on my lips. His lips were so soft and kissable. The bad Raven wanted to make out with him for the next twelve hours until we had to leave. But the Raven who had learned some hard lessons, she thought better and turned her head to the side.

Cameron tensed. "Shit, I'm sorry. I shouldn't have done that."

I bit my bottom lip on the side and spoke to the hospital bed. "I can't."

I could see Cameron's head bobbing up and down from the periphery, but I couldn't tell if he was mad or disappointed.

"I know. That was so out of line. It's hard for me to be near you and not kiss you. It's no excuse though, Raven. I'm sorry, babe."

A large grin spread across my face. "I get that more than you understand. I just, I can't be in a relationship right now. I don't know if I'll ever be able to be in one again, but I do know that I need to get healthy, both physically and emotionally." I turned my face to him to find him staring at me. His lips tugged up at the side and his blue eyes soft. "I've spent my entire life bouncing around, trying to blend in with my surroundings, so I didn't cause a stir. In foster care, no one wants to keep a brat, so I became pliable. In Trent's house, it was dangerous for me, so I became compliant. I've only ever catered to other people's feelings, and I don't even know who I really am without that." I had cried a lot these past few weeks, and apparently today was no exception. The tears came streaming at the admission, the recognition that I didn't know who I was.

"Oh baby, I want that for you. I'm not going to lie to you and say that I don't want to be with you, that I didn't fall in love with you, because I do, and I did. But if you can't be with me, I respect that. I respect *you*. Christ, if you only knew what I saw when I looked at you, you'd see how truly strong you are, how everything you are. You've been to hell and back, and you not only survived, but managed to get yourself out of it." He breathed out a large breath, his lip quivering. "You're one of a kind, and if we can't be together again, I'll understand. I still want to be in your life somehow. I need to be in yours and Zara's life. I love you both, and I'll take whatever I can get. I'll be your friend if you'll let me."

Friends? The idea was both a slap to the face and a tempting offer. I wasn't sure we could be just friends. Our chemistry was all-consuming.

"I would like that." *I would? Okay then, I guess we're doing this.* I was sure that if I didn't accept his offer of friendship right then, I would still find a way to keep him in my orbit. I was drawn to him.

He sighed, a full exhale escaping his lungs as if he had been holding his breath for me. "Good, that's good." He stood up and started pacing the room.

"You're going to need a lot of help these next six months. I've already talked to Tessa and Mika, and we worked out a joint schedule to help you get back on track with school. Since Tessa's in the final month of her classes, I'm going to take up her night shifts with Zara, and Mika is off on weekends, so when Tessa isn't available, she's going to be with Zara. If you're on a night shift, I will be there when you get home to walk you from your car to the house." He was talking a mile a minute, intensely focused on his plan.

"Cameron, you don't have to do that. That's a lot."

He waved me off and kept talking. "We can do this, Raven. If we stick to the plan, and you stay open with us about what you need, we can make this work."

We. I was part of a "we." People that wanted nothing from me. It wasn't even an exchange. I couldn't offer them anything. I would try, and I planned to pay them back in any way that I could, but right now, I needed them. I'd never had people in my corner, no family to fall back on when times had gotten hard. Zara never had that either, other than Tessa, of course. And now, we had three people in our lives helping us pick up the pieces and put them back together. My heart was full.

After being taken by Trent, I wasn't sure that I'd ever feel good again, and now, my heart kept beating because of my friends. Cameron was still talking about the plan, but I was too deep in my thoughts to have heard anything else.

"That sounds good?"

I nodded, in a bit of a daze.

"It's gonna work, Raven. It'll be good, I promise."

"Yeah, I think so." And I did. For the first time in weeks, I felt it. That gnawing spark of hope that refused to leave me.

****

In the weeks after getting home, everything moved fast. Cameron was not kidding that he had formed a plan, and everyone was on board. I hadn't missed much school, and by the time the spring semester began, I was back at the Blue Rose weekend mornings, and I had started seeing a trauma counselor twice a week. It felt like overkill initially, but after the first few awkward sessions, I tried really hard to open myself up. I had never recognized how closed off I had become over the years.

The woman was a saint. She never got mad. When I lost my cool, she just smiled and told me, "That's good, that's honest, Raven. Good job!"

Counseling became a safe place for me to express some of the anger. But instead of me taking it out on the counselor, she found ways for me to do it safely.

Cameron was meeting me at home *every* evening after school. Most of the time he was already there, watching Zara when Tessa had work or classes. He worked out his schedule with the Sheriff, requesting to work the morning shift at the station so he could help me at night.

"Hi, baby girl! How was your day?" I asked, beaming at Zara, who was busy munching on what appeared to be a few sticky cheerios.

"Good, good, good!" Zara threw her arms up dramatically, confirming the cheerio situation when not a single one flew from her hands. "Camyun go on time out, but he's a good boy again, and he got a big boy treat!"

I looked at the man. "He did?" I put my hands on my hips and widened my eyes, feigning shock. "What did he do this time?"

She loved to put him on time out for *everything.* She didn't do this to anyone else but him. Zara loved to boss him, and he let her do it because she had him completely wrapped around her tiny finger.

"He make me eat spinach!" Zara said as she screwed up her face and stuck out her tongue.

I picked her up and removed the remaining snack from her hands before kissing her cheeks. "Wow! Cameron must really love you to try and make you so healthy!"

Zara smiled and reached for Cameron, wiggling out of my arms and planting her hands on his cheeks when he took hold of her. "Yeah, but I still not yike spinach."

His deep voice was a rumble that spoke straight to my lady parts. "I told you, little Z, spinach is going to make you grow so big, like Superman."

306

"I not want to be yike Soup Man. I wanna be a pwincess, yike Mommy. I's gonna take care of all the people in the hopsidal just yike Mama does."

"You know your mama eats spinach so she can take care of all those people so good, right?"

Zara's wide eyes flashed, and she looked at me.

I nodded. "It's true. I eat so much spinach. Cameron and Mommy love you so much that we want you to grow up healthy."

"Aunty Mika yuv me too because she give me peas, and I's don't yike peas but Aunty Tessy not yuv me vewy much, and she give me yoyyipops and gummy bears."

I smiled softly at her. "Well, sometimes we have to have lollipops and gummy bears too. Both of your aunts love you, and so do Mommy and Daddy."

We both froze. A misstep, a hammer straight to the heart. I chanced a glance at Cameron, expecting to find horror, that same horror I felt at my own words. But when I looked at him, I didn't see fear or confusion, just a listless look off into the distance. He was a thousand miles away, yet right here with us.

"I yuvs my Aunties and Mommy and Daddy too." Zara squeezed us all together. I avoided his eyes, sure I would have to address this with Zara later, but for now, ignorance was bliss.

"I grabbed your mail, baby."

His soft voice pinned me in place. He was still calling me "baby" like we were a thing. We were stuck somewhere between being a real thing and being friends, except I couldn't help but feel that what he and I were building now was the most real thing I'd ever had. I wanted him, but between my messed up life and the death of his wife, neither of us was well.

As far as I knew, Cameron still slept on his couch. I deserved better than someone who could give me only a part of themselves. Both of us needed time to heal. We were friends, and that's what we needed to be. He had become one of my best friends now that he knew everything about me. Our friendship had grown to something real and comfortable. Aside from the sexual tension, we had an ease when we were together, operating like we were on the same wavelength. And that felt good.

"Okay, thanks." I answered with a small grin. "Anything good in there?" I asked, trying to keep things light, but worried that what I'd just said to Zara had suddenly made things weird between us.

Cameron didn't answer me. Instead, he set Zara down and handed her the sippy cup sitting on the coffee table. "Finish your milk, okay? It's almost bed time."

Zara grabbed the cup and wandered off to the spot in front of the television where Maus was laying.

When he stood back up, he was still silent, watching me, looking like he had something to say.

"What's going on?" I asked. "If it's what I said to Zara, I'm sorry. I just-I misspoke."

He furrowed his brow, searching me tenderly. "It's not that." He took in a sharp breath, shifting the mood from serious to light with just a simple expression—a half-smile on his handsome face. "You want a glass of wine, babe?"

"Um, sure. Do I need a glass of wine?" He raised his brows and opened his mouth to speak, then hesitating, he closed it.

"So that's a yes," I told him, feeling my body tense.

"Let's just have a drink together, and then we'll talk

about it."

"Yeah, but I'm not going to be able to relax now that I know there is something that is going to stress me out so much that I need wine. Is this a one or two drink kinda news?" His silence only confirmed it. "Ah…so three?"

"It depends. In the end it's going to be for the best, but short-term…" He trailed off.

"Okay, wine please. And while we do that, I need to feed and bathe Zara." I snatched her up playfully from the floor, and she squealed with surprise and delight.

"She's done both already." Wait, what? "She was hungry, and then after she ate, babe, wow, our girl can make a real mess." He laughed while he ran his fingers through her soft hair. "I gave her those ravioli things that she loves and, of course, spinach, which she hates me for."

"Oh," I said, slightly taken aback by all he had done.

"Hey, I'm sorry. I didn't think that you might want to have that time with her. I was just trying to be helpful."

Zara squirmed in my arms and I sat her back down next to Maus. "Don't apologize." My voice cracked. "Not for taking care of Zara. You've been making my life easier and helping me more than you know." Before I could stop it, the tears came pouring down. Cameron was at my side in a split-second. He was always at my side now.

"Okay, okay, it's all right. You know Zara's my girl, and I would do anything for her."

He kissed the top of my head while I broke down. This was my life as of late, so much crying. My therapist said it was normal, and that my emotions would eventually stabilize. I couldn't wait for that day.

"Shhh, baby, shhh." He kissed my temple. The

closeness was almost too much, memories of us flooding my mind. Of him on me, in me, licking up and down my body.

"Don't cry, sweetheart." He was moving down, and I was moving...my hips? His lips felt divine and I was going to lose it. He kissed the tears off of my cheek, and my resolve was weakening. He kissed the corner of my mouth, and I leaned my head back in pure delight, exposing my neck like an offering. My mournful whimpers turned to moans as he hovered over my lips. So close our breaths became one. *Kiss me Cameron, just please kiss me.*

"Mommy!" Zara yelled from below us. We jumped apart, frozen, stunned, and in a daze, trying to exit the fog of what had almost happened. Then she tilted her head in questioning.

"Daddy, you blow Mommy up yike my water wings?" Oh boy. My hand flew to my mouth and our eyes connected with Zara's words registering. Daddy?

"She was low on air, little Z." Cameron smirked at me, moving right through her words like they were nothing at all. And I couldn't blame him. How did I explain to her what he was to us, to her? Before I could fall further into my thoughts, I scooped Zara up and hugged her to me. I moved to land a kiss on her chubby cheeks, but she caught me first, planting her lips on my face and blew.

"I blow Mommy up too!" She squealed.

Oh, this kid. I fell down in a fit of laughter, Zara continuing to blow raspberries on my cheeks. The three of us chased each other around the house for the next hour, having tickle fights and blowing raspberries until Zara's bedtime.

She wanted us both to put her to bed, so we took turns singing her favorite songs and giving her bedtime kisses. And Cameron, well, he was easily manipulated by her. He got her water, stuffed animals, water again, and more kisses, before I had to cut him off and threaten him with the nighttime pull-up changes if he got her one more glass of water. And I couldn't help but wonder if this is what I had been missing out on all of my life.

Chapter 22

Cameron

"Okay, time for wine and whatever it is you have to tell me."

I poured two glasses of wine, trying to wrap my mind around what almost happened between us earlier, trying to register the fact that Zara had called me "Daddy" and it all just about destroyed me. Any plan I had to take it slow with Raven was being ruined by my love for these girls. I was so close to forgetting everything and giving in to my need for her. She raised her glass in a toast with a look that said, "All right, let's do this." We clinked our glasses together and chugged the wine like we were the classiest frat boys ever.

"Another?"

She tilted her head and twisted her lips, looking expectantly at me. "Yeah, maybe one more."

I poured us both a full glass that finished off the bottle. We cheered and tipped our glasses up, finishing the wine in a single drink.

Raven made a sour face and shook her head. "Bad idea. I'm gonna have to let that settle a minute. This is why people do shots to get buzzed quickly." She took a breath in and sat down. "Okay, lay it on me." She had her palms up and wiggled her fingers in that gimme motion.

I swallowed hard because I knew that no matter what, this wasn't going to go well.

"A courier came today while you were in class." She cocked her head to the side. "They scheduled his trial." We never said his name and only referred to Trent as "him." "And you need to be there to testify." Before she got rattled, I continued. "It's a closed hearing, so your identity is still protected."

"No, no, no. I can't, I can't. I know I struck a deal, but no. Cameron, I can't see him. No!"

Raven began to shake as her eyes clouded over. I ran to her immediately and lifted her into my arms. The judge had ordered him to be held without bail, so Raven didn't have to worry about him hurting her, but I knew the trial would trigger her memories and anxiety.

"Cameron, I can't," she wailed. "I can't see him. I can't handle it. I won't be able to do it. Then what? He'll go free? He'll come for me and Zara."

"Hey, hey," I cooed, rocking her in my arms. "I am *never* leaving your side. He has no chance of going free. I spoke with the DA, baby, and the only question is how many life sentences he will get. He killed a man, at least one that we know of, and that's on video. That's evidence and the courts won't ignore that. The rest of it, the pounds of drugs they found in the raid of his business, his contacts, all the witnesses being subpoenaed by the DA, that's the nail in the coffin. He's done. You're free of him. Zara is free of him. Divorce papers are final, and he's been stripped of his parental rights. The only thing left for you to do is to be as brave as you can and testify. This is the last thing you have to do. I'll never let him hurt you again, I promise."

Her breathing slowed, and her loud sobs became soft

whimpers until she was quieted, relaxing into my arms. Exactly where she belonged.

I moved her hair to the side. "There's one more thing."

"Just tell me, honey."

Honey. Yes.

"It was Laurel that led him to you."

Raven's body tightened in my arms, and she pushed herself up and away from my grasp. "I'm sorry, but say that again, because I swear I just heard you say 'Laurel.'" Raven's body started to convulse as she fell into hysterical laughter. "Bitch-brows? *She* was the catalyst to my nightmare?" She laughed harder, until her body surrendered to the couch. Her laughter faded, and she fell silent.

Shaking her head back and forth, she stared off, the light in her eyes dimmed. "I didn't realize she hated me that much. I never did anything to her except love you. How can love be bad?" Her voice came out like a whisper, and my already destroyed heart couldn't take it.

I wanted to kiss her and tell her that I would always love her. I wanted to beg her to be with me, to let me take care of her and Zara in every way possible. And did I want to be Zara's father? More than anything. But I knew that's not what she needed now, so I said nothing and just held her instead. Moments later, she'd fallen asleep. I carried her to bed, but when I pushed off the bed to leave, her delicate hand grasped my forearm.

"Stay. Don't go, please? I need you tonight," she asked in that sweet, sleepy voice.

She didn't have to ask. I'd planned to sleep on the couch anyway, but I was all for jumping in bed with her.

"I was going to sleep on the couch. Do you want me

in here or on the couch?"

"Here."

She sat up, her eyes at half-mast, and pulled off her clothes, leaving her only in a matching maroon bra and a useless scrap of panties that dipped below her small curves and had me coming apart. I wasn't going to be able to handle this, not without some serious self-restraint.

"Raven." My voice came out low and gravely. "I don't think that I can," I swallowed the lump in my throat, "sleep in here with you."

"Then bring me to the couch."

Christ, if I brought her to the couch, it would be to bend her over and fuck her on it until neither of us could think of anything else but my cock buried deep inside her. Bad idea. Good time, but wrong time.

"No," I told her roughly. I needed to put some distance between us. "Go to bed," I demanded.

"But Cameron, I…"

I bent down and clasped her face in my hands, so close to her that I could almost taste her lips.

"Are you trying to kill me?"

"No."

"You're almost a nurse. Tell me, baby, can people die of blue balls?"

She giggled. My favorite sound. "I don't think so."

"If I lay down next to you, I'm gonna want you, and I know we aren't there yet. So please, have mercy on me, woman, and give me a break. Let me sleep on the couch."

She bit her lip and widened her eyes at me, nodding. I noticed her squirm a little and squeeze her legs together as her gaze fell to my cock that was pressing against my jeans. We both wanted it. And we both knew that it was a terrible idea.

"Okay then. Goodnight, Cam."

"Night," I gritted out, annoyed with my dick, which had begun to harden the very second I picked her up and carried her to her bed. And now it was painful.

I lay on the couch, willing my dick to calm down and trying to let my exhaustion drag me down. Eventually, I fell asleep but woke up some time later to find Raven on the floor next to me, fast asleep, her hand in mine. It was a small mercy, but I was grateful that she was wearing a loose-fitting shirt and a pair of tiny shorts. It wasn't much, but it was better than nothing. I dragged her up to me, planting her firmly on my chest. Her legs straddled one of my legs, and her arms rested on my shoulders. Kissing her head and stroking her back lightly, I whispered into her. "You're hotter than ever, and you're pissing me off with this. But I love you, and I promise that I'll always do right by you."

I swear I felt her mouth move into a smile on my chest, but when I looked down, she was fast asleep.

****

It had been nearly two years since Callie died. It had also been nearly two years since I visited her resting place. I'd made a lot of changes in my life since then, attending counseling myself and trying to move on from my past. The cemetery was green and well-kept. For a place filled with so much loss and grief, it was pretty.

I walked to where we'd laid Callie to rest, each footstep sinking into the dank earth. I never returned after that day, the day I buried her, but I remembered exactly where she was. Placing a single yellow rose where she lay, I sat down next to her and looked up at the clear blue sky.

"So, this is what you've been doing this whole time?" I laughed. "Not a bad view."

I cleared my throat.

"I met someone. She's, well, she's everything." I shook my head and chuckled. "She's not really anything like you, which is strange, because I loved everything about you. I still believe that you were absolute perfection. She is sweet and caring like you. A good mother, like you would've been. A kind woman. I fell in love, but I've been holding myself back because of the anger I had toward you. You broke me, Callie. You destroyed me. I know you tried, but in the end, it was too much for you."

I ran my hands through my hair and buried my head in my knees.

"I have to let you go. I have to let go of all the pain and the lies and the hurt. I loved you, Callie, but now I'm going to take that love and give it to Raven and Zara. I hope that you're good with it. I—" A hand gripped my shoulder, and I startled.

"It's me Cameron, relax."

I knew that voice. My whole body tensed, the kindness I found in it more shocking than the realization that I wasn't alone.

"Susan?" I turned to look at her.

She was standing there with a bouquet of blue hydrangeas—one of Callie's favorites, second only to yellow roses. Susan released her hand from my shoulder and knelt next to me. We sat in silence for a few minutes, neither of us making eye contact. Then, she spoke.

"It wasn't your fault."

Her voice was shaky and soft. Her words, a balm to my broken soul, my guilty spirit that begged for the lifeline she was giving me. Or a sign from Callie. A way out of the tangled mess I'd been trapped in since she died.

"She was struggling. Don't you think I knew that?" She sniffled. "I knew it was bad when she came to my house one day and disappeared into my bathroom first thing. When she abruptly left, I went to see what she had done. My pills were emptied. I didn't even have the stuff she was probably looking for, but she was so desperate, always chasing that feeling."

Susan squeezed my hand and closed her eyes. The sadness she carried in plain view.

"I never blamed you for Callie's death. Not once. I just wanted to know what happened. I could guess. I saw the toxicology report, but I wanted to know for my own closure."

Sighing, I told her about Callie's last day and how it happened. I lost it when I admitted that I gave her the final dose that did her in. Susan cried, still reminding me that it wasn't my fault. As hard as it was to let go of that belief, I was understanding more and more that it wasn't me who had killed her. Callie developed an illness, and that's what killed her.

Susan and I hugged and cried for what felt like an hour, maybe longer. We were healing. Together. Finally doing what we should have done two years ago—we were leaning on each other.

"She would want you to be happy, honey. She would want you to move on with that lovely girl and her daughter. I know it. I can feel it. And as for me, I want you to be happy too, and I can tell you are." There was no judgment, no bitterness to her statement, just pure love.

"That means more than you know, Susan. I'm worried I messed it up already, though."

Susan shook her head at me and smiled. "You know, I heard about what that girl went through and how you were part of the team that saved her. I don't think many women would forget that, not if she's really the kind of person that everyone has been telling me about."

"She is."

"Then show her that you're serious about her."

"I've been trying. I've been with her every day."

"Women respond to large gestures, Cameron. Keep doing the little things. Those are important, and I know you are doing them because you're a good man. But go big and prove to her that you're gonna stick. Single mothers can't mess around. You're either all in or all out, because for single moms, it's about what's best for their baby. If you really love her and her daughter, show them. Be committed, be *all in*."

Susan was right. I needed to show Raven that I was in it for the long-haul. If I was getting a second chance at love, I would wait for it. And while I was waiting, I'd do everything in my power to show her that I was all in.

"You are like a son to me, Cameron. And I know that these past few years have been rough, but I want you in my life. And I want whoever is in your life in my life, too. Callie was not a jealous person. She was a gentle, loving, kind soul. I know she would want us both to be happy."

"I want that, Susan. You were always like a second mom to me, and I never wanted to push you away the way I did, to lose you."

"You haven't."

When the clouds started to roll in, it was time to go.

I had a lot of stuff to do, and I needed to start planning. I walked Susan to her car, and we made plans for lunch the following week so we could catch each other up on our lives. After she drove off, I grabbed my phone and sent a text.

Me—*You have some time to meet?*—

Mika—*Sure. Is everything OK?*—

Me—*Everything is great, but I need your help with something.*—

Mika—*All right. Tell me when and where.*—

Me—*Shea's. 7? Come alone.*—

Mika—*This sounds like a spy thing. Should I bring the files and my pager? Lol.*—

Me—*Haha...It is kind of a stealth mission. Can you keep it from Tessa for now?*—

Mika—*Boy, you know it's bad news to keep things from your girl.*—

Me—*Promise, it's nothing bad. Tessa will be happy in the end.*—

Mika—*If this goes south, you're explaining to my woman why I had to lie to her.*—

Me—*Done. See you at 7. Beers are on me.*—

Mika—*Fine, I'm convinced. See you then.*—

Chapter 23

Raven

Opening the patio door, I saw Cameron and Zara kicking a ball back and forth. Well, mostly Cameron was doing the kicking while Maus would chase the ball as Zara ran after them, ending in a tumble. Cameron walked my way, and I handed him a margarita, which he looked at like it was some foreign object.

"This is a strange beer."

My lips ticked up into a grin. "It's a margarita. What, are you too much of a manly man for a little sugary tequila?"

He grunted and took a sip as Zara zipped past us, running inside with Maus trailing her.

I was about to sit down on the chair next to him when his arms grabbed my waist and yanked me onto his lap. I wasn't about to fight it. I couldn't fight it even if I had the will to. I was two margaritas in and hard up for this man. If he wanted to casually sit me on his face at this point, I wouldn't protest.

"Hey, you." The words rolled off my tongue like a purr, sounding way more seductive than I'd planned.

"You look beautiful today." His hands spread out across my stomach, pulling me deeper into him. "I love this dress you're wearing."

I was wearing a white sundress that had thin straps

at the arms and was tight at the waist before flaring out and only going down to my upper thighs.

I'd picked it out for him, but I wasn't about to admit that. Instead, I asked, "You do?" and pretended to be surprised.

"I really do," he growled, nipping my ear, and then moving his hands slowly from my stomach to my inner thighs. Lust poured over me. The weak-ass threads that held my self-control together were frayed, barely hanging on.

"Ah." My breath hitched at the contact, and I jumped up a little. Or I thrust into his hands. I couldn't be too sure, and I really didn't want to know. I didn't want to think.

He pressed a wet kiss to my neck. I tilted my head to one side, giving him as much access as he needed. He ran his fingers down my neck, trailing a path from my ear to my collarbone, and then followed it with soft kisses.

"Cam."

I was drenched and pretty sure that I was dripping all over him. His hands, splayed out across my inner thighs, slowly began to move up my dress. I moved, writhing on him, desperately needing some friction. I rocked my ass back into him, forgetting all reason and feeling no shame. He put one hand on my lower back and pushed me away every time I pushed back on his hard cock. We fell into a rhythm, and I unabashedly dry humped the man right in the open. His fingers grazed my panties, and he moved one finger past the hemline. Torture. Such torture.

"Hey, you two!" Tessa yelled as she walked out, extinguishing all of the flames and bringing us both back to reality.

She had a shit-eating grin on her face, and I was positive that I never realized how truly evil she was until right then. I sprung away from Cameron at the sound of her voice and smoothed my dress. She looked between us, pointing to me and then Cameron.

"Well, you look guilty, but he looks pretty damn pleased with himself. Sorry to break up the party."

I shook my head at her. "There was no party. We were just talking."

"Oh yeah," Mika laughed. "Tessa and I have all of our best conversations with my hand up her skirt."

Cameron and Tessa laughed, annoying me further. "Wow, Mika, Tessa's rubbing off on you." I shook my head and gaped at her.

Tessa winked. "That's the goal." Then she bounced around, setting out some chips and salsa.

"We need music," Mika said, reminding us all that she had set up Bluetooth speakers on the deck a few weeks ago. Now that the weather was perfect, we were out here listening to music and relaxing almost every day.

Tessa hit a playlist on her phone. "Yeah!" by Usher started to play and, just like a Pavlovian response, we both jumped up to dance. Tessa pulled Mika up to dance with her, the two of them entwined together in their own little world. I turned to Cameron and, sticking out one finger, I motioned for him to get up and join me.

"Oh, I don't know about that. I'm not a very good dancer."

I sauntered his way, channeling my old self and giving him a bit of a show. Once I got to him, I leaned down and whispered in his ear. "Remember, no touching," I teased, and his body visibly stiffened.

"So, you *are* trying to hurt me?"

I smirked at him. What I was trying to do was get laid. "Oh, I don't think any of what I'm about to do is going to hurt."

He closed his eyes for a second and breathed in deeply before releasing a long breath. I started to give him a very mild and innocent lap dance. That's what I told myself, and by the looks on Tessa and Mika's faces, it was still sexy. Not that those two had any room to judge—they were grinding and kissing like no one was watching. After torturing Cameron for a few reckless minutes, the song ended, and he looked just as tormented as me.

A cover by Haley Reinhart of "Can't Help Falling in Love" came on. Cameron stood up, adjusting himself while narrowing his eyes at me. "Slow songs I can do."

He grabbed me by the waist and pushed me away from the chairs, taking both of my arms and placing them on his chest, while he held onto my waist. Cameron's hands were wrapped almost all the way around me, his fingers resting just above the curve of my ass. Time was suspended as we stared at each other, swaying side to side, the words sinking into my heart.

Cameron opened his mouth to say something when I felt a tug at my dress. Zara was standing there, smiling up at us.

Cameron reached out for her. "Wanna dance, Z?"

"Yeah, I dance with you and Mommy."

He hoisted her up before pulling me back in with one arm. Zara held onto him and rested her head on his shoulder while I hugged him and rested my head on his chest. The three of us danced like that for the rest of the song. It felt right, like it was always meant to be us. It was a moment I would never forget. I was completely in love with this man, and I knew right then that I needed him. I was sure of it.

****

Cameron was nowhere to be found. Over the past six months, he had become a part of my close circle, but over the past week, since that perfect dance, he had pulled away. Without him here, I felt a void. Stupid scenarios started to play in my mind. Maybe he had met someone else, and he couldn't go running off to his ex-whatever's graduation with someone else in the picture. My chest heaved at the thought of him with someone else. Anger and jealousy burned, and I felt like I was going to detonate.

He said he loved me. Again.

And then he left. Again.

But I wasn't going to let a man ruin any more of my days, especially this one. I had three of the most important people show up for me, and they were my world, everything I needed. Sitting down in my assigned seat in the center of the stadium, I looked up to find Mika and Tessa waving at me and Zara holding a sign that I couldn't quite make out, but it definitely looked like her original work. I smiled and scanned the crowd until my eyes landed on a handsome man in uniform, standing in the front row with a ridiculous camera.

He was here.

I couldn't stop the embarrassing smile that spread across my face just as he pressed a button, capturing my dopey face. He set the camera down a bit and looked at the screen and then laughed, throwing his head back. Oh, that face, that laugh. That man.

But my smile faded, and I turned to face the stage. Where was he this entire week after promising me that he would always love me and never leave me? Now wasn't the time to fall deeper—it was time to cut myself off from him. *Protect yourself, Raven.*

"Raven DeLuca!" I shot up when I heard my name and walked up to the stage. It was happening. I was actually going to be a nurse. I had passed all of my finals and only had to take the NCLEX. I shook the Dean of Nursing's hand and posed for the camera.

When the ceremony was over, I found Tessa, Mika, and Zara waiting for me outside the auditorium where the families had gathered to wait for their graduates.

"I'm so, so proud of you, babe." Tessa sniffled and wiped her eyes.

"Raven, you're an inspiration. I hope you know that. I'm so proud of you." Mika didn't even bother trying to wipe her tears.

I dragged them both close to me, with Zara caught in the middle.

"I couldn't have done it without you guys. I truly mean that. *We* did this. And Cameron too, wherever he is." My eyes shot downward.

"Aw, Raven, he was here, but he's on duty and had to leave right after the ceremony." Mika told me this like it was no big deal. And I guess it wasn't, except I knew he had arranged his schedule for me for six months and now this one day, he couldn't manage to be here? I knew that I was being bratty about it, but something had shifted with us, and I was terrified about what it was.

After getting several pictures of the four of us, Tessa and Mika headed out to meet me back at the house. I was so ready to get home. The blaring of a police siren and flashing lights grabbed my attention.

What? No! This cannot seriously be happening right now. I pulled over to a safe part of the side road and bent my head down over the steering wheel, cursing my luck. If it was Gray, I could probably get out of it. If it was Bram or Phillips, I could *definitely* get out of it.

"Excuse me, ma'am."

Well, that was a voice I would know anywhere. My jaw was clenched as I shot my head up to look at that hot cop, the beautiful man who had stolen my heart and then crushed it underfoot. Sure, he was gorgeous, but I was fuming. I had no words.

"Do you know why I pulled you over?"

Was he for real? I changed my mind. I did have some words.

"Because you're a dick?" I said, not bothering to hide my contempt. Acting like he didn't even know me, he peered into my backseat.

"How old is your baby?"

My eyes widened in disbelief. Was this a joke?

"Cameron!" I yelled at him.

He raised his eyebrows, tilting his head to one side and pointing to his name tag. Oh, the nerve of this man.

"Officer Jameson," I gritted out, the words barely escaping from the confines of my teeth. He pointed to his body cam. "She's almost three. You know this though, because you bought me this car seat last year, you know, when you were giving it to me on the regular?" Screw him and his body cam. He nodded his head.

"Ah, that's right. Well, if I could have your license and registration, please, I'll just be right back."

I dropped open my glove compartment, grabbed my documents and slammed it shut. I wasn't oblivious to the fact that he wouldn't be acting like this unless he'd moved on. He had been there for me every step of the way, and now it was like he didn't even know me. After taking my documents to his truck, he returned with a piece of paper.

"I had to write you something. Sorry." I pursed my lips to the side, holding back the swear words that wanted to exit my mouth. I nodded my head.

"Thank you, Officer. I hope you have a nice day." I said the words in my most saccharine voice, hoping he could sense the anger behind them. As he walked away, he stopped for a moment.

"And Ms. DeLuca, it's really important that you take care of that ticket right away. Read it carefully please. I wouldn't want anything to go permanently on your record."

I gave him a one-finger salute, and he walked away, a tiny smirk on his annoyingly handsome face. I watched him in my rearview mirror, taking in every ripple of every muscle as he moved. His ass looked so sinfully good in his uniform. And his arms. Those biceps bulged out of everything the man wore. I was going to miss that body.

I waited for Cameron to drive away and then crumpled the ticket. A minute later, while I sat, still befuddled, my phone pinged. A text from Cameron.

"Ahhhhh!" It was more of a whisper scream because I didn't want to wake up Zara. I unlocked my phone to see what he had to say.

Cameron—*Uncrumple that citation, babe.*—

I looked around like a paranoid lunatic, as if he could still see me. He couldn't see me; he just knew me too well at this point.

Me—*I don't know what you're talking about and don't call me babe. You can save that for your girlfriend!—*

"Ugh!" I whined into my steering wheel and tossed my phone to the back seat. Why did I say that? Why couldn't I be one of the girls that didn't wear her bleeding heart on her sleeve? For once in my life, I wanted to play it cool, hold back my hurt, and pretend I wasn't dying on the inside.

I unfolded the scrunched-up ticket and looked for the so-called important information on it. Except, I didn't see information for the ticket, only a note:

Raven, come celebrate your graduation with your Brooks Falls friends at Shea's. We've reserved the bar for friends and family to celebrate your accomplishment.

My heart sputtered in my chest. I wasn't expecting that. Feeling a little embarrassed, I reached back for my phone so I could send Cameron an apology and also a thank you, but I had already received another text from him.

Cameron—*Ah, okay. But just to be completely honest with you, it's much more serious than that.—*

Goodbye heart, hello loneliness. The thought of someone else touching him made me sick. My shoulders slumped, feeling the loss of him in the deepest parts of me. The only love of my life, and I had lost him.

When I got to Shea's, I rubbed Zara's puffy cheeks that were red from leaning on her car seat.

"Baby girl, wake up, we're here."

"Mommy, where Daddy?" she asked sleepily.

And oh, my heart. What had I done confusing her the way I did? I hated myself for it. It was no one's fault but my own. Thankfully, Zara was still half asleep, so I could avoid the question for now and explain to her later that it's just her and me. My heart splintered thinking of how I would have to one day tell my daughter that she didn't have a daddy. Trent certainly wasn't her dad. She didn't even know who he was, and she wouldn't for a long time.

"Hey, guess what? We are at a party for you and Mommy!"

Her eyes shot open at the word party, and her whole body came to life. How was she *my* kid, but so much like her Aunt Tessa? Loved to party, loved to talk, and loved her dresses.

"Party? Is a cake?"

I laughed as I unbuckled her. "Probably. I'm not sure you can call it a party without cake!" She smiled and wrapped her arms around me as I knelt down to set her on the ground.

I'd let her pick out a present for Tessa, Mika, and Cameron as a way to say thank you for helping me accomplish this dream. For Tessa and Mika, we designed a collage of photos of all four of us, placed in a frame that said *Family.* I loved the pictures that Zara chose, one of all of us looking ridiculous on Halloween dressed as zombies, one of Zara and Mika snuggling on the couch together reading, and several others showing the love and care we all had for each other. It brought tears to my eyes just looking at it, knowing that times were going to change. I couldn't stay with Tessa forever, especially now that she and Mika were serious. They'd want to get married and start a family eventually, and they would need their space to do that.

Zara opened the box that held the gift she got for Cameron. I closed my eyes, taking in deep breaths, trying to keep it together. I chose the frame, and she chose the pictures. It was a double frame. On one side I placed a picture of Zara, smiling this huge grin, her round little face only made more round by that huge sunflower headband framing it. That side of the frame said "Little Z." The other side said "My Hero" and held a picture of the three of us dancing—a picture Mika had taken the day of our barbeque. We were looking at each like we saw the world in one another's eyes. I needed to get this over with and let it go.

"Shall we?"

"Yes, yet's go, Mommy. I's ready for party."

When we walked into Shea's, I was greeted by what felt like all of Brooks Falls. A large *Congratulations Graduate* sign hung from the rafters, and balloons were tied to the chairs. Every table had a tray of cookies made into little graduation caps. I looked around to see all of my friends beaming with love and pride as I wiped tears from my eyes.

"Wow, everyone. Thank you so much. This is so beautiful and kind. I don't know what to say other than thank you, and I'm touched beyond words."

"I'd like to touch you beyond words," I heard Gray mumble from the side as Bram shoved him away, and Cameron—yes, that's right, Cameron—glared at him.

There he was, already changed out of his uniform, wearing fitted jeans that accentuated his grabbable ass and a black Henley that I wanted to tear right off of his body so I could lick every part of him. I stared at him adoringly, not really caring about anyone else in the room, too focused on getting back to this man. But when I started to walk toward him, he broke eye contact and looked to his right at the tall, blonde, and perfectly tanned woman who was trying to get his attention.

What was happening? My heart didn't just fall. I was pretty sure it left my body entirely and just died alone somewhere in the wilderness. From pictures that I'd seen of Callie, this woman was Callie 2.0. They looked perfect. They chatted about something, and he nodded before she walked out of the bar. I fiddled nervously with the boxes I was holding as he walked over to me. I was sure he could see my crest-fallen expression. Honestly, I wasn't certain if I was still standing.

"Hey, Raven."

Raven. I hated hearing him say my name. Sure, I told him expressly not to call me "baby," but when had he ever listened to that? I wanted to be his baby again.

"I gotta run and take care of something. I'll be back in like thirty minutes tops, I promise." My nostrils flared and I could feel jealousy poking holes in my soul with the hot side of a fire iron.

"Yeah, okay." I swallowed back the tears as he leaned in and pressed a kiss to my cheek.

I watched him walk away, and then drive away, following Callie 2.0. We had been through too much to throw the towel in on this. He was not going to ride off into the sunset with some gorgeous blonde who wasn't me. He and I had a history that could not be erased. We had chemistry. We *still* loved each other.

"I'll be right back," I told Tessa.

Her eyes widened in shock. "What? Where are you going?"

"I'm going to get him back, Tessa. He doesn't love her! He loves me, and he's still mine. I'm going to remind him of the promises he made to me, to Zara. She doesn't get to take *my* man. Can you watch Zara while I deal with this?"

Tessa furrowed her brows, and I swore I saw her lips tip up a little before she straightened up and frowned. "Yeah, you know what, you go tell him what's what! And don't back down!"

Mika interjected. "Tess, baby, you know that—"

But Tessa cut her off, shooting Mika a look that I didn't have time to decode. "No, honey, she has to do this. That chick has nothing on you, and he knows that. You go get 'em, I'll watch Zara."

She smacked my ass as I walked away. I shook my head at Tessa, ran out of Shea's, and jumped into my car. I had been fighting for everything that I wanted for the past two years, except Cameron. I had nothing to be afraid of now, and it was time to fight for love. It was about to go down.

Chapter 24

Cameron

"Wow, thanks, Anna. It's more than I expected. I can't thank you enough."

"Of course, it was my pleasure. I really enjoyed it. This is one of the more emotional projects I've taken on. I can tell there is a lot of love in here, and it was a delight to be a part of that in some small way."

I went to shake her hand but was interrupted by a loud banging on the door. I wasn't expecting anyone, and I definitely wasn't expecting anyone angry. The banging was steady and getting louder.

"I'm sorry, I better go see who that is." I swung open the door, and there she was with those wide, brown eyes staring back at me, that long black hair, and that body wrapped up in a short, little dress that accentuated every curve. She was beautiful. She was mine. She was— *seething?*

"Babe?"

She pointed her finger into my chest, pushing me and backing me up into the house. Sure, she was little, no more than five foot two, but for a tiny thing, she was terrifying when she was pissed.

"Don't you 'babe' me, Jameson!"

Jameson? Oh, this should be fun.

"Where is she?" She whipped around the house,

looking for something and coming to a screeching halt when her eyes landed on Anna. "And you! How dare you swoop in here with your long legs and your perfect teeth and your flawless manicure and your model looks and take *my* man! What, you've known him for two seconds, and you think you can just, you can just like, take him from me?"

Anna opened her mouth to speak, but Raven continued.

"The answer is a *no*. No, you may not have him. He. Is. Mine. And I belong to him. So the sooner you understand that fact, the better off you are! You seem like a, well, you seem like a person that I don't know, so I can't really say whether you're nice or not, but seeing as Cameron likes you, you're probably a good person…"

She trailed off in that cute way she did when the wheels started to fall off of her rants. She would start angry, and by the end, she was thoughtful and calm.

"But-but the thing is, good or not, Cameron and I are in love, and we belong together. So…I think it's best that you just go…" She shooed her hands toward the door and Anna pressed her lips together and quirked her brow. Raven sighed and let out a frustrated growl as she put her hands to her flushed cheeks. "Ahhhh. I'm sorry, what's your name?"

"Anna."

"Okay, I'm sorry, Anna. I don't want to be mean to you. It's not your fault. I mean, look at this man," Raven pointed to me, running her hand up and down, showcasing my body like she was Vanna White. "He's gorgeous and kind and fun and, oh, he's so good in bed. The things he can do to a woman." Raven's eyes flashed as she studied Anna's face. "You better know nothing about that."

Anna put her hands up in surrender. "I don't."

"Good. I gotta be honest with you. I will *always* love Cameron, and I won't go away easily."

Anna bit her lip and nodded. "That's fair."

"It is fair! Wait, it is?"

"Yeah, I suppose I should probably go then. It was lovely to meet you. You are every bit of the woman that Cameron said you were."

Raven jerked back and glanced at me. I shook my head at her and chuckled.

"Thanks for everything, Anna." I extended my hand to her once again, giving her a nod and a firm handshake. Opening the door, I ushered her out and turned to Raven, who was standing in the same place, biting her bottom lip.

"Ummmm."

That was all she said as she looked anywhere but at me. The moment I saw her face change from confusion to surprise was the exact moment I had planned for. I originally planned to do it after her party and in a much more formal fashion, but this was Raven and me. We didn't seem to ever follow the rules together.

"Cameron," she gasped as she took in the room.

Turning to the new fireplace, she threw her hand over her face as she gazed across the mantle. "It's, oh, it's us."

All across the mantle were pictures of our family. There were pictures in various combinations with her key people in them—Zara, Maus, Tessa, Mika, and me. In the center of the mantle, blown up, my favorite picture sat in a frame surrounded by heart cut-outs. It was Raven, Me, and Zara holding each other as we danced. Mika had snapped it and sent it to me for the mantle centerpiece. It was perfect. One picture that captured everything I wanted.

"That picture! I'll be right back." She ran out my door.

Seconds later, Raven came back with a box that she handed to me. "This was meant to be a thank-you for helping me get through school."

I opened the box. Perfection. Adoration. Everything in one picture. My life, my bleeding heart, my girls.

"Baby." I ran my hand down her cheek, wiping away a few tears. "This picture, it's everything we are."

"Yeah, I guess we both had the same idea, huh?" She smiled, blushing. "I'm sorry I yelled at Anna, the...?"

"The interior decorator."

She looked down at the floor. "That makes sense. I'm so embarrassed. I just thought that she was well...and that you two were..."

"Don't finish that sentence. Don't you remember how I told you that it's only you, baby, that it would only ever be you?"

"Yes, I do."

Without a word, I put Raven's hand in mine and walked her down the hallway to the room that Zara slept in when they stayed over. I pushed open the door to reveal a room covered in sunflower stencils. She squeezed my hand and burrowed into my side.

"What is this? There's furniture." She put a hand over her mouth as she took it all in.

"Yeah, baby, there's furniture." I had furnished the room in distressed white furniture, ideas I got from Raven's Pinterest. "And if you don't like the color or anything, I checked, and we can exchange it and get anything you want."

She shook her head. "No. It's perfect. I don't want to change a thing." She hugged me tightly before letting go to walk around the room, running her hand across the dresser. She stared at the large words that hung above the dresser from a yellow ribbon—*Little Z.*

"It's, it's so beautiful. The colors are perfect. How did you know?"

"I follow you on Pinterest."

Her eyes widened. "You what now? You are full of surprises, Jameson."

"Still Jameson, huh? I think I better show you the rest so I can be Cameron again."

"The rest?"

"We aren't done, sweetheart." I pulled on her hand to follow me. Earlier, I'd set up a painter's cloth over the second hallway, just for dramatic effect. When we got there, I pulled it down, and she turned to me, stunned. I could tell she was refusing to look down the hallway because she put her hand up as a blinder.

"Honey, are you sure you want me to go in there?"

"I need you to go in there, baby."

Slowly, she dropped her hand to her side and turned to face the hallway. I walked her down to our bedroom, which was completely remodeled, and I'd hoped she could see that everything was new.

"Wow, it's beautiful in here." She spoke in gentle reverence.

And that was the thing about this woman. She understood what this meant. She understood that I'd let go and moved on, but she also knew that it was something complex. Aside from the decorating, I had a large bay window installed in our room, so we had plenty of natural light and a view of the nature reserve.

"Everything has been replaced. It's all new. I donated the old items and got all new things for us." Now I was getting a little nervous. Throughout the entire process, I never considered that she might say no to me or hate what I'd done to the place. "Do you like it? Because if you don't, we can change anything you want."

She smiled and touched my forearm, her sweet voice a whisper, her eyes scanning my face and searching my soul. "I love it so much. I love the colors and the furniture and the lighting. It's so peaceful and beautiful in here."

I breathed out a sigh of relief. Raven looked to the side before peering right through me again, piercing my spirit with her kindness. "Are you okay? I know this couldn't have been easy for you, honey. And you know, you deserve time to heal too. I would never want to push that. I'm not going anywhere. I'll wait. You are the only one. It's always been you, and it's always going to be you."

This woman. I loved her so much, sometimes it hurt just to look at her.

"Thank you for saying that. It means a lot. But the truth is, I'm so in love with you, and I don't think I can live another day without you. That's the truth."

Her soft smile expanded into a full-on grin before she gave me a slight nod of understanding. Perfection.

"Now, come see the bathroom." She narrowed her eyes at me. "Not for *that*. Not right now anyway," I mumbled under my breath. Dragging her to the bathroom, I put my hands over her eyes, and when we got there, I pulled them off.

"Oh. My. Word." Her jaw fell to the floor, and I understood it. This was my favorite of all the rooms—the most decadent for sure. Mika and I had installed a huge clawfoot tub, big enough for two. And next to it, a standing shower with side sprayers, a rain showerhead, and a normal showerhead. I also may have installed a few handholds at various levels. She instantly noticed those and giggled.

"Is this a shower or a sex dungeon?"

I shrugged. "Why can't it be both?"

"It absolutely can." She got onto her tip toes, and I bent down so she could press a kiss to my lips. "Cam, this is everything I have ever wanted. And I don't mean the house or all the things in it. I had a house. It just wasn't mine, not really. This place, though, this place feels like a home."

"Baby, you don't know what it means to hear you say that. I've been nervous all week the closer I got to being done. I don't want to lose you again. I want you and Zara with me all the time. Will you stay?"

She nodded her head voraciously. "Yes! You'll never lose me. I don't think you'll ever be able to shake me off, even if you wanted to."

"I won't want to."

Raven leaned into me and pulled my ear down to her lips. "Cameron?"

"What, baby?"

"I need one more thing."

"Anything."

"Take me to our bed and—" Raven squealed as I tossed her over my shoulder. "Fuck me," she finished with a laugh.

Raven's giggles filled the room as I hauled her to the

bed. To *our* bed. She let out a surprised yelp when I dropped her onto the mattress.

"You're practically a caveman," she said, her voice teasing and light.

I looked down at her and grunted. I couldn't help it. It had been so long since I'd been inside her, and I didn't know what I wanted to do first. I stood staring, enjoying the sight of her petite body spread out across our bed.

"Umm, Cam?"

"Hmm?" I asked, my mind preoccupied, contemplating my next move.

"In order to do that, you're going to have to join me in the bed."

"Right. Just trying to regain some composure so I don't hurt you."

"Who said I don't want to feel a little pain?"

I worked my jaw back and forth. For months I'd been nursing the worst case of blue balls that not even jerking off could remedy.

"You won't hurt me, honey. It's been forever, and I've thought about it almost every second of every day for the past four months. I just need you to get inside me."

Christ, I felt like a beginner. "Fine. Okay, but just don't talk too much. I just—I'm gonna come in two seconds flat if you open that sexy mouth." My voice had gotten low and dark.

She pressed her lips together as I threw off my shirt and unbuttoned my jeans immediately. My cock was painfully hard, and I needed to get a little relief. I stood on the edge of the bed, in front of her, with only my briefs.

"Take me out, baby."

Raven bit her lip and squirmed on the bed. She hopped off the bed and turned around, her back to me. "Unzip me first?"

I leaned down and took my time unzipping her dress, kissing down her back as I pulled the zipper down. Her dress fell to the floor, revealing some crisscrossed strappy little joke of a bra that barely covered her tits, and a matching pair of panties that crisscrossed below at the hip a few times, with just a tiny piece of fabric covering her pussy.

She smirked. "You like these useless panties?"

"I love them, but I am going to destroy them."

She pouted. "My turn." She ran one finger down my chest, slowly, staring at my body like it was her own private oasis. Dipping her finger into my briefs, she pushed them down unhurriedly, but with so much intention.

"I'm gonna lose it. You're gonna make me lose my mind and I can't promise what happens after that." My cock sprang free as she finally got me all the way out. A gasp left her lips.

"I forgot how beautiful you were. It's been too long," she told me, licking her lips.

I grabbed my length and gave it a stroke, knowing exactly how to drive her as crazy as she was driving me.

Her lips parted. "I could watch you do that for hours."

"I'd rather do you for hours." I grabbed her hips and ground myself into her, into something or somewhere on her body. At this point, anywhere would do. "Christ, you're so sexy. I don't know if I'll be able to contain myself right now."

She pushed back into me and leaned her head back,

tilting her head to the side, allowing me access to her long, elegant neck. I had to keep myself from biting it.

"I don't want you to hold back. I want you to own me. I want you to take every part of me and make it yours. Lay down on our bed, Cameron, and hold the headboard." Christ.

I smirked at her. I loved that she was taking control of this. There was nothing hotter than knowing she was just as turned on as I was. I lay down on the bed, doing as she said. She crawled on top of me and started with my mouth.

"I missed your mouth," she said, hovering over my lips.

I slid my tongue across her lips as she parted them for me, allowing me to get more of her. I sucked her bottom lip between mine, tasting her, exploring her as we consumed each other. She rocked her hips on top of me, and my dick was bobbing and sliding into the crease of her ass. She liked it, because she circled her hips back into it.

"You want that cock, baby, don't you?"

I knew her answer when I could barely get the words past my lips as she kissed and licked down my neck, biting ever so gently at the crook. It was careful, but filled with need. She was getting lower, kissing down my chest and stomach, running her hands along the ridges of my abs, getting reacquainted with my body.

I was sure she was going to go farther and wrap her sexy lips around my aching cock. I was desperate for her. But she stopped and sat up briefly to pull her useless bra off, her breasts falling perfectly as she did. Those tits that I wanted to bury myself in, to suck and lick and bite.

She bent down and used her tongue to circle the dot

of pre-cum on my cock and spread it around my tip before she pulled away again. If she was trying to push my limits of self-restraint, she was doing it well. Raven gathered her breasts, pushing them together with her hands, and bent down over me before shoving my dick between them.

"Oh Jesus!" I gasped.

Muddled words left my mouth as I left my body. It wasn't nerves, though. I was over-excited, and by the look on Raven's face, so was she.

"I'm gonna make you come like this. Tell me when you're close."

"Don't talk, baby, please."

She grinned. She was moving up and down the full length of my dick. The sounds alone were going to put me over the edge. My balls slapped on the underside of her breasts, and I could hear myself sliding in and out from between her as she pressed her breasts closer together, squeezing my shaft. I started to thrust my hips up into her, increasing the speed and friction before I had to take full control. I flipped her over so I was on top of her, bucking wildly into those beautiful breasts while she held them together, my cock jutting barely in and out of her mouth as I thrust.

"You wanna come on my chest or in my mouth?" Raven asked through breaths.

"Tits. No. Mouth," I groaned out as I continued to thrust into her.

I moved faster, my balls tightening under me as my orgasm was building. Bursts of energy released through my entire body, and I knew this was something new, something different.

"I'm. Gonna. Come." I tried to tell her while

thrusting and panting. The first few squirts of cum unleashed onto her chest before she dug her nails into my ass and pulled me between her lips, shoving me deep into her mouth and sucking every last drop of cum from my cock. She wrapped her hand around my base and gave it a pump, taking everything she could get out of me. My body twitched, and as she released me from her mouth, she licked her lips, looking down at her breasts.

"So, I guess both tits and mouth?" she teased.

I fell off of her, feeling wild and unrestrained, all kinds of dirty and right. I pulled her into me, ignoring that she was still covered in my cum.

"I'd like to come many other places as well." I kissed her perfectly soft lips as she rested her head on my chest.

****

Raven

I lay there, soaking it all in. It was everything that I wanted. A man who loved me for me and accepted my past. A father who loved Zara and could give her a safe home that was full of love that she could grow up in. And for the first time in my life, I felt like I was getting what I deserved, because I finally believed that I deserved good things.

"I'm not done with you, baby," Cameron growled into my ear. "I won't be done until I'm buried deep inside of you."

I squeezed my legs together. His voice alone made me wet but add those threats of pleasure and his perfectly gorgeous everything, and I was drenched in desire.

"You don't need a break?"

He glanced downward, and I followed his gaze to

find his already hard cock. I inhaled sharply. I didn't even know that was possible. He came in my mouth no more than ten minutes ago. It was no small amount either; I was covered and filled.

"Seriously? How?" I was truly wondering how he'd recovered so quickly.

"You, that's how." He pushed me off of his chest and hovered over me. "I love you, Raven. More than I've ever loved anyone."

I let that settle in and resolved not to overthink it too much.

"You are the only man that I have *ever* loved. You're the only man that I *will* ever love. Make me yours. Please," I begged him. I needed him to claim me, to show me that this was it.

Without a second thought, he pushed my thighs apart, grabbing greedy handfuls of my ass with both of his hands.

He shook his head and grumbled to himself. "I don't even know where to start." After a few torturous seconds, he made his choice. Lowering his face to my center, he licked my pussy, flattening his tongue against the opening, licking like his life depended on it.

"Honey!" I writhed beneath him, but he pushed down on my stomach, keeping me in place. "Cameron, I have to move!"

He pushed down harder, torturing me in the process.

"Mhmm," I moaned, accepting my tongue fucking and not thinking about anything else. He slipped two thick fingers inside me and pumped in and out of me hard.

"Yes, that's how I need it." I ran my fingers through his hair, pulling and pressing his face harder into my pussy.

Cameron sucked my clit into his mouth, and I screamed out a breathy "yes." Adding a third finger, he filled me up as he licked and sucked and pumped. I squeezed my legs tighter, and he pulled his fingers out of me to push my legs apart again, shooting me a warning look.

"No, don't go." I begged, not even caring about the arrogant smirk on his face. I needed his mouth back on me. I had no shame, not when he was making me feel so good.

"Keep your legs open for me, baby. I need to be able to taste you as much as I want."

"Okay, just lick me already!" I said impatiently, ignoring his small chuckle.

He buried his face in me, licking voraciously. Without easing me into it at all, he pushed three fingers back into me and started working me unapologetically with them. His other hand moved to my ass, circling around my anus, sending me straight to the stars. I was ablaze, caught in the wildfire of sensations.

"Yes, that. I'm gonna." I was moaning and shouting like nothing else mattered. Cameron pressed more firmly into my ass and pumped me harder, licking me like it was his passion. It felt like mine.

"Cameron! Jesus, ah!" I screamed, my pussy, my ass pulsating around him. Before my orgasm ended, he pulled away and pushed his cock into me, driving me over the edge. I screamed so loud that I was sure the neighbors' miles away would hear, but I didn't care. The pleasure coursing through my veins was a pleasure I had never felt before. He was relentless as I rode a never-ending orgasm all the way into oblivion.

"Look at me, baby. I need to see you when I come inside of you. I need to make you mine."

I stared into his eyes as best I could. My whole world was tilted, knocked off of its axis.

"Yes," I answered breathlessly.

Cameron was relentless. And I was pressed underneath him. He grabbed my legs and tossed them over his shoulders, slamming into me at an angle I could barely handle.

"Do you want this?"

"Yes! I'm full, baby. I'm so—Ah!—full."

He didn't stop. "Can you take it? Can you take all of me?"

"Yes, give me everything, please! I need you, baby. I need it all."

"You need me to stop?"

"No, never."

He continued to pound into me, circling his hips and thrusting at the same time. "I'm not coming until we come together, baby."

"Yes." That was all I could say.

I wanted to feel him release everything he had into me, to spill himself into me while I convulsed around him.

"Cameron, I can't—I have to come. I. am."

"Come with me, baby, come all over my cock. I need to feel you. I need all of you."

"You have all of—ah—me!" I cried out as I came so hard that I saw his eyes widen when my pussy squeezed his cock.

"Good!" He growled, still pumping into me. I felt a stream of warm cum shoot into me, strengthening my own orgasm. I didn't think it was possible.

"Yeah, baby, give me everything you've got," he ground out in that dark, needy voice. He was *still* going. He was *still* coming. After a few moments where I lost all sense of time and space, he slowed his pace. His large, muscular arms were still holding up my legs and slowly driving into me, not wanting this to end.

"I want to stay inside of you forever," he said hungrily, looking at me like he was ready to devour me again. Placing my legs down, he stayed carefully inside me and rolled me over on top of him, maintaining our connection.

"I'll never get enough of you, Jameson," I teased half-heartedly, my voice and body so weak.

He kissed my lips softly. "Good. But, babe, you're kind of missing your party."

"Oh right!" My party. I felt like the biggest jerk in the whole world. My friends had gone through all of this trouble to throw me a party, and I just left. I was suddenly riddled with guilt. "How long have we been gone?"

"Mmmmm, about a half hour. Let's clean up real quick and get you back, okay?" I jumped up, and with a sense of urgency, I cleaned myself up, put on my clothes, and tried to hide the fact that I had just been properly, and thoroughly, fucked. It was useless. My hair was a disaster, and my makeup was ruined.

"Let's go, baby," Cameron grinned, and took my hand.

Staring down at our interlaced fingers, I suddenly forgot that I was a mess. A smile spread across my face, and I felt like I was floating. Finally, we were back together, where we both belonged. With my hands in his, we walked out of our home.

Epilogue

Cameron

"Daddy!" Zara jumped into my arms. She was growing fast, but still a tiny little thing, just like her mom. One year ago, I had officially made Raven mine when I married her at an outdoor ceremony. She was beautiful that day, just as she was every day. Six months after we were married, my adoption of Zara went through. We were all officially Jameson's.

"Daddy!" Zara tugged on my shirt. "I wanna go to the splash pad park now. Please?"

"Z? Did Mommy say no?"

She squirmed in my arms, her eyes darting and looking everywhere but at me. Her little tell.

"Uh. Mommy? Mommy who?" She asked with an exaggerated shrug.

This kid. She was too smart for her own good and seriously funny, just like her mother. I set her down and narrowed my eyes at her.

"Mommy who, huh? How about we settle this with a...tickle fight!"

She squealed and ran out the back door as I chased after her and Maus chased after me, barking playfully. I pretended I couldn't catch her for a while, before snatching her up and tickling her silly.

"Hey, guys." Raven walked out with heavy eyes.

350

"Oh, sorry, baby, I didn't mean to wake you." I walked over and bent down to kiss my wife, who had been working the night shift at the hospital.

"You didn't. I was awake. I was just reading a little."

"Mmmmmm. Was it one of those sexy romance novels?"

She laughed as her cheeks reddened.

"Ah, I see. Send me the really dirty chapters so I can see if there's anything we need to try."

She shoved my arm and smiled.

"Hi, Mommy! Are you ready to go to the splash pad now?" Zara strolled up to us with Maus on her heels.

"Yeah, baby girl. I just gotta go get changed into my bathing suit."

"Is Nash gonna be there?" Zara and Nash were basically the cutest best friends now. Even though he was a few years older, he still played with her and ran around however she wanted. Jet was still raising him alone, so we tried to help him out as much as we could. And it helped us, because Zara always had a buddy.

"He sure is! Want me to put on a cartoon for you while I get ready?"

"Yay! C'mon, Mausy, let's go watch cartoons."

We went inside, and Raven got Zara set up, before turning to me. "Hey, baby? I'm not sure what bathing suit I should wear. Do you mind helping me?"

Her eyes darkened. Mine widened at the thought of her sweet pussy riding me, just like she rode my face two nights ago. Instantly, my cock was hard, and I didn't even bother to play it cool. I jogged behind her, and she giggled as I smacked her ass, kicked the door closed with my foot, and tackled her to the bed. I had started taking my clothes off in the hallway, so she laughed harder when she opened her eyes to see I was already naked.

"What? How?" She giggled. "You're like a sex magician. How did you even get your clothes off that fast?" She stood on her knees on the bed and grabbed my neck, pulling me down to her. Arching her back, she pushed her breasts into me as I thrust my cock into her stomach.

"Mmmmm, Cameron," she moaned softly. "I missed you last night."

"I missed you too. Getting tired of you being on nights. Now take off those clothes."

She put her arms in the air, signaling me to take her shirt off. I peeled her shirt off and stared. How was it that every time with her felt like a first? She wasn't wearing a bra, and her breasts looked so beautiful and full.

"Damn, baby." I sucked one nipple while grabbing the stiff peak of the other and rolled it in my fingers.

She started unbuttoning her pants and as I sucked and pinched her nipples harder, she managed to wiggle out of the rest of her clothes. Kneeling on the bed in front of her, I lay her naked body down and hovered over her. So beautiful. Perfection.

I captured her mouth with mine and kissed her hard as she parted her mouth for me. Our tongues wrestled for control. I was pulled into her as she tilted her head to one side, allowing me to kiss her more deeply. I ran one finger along the delicate fabric of her panties to see if she was ready and oh yeah, she was ready, wetter than ever.

"Get inside me, Cam."

I loved when she demanded sex from me. Sure, it turned me on, but it also gave me an opportunity to torture her. I stood on my knees over her and grabbed myself, stroking my cock slowly, enjoying the tease.

"Is this what you want inside of you?"

"Cameron." She writhed below me, and I smirked at her, grabbing my balls and staring at her.

"Is this what you want slapping against your tight ass while I pound into you?"

"I'm going to kill you." She moaned in defeat, but then her eyes glinted.

Raven smiled at me as she reached over to her bed-side drawer and pulled out a vibrator. My jaw dropped as she got off of the bed and put it in her mouth as far as it could go. This woman. Then she turned it on and slowly ran the buzzing toy from her nipple down her stomach and finally down to her pussy, where she slowly pushed it in. I was still stroking myself, and I couldn't stop watching her as she filled herself. Then she knelt in front of the bed with her vibrator still between her legs.

"Get your dick in my mouth," she commanded.

I was in a trance, ruined and commanded by this woman. And also, in no position to argue. I stood up in front of her and let her take me in at her own pace. She sucked me in, hollowing her cheeks, sucking just the tip.

"Mmm, Raven."

Then, in one motion, she engulfed my entire cock in her mouth, letting my length slide down her throat. She sucked hard and swirled her tongue around me. I thrust gently into her, looking down, not wanting to miss any of it. I was going into sensory overload and was going to blow.

"I'm gonna come, baby. You want it in your mouth or your pussy?"

She released her mouth from me and said breathlessly, "Pussy," as she pulled the vibrator out of herself and threw it to the side. I lifted her up into my arms, and she wrapped her legs around my waist as I planted myself inside of her.

"Ease me in, baby," I whispered as she gasped at the sudden connection.

We slowly lowered her until she had fully taken me inside of her, and then we thrust into each other.

"Ah, that's what I need!" she whispered.

I held her up, pushing into her with needy thrusts. Her slick warm heat surrounded me, reminding me why I couldn't get enough of this woman. Electricity pulsed around us as I felt her unfurling in my arms, getting ready to release. I gave it to her hard, her nails digging in my back as I rode her through her orgasm, feeling my whole body tense as I arrived there with her.

"Sweetheart, goddaaaamn." My voice was deep and the sound guttural as I shot deep inside of her. She grabbed my ass, pulled me into her as she squeezed around me.

"You are everything, baby. I love the way you love me. I love the way you make love to me," she whimpered.

I captured her mouth in a soft kiss as I slowed my thrusts. "You're my world, my whole world." I set her down, breaking our connection. My cock bobbed and slapped against my abdomen.

"Seriously? Are you ever not hard?"

"Not around you." I slapped her ass, and she squealed.

"All right, you, let's get ready to go to the splash pad. You need to keep that thing zipped up before I get distracted again."

Right when we were about to leave, Raven stopped us.

"Wait just a minute, I forgot. I have something for Zara to wear!"

When she came back, she had a folded shirt. She took off the shirt that Zara was wearing over her bathing suit and placed the new one on her. Turning Zara around to face me, she asked, "What do you think?"

I bent down and narrowed my eyes to read the shirt. *Big Sister to Baby Jameson.*

What? My head spun, and I looked up at Raven. "Baby?"

She beamed and nodded. I grabbed my wife and hugged her tightly to me. She was everything. She was absolutely everything. She and Zara were all I ever needed, but another baby to add to our family—it was more than I ever expected.

Zara looked at her shirt and jumped up and down. "Why am I jumping?"

Raven and I both knelt down to our little girl.

"Because, honey, you're going to be a big sister," Raven said as she patted her belly.

"A *baby?*" she screamed in delight.

I picked up my little girl and spun her around. "You're going to be a really good big sister, Zara Jameson!"

"And you're a good Daddy!"

I smiled. Life was good. I had my girls and a baby on the way. I kissed my wife, and she smelled like coconuts and tasted like a second chance.

My second chance.

A word about the author…

Sonnet Harlynn was born and raised in San Diego, California. After spending eight years in the Army as an intelligence analyst, she settled in Raleigh, North Carolina where she spends her time writing the stories she dreams about all day. Her incessant writing is fueled by coffee and a determined drive to bring the characters in her head to life.

http://golddustliterary.com

Thank you for purchasing
this publication of The Wild Rose Press, Inc.

For questions or more information
contact us at
info@thewildrosepress.com.

The Wild Rose Press, Inc.
www.thewildrosepress.com

CPSIA information can be obtained
at www.ICGtesting.com
Printed in the USA
LVHW012057101022
730380LV00013B/468